We hope you enjoy this book. Please return or renew it by the due date.

You can renew it at www.norfolk.gov.uk/libraries or by using our free library app.

Otherwise you can phone 0344 800 8020 - please have your library card and PIN ready.

You can sign up for email reminders too.

D1375309

NORFOLK COUNTY COUNCIL
LIBRARY AND INFORMATION SERVICE

Also by Celia Rees

Children's or Young Adult
Every Step You Take
The Bailey Game
Colour Her Dead
Midnight Hour
Ghost Chamber
Soul Taker
Truth or Dare
The Wish House
The Stone Testament
The Vanished
The Cunning Man
Sorceress
Witch Child
Pirates!
Sovay
Blood Sinister
The Fool's Girl
This is Not Forgiveness
Daughters of Time

Trap in Time series (first published as the H.A.U.N.T.S series)
City of Shadows
A Trap in Time
The Host Rides Out

CELIA REES

Miss Graham's
WAR

HarperCollins*Publishers*

HarperCollins*Publishers* Ltd
1 London Bridge Street,
London SE1 9GF

www.harpercollins.co.uk

HarperCollins*Publishers*
1st Floor, Watermarque Building, Ringsend Road
Dublin 4, Ireland

This paperback edition 2021

1

First published as 'Miss Graham's Cold War Cookbook'
by HarperCollins*Publishers* 2020

A catalogue record for this book
is available from the British Library

ISBN: 978-0-00-835432-9

Set in Sabon LT Std by Palimpsest Book Production Ltd,
Falkirk, Stirlingshire

Printed and bound in the UK by CPI Group (UK) Ltd, Croydon CR0 4YY

MIX
Paper from
responsible sources
FSC **FSC™ C007454**
www.fsc.org

This book is produced from independently certified FSC™ paper to ensure
responsible forest management.

For more information visit: www.harpercollins.co.uk/green

To Nancy Elizabeth Marguerite Goodway
(1 January 1900–4 January 1984)
My 'Lion Aunt'

What country, friends, is this?

WILLIAM SHAKESPEARE, *TWELFTH NIGHT*,
ACT 1, SCENE 2

Dining Room, the Grand Hotel
Mirabeau, Lausanne

10th November 1989

```
Fried Fillet of Perch
Perch fillets dipped in egg, then flour,
salted and peppered with a hint of paprika,
fried in butter . . . Speciality of the
place. A finicky fish - hardly worth eating
- bones like needles. Tastes of the riverbed.
```

She put down her pen and pushed her plate away. She wasn't here to eat the food or drink the wine. She had no appetite anyway. She'd come by way of Natzweiler-Struthof, a Nazi camp two hundred miles north of here. A *Nacht und Nebel* place, Night and Fog. Apt name. Four British girls had died there, forgotten by almost everybody, tucked away in the back pocket of a secret war.

She'd laid four red roses in the black maw of the rusting oven. A pilgrimage of sorts.

If these do not die well, it will be a black matter . . .

They had not died well.

A ragged cheer burst from the kitchen. Through the flapping doors, she could see white-coated backs in front of a portable television. From the foyer, tinny, muffled commentary, crowd noise, clinking and chanting, mixed with the excited chatter of guests and staff clustered round a larger screen, drawn by the need to witness the drama taking place in Berlin, history erupting into the present, breaking through the muted formality of this grand hotel. An ending? A beginning? Both? Impossible to tell.

Not that it mattered. Very little mattered anymore.

'Are you finished, Madame?' The elderly waiter hesitated before taking her plate. 'The dish not to your liking?'

'I'm not hungry.' She capped her pen and lit a cigarette.

'You have been here before?' He asked as he refilled her glass. A Chasselas. Swiss wine, none the worse for that.

'Once. A long time ago.'

Just after the war. She doubted he would remember. How many people did he encounter? She'd been here under another name. A different person. A different time. She remembered him, though. His name was Joseph. She had a good memory for faces. She'd needed it in her line of business. A slender, solemn, graceful young man then, dark, thin-faced, with a pencil moustache. His hair silver now, the moustache still there – a thin line sketched in graphite. French, she recalled, and Jewish. He'd found safety here in Switzerland. She wondered if his family had been as lucky.

'Anything else for you, madame? A little dessert, perhaps? Coffee?'

'No, thank you.' She knocked the glass, her hand suddenly as useless as a bat. Wine spilled across the table. Joseph sprang forward to repair the damage. 'No need.' She shook her head. 'Clumsy of me.'

She held her hands on her lap and looked around at the immaculately laid tables, the stiff, starched linen, the gleam of the heavy silver cutlery, the glittering glassware, her fellow diners. Some of them frail, in wheelchairs, she noted, the staff must be used to different degrees of infirmity. She pushed herself back

2

from the table. Anticipating that she was about to leave, Joseph was immediately at her side, whisking her chair away, offering her his arm.

She declined his help and made her way slowly, Joseph hurrying in front of her, nodding to two young waiters to open the double doors. He bowed as she left. She smiled her thanks and wished him farewell. This was the last time she would be eating here, or anywhere. In a little less than twenty-four hours, Stella Snelling, restaurant critic and cookery writer, acclaimed and feared in equal measure, would be no more.

She'd taken a suite with a view of the lake. The Art Deco furnishings were just shabby enough to be authentic. She'd had the black lacquer writing desk reversed, so that it faced away from the fussy, fluted fan-shaped mirror. She found her appearance disconcerting. She had never expected to get this old, to live this long. Even with ten years knocked off Stella's passport, she was looking her true age now. She wore no makeup, her black hair an untidy grey mane; the dark eyes, deep and hooded, had seen too much; the grooved lines etched on the forehead, by the sides of the mouth, carried too much pain. She hardly recognized this person she had become. In her dreams, she was always young.

She opened the overnight bag that she'd brought with her, taking out a small green medical case. She removed the top tray holding the plasters, scissors, antiseptic cream, paracetamol and tablets that any traveller might carry, to reveal a number of disposable hypodermic syringes, ampoules of diamorphine, and more of the drug in capsule form. She placed the drugs in the small refrigerator and took out the Koskenkorva vodka. She poured a glass, lit a cigarette and went out onto the balcony.

The light had almost gone. The lake was a dark pewterish-purple, the mountains opposite lost in a cold, bluish haze. A mist had risen, diffusing the last of the sunset, layering the lake with bloodied gauze.

She sipped her drink, savouring the sharp, clear spirit. There were clinics here in Switzerland that offered a discreet service for the end of life. Such facilities were not openly advertised. She was wealthy, with no living relatives, and believed strongly in a person's right to choose how he or she wanted to die. Arrangements had been made, monies forwarded (for certain services, the clinic demanded prepayment). Tomorrow at 10.30, she had an appointment. A substantial further donation had guaranteed the director's personal attention. Nothing would be left to chance. Hence the diamorphine. The lake had turned to glittering blackness, the coloured lights of the quay dancing on its restless surface. Time to go back inside.

She opened a leather attaché case and began to lay out the contents on the desk. A brochure for the Endymion Clinic: situated on the beautiful shores of Lake Geneva, offering proven anti-ageing treatments and unrivalled levels of expertise in the areas of fertility and sexual health. The name of the director had been circled, *Other services available on application*, doubly underlined. The brochure had arrived at her Paris flat with an accompanying note from Adeline in New York. *This is what we've been waiting for!* in Adeline's arthritic scrawl, with instructions to go ahead and make arrangements. They would do it together, Adeline had said, but she was doing it alone. Within days, it seemed, she was reading Adeline's obituary.

ADELINE CURTIS CROFT PARNELL the celebrated female war correspondent, who covered every major conflict from World War II to San Salvador, died on Sunday in her New York West Village apartment aged 79.

Adeline Parnell was one of the first journalists to enter Germany with Allied Forces. She reported honestly and fearlessly about events as they were happening, including the liberation of Buchenwald and Dachau. She went on to report on the Nuremberg trials and won a Pulitzer for her reporting from Korea. She covered the war in Vietnam and the conflict in San Salvador until ill health forced her retirement. She

4

continued to photograph her home city of New York, which she described as 'her war zone'.

Born Adeline Curtis Croft in 1910, in Poughkeepsie, New York State, she was educated at Bryn Mawr and Columbia University. She went on to work for various newspapers, including the *New York Times* and the *Herald Tribune*, as well as *Life* magazine. In 1942, she married fellow journalist Sam Parnell who was killed in 1944. She never remarried and leaves no close relatives. Her estate and considerable archive are bequeathed to Columbia University.

It was no surprise. She had last seen Adeline in her New York apartment a month or so before. She had tried not to show her shock at finding her old friend so diminished; slumped and twisted into her wheelchair, so thin that her blue shirt and fawn cord trousers seemed empty, like clothes on a puppet, her thick, blonde curly hair reduced to white wisps, her rings loose on the bird-claw fingers that twisted round the controls of her power chair.

'Look a state, don't I?' Adeline looked up; her blue eyes, once so sharp, milky with cataracts. They both knew that this could be their last meeting. She'd turned away to hide the tears in her own eyes.

''s OK.' Adeline gave a ghost of her old smile. 'As long as this still works,' she tapped her temple, 'I don't mind. "God, grant me the serenity to accept the things I cannot change" and all that yadayada. Come, come over here where there's more light.' She manoeuvred herself through her 'archive'. Piles of newspapers, files and clippings stretched from floor to ceiling. She halted in front of the brownstone's tall window that looked out onto the West Village. 'Something I want you to see.'

In the bay, the heavy wooden table was free of clutter. A Tiffany lamp, balanced by a gold and ivory Favrile vase of canna lilies, stood on a faded green-and-purple velvet runner. In the centre of the table lay a book; the brown cloth cover blotched and stained, the title in faded gilt.

The Radiation
Cookery Book
For use with the 'New World'
Regulo Controlled Gas Cookers

The inside cover was flecked and rust spotted, there was a name written along with a place and date:

Lübeck, British Zone of Occupation, Germany,
January 1946.

The name almost illegible. Time erased.

'It was on top of a pile of other stuff, as though someone had just put it down. It wasn't there the day before, I swear . . . Then I found these,' Adeline pointed to a folder of photographs. 'Just spilled across the floor. After all these years. Gotta mean something . . .'

She opened the folder and felt the same frisson. They both knew that coincidence, synchronicity, serendipity, whatever you wanted to call it, was not to be undervalued, that intuition counted for more than cold logic. In her experience, it could be the difference between life and death.

'I took another look, into what happened, you know?' Adeline spoke into the gathered silence. 'I think I'm onto something.' Her eyes showed a little of their old spark. 'I'm waiting for confirmation. Now pour us a drink. There's bourbon over there. Here's to it!' Adeline lifted the glass between her two hands. 'If I'm right, we'll do it together!'

Adeline hadn't made it. It was all on her now. She placed the *Radiation Cookery Book* on the black lacquered desk and opened the brown cloth cover. Such a nondescript exterior blotched and stained with water damage, still smelling faintly of smoke. There were handwritten recipes, clippings from magazines – *Stella Snelling's dozen delicious ways with canapés* – menu cards slipped like memories between pages still grainy and pilled with

6

ancient flour. Each one perfectly innocent-seeming but so freighted with other meanings that they might have been scribed in blood. Everything lay between these covers, not least the reason why she was here.

She put the book down, dark drops spotting the cover. Tears came more easily now than they ever had in the past.

Blinking to clear her sight, she shook photographs from a manila envelope, fanning them across the desk, sorting them like a pack of cards.

What she'd found in Germany, how it had unwound, was here to see.

Images of a ruined city: acres upon acres of devastation; tumbled bricks under a dusting of snow; a few distant buildings showing black, fretted against the sky; a house number – 24 – painted on a chunk of fallen masonry. A man stared at tangled twisted steel girders that reached towards him like the arms of some toppled metal monster. Capsized ships lay in a harbour, half-submerged, funnels flush with the water. Snapshots of some terrifying dystopia taken in Germany 1946. A Caspar David Friedrich frozen sea, the Baltic presumably, frost-foamed waves looking uncannily like the snow-covered masonry piled in jagged heaps. *Niflheim*, the realm of ice and cold.

The photograph of Adeline herself was the one that had accompanied her obituary. Taken by somebody else on some moving battlefield. Adeline with her combat-jacket collar turned up, most of her face obscured by her Leica, blonde curls stuffed under a forage cap, a tank in the background.

Adeline was never without her camera. She had an eye for a picture, was famous for it, but it was more than that with her. It was as though she felt compelled to catch memories in the net of time. Here they all were. Snap. She'd caught them all.

There *she* was smiling, happy, sitting at a table in a sunlit square, the photograph taken in three-quarter profile, blue-grey eyes looking off to the right, the dappled light catching the planes and shadows of her face and the sun glinting on her golden hair. It was a good picture. The last one taken of her.

And a younger self, looking glamorous in a low cut Schiaparelli she'd bought for a song from a Parisian countess living in a cold-water flat in Maida Vale. New Year's Eve, 1945.

There was handsome Harry Hirsch at the same New Year's party. Jewish Brigade and later Mossad, looking boyish, if slightly sunken-eyed, a bit dishevelled, black hair flopping in his eyes, tie loose and shirt sleeves rolled. He had been acting as bartender, dispensing hooch to the spivs, émigrés, service types and general ne'er-do-wells there assembled. Next, the American, Tom McHale, in need of a shave and hungover, the photograph taken the morning after, no less boyish but looking altogether more slippery and deceitful which, of course, he was. Then Leo Chase. Came to a bad end. Dying in some ghastly Moscow flat, liver turned to foie gras. She smiled slightly, proud of the part she'd played in his demise. Adeline was lucky to get him. Leo didn't like being photographed, now everyone knew why, but here he was, eventual disgrace far in the future, his collar turned up against the New Year's Eve drizzle, rain drops glistening on his bowler and overcoat collar, photographed coming in to the party, pale eyes shifty, peering sideways behind his glasses, weak mouth caught between a grimace and a smile.

Next, the von Stavenows. Elisabeth in evening dress, head tilted to one side, large eyes gazing off somewhere, as lovely as a Nordic film star. She placed her next to the first photograph and looked from one to the other. Take away Elisabeth's gloss and glamour and they could have been sisters. Apart from the eyes. Hers were icy; the other's kind. Below them, came Kurt as Sturmbannführer, handsome as a viper in his black and silver. Underneath this, a much younger Kurt von Stavenow, looking very fetching in a cricket sweater, all blond hair and chiselled cheekbones. No wonder she'd fallen for him. The photo was passport size and had been paperclipped at some time: a long hook of reddish-brown spots marred his white shoulder. Rubbing with a thumb made no difference. Some stains are impossible to erase.

She'd laid out the photographs in a pyramid, like a Tarot

Spread. She placed the smiling woman in the sunlit square at the apex, the others ranged below. A reading would be impossible. There were no good cards here.

Oh, my dear girl, what did we do to you?

There was a reckoning to be made. A debt to be paid.

LONDON

1945/6

1

Government Offices, Marylebone

31st December 1945

'Do you know this man?'

Edith Graham looked back at the implacable black eyes staring into hers, then down at the photograph. A Greek *kouros* in a cricket sweater. A young man caught in the full beauty of his youth, or so she'd thought when she fell in love with him that very afternoon. She remembered the photo being taken. 1932. The Parks in Oxford. He was standing at the edge of the pitch, hands in pockets, face in profile, fair hair waving back from a high forehead. Shadows showed beneath his brows and defined his high cheekbones. He was frowning slightly, his mouth a straight line.

'Why yes, I do know him. That's Kurt von Stavenow.'

'Are you sure?'

'Oh, yes. Quite certain.'

'And your *relationship*?'

'We – we were lovers for a while . . .'

The woman made a note with her green marbled Sheaffer. Edith left it at that. She wasn't about to confide in this austere stranger with her cold, appraising eyes.

'For how long?' she asked with the air of someone who knew anyway.

'Not long. A year, if that,' Edith replied. He'd been her first love, only real love, come to that. Strange to think their time together had been so short. It took a far greater space in her recollected life.

The woman made another note, put down her pen and looked back at Edith, head on one side. She was strikingly good-looking, black hair swept back from a porcelain-pale face, large, dark eyes, slanted and slightly hooded. She wore red lipstick, the sort of shade that Edith's sister, Louisa, favoured; other than that, very little makeup. The set of her mouth suggested that she rarely smiled. Her dark-grey costume was cut with the severity of a well-tailored uniform. Any suggestion of mannishness was offset by the ivory silk blouse, the Peter Pan collar pinned with a small pearl brooch. Edith admired the subtlety. *I'm a woman in a man's world,* the outfit said, *in a position of some seniority.* The woman put a hand to her throat, an unconscious defence against Edith's scrutiny.

'I say,' Edith broke the silence. 'What is this all about?'

'You're here to answer questions not ask them.'

Edith shifted in her seat. This was beginning to feel less like an interview, more like an interrogation. She had no idea why she was here, or even where 'here' was.

She'd been brought from Control Commission, Germany Headquarters in Kensington, pulled out of the final briefing without explanation, and delivered without a word by a young man in a double-breasted suit and a Guards tie. He'd just pointed to a porticoed entrance.

'First floor. Corridor on the left.'

They were government offices of some type, although the proportions were all wrong for offices: the corridor too wide, the ceilings too high. The room they were in might once have been a grand sitting room. A small gas fire stood dwarfed in a wide fireplace, any heat swallowed by the yawning, cavernous chimney, and the muffled clatter of a typewriter filtered through thin partitioning plywood. No nameplate for the offices, no numbers on the doors. Something to do with cousin Leo. Edith would put money on it. They were second cousins, really, several times removed, but had grown up together, their mothers close. Leo was always vague about his work in the government but everyone knew it was hush-hush.

Edith sat facing a large, plain desk, clear apart from a single pad, fountain pen beside it and two manila files. The woman behind it opened the second folder and Edith caught a glimpse of her own passport photograph.

'You are due to leave for Germany soon to take up a position with the Control Commission, Education Branch,' the woman read from her file. 'That is correct?'

She spoke in German now. Edith replied in the same language. The interview was taking a different tack.

'Before that you were working in a girls' grammar school, teaching Modern Languages?'

Edith agreed again.

'For how long?'

Edith answered her questions, going through her education: her degree in German from Bedford College, London. Time spent in Germany, dates and places. Finally returning to her application to join Control Commission, Germany.

'Why?' the woman asked.

'Why what?'

'Why did you apply? It's a simple question, Miss Graham.'

'Those are often the hardest to answer,' she said. Her smile was not returned. 'I spent the war at home. This is a chance for me to do something. Make a contribution.'

Even to her own ears, her words sounded trite, banal. How could this woman with her important job, involved in goodness knows what, possibly understand the tedium of life as Senior Mistress in a provincial girls' grammar, with responsibility for Languages, Ancient and Modern, and the lower school? And when she wasn't doing that, she was looking after her mother while everyone else, it seemed, was off somewhere *doing* something. Dangerous, maybe, even deadly, but exciting, even so.

Looking back, that time, wartime, seemed melded into one

big mass, like the congealed blobs of metal and glass one found after a raid, impossible to see where one thing begins and another ends. So it was with the succession of days. Even raids had a tedious sameness. The dismal wail of the siren, getting Mother up and down to the shelter, listening for the drone of the bombers with that nerve-shredding mix of dread and boredom that came from not knowing when they would come, how long it would last, when it would be over. Then an hour or two of fitful sleep before the exhausting journey across town to work, on foot or by bicycle, with the plaster and brick dust hanging in the air, depositing a fine film everywhere, rendering pointless Mother's constant dusting and cleaning. Some nights, she would get Mother settled in the shelter and then return to bed, not caring if she was blown to smithereens, in some ways wishing for it. The only relief had been rare escapes to London and Leo.

'And how did you find out about the Control Commission?'

'A colleague. Frank Hitchin.'

'Who is he?'

'My opposite number in the Languages Department at the boys' grammar school.'

'They're looking for teachers,' Frank had told her, 'German speakers, to go there after it's all over, help sort out the mess it's bound to be in. I'm going to give it a go. They'll probably be taking women, too. Spinsters, you know. No ties and nothing to keep 'em. Fancy free.' He'd winked. 'Why don't you apply?'

Fancy free? If only he knew.

She'd pedalled home that evening, parked her bike in the garage with Mother waiting for the click of the garden gate. Tea on the table. Then cocoa and the six o'clock news on the radio. More V2 bombs in London but the Allies were crossing the Rhine; the Russians had reached the Oder. Surely the war was nearly over? 'Then we can get back to normal' her mother had announced with some satisfaction as she turned a row in her knitting. By that she meant, *how things were before*. To Edith, the prospect of peace felt like a closing trap. The Control Commission offered an escape. For a spinster teacher in her thirties, such opportunities did not come often. She was as well-qualified as Frank Hitchin and she'd spent time in Germany before the war, which was more than he had.

She'd said nothing to the family. They'd only try to stop her.

She'd had a reply almost by return, forms to fill, an interview. Nobody at home had the least idea. She didn't tell them until it was too late and she'd given in her notice.

'And what will your job entail?' her interrogator enquired. 'Teaching?'

'The teaching will be done by the Germans,' Edith replied, referring back to that day's briefing. 'We are there as administrators. Inspectors. Our job will be to set up schools where there are none, get them up and running. Vet staff. Get the children in.'

'I see.' The woman glanced back at the file. 'And a high position. Senior Officer, equivalent to the rank of Lieutenant Colonel.' She sat back, fingertips together, assessing. Then she smiled. 'You speak German very well,' she said in English. 'Very fluent with a good accent.'

Edith nodded in acceptance of the compliment. She had a good ear for languages and accents. Something in this woman's speech said she was not British. There had been a lecturer at college who could have been her brother.

'I could say the same thing. I've been trying to place your accent. Romanian perhaps?'

A lucky guess. The woman coloured slightly. There was a pause. Then she gave a slight nod, as though she had decided something.

'I would like you to read this and sign.' She took a form from the top-right desk drawer and pushed it towards Edith.

'What is it?' Edith asked, taking it from her.

'It's the Official Secrets Act.'

Edith glanced down the page of regulations. 'What is this all about?' she asked again.

The woman allowed herself a thin smile. 'We can go no further until you have signed.' She offered her pen. 'Here. And again here, if you would. And your name, clearly printed. Thank you.' She took the document and slipped it into a file. 'I am Vera Atkins.' The name meant nothing to Edith although it was clearly meant to command recognition and respect. 'From now on, all proceedings are covered by the Act and cannot be repeated, now or at any time in the future. You understand? Perhaps you need more time to consider . . .'

Edith shook her head, impatient to know what was going on.

'Now, back to Kurt von Stavenow. Or should I call him *Graf* von Stavenow. A man of many titles, it seems.' Miss Atkins pushed his file across the desk towards Edith. 'Do you recognize him here?'

Edith wanted to think that she didn't recognize him, didn't want to recognize him. His extreme good looks were heightened to a sinister glamour by the black SS uniform: the silver epaulettes, the lightning rune on the right collar, and the four silver pips on the left to show his rank. But of course she did. His blond hair looked darker and was dressed differently, combed to the side and cut shorter. His face had filled out, but still retained a certain boyishness; those high cheekbones, that cleft in the wide, square chin. He was not looking straight at the camera but off to the right, a look of resolute aloofness, his deep-set eyes pale under dark sweeping brows.

'Did you know that he was a high-ranking member of the SS?' the woman asked with a crimson slash of a smile.

'No, of course not.'

Edith felt her cheeks grow hot. She was close to losing her temper with the testing, teasing nature of the interview but it wasn't that which was bringing the blood to her face. Her grip on the photograph tightened, denting the corners. She'd known him. Known him well. They had been lovers. Whatever had happened between them, she'd thought him fundamentally good. She'd often wondered what he might be doing but she could never have imagined this. The glossy paper creased further under her fingers. An officer in the SS? The opposite, if anything. She'd worried he'd get mixed up in something. End up in a concentration camp. She would *never* have thought *this* of him. Never have dreamt it. How could he? How could this be? Her stare intensified as though the image might speak to her. She glanced away and back again. Perhaps it was a mistake. Perhaps it wasn't him. But that was even more foolish. She felt some of her certainty about the world and her place in it shift. It was him all right.

'When was the last time you were in contact with Sturmbannführer Kurt von Stavenow?'

'I didn't know him as Sturmbannführer von Stavenow.'

The woman sighed in obvious frustration, but Edith felt she needed to make the point.

'Very well, when did you last see *Kurt* von Stavenow?'

Edith thought for a moment. 'It would have been 1938.'

'You don't seem too sure.'

'It was 1938. In the summer.'

'Not since then?'

'Of course not!' Edith snapped. 'We've been at war!'

Perhaps he hadn't done anything terrible, part of her mind continued to reason as she answered questions. Perhaps he *had* been involved in some form of resistance, a plot against Hitler. Perhaps that was the reason for this current interest. Yet there was something in those slanting black eyes, a slight twisting of the lip that spoke of a deep contempt, even hatred, for anyone who had even been associated with this man, who might ever have called him a friend. Such loathing was not aroused by innocence. What had he done?

'Ah, here you are!'

The connecting door to the next office opened and there was Leo, coming through in a bustling hurry. Edith had the feeling that he had been there all the time.

'Sorry I'm late! Meeting ran on and on. How are you two getting along? Like a house on fire, I shouldn't doubt.'

He rubbed his hands together, choosing to ignore the frigid atmosphere, or failing to notice it.

'I think we've finished.' Vera capped her pen.

19

'Everything satisfactory? Edith pass with flying colours?'

'Perfectly.' She stood up. 'And yes.'

'In that case, thank you, Vera,' Leo at his most avuncular. 'Now, don't let us keep you. I'm sure you have plenty to do, gathering your bits and pieces and so on.'

Vera looked around the empty room. 'I've already done so. As you can see.'

'Hmm, yes, well . . .' Leo rubbed his hands again. 'Don't let us keep you, as I say . . .'

Vera held Leo's eyes in her level black stare before slowly fitting her pen into her briefcase. It was unclear who was dismissing whom.

'Oh, and leave those files on the desk, would you?' Leo added.

'I had every intention of doing so,' Vera said as she put on her coat, 'since they no longer have anything to do with me.' Quite unexpectedly, she turned as she moved to the door and proffered her hand to Edith. '*Auf Wiedersehen*, Miss Graham.' Her handshake was firm and strong. 'You have a formidable task in front of you with the Control Commission. A great responsibility.' Her grip became more emphatic. 'May I wish you good luck.'

'You mustn't mind our Miss Atkins,' Leo said as the door closed behind her. 'She's got a good eye, old Vera. Good instincts.' He collected the files from the desk. 'Particularly good with the girls. None better. If you pass the Vera test, you're on your way.'

'On my way to where?' Edith asked as she followed Leo out into the corridor. She caught his arm, slightly disoriented, still shocked by what she'd heard about Kurt. 'What am I doing here, Leo? What's this all about?'

'When you said you were off to Germany, I had an idea, that's all. It's a frightful mess over there. Chaos doesn't begin to describe it. Our zone is full to bursting, God knows how many from God knows where – the unfortunate residents of the bombed-out cities, demobbed soldiers, ex-slave workers, refugees from all regions east who've fled from Uncle Joe's forces and who can blame them for that?' He frowned. 'Among them are some bad hats, some very bad hats, taking advantage of all the chaos and confusion. Hiding in plain sight. Nothing suits them better. Our job, or part of it, is to winkle them out. Simple as that. We need all the help we can get, quite frankly.' He looked at her, blue eyes magnified by his glasses. 'Since you're going there, I thought you might do us a little favour.'

'Is Kurt one of these bad hats?'

'Most emphatically, I'm afraid.'

'But what has he *done*?' She held onto his arm, wanting, needing an answer. How could this possibly be? The Kurt she knew transformed into Sturmbannführer von Stavenow?

Leo glanced round. 'Not here. I'll explain later.'

Edith looked down the deserted corridor, the parquet dulled and scored, marked with cigarette burns. The tall windows filmed with grime, still criss-crossed with peeling tape.

'What is this place, Leo?'

'It's a place that's never existed officially and is about to cease to be entirely.' He nodded to a pile of boxes stacked by the door.

'Secret, you mean? Hush-hush?'

He nodded.

'What am I doing here? What do you want *me* to do, exactly?' Edith asked, a sudden, cold realization dawning. 'Be some kind of spy?'

'I wouldn't go as far as that. Not in the accepted sense.'

'The Official Secrets Act?'

'Oh,' Leo waved a dismissive hand. 'Everyone signs that. People get the wrong end of the stick about intelligence work. Most of it's done by perfectly unexceptional types: businessmen, travel agents, teachers, clerks, typists, shop assistants, anybody really. Ordinary men – and women. It's mostly a matter of keeping eyes and ears open, passing on information. Women are excellent at it. Superior intuition.'

Edith frowned. 'How do you know I'd be suited?'

'Oh, you'd be perfect.' He looked at his watch. 'Better get the old skates on. You'll find the driver waiting.' He kissed her on the cheek. 'I'll pick you up from Dori's at eightish. Wear something nice. I've booked a table at The Savoy.'

Edith sat in the back of the car. The driver seemed to know where he was going without her instruction. What was this about? She'd done favours for Leo before. Attended meetings at university, dropped off a parcel or two, collected ditto. Sat on a certain park bench until a man walked by with a dog. Another park, another town. Wait by the floral clock. Same man. Different dog. What did Leo want? The Official Secrets Act suggested something serious. In Edith's experience, the swankier the place, the bigger the favour and it didn't get swankier than The Savoy on New Year's Eve.

2

34 Cromwell Square, Paddington

31st December 1945

Ration Book Canapés
Quickly made from readily available ingredients, serve these delicious savouries to your guests with drinks or before dinner. Hand round fried cubes of spam, speared on toothpicks; triangles of thinly cut hot toast, crusts removed, spread with fried corned beef or tinned snoek mashed with pepper and vinegar. Keep the crusts to make breadcrumbs.
Stella Snelling's A Dozen Delicious Ways with Canapés
Women's Journal, week ending 23rd January 1943

Dori's square was close to Paddington Station. One side was a great yawning cavity, the buildings flanking the gap shored up with beams wedged against the walls. Dori's row was more or less intact, although some of the houses were boarded, either unsafe or waiting for their owners to return. Dori's was second from the end, the cream frontage in need of repainting with chunks of stucco missing. All the result of the bomb that had brought Edith here in the first place.

Edith thanked the driver and went down the basement area steps to the kitchen. She didn't feel ready yet to join the party going on upstairs. Dori's parties started early and went on late.

Easter time, 1941, she'd stumbled down these very steps with bells clanging, wardens shouting, half the square smoking rubble and the trees on fire. After a weekend in Leo's flat, she'd been trying to get home when she'd been caught in a raid and been diverted, herded into the shelter of the tube at Paddington. Adeline had been on the platform, taking photographs. An unmistakable figure, her flying jacket hung about with cameras, her white-blonde hair jammed under a soft peaked cap. Edith had first met the American journalist through Leo and they'd hit it off immediately, meeting up when their paths crossed in London. Edith waved, relieved to see a friendly face among so many strangers. Adeline smiled, equally as pleased to see Edith. Adeline shared her small silver flask of bourbon and they'd settled down together to sit out the raid, talking about who they'd seen, where they'd been and everything in between.

After the all clear sounded, they'd emerged to fires raging. Then, guided by some kind of premonition, Adeline had hauled Edith into a deep doorway just as another bomb went off, very near. A delayed fuse, a tail ender dropping the last of his load. The explosion had sucked all the air. They had clung to each other, the vacuum pressing them together like giant hands, while bricks flew, bouncing past like children's toys. Adeline had taken her by the hand and they'd stumbled through fallen masonry and abandoned cars towards the entrance to the square. A warden shouted: 'You can't go no further!' and Edith had baulked but Adeline had just gripped her hand tighter, pulling her down steps with the warden still yelling.

Half the square were in Dori's basement. 'Waifs and strays, orphans from the storm!' Dori had waved a bottle of gin in greeting. 'Come and have a drink, darlings. It's the only thing to do!'

Adeline had gone straight back out. She had to capture what she'd just seen: the destruction of the square, the flames in the trees, the faces of firemen and ambulance crews strained and white in the flashlights' glare, even the irate ARP warden, would appear on American breakfast tables in the pages of *News Illustrated*. Edith was just relieved to be out of it, glad of the shelter and enjoying the impromptu party. So much better than being at a freezing station, waiting for the trains to start running; so much more fun than sitting in the air-raid shelter at home.

By the time the trains were running, Dori had taken to Edith: 'You can *cook*! Come any time!' she'd said and meant it. Edith was equally taken with Dori; ebullient and flamboyant, she was fascinatingly different from anyone else Edith knew. She took to dropping in whenever she was in London and needing to find somewhere to stay when she was in the city, she joined the ever-changing group of people who periodically lodged with Dori. It was never for long: a day or two, a weekend here and there, a week at the most, but it became her lifeline.

Edith let herself into the kitchen and found a couple of young things standing by the kitchen table looking bewildered.

'Is that you, Edith?' Dori came from upstairs. 'I thought I saw you sneaking in.' Her voice was slightly slurred, as though she'd started the party early, but when she appeared in the kitchen doorway, she looked lovely. Her green silk dress cut low, her black hair falling in deep, soft, sloping waves. A light dust of powder gave a hint of colour to her pale, ivory skin; eyebrows defined to accentuate the tilt of eyes made to look even darker and larger by a sweep of liner and liberal use of mascara. 'Meet Pam and Frankie.' The two girls bobbed their heads slightly, as though Dori was royalty. 'You couldn't help them rustle up some of those delicious canapés, could you, darling?' She gave Edith her best red lipstick smile. 'I'll pop the geyser on and run your bath.' She disappeared up the stairs again. 'And check on my goulash!'

The girls turned to her expectantly. FANYs most probably. Dori had lots of friends in the First Aid Nursing Yeomanry.

Whatever their duties might have been, they did not appear to have included catering.

Edith went to the Aga and lifted a lid. 'Good God! What is this?'

'The goulash?' The taller girl volunteered.

Edith inspected the thin stew, feebly bubbling on the Aga. Dori was proud of her national dish, but she was no cook.

'What do you want us to do?' The other girl asked plaintively. Edith directed them to the larder to fetch corned beef and spam. She'd prepared something similar that first night to pay back the generosity of her hostess. She'd been surprised and delighted by Dori's genuine pleasure in her skill at making something from nothing – canapés, a flattering term for titbits on toast.

'Ooh, Stella Snelling's canapés.' The girl smiled. 'My mum did those at Christmas. She collects all her recipes.'

'You'll know what to do, then.' Edith smiled back.

Edith went to her own shelves in the pantry for OXO cubes, Bovril and her precious bottle of Worcestershire sauce. She raided Dori's cupboard for the fiercely guarded tin of paprika pepper. A couple of teaspoons more wouldn't hurt.

'Go upstairs, would you?' she asked the tall one. Frankie, was it? 'See if you can find me Angostura bitters.' *Just a drop works wonders! (Stella Snelling: Tips to Cheer Up Tired Dishes.)* Pam was ready with the titbits. 'Under the grill. Not the Aga. The gas cooker.'

A recent addition to Dori's kitchen. The Aga had become increasingly temperamental and there was the shortage of fuel.

Pam opened the oven door. 'There's a book in here!'

'Well, take it out! When you've done that put some potatoes in to bake.'

Hanging above the Aga were herbs Edith had scavenged from a bombed-out garden. She broke off thyme, sage, rosemary, bay. The scent reminded her of home. She put that out of her mind. Mother would be round at Edith's sister Louisa's by now sipping a festive sherry, already getting on her younger daughter's nerves,

26

complaining about Edith's imminent departure for Germany. She would not feel guilty. Their problem now.

Edith took the narrow stairs up to the Bolt Hole, the tiny attic room she rented at the top of Dori's house. It was her refuge. It offered a place to stay on her trips to see Leo or when she needed to escape the suffocation of home. It was paid for by the money she made from her recipes: she'd said nothing to the girl in the kitchen, but she'd been writing cookery tips as Stella Snelling for years now.

The great thing about Stella was that she had been a real person in Edith's life – a friend from college who then became a fictitious, handy pal in London and holiday companion. The family had met Stella, so they never questioned Edith going to see her in London or their holidays abroad: cover for her trips with Leo. Even though he was family and they'd been in prams together, jaunting off with him would have caused more than a few frowns. Edith discovered that having a phantom female companion freed her, for a while anyway, from the dull routine of work and the constraints of the family.

The real Stella had married and emigrated to New Zealand but Edith conjured her again when she began to submit wartime recipes, in answer to an invitation in *Woman's Journal*. Edith enjoyed cooking and liked to think of ways to make the ration go further. There was no dearth of tips. Every woman she knew had their hints and tricks: her mother, sister Louisa, Mother's friends in the W.I. and the Townswomen's Guild. The magazine accepted her writing and wanted more. She sent her recipes as Stella Snelling, hiding behind the pseudonym's anonymity. She didn't want anyone at home to know and she liked the idea of Stella as much as she disliked the way people made judgements about her based on her job and her unmarried status.

She stripped off Edith's tweed costume and sensible blouse, balled her lisle stockings and wrapped herself in the burnt-orange shantung robe she'd come to think of as Stella's. The tips and recipes didn't interest Dori but she'd immediately loved the idea of Stella, intrigued by this hidden aspect of Edith and happy to help find what Edith increasingly identified as her 'Stella side'. They had gone shopping for 'Stella'. Dori knew all sorts of unfortunates ready to sell the most wonderful clothes for next to nothing. Any qualms were firmly squashed with a 'Nonsense, darling, you'll be doing them a favour'. Dori had taught her about labels and fashion houses, shown her how to wear her new wardrobe, put on makeup, do her hair. Become a very different version of herself.

Dori seemed to have a talent for this chameleon-like change from one personality to another. Nothing was certain about her: who she was, where she came from, how she had tipped up in London, what she did exactly, even her age was a matter for conjecture. The stories changed depending on who was doing the telling. She was a Hungarian countess who had been married to a Polish cavalry officer who had fallen in the last charge. She had fled the Nazis, pursued on skis across the mountains. No, she was Hungarian all right, but Jewish, and had escaped through the Balkans. No, that was wrong. She was Polish, not Hungarian. She'd married a White Russian and had lived in Paris, got out just before the fall of France. The stories fed on themselves, each one more exotic. The only common thread? Dori was a spy.

This was true, Edith knew. Dori had spent time in France during the war. It accounted for her mysterious disappearances and Edith had seen the scars on her body and the ones inside that she strove to hide. Once, she'd come back from one of these absences ill and weak, unable to sleep, dark eyes deep and wide with the horrors she had seen. Edith, down in London for the weekend, had come in to find her gaunt and wasted, hunched and shivering with a rattling cough. Edith had not asked where she'd been, what might have happened to account for the state she was in and Dori hadn't offered to tell her: *Careless talk costs lives*. She'd just reached out a thin hand and Edith had answered her unspoken need for a friend. She'd stayed to nurse her, cabling Mother that she was caring for a sick friend. She'd sent Anton out to beg bones from the butcher for broth. When Dori was on the mend, the household had pooled their meat coupons and Edith had found paprika to make the goulash that she craved.

It was the Easter holidays. Edith stayed one week, then another. During this time of illness and convalescence, Dori had begun to reveal more about herself. She was from Hungary but had moved to Poland. She'd fallen in love with a British Flying Officer, Robert Stansfield, who was training Polish pilots. They'd left together when war broke out, made their way through the Balkans to Greece, then Alexandria where they were married before coming back to England.

Bobby had been killed in the Battle of Britain. He'd left her this house in Cromwell Square. That's where the story, as told by Dori, stopped. A few weeks later, Adeline supplied the rest. With Dori, it was personal. The Germans had robbed her of her adopted homeland and the man she loved. She regarded them with a visceral, implacable hatred. She wanted revenge.

'She wanted to be able to kill 'em,' Adeline had told her. 'So she volunteered for a secret outfit who'd let her do just that.'

Now it was all over, but ever since VE Day, Edith had sensed a restive dissatisfaction, almost despair about Dori, as if life was finished and everything to come would be merely a diminishing echo. Edith knew that others felt this too, but no one exhibited this restless ennui as strongly as Dori.

Edith went down the stairs to the bathroom. She could smell the *Et Noir* bath oil through the door. All the way from Paris. One of Dori's sidelines. *Got to make a penny somehow, darling!* It was more than a sideline and Dori was making more than pennies. Not just bath oil. Perfume, makeup, nylons, silk stockings. But it was a risky business and Dori was in deep and getting deeper. Impossible to stop her. She needed the money, but she needed risk even more.

Back in the Bolt Hole, after her bath, Edith opened the drawer reserved for what she thought of as 'Stella's things', unrolling precious silk stockings and laying out silk underwear. *Silk, darling, always silk*, Dori insisted. Then she flicked through her rail of clothes to find something nice for Leo: the midnight blue silk, long and tight across the hips with a slight flare in the skirt, the shawl collar dipped to expose her décolletage.

Satisfied with her choice, she moved to her small dressing table to do her hair, brushing out the dark-gold waves, smoothing and pinning up the sides, teasing the front section into rolls. She leaned into the mirror to apply her makeup in the way Dori had shown her: eyebrow pencil for definition, the merest hint of rouge. As a final touch, she uncapped a tube of Marcel Rochas lipstick in a silver tube and applied a shade she never wore in her everyday life. She worked her lips together and smiled at her reflection. The final transformation. This was the moment she relished most. She doubted that many of her colleagues at the Headmistress' New Year's reception would even recognize her as they sipped Miss Lambert's sweet sherry and nibbled on sparsely-filled mince pies and meagre sausage rolls.

3

Cromwell Square, Paddington

31st December 1945

Winter Goulash

A good, filling beef stew is always welcome
on a night that might be spent at the Warden
Post or in the Air Raid Shelter. This delicious continental dish makes a welcome change
to more traditional recipes and can be made
with the cheapest cuts of meat. It is
simplicity itself to prepare: A pound of
onions, a pound and a half of stewing steak
(shin or the cheapest cut available - skirt
will do) and any amount of root vegetables
browned well for colour and flavour. A little
flour to thicken, a sprig of thyme if you
have it; salt, pepper, paprika if possible.
Canned or bottled tomatoes, a dash or two
of Worcestershire sauce and (my secret ingredient) a dash of Angostura. Enough stock to
cover, made up from those kitchen stalwarts
the Bovril bottle or the OXO cube. Simmer

on a low heat or in a moderate oven (regulo
2 or 3) for two or three hours.

Warming Suppers by Stella Snelling,
Home Monthly, November 1944, No. 36, Vol. 24

In the basement, the goulash was doing nicely, potatoes baking. The canapé plates had come back empty. Time for a drink.

The screen separating the downstairs rooms was opened up. Jazz issued from the gramophone, a tune Edith almost knew picked up and whirled away by a tenor saxophone. A couple were attempting to dance but there was scarcely room to move. Men in chalk-striped suits with thin moustaches, Dori's new friends, trailed girls with peroxided hair. Poles stood by the door smoking furiously watched by a tall old man with long white hair, sunken blue eyes and a sardonic smile under his yellowing moustache. Anton lived on the first landing and paid no rent. He supplied the paprika. He bowed to Edith, saluting with his ivory-topped cane.

The rooms were stifling, thick with cigarette smoke, perfume and body odour. Edith drifted through enjoying it all.

'Canapés went down a treat. Come and have a drink. There are impossibly gorgeous men I want you to meet.' Dori took her over to the drinks table. 'This is Edith,' she said to the young man serving. 'Perfect genius in the kitchen and one of my best friends in the world. Get her a drink, would you, darling? Not the punch. The Poles have tipped a whole bottle of some dreadful hooch into it.'

'Pleased to meet you, Edith. I'm Harry Hirsch.' He reached under the table and brought out a bottle of Gordon's. 'Will this do?'

'Very well.'

'What would you like in it? Not a lot of choice, I'm afraid.'

'Lemonade's fine.'

He gave her a wide smile, which Edith returned. Not tall, quite slightly built, but there was a wiriness about him. Good-looking in a delicate sort of way: very pale with thick, black hair falling across his forehead in a boyish cowlick. He was probably older than he seemed at first glance. It showed in the frown marks arrowing down over his nose; the purple smudges like thumbprints beneath his deep-set brown eyes. Edith watched his hands as he poured, his corded wrists, the way the veins snaked over the sliding muscles of his forearms, the skin burnt brown, as if he had spent time in the sun with his sleeves rolled back.

'Where were you overseas?' she asked.

'Oh, Italy,' he said, 'Egypt, before that. And Germany. Just back.' He added a dash of flat lemonade. 'I could add bitters to jazz it up, but it's disappeared.'

She took the proffered drink. 'What's it like there? Germany, I mean.'

'It's a mess.' He frowned.

'Really? I'm due out there in a few days.'

'Are you?' His eyebrows quirked up, making him look younger. 'In what capacity?'

'To take up a post with the Control Commission. You couldn't tell me a little more, could you? I really don't know what to expect.'

'Of course. Happy to.'

He rolled down his sleeves and slipped on a tweed jacket. Moving out from behind the drinks table, he took her elbow lightly and led her to a quieter spot in the throng. His grey flannels had long lost their crease, if they'd ever had one. His white shirt was open at the neck and he wore no tie. Blueish shadow shaded his jaw and upper lip. He had a slightly raffish, bohemian quality that definitely wasn't British. His English was faultless but spoken with an accent that Edith couldn't quite place.

'What will you be doing in Germany?'

'D'you know?' She gave a rueful shrug. 'I'm not quite sure.'

He laughed. 'You'll be in good company. Where will you be based?'

'In Lübeck. Schleswig-Holstein.'

'That's a coincidence. I'm going there myself soon.'

'You're stationed there?' Edith asked casually, hoping he'd answer in the affirmative. He really was rather attractive.

'B.A.O.R. VIII Corps District.' He gave a mock salute. 'I'm

33

a captain. Jewish Brigade. We're conducting interrogations there. I am originally from Latvia, you see, and Northern Germany is full of DPs, displaced persons, from the Baltic countries. We have to sort them out. Sheep from goats. Good from bad.'

'That must be difficult.'

He grimaced. 'Almost impossible. But necessary.'

'Some of the goats are very bad?'

'Wolves in goats' clothing, you could say.' He folded his arms, suddenly serious, his dark eyes shadowed. 'When are you off?'

'Fourth of January.'

'I'm due out a week later. Belgium first, Kiel, then Hamburg.' His face brightened. 'I say, perhaps we can meet?'

'Yes, I'd like that,' Edith smiled, knowing that she really would.

'Yoo-hoo! Edith!' Dori was waving from the other side of the room.

'Over here!' Edith waved back. She turned to Harry. 'I have to go.'

'I meant it about meeting.' He held onto her hand to prevent her from leaving. 'CCG Education Branch. Lübeck?'

'That's me.' He really *means* it! Edith thought with a catch of her breath. Not only that, but she will be in Germany. In that moment, she felt her life turning. This is really happening and it's happening to me . . .

'I'll find you.'

Edith hoped he would.

'If I don't see you before,' his grip on her hand tightened, 'Happy New Year!'

His mouth was warm on hers. The kiss lingered a fraction longer than it should have. The intensity surprised them both.

'Happy New Year.' Edith didn't quite know what else to say. 'Perhaps I'll see you in Germany?'

'You certainly will.' He kissed her hand. 'I better get back to being barman.'

'You're a quick worker, I must say!' Dori was at her side. She nodded towards Harry Hirsch. 'What was all that about?'

'I'm not quite sure,' Edith replied. 'I was a bit startled myself.'

'I rather had my eye on him. But no need to worry. All's fair and the night is young! Also, Leo's here. Cab's outside. Have a lovely evening, darling.' She dropped her voice and her grip on Edith's arm tightened. 'Tomorrow, we need to talk.'

'What about?'

'Not here,' Dori breathed in her ear. 'Not now. New guests are arriving.'

Edith turned and nearly collided with a tall, elegant woman in a long black gown and a fur stole. She was with a curly-haired young man in evening dress.

'Oh, I am sorry. I do apologize.'

'That's quite all right. No harm done.' Vera Atkins peered closer. 'Miss Graham? I hardly recognized you. What a transformation. Going on somewhere?'

Her eyes turned to Leo as he came through the door, shaking moisture from his hat.

'Bloody weather! Fog's turning to horrid drizzle. Edith? Are you ready? I've a cab waiting.' He glanced at the woman by Edith's side. 'Vera. And Drummond. Well, well. Everyone knows everyone, hm?'

The two men shook hands.

'Leo. How unexpected.' Vera Atkins looked from him to Edith, her dark eyes sparking amusement. 'How do you two know each other? Remind me.'

'Sort of cousins. Ready, Edith?'

Leo didn't elaborate further. Neither did Edith. Childhood friends, cousins at several removes. Sometime lovers. As children, they had been co-conspirators, although Edith had learnt to be a wary one. Leo ultimately owed allegiance to no one and there was a streak of cruelty in him. He'd had a knack of drawing her into trouble. She had a feeling he was about to do so again.

4

Savoy Grill, London

31st December 1945

Menu
Consommé
Steak Diane
Noisettes d'Agneau, Pommes Duchesses,
Carottes Juliennes
Glacés
Tergoule de Normandie

One for Louisa!

'The steak, I think,' Leo announced. 'How about you?'

'The lamb.'

Leo nodded, engrossed in the wine menu. 'A Riesling, since you're going to Germany. Then a Duhart-Milon Rothschild, '34.' He snapped the menu shut. 'Had it the other night. Not bad.'

The Savoy Grill was crowded. Leo acknowledged people on nearby tables. There were people here whose fame gave their faces a vague familiarity. Edith tried not to stare. Leo would introduce her as his cousin, if he introduced her at all.

'Thin stuff,' Leo announced after two spoonfuls of consommé. 'I prefer a proper soup.'

'I was just thinking how different it was from soup,' Edith looked up. 'As different as the names. Soup sounds opaque. Thick.'

'Hmm. That's how I like it.'

'What's this about, Leo?' Edith said as she finished her consommé.

Leo put up his hand to silence her as a waiter arrived to clear the table and another approached with a trolley.

'Ah, the Diane! Best way to eat it. You can see what the buggers are doing.'

Leo sat back to enjoy the drama as the deft young waiter fried the steak in butter, executing the flaming with the flourish of a stage magician before transferring the dish to the plate and completing the sauce with efficiency.

'How is it?' Edith asked, once they had been served.

'Not too bad.' Leo chewed. 'Better than the one I had at the Club last week – you could have soled shoes with that. How's the lamb?'

'Fine.'

It was still pink. At home, the sight of blood brought on universal shudders.

Leo reloaded his fork. 'Mash a bit fancy for my liking. Club does it better.'

Edith took a forkful of the duchesse potatoes, smooth and rich under a thin golden crust. Trust Leo to prefer lumps. Enough prevarication.

'So, are you going to tell me?'

'Not here!' Leo looked to the nearby tables. 'You never know who's about. Let's just enjoy this, shall we? It's a bad business.' He added, sweeping slivers of carrot aside, he was never one for vegetables. 'Not something to talk about while one's eating. It's all in the file back at the flat.'

By the time they got to the flat, Leo had other things on his mind. His attentions started in the cab and their lovemaking was quick with the ease of long familiarity. They had been lovers, off and on, since fumbling adolescence. They were comfortable with each other and the arrangement suited both of them. Edith enjoyed her escapes to London and Leo liked the diversion. He had his life nicely organized in compartments: Sybil in the country, the boys at boarding school, flat in Marylebone for his week in London, mistress up in Hampstead and Edith when she was in town. Edith knew Sybil, of course. They met at family occasions, weddings and funerals, which diverted Leo even more.

Edith left him snoring, wrapped herself in his dressing gown, poured herself a glass of champagne, then turned on the desk light and opened the file marked 'Kurt von Stavenow'.

She held the photograph of Kurt in a cricket sweater close to her eyes so that she could study it with an intensity that had been impossible before. She'd gone to Oxford on the train to visit Leo. Kurt had been in the Parks watching cricket. Leo took a photograph. The snap was in black and white but Edith's memory was in vivid colour: blue sky, green grass, the cream of the sweater, Kurt's hair shining a soft, deep yellow like old gold. When he turned and smiled, the world seemed to stop and start again. Edith couldn't quite look at him; it was like staring into the sun.

He had begun studying Anthropology at Heidelberg University, he told her in his careful English, but had changed his course of study to Medicine. 'I want to find ways to bring the two disciplines together,' he said, interlacing his fingers. 'To help people, you know? Make them better.' He'd smiled again. Perfect teeth and dimples. Edith had never thought that a man could be so beautiful. She was scarcely listening as he went on to explain that he was in Oxford to perfect his English and to study his other love, Anglo-Saxon. He talked excitedly about Old English, Norse myths and his new obsession: Arthur and the Knights of the Round Table.

'He wants to find the Holy Grail!' Leo roared with laughter.

Kurt's brows furrowed, his answering smile uncertain, as if he couldn't see the joke.

That was the moment Edith fell in love with him.

'Leo has promised to show me the important places,' he said, looking down at her. The focus of his attention melted whatever was left inside her. 'Perhaps if you are also interested, you might like to come along.'

That's how it started. In the long vacation, Kurt stayed with Leo at Gorton, Leo's family home. Edith often stayed overnight. Their excursions demanded an early start. They visited the Rollright Stones, Wayland's Smithy, the White Horse at Uffington, then further afield to Stonehenge, Avebury, Templar churches in the Marches. Kurt took these expeditions very seriously, delving into his haversack for binoculars, maps, ruler and compass to work out alignments, notebook and camera for sketches and photographs. Leo took less of an interest, installing himself at a local pub, leaving Kurt and Edith to explore by themselves.

They would return to Gorton for supper. The house was enchanting, Kurt announced. *Ein nettes kleines Haus.* The remark stung with Leo. He didn't think it at all small, although Gorton had gardens rather than grounds; it was large, but not remotely stately; looked old but was relatively new. Leo was annoyed, as if he'd been found out in some way. Kurt belonged to a fearfully aristocratic and ancient Prussian family and talked of house parties and hunting parties in great castles. Leo became increasingly huffy. Kurt wasn't aware of it, but his remarks struck at deeper insecurities: Leo's father was a Brummy, a generation away from the bacon counter. Leo had begun to move in circles where such things mattered.

'I'm letting him have the run of the place,' he'd muttered to Edith, 'taking him all over the country and the little blighter insults me! Boasting about his bloody schlosses.'

One particular evening, things got so tense that even Kurt noticed. Later, he came to Edith's room and sat on her bed. It was a hot night and his pyjama top was open. The moon was full, cutting through gaps in the curtains, casting bars of silver over the smooth skin of his bare chest.

'I upset Leo in some way,' he said, frowning. 'This evening, he was off hand with me. That is the right phrase?' He looked up for confirmation. Edith nodded. 'I don't know why he is angry.'

Edith tried to explain. She didn't think any slight had been intended, but she feared that he, Kurt, might have given the impression that Leo's house, the way of life here didn't quite, well, measure up.

'Nothing could be further from my thought!' Kurt looked stricken. 'It is my English. I only say these things because I'm proud to be Prussian. I would love so much for you to come and visit me there. My two best friends.' He drew closer, taking her hands in his. 'You believe me, don't you?'

'Of course I do.'

'I thought he was cross with me because of you.'

'Because of me?'

'Yes. I thought you and he were, you know, and I'd come between you.'

'Oh, no!' Edith had to stop herself from laughing. 'We were, have been, but . . .'

She let her words peter out. It was difficult to explain. They'd been very young. It had all been Leo's idea and she hadn't liked it very much. Since Leo had gone up to Oxford, he'd been less attentive, pursuing something else Edith suspected, although didn't really care to ask.

'But not now?'

'Not now,' Edith confirmed. 'I think he has,' she hesitated. 'Other interests.'

Kurt had nodded. 'I understand. Many of the fellows in the college are, ah . . .' it was his turn to pause, 'of similar inclination. Is that correct?'

'Completely.'

'I'm glad Leo is, too,' he leaned towards her and they were kissing.

'Let's go out.' He took both her hands in his. 'Let's go outside.'

They walked barefoot in the moonlight, across the silvered lawn to the lake which lay as still as mercury. 'Let's go in,' he whispered. They kept on walking, the water soft as silk on the skin. The next night they swam to the island. They made love on an old picnic blanket that Kurt had brought out earlier in the day. He was so *very* different from Leo . . .

They tried to be discreet but Leo knew right away. He didn't seem to mind at all. He was glad to have Kurt off his hands. *He's all yours, old girl.*

Kurt came to see her in Coventry on an old motorbike that he'd found in the stables. If Gorton had seemed small, Edith's house must have been *sehr klein* indeed, but Kurt seemed to enjoy his visits. He'd spend ages working on the bike with her brothers, Ron and Gordon. They were mad about engines. 'I like your father and brothers,' he told her. 'They are *workers*.' He held up his hands. 'They *make* things.' He liked talking to them about cars and the motor industry. In a city famous for car manufacture, the boys had followed their father into the works. Gordon to the Standard and then to Whitley. Ron had an engineering apprenticeship with a firm in Rugby making turbines. They were proud of what they did. Keen to show Kurt. He followed with his haversack, making notes, taking photographs, as interested in the factories as he had been in Avebury.

Now she knew why.

There were maps in his file. Coventry and surrounding towns, the factories marked for the Luftwaffe. The Lockheed in Leamington Spa, BTH in Rugby. Her family had liked Kurt, made him welcome. He had a way with him: flirting with Louisa, complimenting her mother on her cooking. He knew how to get along with men and how to please women. They had been kind to him yet her father, her brothers could have been in those factories when the bombs rained down.

How naïve she'd been. How impossibly stupid. It was all here.

von Stavenow, Kurt Wolfgang
1931 – Joined National Socialist German Workers' Party
1937 – University of Heidelberg – Doctor of Medicine
1936 – Member of the Schutzstaffel (SS)

1937 – SS Ahnenerbe (and a helpful addition in pencil: *pseudo-scientific institute founded by Himmler to research the archaeological and cultural history of the Aryan Race*) *Sicherheitsdienst des Reichsführers SS (Ausland-SD)* (another addition: *Foreign Intelligence – see over*)

It had been lies from start to finish. For each action, an equal and opposite motivation: Principia Mathematica of the human heart. The shock of it jarred; old fracture lines started to crack open until she was fighting back tears.

At the end of the summer, Kurt had had to go back to Germany, departing with unexplained suddenness and abundant promises. He would write. She would come to see him. They would walk by the Rhine and the Neckar, hike in the Odenwald. He would recite eddic poems, heroic lays, stories from the Nibelungen. They would sleep in little lodges smelling of pine and resin. They would go to the Black Forest and the Harz Mountains, camp on the Brocken, climb to greet the May Day dawn.

Before he left, they agreed she was to go out the following year. She remembered the fierce excitement she'd felt anticipating their meeting. They would be able to spend all the time they wanted together. The rest of their lives.

It didn't work out like that. What in life ever did?

She blinked to clear her sight and focused on the next file, hardly noticing the peal of nearby church bells, silenced by long years of war, ringing out the old year, ringing in the new.

She detached the photograph of Kurt as an SS officer and read through his war career.

1939-45 – Sturmbannführer Kurt Wolfgang von Stavenow

What rank was Sturmbannführer? She had no idea.

1939-40 – Friedrich Wilhelm University, Berlin. Psychiatry/ Neurology

1939-41 – SS Special Purpose Corps. Aktion T4
1941-43 – Medical Officer with Special Responsibilities
1943-45 – Assistant Director to the Medical Superintendent.
 Charité Hospital, Berlin.
April 1945 – Last seen Berlin, present whereabouts unknown.

Underneath lay closely typed papers, some stamped with the Reichsadler, spread eagle and swastika, the lower half of some of the pages discoloured, rucked and crisp, as though the paper had been in contact with water then dried, rendering the typing even harder to read. Supporting evidence. She read what she could, the typing blurring still further as she scanned the pages, flipping back and forth.

She rubbed her arms at the bone-deep chill spreading through her. It either made no sense, or it made the most dreadful sense of all . . .

She didn't know how long Leo had been standing in the doorway watching her expression changing from puzzled to incredulous, finally settling into frozen horror.

'Make sense now?' He poured two whiskies. 'Here, drink this. You look as though you need it.'

'You never suspected?' Her voice sounded thick, distant. 'That he was a Nazi?'

'Did you?'

Edith shook her head slowly.

'He played us for fools, old girl. Pulling the wool. Acting like butter wouldn't melt. I suppose we should have known. His interest in the occult and Aleister Crowley – well known bad hat. When I look back on that summer – King Arthur, the Templars, Druids – it all fits. Remember the arguments?' Edith nodded, she and Leo insisting that it was myth and legend, Kurt replying that, on the contrary, it was history, a shared history. The history of the Aryan peoples. 'He was deadly serious. We couldn't see it the time, why would we? We didn't realize the reasons for his interest. He was a member of the Thule Society. Did you know that?'

'I've never even heard of it.'

'Exactly. He kept it secret. *The Study Group for Germanic Antiquity*. All those ridiculous theories.' He paused. 'Remember those trips he made us go on, haring all over the country . . .'

Edith closed her eyes. Yes, she remembered, standing at the very top of Glastonbury Tor as Kurt wove a net of romance and mystery around the death of Arthur. With the sweep of his arm and the passion of his words, the world transformed. The land before them became a vast mere spreading from horizon to horizon, still as a mirror. The only sound, the slow, soft, muffled plash of the oars on the dark funeral barge bearing the mortally wounded king. Two heavily veiled queens sitting at prow and stern, motionless as tableaus, while another stepped with bare white feet onto the stony shore to welcome the King to the Lake Isle of Avalon . . . They'd stood together, hands linked, as the sun fell towards the west. Shafts of light shone through the lens of the clouds and she'd experienced a moment of transcending wonder, caught in the pure magic of the place, the time, and him.

'. . . turns out it's just an excuse to spout theories of Aryan supremacy,' Leo was saying, 'and indulge in anti-Semitism of the most unpleasant and virulent kind. Joined the Nazi Party in '31. Plenty there of similar mind, including Heinrich Himmler. Every one of them firm believers in the Master Race, and all that. Tommyrot, of course, but dangerous tommyrot. Tommyrot that would cause the deaths of millions of people . . .'

'But he was training to become a doctor.' Edith shook her head quickly, denying the thought even as it was forming. Another came instead. Her mother burning herself on a tin from the oven, hiding the injury, making light of it.

'It's nothing, really,' she'd said.

'Let me see.' Kurt insisting, high, broad brow creasing with concern as he took her mother's hand with his slender fingers to see the burn. Edith remembered being proud of his patient skill, his confident, gentle touch as he applied salve and carefully bandaged the hand.

'You'll make a wonderful doctor, Kurt,' her mother had said, as she turned her wrist this way and that to admire his neat work.

44

'His chosen vocation had very little to do with the Hippocratic Oath.' Leo was pointing at the notes in front of her. 'The clue is in his specialism.'

Edith glanced down, frowning. 'Psychiatry? I don't follow . . .'

'Why would you? No right-minded person *would* make sense of it. Kurt was involved in something called Aktion T4, before the war and during.'

'I saw that in the notes.' Her frown deepened. 'What does it stand for?'

'It's an address in Berlin: Tiergartenstraße 4, sounds innocent, neutral. Headquarters of the Gemeinnützige Stiftung für Heil- und Anstaltspflege.'

'The Charitable Foundation for Medicinal and Institutional Care?'

'They were good at that kind of thing, the Nazis, inventing euphemisms to hide their filthy business. They called it the Euthanasia Programme. The taking of life on an industrial scale based on ideas about who should live and who shouldn't. They had a term for it: Lebensunwertes Leben: Life unworthy of Life. It's all there in black and white. It all makes sense now. It all fits.'

Life unworthy of life. Edith rubbed at her temples, trying to massage the words away, her eyes closed against the dreadful realization that the words meant exactly what they said.

'I'll admit, it beggars belief. It began in the Mental Institutions with the mentally deficient, adults and children with disabilities. Enforced sterilization. All to do with the purity of the race. Doctors have walked some very dark corridors, in the name of research, in pursuit of knowledge, trying to prove some misguided ideology. Our friend Kurt among them.'

'Medicine and Anthropology, melded together.' Edith looked up at Leo. 'He told us the first time I met him.' A memory, his long fingers folded together. *I want to bring the two together.* How could she have missed the darkness within him? He'd told her himself.

'Mixed up with Eugenics. And those other cock-eyed theories.'

'I suppose that's all we thought they were . . .'

'Indeed. We didn't think that they were about to put theory into practice. And we were in good company. Nobody did. Although it's all there, in *Mein Kampf*. Sterilization and the rest of it. And then even that wasn't good enough, they might not be able to breed, but they were still a burden on their families and the state. So they decided to kill them.'

'Who? Who decided this?'

'Well, Hitler gave the order, but it couldn't have been carried out without the co-operation of the doctors and nurses in the institutions.'

'They killed their own patients? How?'

'Starvation. And if that didn't work, lethal injection. And gas.'

'How . . . how many?'

'Tens of thousands in Germany, hundreds of thousands probably, we don't know, and goodness knows how many in the wider Reich.'

Edith stared at him, incredulous. 'I didn't know about any of this.'

'Few did. They kept it all well hidden, even from their own people. It gets worse.'

Edith looked down, slowly moving her head. How much worse could it get?

'Easy to see how it spread to other "undesireables",' Leo went on. 'Untermenschen: Jews, gypsies, homosexuals, Slavs. They moved the whole thing to the east, lock stock and barrel, used the techniques, the equipment, the personnel, to set up Extermination Camps for the Jews.'

Edith leaned forward, forehead in her hands, fingers tugging at the roots of her hair, knowing, dreading, what he was going to say next.

'And Kurt was involved.' He tapped the file. 'We've got chapter and verse.'

She knew what Leo was talking about. She'd seen the newsreels. Had been moved to tears by Richard Dimbleby reporting from Bergen-Belsen. Shock, anger and indignation shaking his

46

voice as he described the horrors that he had witnessed.

It wasn't cold in the room, but Edith could not control her shivering. The evidence was in front of her. There could be no possible doubt. And yet. And yet. To have been responsible, directly, or indirectly, for the deaths of millions, how could she believe that of anyone, let alone the man she had loved? She swallowed hard to keep down the whisky burning up into her throat.

'Where do I come into this?' she asked when she could trust her voice.

'Keep your eyes and ears open when you get to Germany. Put out feelers, see what people know. Softly, softly. You know? Shouldn't be too difficult. Most of them would sell their own mother for a tin of bully beef.'

'And if I do find anything?'

'Adams is your contact. Captain Adams. He'll be in touch. Oh, and keep a look-out for Elisabeth.'

'Elisabeth?' Edith had not been expecting that.

'His wife. You remember her?'

'Of course I remember. I just wasn't expecting her name to come up.'

'She had a cousin, or something, lived near Lübeck. She could well be in the area, since they've all been booted out of East Prussia. That's if . . .'

'She survived?'

'Well, yes. Obviously. The Frauen are turning out to be quite an asset. Find the Frau, find the Mann.'

'Do you think *she* was involved?'

'Not directly. Lots of the wives preferred to turn a blind eye. She struck me as very much the Juncker. Thought Hitler hopelessly vulgar and nothing existed outside of Prussia. All she cared about was her estate and her horses. She probably stayed up there looking after them until the Red Army arrived at her gates. Can't know for sure, of course.' Leo shrugged. 'When you find her, it'll be up to you to judge.' He refilled their glasses. 'Happy New Year, by the way. And happy birthday.'

5

Cromwell Square, Paddington; Service Women's Club, Lower Sloane St

1st January 1946

Corned Beef Hash meets Bubble and Squeak
Traditionally made from Sunday lunch leftovers: cabbage, potatoes and cold cuts from
the roast, it can be a satisfying supper for
any day of the week with the addition of
cubed corned beef. Combine together with a
liberal sprinkling of salt and pepper, form
into a large cake, fry both sides until
browned and beginning to squeak.
          Stella Snelling, Ideas for Leftovers

When Edith returned the next morning, Dori was sitting at the kitchen table in silk pyjamas and dressing gown absent-mindedly drinking a glass of flat champagne. Even dishabille, her makeup and hair were immaculate. Edith felt tired, drained. She'd spent the rest of the night next to a snoring Leo unable to sleep for the weight of the knowledge laid upon her.

'How was dinner with Leo? Go anywhere nice?'

'The Savoy Grill.'

'Oh, very grand. You couldn't rustle something up, could you, darling? We're starving.' Dori waved her coupe. 'Happy New Year!'

'We?' Edith questioned.

'Adeline's here. It's a wonder you didn't see her. She's out in the square taking photographs again.'

Edith went to the pantry and found leftover potatoes, a tired-looking cabbage and the inevitable corned beef. She cut the cabbage fine, put it in a frying pan and added the flesh from the baked potatoes and cubed corned beef.

'Happy birthday.'

Edith looked up in surprise and smiled to see Adeline coming in from the basement area wearing a uniform jacket, olive slacks, and tennis shoes. She put her camera down on the table.

'I'm amazed you remembered.'

Adeline put an arm round her shoulders and kissed her on the cheek. 'You know me, I don't forget much. I got some nice shots. Before and after, you know? Nice to see the trees growing back. I like the fog. Goes well with the folks back home. Foggy London Town. Good thing I had my pack with me. Too cold to go tripping about out there in party clothes.'

'Is he still asleep?' Dori pointed at the uniform jacket.

Adeline shrugged. 'Far as I know.'

'You must have worn him out, darling.' She turned back to Edith. 'You missed a marvellous party. Didn't she, Adie?'

While Edith found plates and knives and forks, Dori poured two more glasses, emptying the champagne bottle.

'A toast. To Edith and the New Year!'

They all raised their glasses and Edith dished out the food.

Adeline took a forkful. 'Umm, not bad. Kinda like hash with beets. Goes well with champagne.'

'Doesn't it?' Dori stirred hers with less enthusiasm. She put down her fork and folded her arms. 'Now, Edith, time to tell all. Beginning with, who is the handsome Sturmbannführer? And ending with what does Leo want?'

Edith put down her knife and fork. 'How do you know?'

'I was in Vera's office yesterday,' Dori lit a cigarette. 'Imagine my surprise when I see a file with *your* name on it. Imagine my further surprise when I find that it is paperclipped to another file and inside that is the photograph of a high-ranking Nazi officer. *Who is he?* I wondered. *Does Edith know him? What a very dark horse she is.*'

'What were you doing there?'

'I asked first.'

Edith glanced towards Adeline.

'Don't worry,' Dori said impatiently. 'She won't tell anyone. Not above a bit of spying herself, isn't that so, darling?'

Edith had never thought of Adeline as a spy but it was perfectly possible. She could be extraordinarily secretive about herself although she was very good at getting information out of other people. She knew the power of silence and how to flatter by close attention. She was adept at sniffing out a story and single-minded in her pursuit of it. It's what made her good at her job.

'So get on with it!' Dori sat back. 'We're both agog.'

Edith sighed. Dori's flippancy was grating on her and she didn't want to talk about Kurt and what she'd learnt. She was struggling to make sense of the contradictions it contained, between the man she'd known and what he had apparently become.

'I don't know if I should.' She shook her head. 'I've signed the Official Secrets Act . . .'

'Who hasn't! It's a bit late to worry about that now. Who is he? Come on, Spill the beans!'

Edith's sigh deepened. She'd have to give them something. They'd badger until she did. 'He's someone I knew before the war.'

'A friend of Leo's?'

'Well, yes. Originally.'

'And then a friend of yours?'

'We were lovers for a while.'

'Leo didn't mind?'

'No, not really. He encouraged it, if anything.'

'Did he? And what does Cousin Leo want now?'

'*Distant* cousin,' Edith corrected. 'He wants me to look out for him – Kurt von Stavenow, that's his name – when I'm in Germany.'

'And any others of his ilk that you might happen upon, I suppose?'

'Something like that. He calls them "bad hats". He wants me to find out what I can.'

'Hmm,' Dori frowned, suddenly serious. 'I know he's your cousin, and everything, but be careful what he gets you into. Leo is a slippery one. You're an innocent.' She shook her head. 'He should never have involved you.'

'Hold on Dori,' Adeline spoke. '*Innocent-looking folk make the best spies,* isn't that one of Dori's Rules of Espionage? Butter wouldn't melt types. Who would suspect?'

'They also get played, turned, sold down the river,' Dori snapped back.

'This von Stavenow,' Adeline turned to Edith. 'What did he do?'

'He was a doctor. Involved in something called the Euthanasia Proj—'

Adeline put up a hand for silence. They all looked to the stairs, the subtle rustle of bare feet on wood. Someone there. No telling for how long and sound carried.

'Well, look who it isn't!' Adeline raised her camera.

'Hey!'

The tall young man put up his hand to hide his face but he was too late. Just like Leo, he didn't like having his photograph taken but he was captured, caught in that moment, unshaven, in crumpled khakis, reddish-blond hair like stubbled wheat.

'I wish you wouldn't do that, Adie.' He took a swipe for the camera.

'Oh, no you don't!' Adeline whisked it out of his grasp. 'It's going in my archive.'

'I was looking for my jacket. Then I smelt chow. Any for me?'

He took the chair next to Adeline. She put a protective hand over the Leica.

Edith went to the stove and brought a plate back for him. Tom McHale. She'd met him once or twice before. He was one of those young men, vaguely attached to the American military, who came and went in the war. One didn't know what they did. One didn't ask.

'Got any ketchup?' He pushed the food round with his fork. 'Needs ketchup. Or hot sauce. Got any of that?'

'This is Britain, Tom.' Adeline shook her head. 'Of course they haven't.'

Edith went to the pantry and took out tomato sauce and Tabasco.

'Well, look at that!' Tom grinned at Adie through his food.

'Edith's going to Germany,' Adeline said.

'No kidding!' Tom looked up from dousing his plate with sauce.

'Absolutely not,' Edith stared back. There was something unnerving about him. His pale-blue gaze, made enigmatic by his fair brows and lashes, suggested a blankness that was not just in the eyes. 'I've got a job with the Control Commission. Education Branch.'

'I might see you there,' he said between mouthfuls.

'Might you?'

'Yeah, heading out there later today.'

'Me, too,' Adeline said. 'On assignment for the *Tribune*, covering the Nuremberg trials. Among other things.'

'Things like what?' Tom McHale asked.

'Know 'em, when I see 'em.'

'A snapper-up of unconsidered trifles?' Edith offered.

'That's me.' Adeline smiled. 'Kind of like a magpie.'

'Attracted to bright things and carrion in equal measure?' McHale laughed.

'Something like that.' Her smile widened. 'Corpses and paper-clips.'

A look passed between them. His mouth tightened and he stared hard before pale lashes shuttered down on those ice-blue eyes.

'Uh, huh.' He pushed his plate away. 'Well, seems like the place to be.' He got up from the table. 'I need my jacket. You'd better get a move on, Adie, if you want a lift with me.'

'Do you think he heard?' Dori asked after he'd gone upstairs.

Adeline shrugged. 'No knowing. He's sneaky.'

'He's OSS, isn't he? Still operative?'

'Yeah. Although it's not OSS anymore. They're calling themselves something else now.'

'Names don't matter,' Dori frowned. 'It's what they do. He's heading for Germany. Any idea what he might be up to?'

Adeline signalled for silence. Footsteps retreating, a door closing.

'He'll be hunting Nazis but not to bring them to justice. They're looking for particular individuals who might be useful.' She spread her hands. 'To us. The Allies. If Tom's involved that means to the US and not useful to the Russians and Uncle Joe.'

'Who are they looking for?'

'Scientists, mainly. Experts in all kinds of stuff. They've already rounded up all those rocket scientists responsible for the V1s and V2s, or as many as they can find. They're justifying it by saying that they were only involved in designing the things. But these are not innocent guys.' Adeline's hazel eyes became hard as agates. 'They designed rockets that killed thousands indiscriminately, right here in London. Rockets developed and made underground by slave labourers and concentration camp inmates who died in the dark in their tens of thousands? I was at Nordhausen. You should have seen the state of the workers there, half-naked, skeletons, barely alive. Almost impossible to tell the dead from the dying, bodies everywhere, corpses stacked up like so much cordwood. No one is innocent here.'

'What do they do with these scientists, once they've found them?' Edith asked.

'They take them to some special interrogation centre, bleach away any taint of Nazism. Once they've promised to be good boys and girls, they're given a new identity and shipped off to the US. They're looking for others, too. Real thugs who worked for the Abwehr, German Military Intelligence, or the SD – SS Intelligence. The Germans had good penetration of the Soviet Union during the war. We want those networks. The Russians are the enemy now. It's all about getting one over on them. The whole thing's called Operation Paperclip on account of the paperclips they use to fix the new IDs to the files, or that's what I heard, anyway. They've bagged most of the big boys. Now they're going after the smaller fry. Your guys will be doing it, too. It's a race for who gets there first. It's not about punishment, or even revenge. They are taking their reparations in people. A kind of human looting.'

'Adie!' Tom's voice came from above. 'My jacket!'

'I gotta go,' stood up. 'You keep safe now, honey.' She bent swiftly to plant a kiss on Edith's cheek.

'Leo didn't mention anything about this Paperclip business,' Edith said after she'd gone.

'He wouldn't, would he?'

'Did you know about it?'

'It's some time since I knew about anything, darling.' Dori frowned. 'But they will be busying themselves with a similar kind of thing, you can be sure of that.' She rose from the table. 'Time to find out. Meet you in the hall in twenty minutes.'

They got off the underground at Sloane Square. Edith thought that they were going shopping but instead of crossing to Peter Jones, Dori turned into Lower Sloane Street. They walked past a terrace of handsome red-brick buildings and stopped in front of a wide porch ornately decorated in terracotta. Two shields on each supporting column announced that they had arrived at the Service Women's Club.

'Mrs Stansfield and guest,' the concierge said. 'You're expected. Madam is in the Library.'

They were shown through to a comfortable room, discreetly lit with pearly lights in wall sconces and table lamps. Magazines and newspapers lay on a pale-oak table. The newspapers looked as though they'd been ironed. A large fire burned in the wide grate. The effect was warm, cosy after the rawness of the January day.

The woman in the armchair by the fire rose to greet them. She was dressed in a closely fitting black costume, pale-green silk shirt caught at the throat with the same pearl brooch.

'Vera!' Dori embraced her, kissing each white cheek.

'Dori,' Vera Atkins returned a merest peck to either side, 'and Miss Graham. How good to see you again. Do sit.' She indicated the sofa next to her chair. 'Drinks?' She rang a small bell. 'Gin and tonics,' she said to the girl who answered the call. No choice was offered. 'This is a very good place to meet.' She looked up at the portrait of a handsome woman in WAAF uniform smiling down from above the wide mantelpiece. 'The drink is cheap. There are no men about and it is very discreet. I won't beat about the bush,' she said when the drinks were delivered. 'I have a proposition to make.'

She turned towards them. As her black gaze fell on both of them, even Dori's confidence seemed to falter. She was the most elegant and terrifying woman Edith had ever met.

'I did rather put you through it, Miss Graham. Gave you a bit of a grilling but I had to be sure you were the right sort.'

'For whom? For Leo?'

'No. Not for them.' She gave a thin smile. 'For me. I no longer have anything to do with his department. Interviewing you was my last service.' She adjusted the hem of her skirt. 'I have recently been in Germany and will shortly be returning. I'm due to go out there in a few days, just as you are, Miss Graham. I have been tasked with finding out what happened to the girls who worked for Special Operations Executive, F Section,' her eyes flickered towards Dori, '*our* branch of the Service.'

She reached for her briefcase and took out photographs, placing each one on the low table: women in uniform and out of it, some smiling, some serious, some quite beautiful, all of them young.

'These are girls who were sent to France,' she said, her fingers aligning the photographs more exactly. 'Girls whom *I* sent to France,' she corrected. 'And who didn't come back.'

Four pairs of eyes gazed back at Edith. Four women full of courage and pride who had stepped forward to enter Occupied France, that deadliest of arenas. Four lives given to the service of their country. Four families still waiting for news.

'Do you think any of them might have survived?' Edith asked.

'It is possible. Anything is possible. There's always hope.' The black eyes became bleak. 'But I think it unlikely.' She paused, seeming to collect herself. 'We have to find out what happened to our women. Where they were taken, on whose orders, what those orders were, who carried them out. It will be my last service.' Vera's fingers lightly played over the young faces. 'I owe it to their families. I owe it to them.' Her voice had grown husky. 'I mean to see them honoured. I've made a start but new information is coming in all the time. It's too big a job for one person. I need help.' She looked at Dori. 'A person I can trust and I've asked that Dori might join me. We will be working with the War Crimes Commission, tasked with bringing the men responsible to justice, while taking part in a wider search for other criminals of the Nazi regime. Men like your von Stavenow.'

Dori perched on the edge of the sofa. She sat very erect, hands clasped tightly, as if to hold in the tension running through her. She stared at Vera, her face paler than ever, hope and expectation contending with fear of disappointment in her intense, dark gaze.

'I invited Dori to come today for the yay or nay.' Vera picked up a silver cigarette case and lighter and lit a cigarette. 'I'm happy to say it is yay. If it had been otherwise, we would not be meeting.'

Edith didn't take her eyes off Dori. 'You didn't say anything about this.'

'Dori's good at keeping secrets.' Vera drew deeply on her cigarette and let out a stream of smoke. 'As, I believe, you are, Miss Graham, from what Dori tells me. Hidden depths,' she gave one of her thin smiles. 'I like that. I've worked with far less promising material, it has to be said. That's why you are here. Now,' she tapped ash into a cut-glass ashtray. 'Leo has asked you to to keep an eye out for Nazi criminals, has he not? Like your friend von Stavenow, or any of his ilk that you might come across. Yes?' Edith assented. 'All I'm asking is that you tell us what Leo's interest is.'

'Why would you want me to do that?'

'Because I'm not entirely convinced that it completely co-incides with our own.' She stubbed out her cigarette and sat back, hands folded. 'Leo belongs to a different branch of the service now. A branch that is not interested in bringing these men to justice. Rather the opposite.'

'It's what Adeline was talking about,' Dori said, urgently. 'The Paperclip business.'

'You have proof that Leo, his people, are doing the same thing?' Edith asked.

Vera nodded. 'They are calling it Haystack, as in needle in.'

'And if I find something?'

'You still tell Leo, or whatever minion he sends, the only difference is, you let us know, too.'

'So I'd be some kind of double agent?'

'If you want to put it like that.'

'Oh, I don't know . . .' Edith said, uncertain.

'Do you want these men to get away with it?' Dori gripped her arm hard. 'Do you? Do you think it's right when so many died, when they have so much blood on their hands? She stared at the photographs on the table. 'Look at them. Look! Those are our girls, my friends. It could have been me quite easily.' She gave a deep sigh. 'In May, '44, we had a message. From Paris. It was hard to decipher, but some of it said: *They're sending our joes up the chimney*. We took it to mean they were being sent to concentration camps. The Nazis were clearing out Gestapo Headquarters on Avenue Foch, where they took agents. I've been there, seen the blood they didn't bother to clean up, the instruments set out in neat order: scalpels, pliers, hammers and chisels, like a cross between an operating theatre and a carpenter's bench. It wasn't just our girls held there and tortured but countless others. Countless! It's not just the cosh and cock boys we need to go after. That's what they used, didn't they?' Her defiant stare challenged Vera's wincing disapproval. 'Rape and torture? They are not so hard to catch. I want the ones who gave the orders. They are the ones who will escape us if we are not careful. So much death, so much suffering.' Her voice was deep with emotion, her accent pronounced. 'Then these, these *monsters* are free to go and live some nice life somewhere, with a new identity as if nothing had happened. Do you want that?'

Edith had never seen Dori so angry, so passionate about anything. Her face was as white as Vera's, her dark eyes glittering, brimming with tears. She was shaking, gripping so hard that Edith's arm was hurting. Her carefully cultivated insouciance had slipped. Edith could see now that it was just another disguise.

'Of course not,' Edith said, putting a hand on hers to calm her down.

'Then there is no choice that I can see,' Dori slowly released her grip, her voice full of unspilled tears.

'Dori feels strongly about this, Miss Graham, as do I, although I might not use the same language or show my emotions so readily.'

'I'll do whatever I can.'

Vera acknowledged Edith's answer with a slight nod and leaned back in her chair, eyes almost closed. The silence stretched.

'If messages are to pass between us,' she said finally, 'we will need some kind of code.'

'I can't just write to Dori, I suppose?'

'No!' Both women spoke at once.

'Your letters will come through Forces Mail,' Dori said. 'No knowing who might be reading it.'

'That someone will is certain.' Vera's eyes opened. 'Germany is under Mil Gov and Lübeck is right on the border with the Soviets.'

'We need a code and a safe delivery system.' Dori lit a cigarette. 'Something simple.'

Vera gave Edith a long, appraising stare. 'Quite so. Something that sounds innocent but isn't. Something that only means anything to people who know the code.'

'A word code would do,' Dori said.

'Yes,' Vera thought for a moment. 'It would.'

'A word code?'

'One of the simplest but surprisingly difficult to crack,' Dori explained. 'Messages are sent by card, or letter based on some common interest, bird watching, say, or some other type of hobby. The messages appear to be perfectly innocent but the words are freighted with other pre-agreed meanings which convey a completely different message.'

'A word means just what I choose it to mean . . .' Edith smiled.

'Exactly.'

Edith frowned. 'Why all this need for secrecy?'

Dori glanced to Vera, who gave a slight nod.

'In the war, not just individuals but whole networks were betrayed. Men and women sacrificed . . .' She glanced at the photographs spread out on the table. 'Some of the girls were picked up more or less on arrival, which means the circuit was blown, or there was—'

'A traitor at the heart of SOE,' Vera finished. 'Whoever it was might well have moved on to another branch of the Service. *That* is why we need secrecy. Such an individual will act without scruple, doing whatever is necessary to save his own skin. What we are asking you to do is not without danger.'

'We can't risk—' Dori started.

'No, quite,' Vera interrupted. 'It has to be secure. Between us. We will give it some thought, Miss Graham. Now, could you excuse us for a little while? We have things to discuss.'

'Of course,' Edith got up, taken aback. She hadn't expected to be dismissed like that.

'Go for a walk, or something,' Dori smiled, trying to make up for Vera's abruptness. 'We won't be long.'

Edith turned her collar against the chilling dampness coming up from the river and strode off, hardly knowing where she was going, hands thrust deep into her pockets, while she weighed what was being asked of her. She frowned, burying her chin deeper into her scarf. Dori and Vera were telling her one thing while Leo had told her entirely another. She stopped. Or rather, he hadn't. In typical Leo fashion, he had outlined Kurt's crimes, shown her absolute, shocking proof that the man she'd loved had been warped and changed, done the most terrible things, been turned into a monster by the regime he'd served. What Leo had *not* told her was *why* he wanted him found. Nothing about Haystack, nothing about finding scientists to use them, nothing like that at all. That had been left to Dori and Vera. *They* wanted to find men like Kurt to bring them to justice, to make them pay for their crimes. Instantly, instinctively she knew which side to take. She walked on. There was no really choice that she could see. Official Secrets Act, or no Official Secrets Act. No choice at all.

She stopped, mind made up, only to find that she'd totally lost her bearings. She suddenly felt nervous, even panicky, her surroundings unfamiliar, fog coming up from the river. The road was lined with antique shops, most of them closed, windows filled with junk mainly, salvaged from bomb-damaged houses. She hurried to one with lights on and peered through chipped china, dusty pieces of sculpture, jumbled bric-a-brac. The man behind the counter looked up as the bell tinged. He was in his overcoat, his expression flickering between wanting to make a sale and getting to the pub.

'I'm just about to close,' he said. 'Half day.'

'I just want directions.'

'Where to?'

'Lower Sloane Street?'

He gave a wheezing laugh. 'You're a bit out of your way. Here.'

He unfolded a worn map of the area, tracing the route with a nicotined finger. As Edith leaned forward, she dislodged a pile of books stacked in front of the counter.

'How clumsy of me.' She collected as many as she could, then paused, keeping one back. 'How much for this?'

The bookseller turned the book in his hands as though it was a valuable first edition even though it was water stained, smelt faintly of smoke from someone's bombed-out kitchen and he knew perfectly well that it was one of those given free with gas cookers.

'Depends how much you want it, doesn't it?'

'Sixpence?' Edith ventured. It was worth nothing but she did want it. Badly.

'Ooh,' he rubbed the side of his purple, pitted nose. 'I dunno . . .'

'Ninepence?'

'Done.'

Edith handed him a shilling. He reached for brown paper.

'No need.' Edith picked up the book and headed for the door.

''Ere! You forgot your change!'

He shrugged and dropped the threepenny bit into the till.

Edith held the book cradled inside her coat. They had one just like it at home: the cover stained, like this, marked with spillages, crustings of flour, pages interleaved with pamphlets (*Ministry of Food, Dig for Victory*), recipes cut from newspapers, torn from magazines (*Meals from the Allotment, Ruth Morgan's Wartime Cookery, Stella Snelling's Ideas for Leftovers*). They spoke of scarcity, turning the garden over to vegetables, the tyranny of the ration. Besides cuttings, the book held menus collected from restaurants, hotels, RAF messes; recipes written out in Mother's careful copperplate pencilled on lined paper; Louisa's purple-inked scrawl on deckled stationery; Edith's neat, small cursive in washable blue on Basildon Bond. Food, recipes, menus told you an awful lot. Taste and preference defined a person; what was on offer provided a wider context. *Messages based on some common interest. Messages that appear to be perfectly innocent . . .* Didn't this fit that?

They were sitting where she'd left them, enjoying a second round of gin and tonics. The concierge tried to stop her, but she burst in, still in her coat, face pink with the cold and excitement.

'I've got it!' she said, waving the book.

'Got what?' Dori looked up.

'The code. It came to me when I saw this – the *Radiation Cookery Book*. A code based on recipes. Everyone is obsessed with food, have you noticed? What's available, what's not available: on ration, off ration, blackmarket. Rationing and scarcity only sharpens the appetite. If that's true here, I can't see it being different over there.' Edith paused, the better to order and express the ideas that had begun to seethe. 'The very words we use can be read in two ways, sometimes more than two. We talk about being in hot water, being hot, or cold, going from the frying pan into the fire, putting things on the back burner and, I don't know, I'm sure we can think of others. Hot and cold, for example. See here,' Edith turned to the front of the book. 'Regulos control the temperature. Regulo 7 is very hot. Things cook quickly. Regulo 1 or 2, cool, slow cooking. I'm sure we can work out a whole code based on this book, understood only by us, each message couched in cookery terms, and Dori has the same edition!'

'I do?'

'In your larder. It came with the gas cooker. We use it to agree a code. Anything of interest, I send a recipe or menu, with a note, a card, or letter, message embedded. Every woman interested in cooking swaps recipes,' Edith added. 'What could be more natural? Or more innocent?'

'Or more likely to be beneath the attention of possible censors,' Dori finished, 'who are bound to be men.'

Vera leaned back, long fingers laced, her face as severe as ever.

'It might just work.' She gave one of her rare smiles. 'How exactly, will be up to you. Keep it simple. That's my advice.'

After Vera left, Dori ordered more gin and tonics. Keep it simple. Edith would send recipes to Dori and as a fail-safe to her sister, Louisa. The messages didn't have to be complicated. They could be limited to certain categories. A person of interest. Contact made. Developments in this area, or that area. Defined by the recipe sent, refined by nationality. British, American, German and anyone else who happens along. What could be more natural than collecting recipes, menus, dishes, from different nationalities?

'A flavour of the place. A flavour of the people.'

'Taking the temperature, testing the water?' Dori ventured.

'Exactly. With reference to recipes found in here,' Edith patted the book. 'Just so you know that such a thing is important.'

'But I can't cook,' Dori said suddenly. 'Does that matter?'

'Not at all,' Edith smiled. 'It's even better. I'm teaching you . . .'

'Oh, that's good.' Dori grinned back. 'We'll mark pages up when we get back. Decide on prearranged references. Doesn't have to be precise. More like progress reports. How you're getting on, that sort of thing. It's inspired, Edith. I really like it.' She finished her drink. 'More than that, I think it could actually work.'

Back at the flat, they went straight to the basement kitchen. Dori retrieved the *Radiation Cookery Book* from behind the Bird's Custard Powder.

'It's not much of one,' Dori sat back when they had finished the code. 'Rather Heath Robinson, truth be told. It certainly wouldn't pass muster with SOE, or any other intelligence agency for that matter, but that could be all to the better. Enough for tonight.'

The next few days were spent on the mundane: buying clothes and things that might be difficult to obtain: sanitary towels, toothbrushes, toothpowder, talcum powder, decent soap, makeup, perfume and haberdashery: sewing machine needles and bobbins, ordinary needles and sylko. Useful wampum, Dori called it. Then on Edith's last evening, Dori came to her room, a fur coat over her arm.

'I want you to take this. It'll be cold out there. You wouldn't believe how cold. Come, try it on.'

Edith slipped her arms into the sleeves. Her hands automatically stroked the thick fur, slippery against her cheek and under her fingers. It smelt faintly of powder and Dori's perfume,

Guerlain *L'Heure Bleue*, and beneath that, a slight, sharp animal smell.

'Dori, really, I couldn't possibly,' Edith began, although she already felt reluctant to part with the warmth of it, the soft, rich beauty of the fur. 'You might need it.'

'What for? I'm not going anywhere. Not yet anyway. It is never so cold here. I have boots. Proper boots. Nice leather, fur lined, knee high. I want you to take those, too. Try them on. We're about the same size.'

Edith pulled on the boots. They fitted perfectly.

'This is very generous of you,' Edith slipped her hand into the pocket. 'What's this?'

Her fingers closed around cold, smooth metal.

'It's a pistol. The bullets are here.' Dori held out a cardboard box of shells.

Edith turned the weapon over in her hands. 'I wouldn't have the slightest idea how to use it.'

'I'll show you.'

'But is it really . . . necessary?'

'Oh, yes.' Dori said, 'Vera agrees. We think you should take it for your protection. It could get dangerous.'

Edith had never held a handgun before, let alone used one. She looked down at the dull, dark metal of the short barrel, ran her fingers over the curved trigger inside its guard, felt the hatched rubber of the grip against her palm.

'But I can't possibly take it. What if I'm stopped? Searched?'

'Wrap it in underwear, preferably worn. They don't like picking through soiled undies. Or in a box of sanitary towels. They never touch those. And you have a rank. Use it. Act innocent but haughty. Haughty gets you a long way.'

'But I've no idea what to do.'

'I'll show you.'

Edith listened to Dori's instructions, watched as her slim, strong, practised hands handled the weapon. She loaded and reloaded the pistol under Dori's watchful eye, feeding bullets into the clip, taking it out, squeezing the trigger on the empty chamber, noting how the safety mechanism worked, until her hands were grey, filmed with fine-grade gun oil.

'That should do it. You don't have to actually *shoot* a gun,' Dori said, 'just know how it works. Aim at the body. It's a bigger target. Get close enough and even you can't miss. Once he's down, move in for the headshot. That way he won't get up.'

This woman had seen death and dealt it. Edith looked down at the gun in her hand and hoped she'd never have to act on her advice.

'That's enough. Wrap it in your knickers.' Dori stood back to scrutinize. Edith felt like a knight being armed for his first battle. 'There's something else I want you to have.' Dori unclasped the medallion she wore around her neck and handed it to Edith. 'It is Our Lady of Częstochowa.'

In Edith's palm lay a tiny oval icon, executed in jewel-like enamel, encased in gold: a black Madonna, her dark face scored and marked, the Christ child in her thin arms.

'You can't give me this!'

'Take it!' Dori closed her fingers over the talisman. 'Your need is greater. She will protect you.'

'Thank you!' Edith could feel the tears stinging at her friend's kindness.

'Let me fix it.' Dori reached round Edith's neck and secured the clasp. She held her close for a moment and whispered, 'May she keep you safe.'

When Dori released her, there were tears in her eyes, too.

GERMANY

1946

6

Blue Train, Hook of Holland—Hamburg

4th January 1946

```
Blue Train Picnic
Broodje kroket
Rookwurst (Smoked Sausage)
Mustard
Hard-boiled eggs
Genever
```

Broodje kroket: Not unlike a rissole, flecked with parsley. Made with leftover meat, minced or chopped, mixed with onion but bound with a béchamel then formed into a fat sausage, crumbed and deep fried. Eaten in a bridge roll with mild Dutch mustard.

More like a rissole than a croquette. Find under Meat (66, 63). Can be baked at Regulo 7 (or 6 depending on the oven) or fried for 9 or 10 minutes (turn after 5).

Hook of Holland station. A blue enamel token gave her a place on the train to Hamburg. The line of carriages stood the length of the platform; at the head of them the huge engine hissed steam. Travel came down to a game of snakes and ladders. Liverpool Street Station to Harwich. Boat to Hook of Holland. Now she was on the train to Hamburg. So far, no snakes.

She stowed her leather Gladstone in the nets and took a window seat, resolutely facing the direction of travel. The window was grimed from the outside but she wiped at it, impatient to get going. The stationary train conjured other platforms on other stations. She felt herself slipping backwards into memories she'd been trying to avoid. The awkward farewells at Coventry. The family assembled to see her off, the parting stilted, still coloured by the row that had blown up when she had announced her intention to go to Germany and work for the Control Commission.

'Are you out of your mind, Edith? I've never heard of anything so ridiculous!'

Her sister, Louisa, led the attack since Mother had taken to her bed.

Louisa was the beauty in the family. Even as a child, her looks had gone beyond prettiness. Rich, auburn hair, large dark eyes in a heart-shaped face. Louisa had been her father's favourite, everybody's favourite. Spoilt and headstrong, she'd married young. The war had been a godsend to her, allowing her to leave her life in the suburbs and travel with her handsome RAF husband to bases all over the country. But now all that was over. All the glamour had gone. Now this. Just when she was having to adjust to civvy street, normal life again, Edith was planning to swan off. Not only that, but the responsibility of caring for Mother would naturally fall on Louisa. It wasn't right. It was against the natural order of things and it had put her into a towering rage. She had her own family. Edith was a spinster: it was her job to look after Mother.

She had invited herself and the rest of the family round for a Sunday teatime conflab. Perfectly turned out, as always, in a striped silk shirt and pearl-grey costume, her lustrous hair scrolled back and caught at the nape in a snood, she strode about the small front parlour, full of righteous indignation, gesturing with her cigarette.

'What on earth are you thinking of? How could you dream of doing such a thing? What about Mother? How will she cope? You know there's no help to be had these days . . .'

Brothers, Ronald and Gordon, fell in with her as they always did, adding their chorus: 'Lou's got a point there', 'Have you thought it through, old thing?', 'Aren't you a bit long in the tooth?'

'I'm not *that* old . . .'

'Not far off forty!' Louisa laughed, sneering and harsh.

The sisters-in-law, Trudy and Vi, joined in, bleating protests, shocked that she should dare to break away, duck her responsibilities as the spinster daughter of her elderly mother. Their real fear was that they'd have to take over care of Mother, do the housework, the washing, the shopping, the gardening, keep the lawn mowed and the hedges trim.

Edith tried to explain that she was not doing this out of spite, or to shirk her responsibilities. She wanted to *do* something. All through the war, she'd seen others leave to join the forces, do useful work. She'd done nothing. She felt wasted, unfulfilled, as though she'd missed an important experience. Others had risked their lives, done things that meant something, that counted. All she'd done was trudge backwards and forwards to school, call registers, teach the girls, come home, do the garden, dig for victory, manage the ration, cook supper, listen to the wireless with Mother. This was her chance to make a real contribution. All this just earned an exasperated stare from Louisa.

'Oh, for God's sake, Edith! What do you take us for?' Her carefully drawn brows arched higher and her red-lipsticked mouth curled with contempt. 'I've never heard such claptrap.' Louisa turned away to light another cigarette, cupping her talloned fingers as if she was standing in a gale.

Only her brother-in-law, Ted, had been sympathetic. He stood by the mantelpiece, hands in his pockets, as handsome

71

and affable as ever, his dark hair sleek and close to his head, brushed back from a prominent widow's peak. He'd watched the row, a slight smile showing the gap between his perfect white teeth. Louisa had married him for his looks rather than his prospects.

He was the only one Edith could really talk to, the only one with whom she had the least thing in common. He was a teacher, too. He'd volunteered early and got a commission. Louisa didn't want to see her husband diminished by civilian life but Ted didn't seem in the least bothered about swapping his RAF uniform for grey slacks and a sweater and returning to his profession. He was looking forward to the part he might play in the changes the new Education Act would bring.

He carried out the tea things with Edith. Barely touched. A precious tin of salmon had gone into the sandwiches; a whole week's butter ration into the fruitcake. The raspberry buns, Mother's favourite, had been waved away with a peevish, 'You know the pips get under my plate.'

'Never mind,' Ted grinned. 'Kids'll polish that lot off. Let's go out shall we? See how the garden's doing.'

He lit his pipe as they stepped outside. They walked down the York-stone path past the flowerbeds and lawn. Children dodged in and out of the shrubbery. Ted's pipe smoke wreathed up through the cold, damp air like a veil. They stopped at the vegetable patch, brassica stumps still in the ground, a forlorn row of sprouts, the bean sticks showing ghostly in the mist.

'I really ought to dig it over,' Edith said. 'Get the broad beans in.'

'Don't worry, I'll see to this.' Ted knocked out his pipe on the sole of his shoe. 'What does Leo think? Have you been in touch at all? You were pretty close at one time. His ma's in a nursing home, Lou tells me. House and land sold to a builder. Plans afoot to develop all round there. Must have made a pretty penny.'

There was no jealousy. It was just an observation that chimed with the family's perception of Leo; he was the rich one, private school and Oxford. Not like us.

'Met him a couple of times during the war, in London, you know,' Ted went on. 'Always cagey about what he was up to. Got the impression that it was pretty hush-hush.' He looked over at her. 'Thought I saw you with him once, on the Strand. You were visiting your pal Stella. Never said anything.' Ted turned to her with his wide, white smile. 'You go off and do it, kid. You need to get away from here. You've done your turn with your ma. Let the others take over. Lou will grumble, but she'll manage. They'll need good people over there. It's a bit of a mess, from what I hear. You deserve this chance.'

A shrill whistle sounded. Doors slammed. A long blast signalled departure. Edith relaxed into her seat as steam billowed past the window and the wheels began to turn, slow at first then faster. This felt entirely right. The right thing to do. She suddenly knew that she would not be going back. Not ever. She should have made the break a long time ago.

'Mind if I join you?' A young army officer stuck his head into her compartment. 'Not many seats left.'

'No, please do.'

'Phew! Only just made it!' He pulled off his glove with his teeth and held his hand out to her. 'Alex Drummond. Bulldog, inevitably.'

Edith laughed. 'I'm Edith. Edith Graham.'

Bulldog. One of those forces sobriquets: Tinker Taylor, Chalky White. Medium build, not very tall, but there was a strength about him, in the squareness of his shoulders and the easy, physical confidence with which he moved and held himself. His pleasant face was just short of handsome, wide across the eyes and forehead with a strong squarish jaw. More bull terrier than bulldog but the nickname suited him.

'Nice to meet you, Miss Graham.' He lifted his bag one-handed and boosted it onto the nets. He looked down at her, quizzically. 'Haven't I seen you before?'

'I don't think so . . .'

He removed his cap, revealing bronzish hair, tightly curled, like a Greek statue, short at the sides, as though he'd just had a haircut.

'New Year's Eve. Dori's party. As we came in, you were leaving with Leo Chase.'

'Of course. You were with Vera Atkins.'

He smiled, seemingly delighted by her recognition, the connection made. He took off his greatcoat and sat opposite her. Edith smiled back. She had a suspicion that this was more than a coincidence, probably Dori or Vera keeping an eye on her, not that she minded. It was a relief to be watched over and she'd be glad of the company.

'I suppose we both look a bit different out of our finery.' He nodded towards the coat she was wearing. 'Though that is a rather splendid fur.'

'Dori's.' She pulled the coat closer about her. 'She insisted I take it against the cold.'

'Thought it wasn't Control Commission issue.' Drummond glanced at the badge on the cap on her lap: CCG, gold interlocked letters. 'Is that who you're with?'

Edith nodded.

He opened his cigarette case, automatically offering it to her.

'I don't. Thanks.'

'Sensible woman.' He snapped the case closed and lit his cigarette. 'Make sure you take up your ration. Germans would rather be paid in cigarettes than marks. Strictly against regulations but everybody does it. Going far?'

'Hamburg. Then Lübeck. I'm stationed there. Education Officer.'

'All the way, then.' His smile showed a slight gap between his front teeth.

'You?'

'Bad Oeynhausen. I leave the train at Osnabrück.'

They sat in silence. Edith looked out of the window. Drummond finished his cigarette.

The train was taking them through the outskirts of Rotterdam. Evidence of heavy bombing: broken buildings blackened and

74

hollowed, warehouses crumpled as if they were made out of cardboard. In the distance, huge cranes lay, unhinged and twisted, listing into the river.

'Rotterdam took two doses.' Drummond stared out at the devastation furling past their window. 'Germans in '40 then we had a go – shipyards, docks and the E boat pens.'

'E boats?'

'Fast attack craft.' He folded his arms, his jaw set. 'Bloody nuisance to our shipping, so it had to be done.'

They lapsed into silence again. Eventually, the train left the urban destruction behind and they were in a flat, geometric landscape, drab greens and browns with dykes and polders and windmills. Everyone's idea of Holland, culled from geography books and travel guides, but textbooks and Baedeker didn't show the broken bridges, their metal spars sprawled in the rivers as if pulled from their abutments by some giant fist.

'Want some of this?' he took out a flask and two thimble-sized metal cups. 'Genever. Have a drop. Keep out the cold.' He poured her a tot of gin. 'Cheers!' He threw his back and poured himself another. 'Wonderful! Not like that London stuff. That just makes you drunk. This is warming, sustaining. A real aqua vita.'

Edith sipped cautiously. She didn't usually drink neat gin in the middle of the day. The spirit was thick, almost oily, and aromatic with the piney sharpness of the juniper and other flavours she couldn't name.

'Just the thing, eh?' He reached over and poured her another. 'You missed a good party. Pity you had to leave so early. It was one of Dori's best ever.'

'So I hear.'

Edith looked out at the passing villages. Places one might glimpse for a fleeting moment but would never visit. In the middle distance, a man drove a horse-drawn cart, hunched over his reins; in the foreground, a couple of men shod in clogs plodded along a glistening, muddy road. It could be Brueghel. Medieval.

'I say,' he began. Edith turned back to find Drummond smiling at her. 'I was thinking about going along to the dining car, such as it is. Perhaps you would care to join me? Food is pretty poor on these trains.' He picked up his knapsack. 'Luckily, I've brought provisions. You're welcome to share.'

The dining car when they reached it was almost full. They slipped into a table. Drummond took out a napkin bundle tied neatly at the top. He undid the knots and unwrapped a series of packages.

'We have *broodje croquetten* with mustard – meat croquettes wrapped up in a soft white roll, really delicious – and *rookworst* – Dutch smoked sausage – and hard-boiled eggs. I'm always starving after the crossing but can't eat the muck they serve up when we get to the Hook.' He shuddered. 'So I breakfast at this little café. Hot rolls, real jam, proper coffee. Just the job. I have them make a little picnic up for me.'

He portioned the food carefully. He had good hands for a man, broad across the backs, but not fat; neat nails with short, strong fingers. Edith always noticed hands. She hadn't realized how hungry she was. The food was delicious. Different. Continental.

'Are you religious?' he asked, suddenly.

'No, not especially. Why do you ask that?'

'Oh, nothing,' he shrugged. 'It's just that pendant you're wearing. The Black Madonna of Częstochowa, isn't it?'

'Oh,' Edith's hand went to the medallion. 'Dori gave it to me. For protection.'

'We all carry something.' Drummond's hand strayed to his top pocket. 'She must be a good friend to give you that.' He looked at her with a strange kind of respect. 'Let's hope she doesn't need it back.'

'Why should she?' Something about his tone made her look up sharply.

'No reason.' He shrugged. 'How do you know Dori?'

There was a softening round the eyes, the quirk of a private smile as he said her name, that made Edith think that he might have been one of Dori's many lovers. Maybe still was.

'Through Adeline Croft.'

'The American journalist?'

'Yes, do you know her?'

'Met her a couple of times.'

They were having that kind of conversation. People of brief acquaintance, trying to discover people they might have in common.

'And Vera?' Edith ventured. 'How do you know her?'

'How do you?' he countered.

'I don't. I've only met her once.' She hesitated. 'Well, twice if you count Dori's party. I know her hardly at all.'

She omitted to mention the third time at the Service Women's Club. He looked at her again, as though he knew she was leaving something out but respected her for doing so. His smile widened as if she'd passed some kind of test.

'You must have made quite an impression.'

'Why do you say that?'

'At the party. She spoke to you. She cuts people she's known for years. Claims short sight. She can't be bothered, is closer to it.'

'You know her well, then?'

'Well enough.' It was his turn to be evasive. 'People in common, you might say.' He stared out of the window, his face suddenly closed and distant as if they had wandered away from safe ground. Then he looked back, as if he'd decided something. 'Vera and I will be working together. War Crimes Commission.' He looked down at the badge on his cap. 'Find out what happened to our chaps. Hunt down murdering Nazi bastards. Bring them to justice.'

He turned away again, as if that was all he had to say about it. Within moments, he was asleep. The scene outside had turned wintery, dykes and rivers covered with the dull-grey, green gleam of ice, the fields dusted with snow. Like Johannes Janson's *Winter Landscape* but without the skaters. Edith took out her pen and notebook, casting her eye over the debris on the table, selecting the croquette: a meat mixture, good way to use up leftovers. Basically a rissole . . . She wrote quickly, creating the recipe, looking up every now and then as she gathered the ingredients.

Sprawled in the seat opposite, head against the window, mouth slightly open, Drummond looked younger, his body loose, the tension erased from his face. He reminded her a bit of her brother-in-law Ted: the contained strength, the straight eyebrows over greeny-grey eyes, even the slight gap between the teeth.

The train jolted and Drummond was suddenly awake. Edith looked away quickly, not wanting him to think she was staring. The pen jerked in her hand, stabbing the paper, blotting the page.

'What are you doing?' he asked.

'Oh, I— I'm,' she looked at the pen in her hand, the notebook on her lap. 'You know, just jotting down a few things. I collect recipes. Foods I encounter – menus, and so on.'

'Our picnic?' He seemed amused by it.

'Well, yes.' She glanced down at the notes she'd been making. 'Food tells you a lot about a person. Allows you to see beneath the surface display.'

'What does this,' he motioned towards the debris, 'tell you about me?'

'Oh, you're sophisticated, well-travelled, cosmopolitan. You're a bit of a maverick, willing to improvise, cut corners, break rules. Well-educated, good at languages, intelligent. You are charming, especially to women, but men like you too—'

'Spare my blushes!' He laughed. 'You can tell all that? No need for palms?'

'Yes. Food reveals a great deal. It also serves to fix the memory. Better than a diary. Even years later, the recall is instant. Diaries can be dull. Trite.'

'And not allowed.' His look was frank and level. 'I see,' he settled back into his own memory. 'I do see.'

'So?' she asked. 'What do you see?'

He leaned forward again, hands clasped. 'The desert. Been out all day with Long Range Desert Group. Infernally hot. Stopped when the sun went down.' His eyes went distant. 'I can see this long dune, like a knife against a violet sky. We were starving. All we'd got were hard biscuits and bully beef. This Kiwi chopped the tops off the tins with his bayonet. I can see him now, the tattoo on his bare arm. Corned beef had melted to slurry. We scooped it up with biscuits, ate it from the tin. Out there under the stars, it tasted better than foie gras.' The train jerked violently then slowed in a series of juddering halts. 'What's wrong with this damned train? We'll never get there at this rate.'

He rubbed at the glass but removing the condensation made no difference. The world outside had gone a misty, pearl grey. A horde of children appeared like ghosts out of the fog, running alongside the halting train, shouting, '*Haben Sie Brot?*' Some of the occupants of the dining car ignored them but others opened the windows and from all along the train came a shower of sandwiches, cigarettes, loose and in packets, chocolate bars.

'It was bad here,' Drummond said as the children swarmed towards the tracks. 'They were more or less starving by the end of the war. The winter will be making it hard again. It'll be the same thing from now on. Wherever the train stops or slows, crowds of children come from God knows where shouting: "Chockie Tommee! Fags Tommee! Butties Tommee!" The chaps throw them what they don't want, or what they can spare just to watch them scrabbling and fighting over it. Or maybe they feel sorry for the poor little sods.' Drummond threw what was left of the sausage and a couple of children dived for it. 'You'll see plenty like these where you're going.'

One child did not move, just stared up at them. A little girl in a thin cardigan over a summer dress and what looked like sandals. She was just standing there in the enveloping mist, on ground grey with frost. Edith recalled a Control Commission briefing: a tall, sharp-featured woman in battledress tunic and navy skirt, an Education Officer who had just come back. She'd shown slide after slide of urban devastation, interspersed with grubby-looking children, playing in mountains of bricks and fallen masonry. 'You won't know what it is like until you get out there,' she'd said, white faced and solemn, as if she had scarcely believed it herself. Edith had noted down statistics: Cologne 92 per cent of buildings unusable, only 162 primary schools in the whole of Schleswig-Holstein, but it was the children sitting on the rubble, their faces pinched and sullen, who had stayed with her. Whatever else she might be doing, she was there to make a difference to the lives of children. She must never lose sight of that.

The train gained speed. Drummond glanced out of the window. 'Border soon. Papers at the ready.' Edith suddenly remembered the dratted gun. Her concern must have shown. 'No need to look so worried.' He leaned forward. 'They never search or anything. Well,' he grinned, 'almost never.'

The checks were cursory, papers and passports only. Formalities over, the groups around them became more relaxed, passing round bottles of brandy and schnapps.

'It's strange,' Drummond said, nodded towards the window. 'Some places hardly touched, as if there had never been a war.' They were passing Bad Bentheim. It looked just like a postcard, or something from a fairy tale, a great castle standing on a bluff; the red roofs of the town spread out below it, dusted with snow. 'Others,' he shrugged, 'almost utterly destroyed. It's the same all over Germany.'

The next town of any size was Rheine. Here, the marshalling yards had been bombed extensively, the devastation spread out to the surrounding town, the houses and buildings bordering the line reduced to burnt-out, blackened shells. The sidings were filled with the remains of goods trucks and wagons, sides splintered, burnt down to the wheels, derailed engines lay rusting on their sides. Some recovery work was going on. Men cutting up a tender, the falling arc of yellow and red sparks the only colour anywhere.

'Good to see someone trying to do something, even if it's only righting an engine.' A burst of raucous laughter from the people sitting on the other side of the aisle caught his attention for a moment. 'That's what we do here while we're supposed to be sorting out the mess we've created. Get drunk. Dream of other lives.'

Drummond looked away to the men working in the growing darkness.

The devastation grew greater as they approached Osnabrück. The train seemed to slow so that they could get a better look. As far as the eye could see, on either side of the line, only the odd church spire was left standing. In the distance, the jagged outline of what had once been blocks of tenements stood black against the last of the day.

'Serves them right, that's what I say!' A girl's voice, sharp and high, broke the silence that had spread through the carriage. She followed her remark with a fluting note of nervous laughter and there was a subdued rumble of agreement. The light was going, night coming on. The window turned into a reflecting mirror and Edith studied the girl against the scrolling phantasmagoria: smoke curling from her cigarette holder, her vivid lipsticked bow of a mouth frozen in laughter, her eyes dark below thin, pencilled brows, short blonde hair set in sculpted waves.

Drummond watched the group, his mouth set in a straight line.

'The train divides here.' He stood up. 'This is where I leave you.'

He retrieved his belongings and shrugged on his greatcoat. They stood in the corridor, Drummond lit a cigarette.

'You'll be a while. Engine change. The damage here is immense. It gets worse the further north you get.' He nodded towards the dining car. 'Not sure how much help they're going to be. Good war types, shy of civvy street, wanting to prolong the party. Can't blame them, really, I suppose. Pretty dreary back home, what with rationing and all that. Here you can have anything you want.' He stared into the darkness outside. 'And I do mean anything.' He looked back at her, his grey-green eyes hardened to serpentine. 'Don't get me wrong – I'm not soft on them. The Germans. I've seen Belsen, which is more than that lot has. Believe me, everything you've heard about that place is true, and it's not even the worst, not by a long chalk, but this "give them a dose of their own medicine" . . .' He shook his head. 'I don't go along with it. We need civilians. I'm not saying we don't. Military has enough to do. I'm just not sure we're getting the right sort. I don't mean you, of course. You're not like them at all, or the other kind, for that matter.'

'The other kind?'

'Bureaucrats, pen pushers with briefcases full of red tape. Either that, or Colonel Chinstraps.' He smiled down at her. 'Don't let them tie you up in it, Edith. They'll find a hundred reasons to do nothing. Find your own way. Get things done.' A whistle blew. 'I'd better be off.' He pulled down the window and gripped the outside handle to open the carriage door. 'Thank you for making the journey such a pleasant one.' He gave her a mock salute. '*Auf Wiedersehen!*'

He shouldered his bag and turned to wave before he set off down the long platform. Edith was sorry to see him go. She'd liked Drummond. He was intriguing. Easy, amusing company, although he'd been reluctant to talk over-much about what he was actually doing here, or what he'd done in the war. 'Oh, you know, this and that in the usual places.' Some men's reticence came from a desire to forget, get on with life in civvy street. He wasn't like that, the opposite in fact. Still in uniform. Very much the soldier. It was not what was said, but what *wasn't* that mattered. The words unspoken.

Edith went back to her compartment. The blinds were drawn now, blue lights in operation. Most of the carriage was asleep. It was warm enough in there, even stuffy, but cold outside, very cold, she could feel it through the window. She arranged Dori's coat like a blanket, turning her face into the corner. The worn moquette, the smell of dust and smoke, reminded her of another journey she'd taken.

Easter 1933. Going to see Kurt for their long-anticipated reunion after that wonderful summer. It had been cold then but not as cold as this. She'd booked a couchette but had found it taken. Too shy to oust the large Germany lady who occupied it, she had slunk back to her place in the ordinary carriage and sat huddled into the corner, unable to sleep. She hadn't eaten all day. The sandwiches she'd brought had turned rancid. Fish paste. Not a wise choice. But it was not hunger that had kept her awake. It had been nearly a whole year since she'd seen him but now she was on her way, now it was finally happening, her anticipation, her excitement were rapidly evaporating, distilling into fear. She'd wanted to halt the inexorable forward motion of the train, stop the wheels from turning, send them into reverse to take her back to everything that was safe, to the world she knew.

She shifted in her seat, trying to find a more comfortable position. It wasn't just the smell of the moquette, in the cold, early morning, eerie blue-lit darkness, fear was seeping into her like the chill through the seal round the glass. *Had* she done the right thing? Was she really cut out for this? Was she mad to do it? That's what they thought at home. Should she have stayed there? Done what was expected? She'd had a job, a family, security. Chucking it all could turn out to be the very height of folly. She was already feeling at a disadvantage, as though everyone else knew the ropes. They probably didn't, but that was little comfort. There had been a hectic quality about that group in the dining car that she'd found disconcerting, as though they were using brandy and bravado to allay their own insecurities.

What if this journey turned out as badly as that last one?

Gradually, the rhythm of the rattling carriage, the turning of the wheels on the tracks, lulled her into a fitful sleep broken by sudden jolts and starts, voices shouting, whistles shrilling, steam shunting, the hiss and shriek of the engine as it rolled into stations and out again taking her on, deeper into Germany, into the dark unknown.

7

Hotel Atlantic, Hamburg

5th January 1946

Breakfast Menu
Mushroom Omelette
Oeufs au Jambon
Rolls & Comfiture
Coffee

I chose the Omelette over the *Ham and Eggs.
A good choice - made with real eggs, flecked
with tarragon and scattered with champignons.
Everything about it 'continental', from the
deep-yellow yolks to the strongly scented
tarragon to the tiny wild mushrooms.

See recipe for Savoury Omelette in Cheese,
Eggs and Vegetarian p.178. Add 5 or 6 mushrooms (sliced). *Breakfast dishes p.229.

For sweet version see p.180. Simple dish but
needs great care. One has to be as watchful
as when preparing something more complex,

like crêpes suzette, or there is a danger
of ruining it – most unpalatable.

Edith woke stiff and cold as the train pulled into Hamburg Hauptbahnhof. End of the line, she was practically the last person on the train. She collected her suitcase and stepped down to the platform. There was no glass between the vast, curved girders of the great arching roof. The clouds of smoke and steam from the engine billowed up into the blackness. A few snowflakes sifted down, starring the sleeve of her coat.

At the end of the platform, the Rail Transport Officer came out of his small makeshift booth, not at all happy about leaving the comforting warmth of his paraffin heater for the biting cold of the open station.

He barely glanced at Edith's travel documents, just jerked his head towards the barrier. Edith picked up her suitcase and walked on through the cavernous station. She was to break her journey in Hamburg before going on to Lübeck. It was 05.55 by the huge station clock. She looked round the deserted station, at the signs and notices, the heavy gothic lettering, and the doubts and fears of the night journey faded. She took a firmer grip of her suitcase, heard her own heels echoing as she made her way to the main entrance. She was here. In Germany. She had arrived.

She halted. The orders hadn't specified exactly *where* in Hamburg, just she'd be 'met'. There was no sign of anybody and she had been travelling for almost two days. She was cold, tired, in need of a hot bath and coffee and not at all certain what was going to happen next.

'Miss Graham?'

Edith turned at her name. A man in uniform was running after her. She was nearly at the entrance to the station. What she had taken to be a pile of rubbish stirred, a bundle of rags wriggled and burrowed deeper into a filthy corner. There were people here, sheltering from the cold.

'You don't half go at a clip. Thought I'd missed you.' The man touched the peak of his cap. 'Jack Hunter, ma'am. Your

85

driver. I was in the RTO's hut getting warm.' He shepherded her out of the station, skirting round a frozen mound of rubble that had once been one of the towers at the main entrance. 'Car's over here.'

A driver. She hadn't been expecting that. Very grand. She could hear the chorus at home, Edith getting above herself. He conducted her to a black Humber parked by the side of the station. He was tall, well over average height, bulky in his overcoat. Dark hair curled from under the edge of his cap.

He opened the boot and stowed her case and travelling bag. 'You travel light.'

'I'm having the rest sent over.'

'Very wise.'

He held the rear door open for her.

'I'd prefer to sit up in the front, if you don't mind.'

'Suit yourself.' He got in next to her and started the car.

'Would you mind telling me where we are going?'

'Atlantic Hotel. Regional Headquarters. You aren't due in Lübeck 'til Monday. Office is shut. Weekend, see? Miss Esterhazy booked you in here. Recover from your journey, like.'

'Who's Miss Esterhazy?'

'In charge of the Lübeck office. Useful little body. You'll be fine in the Atlantic,' he added. 'All the brass stay there.'

She looked out of the window. It was six o'clock in the morning, still dark, but already a few people were moving about; impossible to tell if they were men or women, just shapeless bundles, wrapped against the cold, one or two pulling little trolleys.

'Trying to stop themselves freezing to death,' the driver commented. They slowed at a halt sign. A hunched figure shambled past them, head swathed, shoulders white with frost. 'Looking for work, grub, coal, firewood, anything they can sell or barter. Early birds, like. You see 'em going about everywhere lugging them little carts.'

'Are you from the Black Country?' Edith asked.

'Arr,' he grinned, broadening his accent. 'Where you from, then?'

'Coventry.' Edith smiled. She liked his accent. Something familiar.

'Got a cousin down there. Works in the Standard. Had it bad, didn't you? Not as bad as Brum, mind. Or these poor buggers.' He turned one corner, then another. 'Some of it looks quite normal, especially in the dark, but them rows is just facades, nowt behind 'em. Other places? Just nowt.' He wove down a narrow path zigzagging between hills of bricks, the headlights picking out the glitter of glass. 'I can give you a bit of tour later, if you'd like.'

'I've seen ruined cities.'

'Not like this one.' The car turned another corner. 'Here we are.'

They drew up in front of a tall porticoed entrance, doorman already coming down the wide steps. There was no damage here. The Atlantic stood just as it had always done, an imposing presence. Its white stuccoed façade swept the length of a city block, banks of balconied windows faced a wide expanse of water, the Außenalster.

'You look done in. I'd get some kip and some grub, if I was you,' Hunter said as he got her case from the boot. 'I got orders to pick you up at 1100 hours.'

'Oh, from whom?'

'Captain Adams. Intelligence. Your company is requested. Lunch at the Club.' He touched his cap in salute and turned back to the car.

Her contact. It had started. She felt an uncomfortable flutter at the name but she was too tired to think about any of that now.

Edith was checked in by a charming German girl. An elderly porter conducted her to a pleasant room overlooking the Außenalster. She hung Dori's coat in the wardrobe, kicked off her shoes, ran a bath. The water was hot, scented soap provided. She filled the tub and let herself float, soaking off the grime of the journey. She wrapped herself in a towelling robe and lay down on the bed.

She woke suddenly with no idea of the time or place. It took moments for the high-ceilinged room, the whiteness of the light, the thick quilt she lay under to make sense.

She ordered breakfast. Omelette. Rolls and coffee. The waiter set the tray down on the low table in front of the windows. The omelette (real eggs) lapped the sides of the plate. Edith buttered a warm white roll and poured coffee from the silver pot. Outside, the frozen Außenalster showed black through the bare lindens. The scene was monochrome, veiled by steady snowfall, it was like viewing an early film.

She was just thinking about dressing when there was a knock at the door.

'Adeline!'

Edith stood back to let her into the room. Melted snow spangled Adie's woollen hat and bulky, padded jacket. She smelt of cold air and smoke.

'What are you doing here?'

'I'm doing a piece on the destruction of the German cities. Thought I'd better take a look at Hamburg. I just arrived on the sleeper from Nuremberg. Saw you'd checked in but thought you could do with a sleep.'

'How did you know? I'd be here, I mean.'

'Lucky guess,' Adeline grinned. 'No, not really. I called your office. Spoke to a Miss Esterhazy? She said you were booked in for the weekend. I was coming up anyway, so thought I'd look you up.' She shrugged off her coat and took one of the chairs set by the window. 'Nice view. I could use some coffee.'

Edith poured a cup while Adeline told her about the trials in Nuremberg, the judges and lawyers, the prisoners in the dock, her fellow pressmen and women.

'But they might as well be show trials, given this Paperclip business. Your guys must be doing the same kind of thing?'

'Yes. They are. They call it Haystack.'

'Very appropriate. This from Leo?'

'No. He hasn't said more than he said before. Just keep an eye out for Kurt and his wife, Elisabeth, and anyone else I might happen upon.'

'And if you do find anything?'

'I report to a Captain Adams. I'm meeting him for lunch. I'm being picked up at eleven.' She looked at her travel alarm. 'I better get a move on. It's half past ten now.'

'So, who told you about Haystack?' Adeline asked as Edith began to dress.

'Will this do for lunch?' Edith took a light-grey costume and peach silk blouse out of her suitcase.

'Very smart. So, if not Leo . . .' Adeline prompted.

'Dori and Vera Atkins.' Edith wriggled into the skirt. 'Is this too tight, d'you think?'

'No, looks fine. I don't understand where Dori and Vera Atkins come into this.'

'They will be working together, for War Crimes,' Edith buttoned her blouse. 'Hunting down Nazis to bring them to justice. Didn't Dori tell you?'

'Uh uh,' Adeline shook her head and lit a cigarette.

'Oh . . .' Edith faltered. Maybe she shouldn't be telling Adeline this either, but it wasn't exactly a *secret*. Was it? 'They've asked me to help them.'

'OK.' Adeline sat back in her chair. 'Let me get this straight. You will be working for Leo, presumably through Adams, who is *not* interested in bringing these men to justice. In fact, the opposite. While at the same time helping Vera Atkins and Dori who are working for an entirely different outfit and who want them brought to account.' She looked up at Edith, enquiring. 'How are you going to stop Leo and co. from knowing what you are really doing? There must be some kind of censorship going on here.'

'We've developed a code based on a cookery book,' Edith said, as she went to the mirror to put on her makeup.

'And how does that work?'

Adeline never made notes. She didn't need to. She could recall conversations verbatim, like some kind of recording machine. She never forgot anything, slotting it all away to be checked, cross-referenced and followed up later. When she was listening like that, she had a certain look: hazel eyes wide and expectant, head on one side, curly locks twirling between her fingers. She was looking that way now.

Edith broke off from applying her makeup. 'Why do you want to know?'

'I'm interested, that's all. And concerned.' She spread her hands. 'It's good you have a system. You never know who else might be taking a look.'

'Like who?' Edith resumed applying mascara.

'Us for a start. Russians, even.'

'Russians!' Edith stopped, mascara brush poised. She looked at herself, startled in the mirror, one eye larger than the other.

'Well, yeah. If we're setting up networks in their zone, and you can bet we are, they will be doing the same and Lübeck is practically on the border.'

'No one said anything about *Russians*.'

'That's because they don't want you to know . . .'

Adeline stood up suddenly and went to the window. For a long moment, she stared out at the Außenalster, the graphite surface scarred with whorls and scribbled scorings although there were no skaters out today.

'I can't do this,' she said as if to herself.

'What can't you do?'

Edith finished her mascara while Adeline continued to stare at skaters who weren't there. She appeared to be weighing something in her mind.

'You know what?' she said finally. 'Fuck it.' She turned back to Edith. 'He can send me back. I don't care.'

'Who? Send you back to where?'

'Tom. McHale. To Poughkeepsie. To the Women's Interest pages of the *Eagle*. He can do it, too.' She snapped her fingers. 'Just like that.'

'What? But why would he want to do that?'

'He's not *going* to. He's threatening to. Unless . . .'

'Unless . . . What?'

Adeline sighed. 'Unless I find things out from you.'

In the depth of her sigh, Edith sensed that she was caught between the relief of telling and disgust at her own vulnerability.

'Things like what? What does he want to know?' Edith asked again.

Adeline laughed. 'Anything. Everything. Knowledge is power. Who said that?' Adeline didn't wait for an answer. 'He must have heard more than we thought at Dori's and what you were saying chimed with his new baby. His new area of interest, or one of them. He collared me after court yesterday, said if I don't find out what you are up to for the Brits, he'll have me back in the States before I can sneeze.'

'Oh Adie.' Edith made a move towards her, but Adeline gave a brisk shake of the head. Edith hesitated, then asked, 'So what *is* his new area of interest?'

'Scientists. Doctors. Involved in all kinds of nasty stuff – poison gas, biological weapons and the effects thereof. Up to now, these guys haven't been a priority. FDR didn't like that kind of warfare but he's not there anymore. They sure as hell don't want the Russians getting their hands on them,' she paused, 'or the British, for that matter.'

'So they might want Kurt?'

Adeline nodded slowly.

'What will you tell him?'

'I'll stall him.' She shrugged, hands in pockets. 'Say you don't know anything.'

'Well, it's the truth isn't it?' Edith's laugh had a nervous edge to it. What would happen if, and when, she did?

Adeline caught her sudden apprehension. 'This is a dangerous game, Edith, but you don't have to get mixed up in it. You don't want to be caught in the middle. You can walk away from Leo. Dori. Me. Go to Lübeck, get the schools going. That's enough.'

'Well, I am, aren't I?' Edith said quietly. 'Caught up in it, I mean. I can't see how I can back out of it now.'

No suitable job for a woman, isn't that what they said? Adeline had taken no notice; she'd fought them all. Now, all she'd worked so hard for, all she'd achieved, could be undone in an instant, tossed aside as if it had no worth and she'd be packed back to where she belonged, reporting on fashion and flower shows. Edith couldn't be responsible for that. Besides, Adeline's reports gave a voice to those who would otherwise have no voice at all. She'd added names and faces to the bald, bloody statistics of war. She would do the same to the aftermath. Expose the venal weakness, cowardice and culpability of the men in the dock at Nuremberg. Tell the stories of the vanquished Germans and how they lived now.

'We'll work something out,' Edith took Adeline's arm. 'Throw him a bone, every now and again, like Dori says.'

They laughed. Nevertheless, the sudden shrilling of the telephone made them both jump. Edith picked up the receiver, half expecting some sinister voice, British, American, even Russian.

'Frau Graham?' The voice was German, light and female – the receptionist. 'Your driver is here.'

8

British Officers' Club, Hamburg

5th January 1946

Officers' Club Lunch
Windsor Soup
Roast Beef
Roast Potatoes
Red Cabbage
Albemarle Pudding
Cheese and Biscuits
Coffee

British but not. Roasted potatoes sprinkled
with salt and caraway seed. Braised red
cabbage. A small jug of mahogany gravy, the
juice from the meat, augmented with red wine,
reduced, made shiny with butter and horse-
radish, but not as we know it. My Officer
companion enjoyed his beef 'bloody'.

Under Meat – Roasting. For RARE - Regulo 8
for 12 minutes to the lb, then Regulo 9 for
12 minutes then rest for 25 minutes.

Jack Hunter was waiting for them in the foyer. He'd swapped his uniform for a double-breasted grey suit with wide lapels, a blue shirt and regimental tie. He looked quite imposing, very tall, with a big, fine head, high, broad cheekbones and strong features. His black hair was cut short at the sides, a few waves already escaping the brylcreem into oily curls. His mouth turned up slightly and his bright-blue eyes crinkled at the corners as if he was enjoying some private joke, very probably at your expense.

'Sergeant? This is Adeline.'

Adeline sketched a wave.

Jack nodded, 'How do?'

'Adeline is an American journalist. She's writing about German cities. Maybe you can give us that tour you mentioned. If it's not too out of our way?'

Adeline was the only person she knew here. Edith didn't want to say goodbye to her just yet.

'I'm here to serve.' He gave a mock bow. His look of vague amusement turned into a genuine grin. 'Be glad to. Snow's stopped. Clearing from the North. Nippy, mind. You'll need your coats.'

He escorted them to the car and drove down to the river. He stopped at various places so Adeline might take photographs: a ship half-submerged in the docks, another, lying on its side, water lapping into the funnels, yet more, or perhaps they were submarines, in dry dock, their sides open, the metal peeled back, as if by an enormous can opener. Everywhere an incomprehensible tangle of rusting metal: fallen cranes, toppled and crushed like discarded Meccano; splayed steel beams reaching out like fingers spread in warning, or to ward off a blow.

'We did that lot,' Hunter commented. 'And I don't mean in the war. Blew it all up, useful or not. Crying shame. Perfectly good gear.'

He turned away from the Elbe into a vast wasteland. The roads were clear. Straight lines in a gridded pattern divided the flattened landscape. It went on for what seemed to be miles on either side of them, the perimeter defined by a serrated curtain wall of ruined apartment blocks.

'See that there,' he pointed out crosses painted on toppled pillars, lumps of masonry. 'That means bodies.' Further along the road a withered wreath lay on the low, fretted remains of a smoke-blackened wall. Everything was frozen, snow lay in the hollows of the uneven surfaces. 'God knows how many are still underneath it. Good thing it's cold,' he added. 'It'll be ponging to high heaven come summer. See that?' A trickle of yellowish grey smoke seeped out from a mound of rubble. 'That's how they're living. In the cellars.'

More stops. More photographs.

They went on. Tall ruins of apartments loomed nearer, gaining dimensions. All the roofs were missing. From above, it would look like a honeycomb with the protective wax sliced away to reveal the naked, vulnerable cells of the hive. Rubble rose either side of the road to the height of at least two storeys. It spread away in peaks and troughs. Edith was reminded of something, not natural, but not human built either. *Trümmerfrauen*, rubble women, stood in lines that followed the contours, passing pieces of broken masonry hand over hand with ant-like industry. In some final, ratcheted twist of irony, they looked like people passing buckets to put out a fire.

'3,000 planes, over eight days and nights,' Hunter continued his commentary. 'Our boys and the Yanks. I've got a pal who was on the raids. Said he'd never seen anything like it. Like flying over a volcano. Great column of smoke rising up to about 20,000 feet and the ground just a sea of fire. Horizon to horizon. Heat that great, they could feel it, smell the burning in the plane. 40,000 dead, so they reckon. Probably more'n that. No one rightly knows. There was this great firestorm, that's what did for most of them. Swept through the city like a hurricane. Winds up to 170 m.p.h.; temperatures hot enough to heat a furnace. I met this chap. Been a P.O.W. in Dresden. Lived through the same thing there. Had to help clear up after. Sights he saw . . .'

He went on with a tour guide's practised ease, recounting the facts and figures, death and destruction: an inventory of horror alternating between gruesome anecdote and the bald statistics of a debriefing session. Adeline was paying close attention but Edith was no longer listening. She had walked to work the day after the bombing of Coventry to find out how many pupils she had left. She had picked her way through the centre of the city, a basin filled with bricks and mortar with the smoke still rising, the ruins hissing in the falling drizzle. She'd seen the temporary mortuary filled edge to edge with bodies. She remembered the scorched wool, charred wood, burnt meat stink of it. She knew what fire did to people, rendering them unrecognizable as people at all, turning them into something naked and desiccated, like disrobed mummies, not human, shrunken and distorted, like fetish dolls fashioned from tufts of hair, wood and rag. Strange what the flames consumed and what they left. The sleeve of a green woollen blazer, barely singed, the embroidered badge still intact. The raid had begun early that evening, catching children out playing, some still in their uniforms. From one moment to the next, it must have seemed, their city had been turned into a cauldron of fire. A second's hesitation, a moment's disorientation was all that lay between death and safety. How many had died on that night in November? 500, 600? It had seemed an unbearable number. But this? This was of an entirely different order.

He swung round towards the lake. As they drove through what was left of the centre, they passed an ugly, modern building that took up a whole city block. The lights blazed out, although all the buildings around were unlit.

'Victory Club. Glorified NAAFI. You can get anything in there. They got plans to make it even bigger by pulling that lot down.' He indicated the buildings around it.

'But those look perfectly sound,' Adeline frowned.

'You got it exact. Welcome to the British Zone.'

They left the ruined city behind them. The destruction had not been absolute. The random patterning of the bombing had left pockets of the city relatively undamaged. They returned to the Außenalster, driving around the western edge. The road was broad and tree lined. Jack nodded to the left-hand side. Grand houses in their own grounds studded the rising slope.

'CCG, or Military Government, every one of them,' Jack said. 'Living like kings, they are.' He shook his head. 'That's where we're heading.' He indicated a house above the bend of the lake. Bright, freshly-painted, the pillared portico, window frames and stonework carefully picked out in white against primrose-yellow stucco. The grounds ran uninterrupted down to the shore. 'Belonged to some rich industrialist, requisitioned for the use of British personnel. Officers' Club. Too busy arsing about choosing the paint to find homes for them poor bastards' back there, 'scuse my French. Don't get me wrong, I ain't soft on them, I seen what they've done, but when you see little kiddies with no shoes, clammed with cold, babbies living in cellars. That's not right.'

Jack was making no secret of where his sympathies and politics lay. Adeline sat in the back taking it all in to write up later, no doubt.

Jack drew up outside the club and opened the door for Edith. A slender army officer was coming down the steps towards them, his uniform immaculately tailored. Jack stood by the car and saluted. The officer barely touched a finger to his cap.

'Miss Graham? I'm Bill Adams.' He stood very erect, a head shorter than Hunter and slightly built. Small hands and feet. Dapper would be the word for it. His head tilted back so he looked down his snubbed nose. 'And this is?'

'My friend, Adeline Croft.'

'Hi,' Adeline extended a hand to him.

'American?'

Adeline nodded. 'I'm a journalist.'

'Ahh.' Captain Adams smoothed his fair moustache.

'I'm covering the trials in Nuremberg.'

Adams gave a yelping laugh. 'Rather a distance, isn't it?'

'The court doesn't sit at the weekends,' Adeline replied coolly. 'I'm doing a piece on the destruction of German cities. Thought I'd see what the RAF had done up here.'

'Righto. Good show.' Adams turned away from Adeline. 'Going somewhere Hunter?'

'Yes, sir. I . . .'

'Not now you're not. Take Miss Croft back to wherever she wants to go and then come back here and wait for Miss Graham.' He turned away. 'Shall we?'

Edith stayed to say a quick goodbye to Adeline. They hugged tightly.

'You stay safe, honey,' Adeline whispered as she kissed her cheek. 'Look after yourself.'

Edith went to join Adams, who was waiting impatiently at the top of the steps.

'Keep an eye on your driver.' He nodded towards the departing Humber. 'Not a fully paid-up member of the awkward squad but not far off it. A bit of a maverick. Useful man in a tight spot but give him an inch and he'll take a mile.'

'You speak as if you know him well.'

'Oh, Jack and I go way back.'

A German attendant sprang forward to open the door for them; another relieved Adams of his cap. A female attendant came to take Edith's coat. Adams stopped in front of an Art Deco mirror and smoothed his neatly parted creamy-blond hair. He ushered Edith into a long sitting room, taking a table by the window.

'Let's make ourselves comfortable shall we?' He twitched his sleeve to expose a thin gold watch. 'Drink before lunch? What'll you have?'

'A whisky and soda.'

'Make that two.' He didn't look at the waiter who had arrived to serve them. 'Nice view from here,' he said as they sipped their drinks. 'Very nice spot. Skating in the winter. Sailing in the summer. One of my favourite clubs.' He glanced at the menu card. 'Not much choice but they do a good roast beef. I hope you're hungry.'

The dining room was crowded.

'Sunday lunch bit of an institution,' Adams said as they were shown to their table. A waiter brought up a cart. A domed silver dish revealed a roast forerib of beef. 'I like mine bloody and plenty of it. The Yorkshires are hopeless and they will mess about with the potatoes.'

Despite his complaining, he accepted large helpings of everything. For a slender man, he had a good appetite.

'What's that?' Adams recoiled as the waiter prepared to spoon a thick, pale sauce on to his slices of beef.

'*Semmelkren*,' the waiter answered.

'Horseradish,' Edith supplied.

'No thank you.' Adams put his hand out to protect his beef. 'Not in my book it isn't. Looks all bready. Ugh!'

The waiter offered the sauceboat to Edith.

'*Ich danke Ihnen sehr, es sieht köstlich aus.*'

'German speaker, then.' Adams looked up. 'You were a school-teacher, I hear. Now with the Education Branch?'

Edith nodded.

'Did Leo tell you much?'

'Not really,' Edith said. 'Just to look out for bad hats.'

'That's old Leo.' He cut into his bloody beef. 'Nail on the head. That's all it is, essentially.' Adams chewed and swallowed. 'The men we're looking for have been devilishly difficult to spot, right from the off.' He sawed off another portion. 'Ditched their uniforms pretty sharpish. Found Himmler disguised as a sergeant with a patch over one eye. Minus the moustache, of course. Spotted by a sharp-eyed squaddie. That's what you need, Miss Graham. A sharp eye.' He put down his knife and rested his forefinger lightly on one high cheekbone. 'As time goes on, it becomes harder to spot 'em. Melting back into the population. We have too few dedicated officers. There's only so much terri-tory they can cover. So much they can do. That's why we need people like you from different branches of the Occupation: Education, Housing, Displaced Persons, interacting with the German population, keeping an eye out, an ear open. Like listening stations, if you like, each one a single beacon. Together, they create a web that covers the entire zone. Clever, what?'

Edith agreed. It was clever.

'Some of our best pickups have come from people like your-self.' He mopped up gravy and bloody juices with a piece of bread. 'Close to the ground, meeting all sorts – Germans, displaced persons, expellees – they've all got children. They've also got wives. Leo's *Find the Frauen* is already bearing fruit.' He looked up from his plate. 'Spot something, hear anything, tell us. We do the rest.'

'What is "the rest"?'

'Get 'em in, sweat 'em. See what they know.' He picked up his glass, swirling and tasting. 'Not a bad red. We're having difficulty, quite frankly. This business depends on informers. They should be coming forward in droves, the Germans, shopping their own mothers for a packet of Players, but they're not. We need to know why that is.' He leaned back as the waiter cleared their plates.

'Any ideas?'

'Albemarle pudding, I think. How about you?'

'I meant any ideas as to why the Germans aren't coming forward in droves.'

'Oh, got you. It could be they don't trust us, which is understandable, given everything, but it could be something else.'

'Oh? Like what?'

'Like they're afraid of something.' He frowned. 'It's as though the people we are looking for, the Nazi bigwigs, the SS, still have influence, power over them.' He glanced towards the German waiter gliding over to take their order. 'I wouldn't trust any of them as far as I could throw them.'

'That far?'

Adams laughed. 'Pudding?'

Edith shook her head.

'You work for me. Find anything, this is the number.' He put his card on the table then addressed his pudding. A light, lemony steamed sponge, studded with raisins, served with a pale sauce. 'You're missing a treat. This really is delicious. At least someone in the kitchen knows what he's doing.' He ate in large bites, scraping together the last crumbs and custard. He let his spoon clatter into his dish. He stood up, straightening his uniform. 'Due in Herford. Time to love you and leave you. Welcome aboard, Miss Graham.' He shook her hand as if to seal the deal.

'Hunter will take you back to your hotel. Oh, and word to the wise,' he leaned in closer. 'We have to be careful who we talk to about this, who our friends are. Careless talk and all that.'

The last delivered with almost a purr. He stepped back, smiling slightly, passing a hand over his thick, pale hair. His high, wide cheekbones and narrow jaw, blunt nose and smoky, slanted blue eyes reminded her of Miss Lambert's blue-point Siamese. Edith had a feeling he had just shown his claws.

Hunter was waiting outside on the drive. He scowled after Adams folding himself into a Mercedes roadster.

'Gave me a rocket for not wearing uniform. Arsehole!'

Edith stared out of the window as they drove back to the Atlantic. The evening yawned. She half thought of asking the sergeant in for a drink but it probably wasn't the done thing.

He must have seen her look in the rear-view mirror. He shook his big head.

'Other ranks not allowed past the foyer. You can come with me if you like. I'm off to meet my wench, Kate. She's a nurse with the Alexandra's. Teaching me to lindyhop.'

'Thank you, sergeant,' Edith smiled, 'but I think I'll have an early night.'

'Probably wise. I'll be along to pick you up Monday morning, ma'am. 0800 hours.'

9

Außenalster Café, Hamburg

6th January 1946

Lebkuchen
A biscuit traditionally eaten at Christmas,
baked with ginger and other spices. Similar
to gingerbread.

Williamsbirne
A delicate fruit spirit made exclusively with
Williams Pears.

Edith went to bed early and slept late. The day stretched
before her. Being alone didn't really bother her. She needed
to think.

She took the path round the Außenalster. Across the lake, tall
spires showed thin and ghostly, spiking up from the city through
an icy haze. There were few people out. Those she met passed
by with their heads down, hunched deep into their scarves and
collars, unwilling to meet her eyes. A man in a long overcoat
and black Homburg raised his hat to her, his face sunk and
leaden, cross-hatched with deep lines of pain and grief. She
nodded her own greeting and went on. Perpetrator or victim?

Innocent or guilty? Impossible to tell. They were a beaten people. All victims now.

She stopped at a café and ordered a coffee and schnapps to warm up. The windows were steamed, the interior cloudy with smoke. Most of the customers were British. RAF men, a few soldiers, plying German girls with cigarettes, coffee, patisserie. The girls sipped delicately and ate greedily, staining cups and napkins with their red lipstick. The men sat back, smoke curling from their cigarettes, watching with a different kind of greed.

The coffee came with a little plate of Lebkuchen, she bit into one. Soft, spiced with clove and cinnamon, so different from British gingernuts. The schnapps was *Williamsbirne*. Its sharp, pear-drop perfume caught in her throat and in her memory, taking her back to August 1938, to Schloss Steinhof and the von Stavenows. Lebkuchen and *Williamsbirne*. As potent as Proust's Madeleine dipped in tea . . .

Edith hadn't known she'd be seeing Kurt, still less his wife. Leo had sprung it on her. They were holidaying together, a Baltic cruise (the family assuming she was going with Stella). Leo never said anything, and Edith didn't ask, but she'd suspected, even then, that these jaunts were more than mere holidays. Leo took photographs as they steamed in and out of different Baltic ports, as ready with his camera as Adeline, as Kurt. Ships, docks, marshalling yards. It all made sense now. When the steamer reached Danzig, Leo suggested that they jump ship; he'd seen all he wanted to see.

'Thought we'd drop in on von Stavenow,' he said with elaborate casualness. 'He lives in this neck of the woods. Knew he was married, did you? Got a son, so I hear. Thought we might go down to Berlin after. Have a nose about.'

Yes, Edith did know he was married. Her name was Elisabeth. Kurt had talked about her at their last meeting. Leo went off to call ahead, highly pleased with himself. Why did he do that? His cruel streak again. That awful meeting in '33. He knew what the outcome of that had been. He knew she didn't want to think about it, let alone talk about it. Leo came back. Von Stavenow and his wife would be delighted. Train to Königsberg then a local service to a tiny village, no more than a halt. A coachman was waiting.

'I am Andreas,' he said with careful formality. Leo's enquiry about the von Stavenow Estate brought a smile. They were to be guests at Schloss Steinhof, the Gräfin was expecting them.

'The *Countess*, eh?' Leo leaned towards Edith as the wheels of the carriage rattled over cobblestones. 'Wouldn't be surprised if it wasn't *her* family. That'd explain a thing or two. Not least why you lost out, old girl. How do you feel now? Still holding a candle?'

Edith ignored this fresh jibe, just stared down at the wheels turning in the dusty road. They were passing through rich farming country. White wheat fields, splashed red and blue with poppies and cornflowers, went on for miles, giving way to green fields and cropping cattle; emerald paddocks with horses standing off at a distance. Beyond the fields, forest covered the rising ground, spreading towards the blue haze of the horizon, texturing the distance like darkly woven tapestry. '*Alles,*' the driver announced, '*die Ländereien der Gräfin.*'

The carriage turned sharply through a high stone gateway. A narrower, gravelled road led into open, undulating parkland dotted about with large trees. The carriage took a slight rise then slowed for the passengers to better appreciate the scene. A lake, surrounded by dark fir trees, made a glittering silver mirror framed in Hooker's Green, the better to reflect the house beyond.

Castles in Germany could be anything, Edith knew, from lowering fortresses and fairy-tale confections perched on impossible pinnacles, to a solid manor house. This was a grand country house built in the Palladian manner. The approach was along a wide avenue of limes. The interlocking branches shaded and dappled the road in front of them. To right and left more horses grazed, the sun turning their bright flanks to satin. Mares with foals lifted their heads at the sound of the passing carriage, flicking their ears and skittering away from the road. All this belonged to Elisabeth. Kurt, too, but only through her. Leo's summation, bald as always, was as accurate as ever.

The carriage stopped in front of the wide, porticoed entrance and a curving flight of steps. The great front door stood open. At the sound of their approach, dogs of all shapes and sizes had come spilling out, yapping and barking, pouring down the steps and surrounding the carriage. They were followed by Kurt in boots and breeches, laughing, trying to call them all to heel.

'Damn dogs,' he called up to them. 'No discipline! Welcome!'

He was as handsome as she remembered. His smile as dazzling as ever. Edith fought an impulse to look away.

The coachman opened the carriage door as Kurt tried to marshal the excited dogs. A piercing whistle quietened them. They trooped back up the steps to sit in a row ranging in size from Great Dane to dachshund, obedient to the command of a young woman in a white open-necked shirt, jodhpurs and riding boots. She swept her blonde hair back from her face and smiled.

'My wife, Elisabeth,' Kurt waved a hand towards her. 'She has a way with animals.' He laughed again. 'I, as you see, have not. Come. Come and meet her properly. Welcome to our home.'

The coachman set their luggage down on the marble tiles of the hall. A butler directed it to be taken upstairs. Kurt had made no secret of his aristocratic background but this was beyond anything Edith could have imagined. She looked to right and left. Rooms led off, enfilades opening onto a series of diminishing interiors, rather in the way that a pair of mirrors set opposite each other give the illusion of infinite extending distance. She'd never been anywhere that remotely compared, only glimpsed stately homes from the road, never passed through their ornamental gates. She felt small, dwarfed by the grandness of it all, at a hopeless social disadvantage. A complete ingénue.

At the rear of the hallway, a tall door stood open and beyond that further wide doors led out to a terrace. Edith glimpsed splashes of colour, different hues of greens, grass and trees in what must be the gardens stretching away into the distance, a vista so intriguing and lovely, that she instinctively moved in its direction, and going outside would allow her to escape the oppressive opulence of the house.

Elisabeth stepped to her side. 'Come. Let me show you around.'

They walked through the open door into a light, airy room with white painted walls and pale, polished wooden floors covered with Persian rugs. A large ceramic stove stood in one corner. A long room, elegantly but comfortably furnished with a piano at one end, a chaise longue, various chairs, a sofa scattered with cushions. A low table held piles of books and magazines.

'This is the Garden Room. The one we use most.'

Elisabeth led Edith onto the terrace. They both gazed out. Edith studied the formal garden rather than her hostess. With that long, silky, honey-coloured hair parted on the side, the large, slate-blue eyes under finely arched brows, the high cheekbones, straight nose and wide, well-modelled mouth, she looked disconcertingly like Greta Garbo. The temptation was to stare, safer instead to fix on the pattern of the flowerbeds arranged round pools and fountains, admire the way that the eye was drawn to a sweep of wide lawns then redirected by bordering hedges and trees, guided towards a tiny gap filled with the glitter of water.

'We sit out here on fine evenings,' Elisabeth said to break the silence. 'My great-great-grandfather laid out the gardens. They say he never got over a visit to Versailles.'

There were cushioned chairs along the terrace ranged to look out. A drink and this view would be pleasant indeed.

At a little distance, a nurse sat next to a perambulator. The sun was warm and she was dozing, her knitting slipping from her knee.

'And this,' Elisabeth introduced the occupant of the pram, 'this is Wolfgang.'

At the sound of her mistress's voice, the nurse rose hastily. 'Madam! I'm sorry!'

'That's all right, Katja.' Elisabeth smiled, putting the nurse at her ease. They all crowded round, peering into the pram.

106

'Formidable name for a little chap,' Leo remarked.

'It was my father's name,' Kurt frowned, he never did understand Leo's sense of humour.

The infant stared back at them with large, milky-blue eyes, the pupils rimmed with indigo. A most unusual colour, not like his father or his mother. He was perhaps eighteen months old, Edith thought, she wasn't very good at guessing the ages of little children, with hair as pale and fine as corn silk. He regarded them with a fixity, a kind of puzzlement as if he felt he should recognize but couldn't quite place the faces looming over him.

'Irenka, the Cook, says he has an old soul.' Despite her laugh, Elisabeth looked faintly uneasy.

As she saw more of little Wolfgang, Edith came to recognize the truth in that observation. It made one almost believe in reincarnation: as though there was an adult consciousness trapped inside an infant body, baffled by this sudden powerless impotence, frustrated, not quite understanding what had happened or how he had come to be here.

'Nonsense! Nothing wrong with him. Is there, little man?'

Kurt seized the boy from his carriage and threw him up into the air, deftly catching him. The child didn't cry, or chuckle, as other children might. He grunted slightly as Kurt caught him but otherwise remained completely silent, maintaining the same expression of perplexed indifference.

'Not sure he likes that,' Leo observed.

They all laughed and the infant was returned to his nurse.

They went back into the Garden Room.

'Left or right?' Elisabeth enquired. 'East or west?'

They elected to go to the left and were conducted from room to room with Elisabeth putting names to the portraits that stared down at them and describing the history and provenance of the furnishings and ornaments. It was evident that this was her house, her title, her lands.

The final room was a gloomy study with a huge desk. Leatherbound ledgers, studbooks and farming manuals filled the shelves of high bookcases. The walls bristled with horns, the wide sweep of antlers and the heads of grinning, snarling animals: bear, wolf, boar. High up above the desk was a portrait of Adolf Hitler.

'This is the Estate Office,' Elisabeth explained. 'That door leads to the outside. Tenants and estate workers can enter without coming through the house.' She glanced up at the portrait. 'We have to have that here. It is expected.'

Her fine nostrils flared in aristocratic disdain. It was the only sign of the ruling regime anywhere in Schloss Steinhof.

Two smiling maids, dressed alike in blue gingham, their thick hair plaited and coiled tightly round their heads, showed them to their rooms. They were not related, they told her, but they could have been twins. Each a picture of perfect German young womanhood with their wide smiles, blue eyes, flaxen hair and flawless skin, brown and freckled as a speckled hen's egg. Gerda laid out Edith's evening clothes while Beate drew her bath.

Edith had fully expected not to like Elisabeth and was prepared for the antipathy to be mutual. All through the tour of the house they had been weighing each other up. But it hadn't been like that. She felt something like relief that the flickering flame that she'd nursed for Kurt, glowing like an altar lamp deep in her heart, could finally be allowed to gutter out. Any tears were confined to the privacy of her bath. In any case, she told herself, she was mourning the emotion not the man. The end of love. She came downstairs bathed, changed, ready to concede the ground.

Dinner was a formal affair with Elisabeth's mother at the head of the table. She came into the room leaning on an ivory-topped ebony cane. They all stood as she took her place. Her hair was a pure white, intricately dressed and pinned with a small tiara. At her throat, she wore a diamond collar. She exuded the opulent elegance of a long-lost era and made Edith feel distinctly under-dressed. She referred to Leo and Edith as 'the English visitors' and more or less dismissed them once she'd ascertained that they had no connections with any of the English families with whom she had been acquainted before the Great War. She was flanked by two elderly ladies, Elisabeth's aunts. They had their own apartments somewhere in the enormous house and only appeared at meal times. They were also dressed in the fashions of forty years previously, ate little and spoke less. There was a great aunt somewhere but she was very frail and almost never left her room. 'It is common,' Elisabeth told Edith later. 'A house like ours is a haven for the unmarried, the widows.'

From the other end of the table, Edith could feel Elisabeth's cool appraisal but it didn't bother her. She knew her own position in love, in life. Kurt was as handsome as ever but somehow he was diminished. Through a series of evasions, vague exaggerations, truth twisting and subtle mendacity, he'd pretended that all this was his. Then he'd married to get it, discarding Edith along the way. Not that she blamed him, Elisabeth was rich, charming and far, far more beautiful, a prize in anybody's book. She really was exceptionally lovely.

'A bit of a cracker, isn't she?' Leo murmured. 'But best not to stare . . .'

After dinner, the elderly relatives withdrew. Leo and Kurt went off to play billiards and the two women were left together on the terrace.

The day was only just fading. The butler brought a tray of decanters and glasses.

'Thank you, Brice. Now, what would you like, Edith? We have whisky, brandy, schnapps?'

Edith decided on schnapps. *Williamsbirne*. It gave off a sharp, pear-drop smell as Brice poured it. A crescent moon was rising, shining like a tarnished silver brooch pinned to violet velvet. There was a quality to the evening light that lent the memory a luminosity, a pellucid quality, so that Edith was always able to recall the perfumed sharpness of pear schnapps in the waning warmth of the day.

There was still a wariness. Nothing spoken, but it was clear that Elisabeth knew that Edith and Kurt had been lovers. Perhaps he'd told her; perhaps she'd guessed. The reticence was not antipathy. Perhaps the opposite. Women who share a lover can often feel the tug of attraction. Not that Edith had those inclinations, apart from the odd crush at school on an older girl, a pash or two at college, but something made her awkward in the other's company, even shy. Some of the feelings she'd had when she first arrived were seeping back now. Elisabeth's wealth, position, her *aristocracy*. 'Alles die Ländereien der Gräfin.'

Elisabeth drank her schnapps in one, Brice stepping forward to refill her glass.

'Thank you, Brice. You may leave the tray. Now we are alone,' she said when the butler had withdrawn, 'I'd like to get one thing out of the way. You and Kurt—'

Edith was nonplussed. She hadn't been expecting that. She groped for an appropriate response, the right words in German but Elisabeth waved her to silence.

'No need to say anything. I don't want my feelings coloured. I don't mean towards Kurt. I mean towards you. We would be starting on the wrong foot.' Elisabeth offered her a cigarette.

'I don't.' Edith touched her chest. 'Asthma.'

Elisabeth lit her own and leaned back in her chair, smoking. She stared off into the vista beyond the balcony, the meadows and woods indistinct now in creeping darkness and rising mist.

'Prussia lives in the past,' she said after a while. 'We've only just given up serfdom and we still practise dynastic marriage. Kurt's family can trace their ancestors back to the Teutonic Knights but in recent times they have not prospered. I grew up here. With all this.' She smiled and stretched her arms out. 'He was brought up in a cramped apartment in Königsberg.' She lapsed into silence. 'I knew. I always knew. About you. He said you had a *schöne Intelligenz*. Very *sympathisch*. And – there's a word in German – *leidenschaftlich*?' Edith translated it as passionate, ardent, fervent. She felt herself blush. 'I can see the attraction. He loved his time in England but when he came back, then he was mine. It was an understanding. We are different, he and I. He likes to travel, meet people, make new friends. I like to stay here with my dogs.' Her hand strayed to the sleek black head of her Great Dane, Helmar, couchant by her side. 'And, of course, my horses.'

Elisabeth's real love was horses. Her family had been breeding horses for the Prussian cavalry since the eighteenth century. She much preferred them to people, Edith came to realize. She was different when she was around them, more relaxed, happier altogether.

'I like to be among my own folk. In my own country.'

She didn't mention the child.

'Kurt and I really are just friends now,' Edith said. 'Anything,' she searched for the right words, '*otherwise* was over a long time ago.' She refilled her glass. Edith did not drink much as a rule but tonight she felt the need to be fortified. 'Kurt is a doctor now? Qualified?'

'Oh, yes. He has his licence to practise. He hopes to specialize in Psychiatry, so continues his studies. First, he was in Heidelberg. Under Steiner. Now he is in Berlin with Bonhoeffer. At the Charité Hospital.'

'What kind of work is he doing?'

Elisabeth shrugged as if it didn't interest her. 'When he is here, we do not discuss it.'

'Do you join him in Berlin?'

'Kurt is ambitious. He wants to advance in his profession. Berlin is the place for advancement. There are things he must do there, people with whom he must associate. Sometimes, it is necessary for me to be with him but I do not like this life. My place is here.'

'When you are apart, you must miss him.'

'Not as much as you might think.' Her smile was tight, guarded. 'He comes back when he can. You must know, Edith, we have an understanding.' She paused. 'You were part of that understanding. There have been others. Kurt is a passionate man.'

'Don't you mind?'

'What is the point of minding?' She shrugged again. 'He is how he is. I know he will always come back to me. That is all that matters.'

Here, conversation lapsed. They were not at the point in a friendship where deep intimacies were likely to be exchanged.

Besides, Elisabeth was not the kind of woman who allowed the doors to her inner feelings to be opened at the least touch. If there were differences between husband and wife, she did not broadcast them. She kept his counsel as well as her own.

How long did they spend there? A week? It seemed longer. They went walking, riding, took picnics in the forest and by the lake. There were excursions: to Königsberg to see Kant's grave and the great, gothic castle founded by the Teutonic Knights; to the seaside to bathe in the achingly cold Baltic and shelter from wind and sun in wicker *Strandkorb* set out on the bone-white sands.

At the end of each day, they would retire to their rooms, bathe and change for dinner then meet for drinks on the terrace. Edith loved this time. She liked to get down before the others and sip her drink, looking out at the soft, amber light rendering the roses gold and ruby against the dark, glowing scarlet of the garden wall. She liked to hear the strange belling song of the frogs just starting up by the lake.

'Beautiful, isn't it?' Kurt was standing next to her, holding the balcony, his fingers almost touching hers. Edith could feel the warmth of his arm next to hers; smell his Vetiver cologne. 'I so much wanted you to see it. I'm so glad you came, Edith. I saw you come down early each evening. I wanted to speak with you. I so regret that we parted like we did.'

They turned, each at the same time. Edith knew he was going to kiss her, knew she wanted him to. How quickly the flame sparked back to life again. The warmth of his lips, the cool smoothness of his freshly shaved skin, made her limbs loosen with desire.

'No, Kurt,' she said, drawing away. 'I don't think this is a good idea.'

He reached to arrange a stray lock of her hair. The intimacy of that gesture, more than the kiss, dissolved the years, taking her back to that summer when she'd been so in love with him.

'I need to speak with you, Edith,' he whispered. 'I need you to understand. I will come to your room. Tonight.'

'No, Kurt,' Edith turned her head to avoid his kiss. 'I mean it! You're married with a child!'

She shook her head. It was not to do with Kurt's wife or his child. It was to save herself. The fire she thought extinguished could burst into life again; the wound, long healed, begin to bleed. She was about to speak again when Leo appeared.

'Thought I heard voices.' His blue eyes were quizzical behind his tortoiseshell glasses. 'Not interrupting anything, am I?'

'No, of course not.' Kurt turned to Leo with a smile. 'We were just admiring the view.'

'Things a bit tricky out there,' Leo whispered to Edith as they went in to dinner.

'Just a little.'

'Randy bugger! I'll take care of Kurt, don't worry. Call him out if need be. Propositioning my woman, how dare he?' The thought of being Leo's 'woman' and him doing any such thing made Edith laugh. 'Either that, or I'll get him so drunk, he won't be bothering anyone.'

After dinner, the men retired to the library for brandy and cigars. Elisabeth and Edith joined them when it got chilly out on the terrace. Elisabeth didn't like to talk about politics but it was difficult to ignore. The swastika was in every town, on every street. Leo questioned and probed, teasing out their opinions, the opinions of others of their class and acquaintance. Elisabeth and her mother regarded Hitler and the Nazis as hopelessly vulgar and mourned the day when Prussia lost its grip on the nation. They still seemed to think that the old families would bring Hitler back into line. What about the annexation of Austria? The trouble brewing in Czechoslovakia? Kurt joined the conversation here. Hitler was merely bringing stability to those areas of Europe that had been destabilized by the Treaty of Versailles. What about the Jews? Wildly exaggerated, falsely reported. There had been no such trouble here. Leo listened, head tilted as the fragrant cigar smoke drifted. 'Might there be a war?' he asked, reaching for the decanter. 'Oh, no,' Kurt was adamant. 'Not between England and Germany.' Russia was the real enemy of both their nations. Leo nodded, pouring more brandy and changed the subject to sport.

That night, Edith heard the scratch of nails on wood, the signal they'd used at Gorton. She lay still, willing him to go away. She couldn't risk it. Once kindled, the fire she thought long dead would rage unchecked.

Edith deliberately avoided him, spending time with Elisabeth, going down at dawn to join her as the great barn doors opened and the horses streamed out to the pastures and paddocks. Elisabeth had been shocked that Edith did not ride and was determined to teach her. They went on long excursions into the forest, knees nearly touching as they rode along together. They stopped to collect wild raspberries and *Hundspflaume*, wild plums, Elisabeth reaching up to help Edith down. They gathered fungi: fluted yellow *Pfifferling*, penny-bun *Steinpilz*, *schwefelgelber Porling*, chicken of the woods for Irenka, the cook. Heads together, fingers reaching for the same mushroom, Edith breathing in Elisabeth's particular scent: horses, gardenia and light summer sweat.

They would take their haul back to Irenka. In Edith's memory, they are either in the stables or in the large, tiled kitchen with its wide shallow sinks, marble slabs, and black iron range. They would sit at the long wooden table drinking strong, bitter coffee, nibbling Lebkuchen made by Halina, Irenka's daughter. They would prepare fruit for jam, mushrooms for drying, working together, hands touching.

By the time she left Schloss Steinhof, Edith was in love with them both.

What had happened to Halina and the rest of them? One had heard the most terrible, shocking stories about those caught up in the Russian advances: the Russians raping every woman they came across, no matter how young or how old. Had that been the fate of the women she had known? No more than they deserved, that's what people said, but Edith couldn't quite square that with Irenka singing in her rich voice as she kneaded dough,

114

her big, strong hands white with flour. Gerda and Beate, laughing as they shook out the feather quilts; the child, Halina, busy working under her mother's direction, beating, mixing, her light soprano joining her mother's contralto. Did they really deserve to be brutalized by Russian soldiers? Their young lives blighted before they had properly begun? As for the elderly ladies of the Schloss, it just didn't bear thinking about. And what about Elisabeth? Was that her fate? Or did she die defending her place and her people, or by her own hand at the sound of the Russian guns?

'*Mehr Kaffee, Schnaps?*' The slap of the coffee pot on the table brought Edith back to the present.

'*Nein danke.*'

Edith left the café and walked on. How much had Elisabeth known about Kurt? Was she a dyed in the wool Nazi, too? She'd shown no sign of it, but neither had he. How much had she been involved? Would it be right to befriend her now in order to betray? Would Edith be able to do it? Would friendship – love, even – overcome any sense of duty? And what about Kurt? Would she succumb again, whatever he might have done?

Edith stopped. She'd walked further than she'd intended. Across the lake, the Atlantic shone like a liner in the distance. It was growing dark. The cold had deepened. Her fingers and toes were numb inside her gloves and boots, her breath hung thick and white in the freezing air. As she set off back round the lake, the path was black with ice, the whitened ground iron hard. The cold was of a different order to anything in Britain, a cold that had come to stay and was set to get deeper and deeper, not letting up for months and months.

Back at the hotel, Edith stopped in the foyer, selecting cards from those on display. The Hotel Atlantic, Hamburg: hand-tinted depictions, viewed from various aspects. Pre-war stock. She enquired at the desk as to the postal services, the price of stamps to England, and took the cards to her room. Once there, she laid the cards out on the desk by the window, took out her travelling writing case, her fountain pen and her copy of the *Radiation Cook Book*.

'It doesn't have to be difficult or complicated,' Dori had said. 'Messages don't have to be long missives. Keep them short, chatty, food, recipes and so on. Postcard length is fine.'

Edith selected a postcard: the Atlantic viewed from the Außenalster, uncapped her pen and began to compose a message.

Dear Dori,

Arrived safely. Journey uneventful. Thought you might like a recipe for Dutch *Broodje croquetten* which formed part of a delicious picnic I shared with a young army officer on the train. You are right. English food *is* boring. I hope there will be more to follow.

The Atlantic is as luxurious as ever. The Occupiers live well. I'm popping in a couple of menus to show just *how* well!

Love, Edith

P.S. So glad you want to carry on our cooking lessons – even if it is by long distance! Stella *is* pleased!

She opened the *Radiation Cookery Book* to code the messages folded into recipes which she added to the observations and descriptions she'd made to aid the illusion that she was just sharing the meals she'd been enjoying. Then she put everything in a Hotel Atlantic envelope and delivered it to reception, sealed and addressed to Dori in London.

Tomorrow she'd travel on to Lübeck, to see what the future held.

Dori

34 Cromwell Square, Paddington, W2

Dori in her hallway, still in her shantung dressing gown. A weak, winter sun casting a slanting light through the frosting of filth on the fanlight.

'Let yourself out, will you, darling?' She hadn't even glanced at the young man hovering behind her. 'I'll call.'

The door opening, shutting. Dori sorting through the post.

Bill, bill, bill, squinting against the smoke curling from her cigarette, adding to a pile of unopened brown envelopes. Then *Dori Stansfield*. German stamp. Postmark Hamburg. That was more like it. She'd left the rest and took the letter down to the basement kitchen.

Atlantic Hotel stationery. Very snazzy. Only just got there and already busy. She had been certain that Edith would come through. Vera had been the tiniest bit sceptical but Dori had no doubts at all.

'You handle her,' Vera had told her. 'She's your Joe.'

Time to get busy. Dori collected the *Radiation Cookery Book* and sat at the kitchen table with pad and pencil. Edith had met Drummond on the train. Identified him as being of interest. Well spotted, Edith. And useful. Vera could do a little cross-checking.

See what Drummond made of their latest recruit. She'd been rather expecting that encounter. The next one was more of a puzzle. Part code, part crossword. *Breakfast Omelette* to be found in *Egg, Cheese and Vegetarian Dishes*, *Ham and Eggs* in *Breakfast Dishes*. Dori flipped to the relevant pages. McHale in the British Zone interested in von Stavenow. He must have heard more than they thought.

Dori had known McHale in France, seen him operating. Seen him go down a line of traitors, collaborators and German prisoners and shoot each one in the back of the neck with a gleam in those blue eyes and a glimmer of a smile, as though he was enjoying it.

Edith had added a note. *Crêpe Suzette* meant Adeline. It was her favourite dish. Edith had invented a memorably disgusting wartime version with marmalade and gin. Danger meant danger. *Most unpalatable*. A threat to Adeline? Adeline was a big girl. She could look after herself. Dori went back to the McHale message. Americans on the hunt in the British Zone? War Crimes would be interested. She'd pass that on to Vera. It would put the wind up Intelligence. Vera would find a way to pass *that* on.

She turned to the next menu. Edith had met one Adams (*Meat: Roasting*). Dori knew him. Of him, anyway. SIS during the war. Now in Germany with Military Intelligence. One of Leo's men. Good to know who was running Edith.

She'd really taken to the work. Dori knew she would. Dori burned her transcriptions in the Aga and slotted the recipes in her copy of the *Radiation Cook Book* next to a cutting for *Stella Snelling's 10 Quick and Nourishing Winter Suppers*.

Dori smiled. She taken a pride in cultivating Edith's 'Stella' side. It was this that made her different, that had intrigued and attracted, an imago emerging, but it was the real Edith that Dori was putting her faith in now. Practical and dependable, her very ordinariness would be her cover. Something that Leo recognized, too, but he'd reckoned without her high moral sense. He'd lost his a long time before, if he'd ever owned such a thing, which was doubtful. Most people wouldn't associate Dori with any

118

kind of morality. Slept around, drank like a fish, racketed about generally. She stared into the glowing heart of the Aga. She'd killed and had killings carried out on her orders, but for all her sins, she'd never been a traitor and there *had* been a traitor at the heart of SOE. Too many agents betrayed, too many circuits blown. Any hopes of finding whom it might be vanishing by the day. Files already disappearing: lost, stolen, strayed, unaccountably mislaid. Dori wouldn't be surprised to hear of a fire in some distant depot or mothballed air station. Either that, or they would be sealed safely away until everyone even remotely involved was dead, gone and forgotten. Or Hell froze over, whichever was the sooner.

The answer lay in Germany. Vera was back there now with Drummond at War Crimes in Bad Oeynhausen, involved in a desperate race to find out what had happened to the girls and men who had disappeared into the camps and who had not come back. The sands were shifting. Drummond's outfit had been officially disbanded; SOE wound up months ago, the likes of Dori out on their ear with a 'wham, bam, thank you, mam', as the Yanks would have it. The Secret Intelligence Service were taking over, Leo and the boys of MI6. As a woman and of foreign extraction, old Dori was suddenly suspect. Vera was still operative but for how much longer?

Dori was desperate to get out there. She felt the obligation to the missing agents as deeply as Vera and civvy street didn't suit her. Ever since VE Day, she'd been restless. Once the euphoria was over, she'd found herself seeking excitement elsewhere: drinking too much, mixing in bad company, dabbling in the black market. More than dabbling. She could do with getting out of London for a while. Then there was the guilt. Always there, no matter how much gin she drank, a darkness running under her waking life, surfacing in dreams where she saw the girls' faces, heard their screams. Last confirmed sighting: Number 84 Avenue Foch.

They both felt duty bound to the missing agents, Dori knew: Vera because she'd sent them over in the first place; Dori because she'd come back. It went beyond finding out what had happened; there was a need to see justice done, to see those responsible brought to book. The ones who'd given the orders were already slipping away.

Dori needed to be in Germany but there was some snafu with her papers. Understandable on the face of it, but all her enquiries were meeting obfuscation or an escalating official impatience. Nothing stated but much implied. If Dori made any more of a fuss, Dori wouldn't be going at all. Cue for Dori to pipe down and toe the line. It went against her temperament but, all in all, it might be no bad thing. With Edith in the field, she might be more useful here. She looked at her watch. Time to toddle to the Special Forces Club. She'd arranged to meet someone who might know something about the girls they were seeking: rumours of a group of women who had been brought to a small camp called *Natzweiler*; a *Nacht und Nebel* place tucked away in the Vosges Mountains, a place where prisoners were made to disappear, where they were *vernebelt*, 'transformed into mist'. Her contact had reported it months ago but his report had been lost, buried or ignored. Now he was collecting evidence on his own account.

Who were these women? How did they get there and on whose orders? That's what she needed to find out.

10

CCG Mess, Lübeck

7th January 1946

```
Lunch Menu
Potage Parmentier
Boiled Brisket of Beef
Mustard Sauce
Dressed Cabbage
Pomme Purée
Spotted Dick, Cream Sauce
Coffee
```

```
Roz's observations: boring, bland, mostly out
of a tin but plenty of it.
```

Edith found the Education Branch Office on Königstraße, housed in a tall, narrow building that was more or less intact. She was to report to her immediate boss, Brigadier Thompson. He had kept his military title, even though he now worked for the Control Commission and was sitting in his greatcoat, swathed in scarves, wearing half gloves on purplish digits. His nose was red and dripping. When he spoke, his voice was thick with cold.

'Miss Graham?' He rose to meet her, his fingers icy. 'Thank God you're here! Come and sit down.' He sneezed. 'Do excuse me.' He sneezed again and blew his nose copiously. 'No heating today, I'm afraid. You might want to keep that fur around your shoulders.' He pressed a button on the console in front of him. 'Can we have some tea? And some of those ginger biscuits.'

'*Lebkuchen*?' Edith inquired.

'The very ones!' He smiled. 'German speaker? Then you are doubly welcome.'

'I thought we all were.'

'Preferable, of that there is no doubt but, alas, not always the case . . .'

'I see.'

It was all she could think of to say. It made no sense, but very little did in this new world which surprised and dismayed by turns.

'Ah, the inestimable Miss Esterhazy with the tea.' The Brigadier's smile of relief exposed prominent, yellowish teeth under his bristling military moustache.

The Inestimable Miss Esterhazy was young, in her early twenties. She regarded the brigadier over her horn-rimmed half glasses as she poured the tea. She had startling violet-blue eyes.

'I prefer gingernuts myself.' The Brigadier dunked his biscuit. 'Find these too soft. Not that the poor devils out there would be complaining.'

Despite his stated preference, he made short work of the Lebkuchen.

'Now, where to start?' He brushed crumbs from the wide lapels of his coat. 'We've got our work cut out, no doubt about it.' He counted the problems off until he ran out of half-gloved fingers. 'No buildings, no teachers, no books, no paper, no boards, no chalk, no desks, no chairs, no heating, no help.' He spread his hands wide in a gesture of hopelessness. 'And more of the little blighters flooding in every minute from points east. Turning into a positive torrent. The whole area is filling up like a tank.' He leaned forward, hands folded now; his already

122

furrowed brow wrinkled further. It wasn't just his cold making him look tired and worn out. 'As Control Commission, Education Division, we have to set up schools where there aren't any and get the *Kinder* in. Most of them haven't been near a school for the last three years, so that's a job in itself. We have to inspect any places that are up and running. Make sure that the staff is vetted. No raving Nazis, secret devotees of Herrn Hitler preparing for the Second Coming. That sort of thing. You need to develop a bit of an eye for who's playing with a straight bat and who's not. As for supplies and equipment – do the best you can. Sounds a lot, I know . . .'

The Brigadier's voice tailed off as if even he recognized the understatement.

'And what will be my role exactly?' Edith was almost afraid to ask. She'd heard all this before but there was a difference between hearing it in a briefing in Kensington and actually being here. She felt a certain heart sinking at the enormity of the job before her and there was an ominous hint of what might be to come in *do the best you can* . . .

'Miss Esterhazy will fill you in. Now, do excuse me, I'm in need of a rum toddy. Medicinal purposes. They do a good one at the club.' Edith followed him out of his office. 'Not much anyone can tell you, really,' he said as he pulled on a balaclava helmet. 'Best to learn on the job.'

He put his cap on over the balaclava and was gone. From her desk, Miss Esterhazy rolled her eyes towards the closing door. She sat muffled in a bouclé coat that came up round her ears. She pulled the coat closer, tucking her chin into the shawl collar. Her liquorice-black hair swung forward from a centre parting so severe that it showed the white of her scalp.

'That's the last we'll see of him today.' She looked up at Edith. 'He really does have a rotten cold but he'd do anything rather than go through this lot.' She put her hand on the pile of papers stacked in front of her.

'What are they?' Edith peered over her shoulder.

'*Fragebogen.* Forms the Jerries have to fill in.' She picked up a couple of the papers. '130 questions covering everything from religious affiliation to the membership of forty-four proscribed Nazi organizations. If they jump through all the hoops, they get a denazification certificate. The Germans call it a *Persilschein*, washed clean. One of our biggest problems, among many big problems, is finding staff. These,' she brandished the forms she held in each hand, 'have to be filled in by anyone applying for anything. Then they have to be checked. Against what?' She swung in her chair. 'Most records have been destroyed, either by the Nazis or in the bombing. Even if such records exist, people have been displaced, their records might be hundreds of miles away in the Russian Zone.' She swung back. 'Before we get the forms, they have to go to Public Safety, who hang onto them forever, mostly because they don't know any German. Then they are sent here, for the Brigadier to look through, which he might, or might not, get round to, then, and only then, we might, just *might* be able to employ somebody.' She let the forms drift back onto her desk. 'Welcome to the Control Commission, Miss Graham. Welcome to the British Zone of Occupation. Welcome to Germany.' She put her hands inside her coat sleeves and shivered. 'Added to which, it's bloody freezing. Let's get out of here.'

They stepped out from the offices onto Königstraße. Edith had visited Lübeck before the war. The old Hanseatic port had been one of the stopping-off points on that Baltic trip. The medieval town was on an island, surrounded by water, bridges reaching over the circling river Trave and canals. She remembered the churches with their pretty green steeples; the conical towers of the Holstentor Gate; the Salzspeicher, salt houses, with their steeply pitched, rust-coloured roofs; the medieval buildings with their distinctive crow-stepped gables. It was a different scene now. Much of the centre of the town was missing, obliterated in a great swathe from the Lübecker Dom to St Petrikirche and the Marienkirche. The towers of the churches loomed gaunt and tall over the razed ground, their sides blackened by fire, the green copper spires fallen, their bricks stacked in great frozen heaps ready for reconstruction, whenever that might be.

'More than half of the buildings in the city were damaged or destroyed in a single raid on Palm Sunday, 1942. They say in the Mess that it could take fifty years to build the place back up again.' Miss Esterhazy looked up at Edith. 'You're from Coventry, aren't you?'

Edith nodded. The bare-ruin'd choirs of the churches, the rubble-strewn emptiness that had once been the tangle of ancient streets between them. She knew what kind of damage a concerted raid on a small city could do.

A bitter wind whined up from the River Trave and whipped down the streets, fluttering slips of paper plastered onto walls, shop windows and lampposts by worthless postage stamps bearing the head of Hitler. Notes put up by displaced persons: refugees, returnees trying to find lost relatives.

Edith stopped to read the little messages: *Ich suche meine Frau, meinen Mann, meine Tochter, meinen Vater, meine Mutter, mein Kind . . . Last seen . . . Last known place . . .*

Some had been there so long that the colour of the stamps had faded, the paper puckered by sun and rain, the message disappearing to invisibility. There was something forlorn and hopeless about them, the chances of reunion so vanishingly small. Did any of them mention Elisabeth von Stavenow? Were any from her? The chances seemed even smaller. Edith's heart sank further at the impossibility of it all.

'The authorities clear them away every now and then,' Roz commented, 'but they keep coming back again.' Miss Esterhazy turned her astrakhan collar against the biting wind. 'Come on, it's best not to linger in this cold.'

Like any bombed city, the damage was patchy. Out of the centre, Lübeck was remarkably intact. The Mess was well away from the scenes of devastation. A large house, commandeered from an architect. Pale oak panelling and parquet flooring. It reminded Edith of a college of the more modern sort. There were rooms upstairs for visitors, Roz explained, and a library, and a dining room.

A German attendant took their coats. Under the bulky bouclé, Miss Esterhazy was tiny, trimly dressed in a smart navy skirt and twin set with a wisp of scarlet polka-dotted scarf round her neck to add some colour.

'I don't know about you,' she said, 'but I'm going to have a large sherry.'

'I'll join you.'

They went into a spacious, pleasant sitting room. A waiter brought their drinks. Miss Esterhazy took off her spectacles to sign for them.

Without her glasses, she looked younger. She was really very pretty with a finely chiselled nose and a pointed chin. Her carmine lipstick gave emphasis to the sculpted shape of her mouth, the upper lip curving like a Scythian bow. There was something East European about the tilted eyes, the flat cheekbones, the canna-lily skin.

'Esterhazy? Isn't that Hungarian?' Edith said to break the silence that had grown between them.

'My father was Hungarian, my mother Austrian; that's how I speak German. We moved to London when I was small. My real name is Rozália – my mother changed it to Rosalind to sound more English but everyone calls me Roz.' She toyed with her glass. 'I was working in an office back home. When I saw this, I jumped at it. I put down Austria; we still have family there. Instead, I end up here, about as far away as you can get!' Her laugh had a bitter edge. 'That's me, Miss Graham.'

'Call me Edith, please.'

'The Brigadier won't like it.'

'Who's to tell him? Call me Edith when we are out of the office,' Edith said. 'And I can't keep calling you Miss Esterhazy.'

'It is a bit of a mouthful.'

'Edith and Roz it will be, then.' Edith raised her glass in a mock toast. 'Would you like another?'

'I'd better not. I still have those blasted *Fragebogen* to get through. There *are* good people,' she said as they went into the dining room. 'Dismissed by the Nazis, Trade Unionists and so on. They're mostly getting on a bit, but they're still about. I think they could be used to recruit staff. They know the difference between those who were dedicated Nazis and those who weren't. Better, at any rate, than a bunch of retired policemen who don't speak German and are only here to add to their pensions. It drives Jeff mad!'

'Who's Jeff?'

'He works in Public Safety. They vet the Germans.'

'Is Jeff your boyfriend?'

'Oh, no. We're not going out or anything! We go to the pictures sometimes, that's all.'

A sudden swipe of rose madder across Roz's cheek said it might be something more.

Before she could say anything, a waiter came to show them into the dining room.

'They feed us well, Miss Graham,' Roz said as she picked up a menu card. 'Mostly out of a tin, bland, boring but there's plenty of it.' She put on her glasses to see what was offered that day. 'Cabbage, now. That won't be out of a tin, nor the potatoes. Beef is another thing. Spotted Dick.' She grimaced. 'I might give that a miss. I've put on pounds since I came out here.' Miss Esterhazy laughed, showing little pearly teeth. 'Food is all anybody ever talks about. And drink, of course.' She gazed out of the window. 'Us in here stuffing ourselves and swilling; them out there more or less starving. The German ration is hardly enough to keep body and soul together. It seems wrong.'

She broke off and looked round at the other diners. She didn't need to say what didn't seem right to her, or to Edith, for that matter, but that was how things were. To the victor, the spoils.

'Staffing is not the only problem,' Roz said as their soup arrived. 'All the textbooks are "contaminated" by Nazi ideology, even the Maths books are useless. Needless to say, there aren't any replacements. Then there's the buildings. Those still standing need repair or are in danger of being requisitioned for other uses. Even when we have got a building, there's no fuel to heat it. There's a shortage of everything. And the children. Lübeck's already overcrowded, more coming adds to a significant refugee problem, children separated from parents and vice versa. And we've got to get them into the schools. Lack of shoes is a particular difficulty, given the winter we're having. Add that to a lack of adequate clothing and nourishment – how can children learn with no food inside them? Most come after no breakfast at all. Sorry.' She smiled her apology. 'I'm running on a bit.'

'Not at all,' Edith said as she finished her rather gluey soup. 'It's best to know.'

Roz laughed as the next course arrived: brown stew, boiled cabbage and mash, carefully marshalled on the plate. 'See? I was right!'

'The Brigadier made it all sound more than a little, er, hopeless,' Edith ventured as the waiter came to collect their plates.

'He's pretty overwhelmed, poor lamb. Just about given up, easier to sit on your hands. It doesn't have to be like that.' Roz moved the cruet with nervous fingers, making patterns on the tablecloth. 'There are things we can do. I've got ideas. But he won't listen. I'm just a secretary.' She sighed and looked at her watch. 'No time for coffee. I'd better be getting back.'

'I'll walk with you.'

They retraced their steps back to the office. It was colder, if anything. A dusting of snow falling.

'Your friend, Jeff?' Edith asked, as they passed the faded messages fluttering in the bitter wind. 'Could he find somebody?' She kept her voice casual. 'A German, I mean.'

'I could ask him.' Roz stopped and looked at Edith. 'Who is it?'

'A woman I knew before the war,' Edith brushed a gloved hand over the little notices. 'From the east. Prussia up near the Polish border. She had relatives near Lübeck. I wondered if she was here, that's all.'

'It's possible. There's a lot here from the east. Give me her name and I'll pass it on to him.'

11

CCG Billet, Lübeck

7th January 1946

Billet Dinner
Beef Broth with Dumplings
Braised Beef
Sauerkraut, Carrots, Peas
Steckrübengratin
Rice Pudding with Apricots

Cooking is done by Germans and the food reflects that. Not all of it popular with the billetees. Instinctively suspicious of the dumplings in the broth, although they were delicious. Disliked the *Steckrübengratin* – made from swede and they share my feelings about sauerkraut!

The billet was in a large suburban villa situated in another untouched suburb. A German girl answered the door and showed Edith in without a word. She took her bag and disappeared upstairs. Another girl took her coat and hat.

'*Danke. Wie heißen Sie?*'

'Grete.'

'*Danke*, Grete.' She smiled but Grete did not smile back.

An English girl in an unbuttoned CCG battledress jacket appeared in the doorway of the sitting room smoking a cigarette with nervous vigour. She regarded this exchange with impatience, prominent blue eyes unblinking. She looked young, despite the aggressive smoking, younger than Roz, the roundness of childhood still in her face. She wore her curly brown hair severely parted, pinned at the sides in an effort to tame it. She was wearing a red roll-top sweater under her jacket and slacks instead of a skirt.

'You must be the mysterious Miss Graham.' She pushed herself off the doorframe. 'I'm Angela. Angela Parker. Friends call me Angie.'

'Nice to meet you, Angela. I'm Edith.'

'Come in. You must be perished.' Angela led the way into a high-ceilinged room, heated by a large ceramic stove in the corner, gratifyingly warm after the cold outside. Angela threw herself down into a leather armchair. 'Make yourself at home.'

She waved a hand towards an over-stuffed settee adorned with a quantity of appliqued cushions. Edith sat down as directed and looked round the room. Empty bookcases but the heavy sideboard was laden with ornaments: ceramic flowers, figurines, decorated vases, porcelain animals: a Bambi, a rabbit and a couple of German shepherd dogs, painted plates showing thatched chalets, water mills, pastoral scenes. Images of an idealized Germany, long gone if it ever existed. A note: *Not To Touch Plse* was tacked next to the display. Her eyes were drawn up to the wall above, to the pale oblong space where the portrait of Hitler must have been.

'Sorry about the get-up.' Angela pulled at the collar of her sweater. 'It's bloody cold in the office. Working in coats, scarves, gloves, the lot.'

'What do you do?'

'I'm a typist in the Legal Division. You?'

'Education.'

'Don't think we've got anyone from your mob. There's six of us now. Seven with you. Not a bad crowd. Would you like some tea?'

'Oh, yes, please. That would be lovely.'

'You!' It took Edith a second to understand that the girl was addressing Grete. 'Tea. Quick. Schnell, schnell. *Comprenez?*'

'*Verstehen,*' Edith said quietly.

'Sorry?'

'*Verstehen,*' Edith repeated. 'It's the German word for understand.'

'German speaker, eh?' the girl said with some distrust. 'Doesn't do to spoil them.'

'Who?'

'The girls who work here particularly, but any of them, really.' She waved her cigarette as if to indicate the German nation in general. 'It doesn't do to be the least bit familiar,' she added with certainty, 'or they'll take advantage.' She stubbed out her cigarette with a quick jabbing motion. 'Still a bit too arrogant for my liking and look where that got them? We're here to teach them a lesson, not pal with them. Don't you agree?'

Edith could not have agreed less, but said nothing. This girl must have been at school for most of the war and probably hadn't been here long but had quickly picked up the prevalent prejudices. In order to be accepted, no doubt, be part of the crowd.

'Put it down on the table.' Angela spoke to the German girl loudly and slowly, enunciating each syllable, as though she was half witted. 'Now. Go. I will pour.' She turned to Edith. 'How do you like it?'

'Milk. No sugar.'

'It's real milk. Not out of a tin,' Angela said with some pride as she poured the tea. 'Don't worry, Edith, you'll soon get the hang of it,' she added, with the brisk patronage of the very young.

'How long have you been here, Angela?'

'Positively ages. Since October. I'm an old hand. I can show you the ropes.' She handed a cup to Edith. 'We like to have dinner about 7.30. Drinks down here at seven. You'll have a chance to meet the others. Oh, and we like to dress. Not too formal but it gives us an excuse to get out of this beastly uniform.'

Edith's room was warm. Warmish, anyway. Heated by a stove in the corner. The bed was made up, her suitcase on the top of the covers, her battered Gladstone by its side. Dori's fur coat swung alone in the hulking mahogany wardrobe. Precious few hangers, she should have thought of that, but plenty of storage space. Even when her trunk arrived, she doubted she would fill half of it.

Steam curled from a china basin and ewer placed for her on a marble-topped washstand. A towel, worn but clean, hung from a rail at the side. The German girl must have brought it up for her. Dinner would be soon. She found her toiletry bag, stripped off her uniform. She seemed to have been in it for days.

She put on her shantung dressing gown and went over to the walnut-veneered, kidney-shaped dressing table and began to set out her things: her Mason Pearson hair brush, Bluegrass talc, box of face powder, claiming the space as her own. The stool was too high. The dusty-pink velvet seat was slightly worn to one side, faintly marked by old spillages, the trace of a lipstick smear. As Edith adjusted it down, she wondered what had happened to the woman who'd once lived here. No one knew or cared less. Got what she deserved, that's what would be said, but Edith could not help but think about her putting on lipstick and powder in that automatic way one does when off to dinner, or a dance, or just shopping, meeting friends for cake and coffee, without the least inkling. Where was she now? Turned out of this grand house, her comfortable life, to go where? She'd had to leave all this. Edith touched the Art Deco green glass trays that furnished the dressing table. The matching frosted glass-lidded bowl still held dusting powder. Gardenia. The scent of the woman who had left it. She was reminded of Elisabeth.

132

The room was at the back of the house and looked out over the garden. Steps led from a wide terrace to the flat expanse of lawn going down to a scatter of fruit trees, their branches black against an iron-grey sky.

Footprints marked a well-trodden path through the snow to the bottom of the garden before disappearing into a tangle of bushes. Perhaps there was a woodpile down there, or something, although there were plenty of logs cut and stacked under the eaves. Curious.

The smell of cooking percolated from below, carrying with it the hint of what they would be eating for dinner, a whiff of beef boiled with root vegetables and beneath that something else. Insidious and persistent, sharp but with a musty under note of decay. Sauerkraut. Her mind shied from the memories it evoked. She found herself swallowing. The slightest hint brought instant nausea. She wondered if she might make her excuses but it was her first night. They were supposed to dress, Angela had said. She reviewed the contents of her suitcase and selected a midnight-blue jersey dress with a shawl collar – not too formal, but not too casual either – and hoped it would do.

She pulled on a pair of heels and went downstairs to cigarette smoke and conversation gusting from the sitting room. As she came in, the room went quiet.

'Edith! Come and join us!' Angela rushed to fill the silence. She'd changed into a tight navy skirt and a silk, spotted blouse tied at the neck. 'Let me introduce you . . .'

Miss Barratt, Miss Potts, Miss Jones, Miss Campbell. Respectively, Lorna, Ginny, Frances and Jo all stared, as wary as a new class. Edith tried to fix them as she would do at school. Lorna Barratt: older, tall redhead, long, pale face. Ginny Potts: young looking, pretty, pointed nose, chin-length light-brown hair caught back with an Alice band. Frances (Franny) Jones: thin face, narrow shoulders, deepset dark eyes, crisp black hair set into tight waves. Jo Campbell: good-looking, slightly bohemian, short dark hair tied with an emerald scarf, scarlet lipstick, large brown eyes outlined with khol. They all worked in clerical or secretarial positions in various branches of the Control Commission: Miss Barratt in Finance, Miss Potts in Public Safety, Miss Jones in the Quartermaster's Office, Miss Campbell in Displaced Persons.

'What's your poison, Edith?' Angela asked, going over to a line of bottles on the wide sideboard. 'We've got most things. Whisky and soda? Gin and It?'

Edith settled for a whisky and soda.

'Bottoms up!'

'Here's mud in your eye!'

They raised their glasses then all spoke at once, eager to fill in the newcomer, impress her with how much they were 'in the know'. The shortages – soap generally, soap flakes in particular, be sure to ask for a box of Lux when you write home. 'Oh, and STs,' Ginny said, with a sideways glance at the others. 'Make sure you get sent plenty of those.'

'Yes, jam rags always in short supply,' Angela added loudly, defying Jo's impatient sigh and Lorna's disapproving frown.

The subject changed to food. Plentiful but monotonous, prone to unaccountable shortages. One week no potatoes, the next? Potatoes but no onions. There was sauerkraut, every nose wrinkled, and root vegetables – especially swede, cue for further nose wrinkling. Everything else was out of a tin. Who cooked? Frau Schmidt, the housekeeper, with the help of the German girls, who also served and did the cleaning, washing, and general housework. None of these girls slept in the house. They went home in the evening and came back in the morning to light the fires, heat the water and prepare breakfast.

'We don't have to do a thing. It's a jolly good life, really,' Angie summed up. 'Better than at home, anyway.'

The others nodded. They were from Leicester, Bedford, Salisbury, Brighton. English provincial. They spoke of their hometowns with pride but little nostalgia. Better here.

Talk turned to Frau Schmidt, a 'real treasure' running the house and keeping the German girls up to snuff. Her husband, Stephan, on the other hand, was altogether useless, didn't do much of anything, unless Molly was doing the asking, then he jumped to it all right! Heaven knew why Frau Schmidt put up with him . . .

Edith had yet to meet the housekeeper, or the mysterious Molly, but at that moment, as if summoned, in the housekeeper came.

'Frau Graham? So pleased you have come, *gnädige Frau*!' She smoothed her palms down her wraparound apron before shaking hands. 'Grete tells me you speak German. Good. Good!'

She nodded. Every word set her glossy, chestnut curls bobbing, the set and texture so unvarying that it had to be a wig. Her smile exposed gleamingly even dentures that didn't quite fit. There was something false about the smile and it wasn't just the teeth. Her eyes remained as hard as onyx. She was a large woman, buxom with a fresh, shiny complexion, as if her skin was about to burst. 'It is how I am,' she would say. 'The way I was born.' Edith wasn't so sure. Most of the Germans bore at least some of the marks of malnutrition. Frau Schmidt was positively rubicund. Not everyone had suffered privation during the war and she wasn't doing too badly now, by the look of things.

Frau Schmidt was charming enough to the residents, rather less so to the servant girls. From the beginning, she regarded Edith with a certain caution: older, more senior and could speak German. Frau Schmidt was not in a position to show any kind of outright hostility but she would not be above making Edith's life in the billet less than comfortable through little, irritating acts of sly subversion: belongings mislaid, laundry misdirected, requests ignored or not carried out.

After the first introductions and the buzz of sharing knowledge with a newcomer, the girls in the billet more or less ignored Edith. The talk swirled and eddied around her. She might as well have been eating alone. The meal that first evening began with soup: beef broth with dumplings. The girls negotiated the thin liquid, carefully avoiding the little dumplings. Braised beef followed, more gravy than anything, served with a kind of swede gratin. 'Swede again!' Miss Campbell grimaced and the others laughed as if at some shared joke. The sauerkraut was even less popular. None of them touched the pile of greyish-green shreds. Even the sight of it, the sour rottenish smell of it, was enough for Edith. She could feel a migraine beginning, the pain in her right temple sharpening, a flickering of the light as though a bulb was about to pop. For once, she almost welcomed it. It would give her an excuse to leave the table. Give it a few more minutes.

Edith tried to focus on the talk around her. One of their number was missing. Molly. Molly Slater. Frau Schmidt had already enquired as to her whereabouts and the talk centred about her: Molly did this, Molly said that.

There was a screech outside and the sound of a powerful engine dying to an idling growl. Ginny Potts ran to the window.

'That's her now.'

Miss Slater came in with much theatrical shivering, clutching what looked very much like a mink coat around her.

'Darlings! It's positively brass monkeys out there.'

'Did you come home on the motorbike?' Ginny ventured.

'In this weather? Dressed like this? Are you mad? Mercedes, *if* you don't mind!'

As if to confirm it, a horn honked twice, an engine roared and wheels squealed.

'You've missed dinner,' Lorna offered.

Molly grimaced. 'Small mercies! Now, will someone please get me a drink before I expire!'

Angie hurried to obey. Molly took her seat at the end of the table. Ginny offered her a cigarette.

'Andy gave me a lift back from the Mess. He's such a sweetie.' She fitted the cigarette into an ivory holder. Lorna leant over to light it for her. 'I say, the path is most awfully slippy. I thought Stephan was supposed to clear it?' She extended an elegantly shod foot. 'I could have laddered my nylons.' She looked up from studying her shapely, neatly seamed leg and her gaze fell on Edith. 'And who is this?'

'This is Edith,' Angela supplied. 'She arrived this afternoon.'

'Did she?' Molly's look was both appraising and shrewd. Although she showed no hint of recognition, Edith knew her immediately as the girl from the train with the film-star looks and the metallic-blonde hair set in shingled waves. 'Well, Edith,' she drawled. 'Welcome to our lowly abode.' Molly turned back to the others. 'Now, you'll *never* guess . . .'

With that, Edith was dismissed. Molly gathered in her audience. When Edith left the table, they hardly seemed to notice, too busy offering Molly eager court. It had been like that at school. There was always one who held sway, the others offering up their ordinariness to her as if presenting bouquets.

'Shut the bloody door, will you!' A voice called after her and Edith heard distinct sniggers. 'And goodnight to you, too!'

If the job looked well nigh impossible, the billet was going to be purgatory. What was she doing here? She hauled herself up the stairs. Had she made the most dreadful mistake?

She blamed the oncoming migraine for her sudden, plummeting mood. She barely made it to her room before vomiting what little she'd eaten. She lay down, no longer able to fend off the feelings that were taking hold of her. When she closed her eyes she saw ribbons of scarlet and black.

March, 1933. Nazi Party banners rippled down the front of Heidelberg station. Kurt was supposed to meet her there. She'd expected him on the platform, at the barrier, but there had been no sign of him. She'd moved heaven and earth to get here arranging an exchange between her school and a Lyzeum in Heidelberg through her friend, Stella Snelling, who was working there as an assistant. Stella was leaving to take up a post back in England. A teacher from the Lyzeum, a Fräulein Rolf, would take Edith's place at the girl's grammar. The Head had been all for it. 'Admirable initiative,' she'd called it.

Kurt had initially been overjoyed at the news. His letters had been full of passion and plans. The walks they would take, the places they would visit, all the other wonders he wanted to show her, share with her. His voice came through his writing so clearly that he might have been whispering to her. His English rushed and slightly stumbling, the words tumbling in his eagerness, with occasional lapses into German when he could find no other way to express what he wanted to say. Then his letters became less frequent, shorter, the English more careful and correct. He had been busy at the University with his work and various societies and organizations he'd joined.

It all made sense now, but at the time she'd agonized over the difference in his letters. She'd read and reread them on that awful train journey to Germany, wanting to keep alive the dreams he'd woven, but deep down knowing that he had changed, just as brilliance in the early morning brings with it the promise of rain.

She waited and waited at the station, at a loss for what else to do. She watched people coming and going, arriving and leaving, the fear she'd felt on the train slowly congealing into dread. When he finally appeared, he kissed her on the cheeks, as if she were a cousin, some female acquaintance. His smile was as ready as ever but he seemed distant, preoccupied. He was sorry not to meet her train but the recent elections had made things difficult. He had to be somewhere right now but he would see her later. He hailed a cab for her and disappeared back into the crowds. Still, she grasped at some small rags of hope. She'd arrived at a bad time. There *was* trouble in the city. There had been elections, fighting in the streets. The evidence was everywhere: slogans daubed on walls, posters defaced or torn, Adolf Hitler glaring down from every lamppost with his chopped-off moustache.

When she saw Kurt later, it would be different.

But it wasn't. They met at a café down by the river. The place was crowded with SD men in brown uniforms, swastika armbands and kepi caps, drinking beer, eating Wurst and Sauerkraut, which was all they seemed to serve. Kurt was sitting at a table under linden trees, the dapple of the delicate, pale-green leaves playing on his blue shirt. The girl who came to take their order was in traditional dress, smocked white blouse, embroidered waistcoat, her black dirndl skirt trimmed with red rickrack. Kurt ordered beer, Bockwurst and Kraut.

'There is a thing you must know,' he started. He had a certain expression when he had something awkward to say, a rictus of the mouth, the lips drawn back into not quite a smile. He had that look now. Edith put down her knife and fork. 'There is no easy way to say it,' he swept his fair hair back from his forehead, another thing he did when he was nervous. 'The thing is,' he paused again, her silence increasing his unease. 'I have to tell you. It would not be fair otherwise to you, or Elisabeth. I'm engaged.'

'Who's Elisabeth?' Edith asked. It was the only thing she could think of to say.

'My fiancée.' He twisted the heavy gold signet ring on his middle finger. It was set with a *carnelian intaglio*; it looked old – and valuable. She'd never seen it before.

'I see.' The 's' sounded thick, as if her mouth was stuffed with cotton.

'I hope we may still be friends, Edith.' His rictus smile widened. 'I value your friendship so much.' He looked down at the ring he was turning and turning on his finger. 'You will never know—'

Edith was no longer listening. The sound around her, the men laughing and shouting, was turning into an impossible roaring. She looked down at the pale length of flaccid boiled sausage, the green and yellow heap of fermented cabbage, breathing in the sour stench of it. Her mouth flooded with saliva. 'Excuse me,' she managed to say and barely made it to the roadside, bent double, heaving, with the SD men laughing, banging their steins on the table, chanting *zu viel Bier*. He did not come to her. When she recovered, he had already left; the girl was collecting the money and the untouched plates.

Edith walked, blinded, the sunlight suddenly dazzlingly bright. The red, white and black banners ribboning down the buildings flapped and flared at the edges, the crooked crosses flexing and twisting. The rotten onion smell gusting from the crowds around her was overpowering. This was the beginning of her migraines.

She would grow to know the signs. She had to stop several times to heave into the gutter, much to the disgust of passers-by. Some blind instinct found her at the Lyzeum. Luckily, there was nobody about. She staggered up to her small room at the top of a twisting staircase, drew the curtains tightly against the stabbing of the light and collected the washing bowl from its stand. Ragged surges of nausea lurched through her. She lay down on the narrow bed, grateful for the pain. It stopped her thinking about Kurt.

A tentative knocking, hours later. The black tide had receded. She struggled to get up and fell back again.

'Are you all right?' A narrow-faced, anxious-looking young woman with dark, curly hair came into the room. She approached the bed, concern in her fine dark eyes. 'I looked in earlier but you were sleeping. Are you unwell?'

'It's a migraine, I think.' Edith glanced helplessly at the sour-smelling basin of vomit at the side of the bed. 'I'm sorry. I—'

'Oh, you poor thing!' The young woman whisked the basin away. She came back with fresh water. 'Drink this then I'll get you some linden tea. It is good for headaches and stomach upsets.' She sat on the side of the narrow, iron-framed bed. 'I am Sarah, by the way, Sarah Weill. I have the room next door.'

Sarah made the Lyzeum slightly more bearable. There was no question of going home. Edith would have to stick it out for the term even though she didn't like it. Not at all. It wasn't just what had happened with Kurt, there was an unpleasant atmosphere in the school. The Head, Fräulein Weber, was near retirement; her deputy, Fräulein Grafstadt, was helping her out of the door. Fräulein Grafstadt was a thoroughgoing Nazi, proud of being an early member of the *Nationalsozialistische Frauenschaft*. She had taken to wearing her swastika armband to school and was followed by others, particularly Fräulein Wilhelm, Head of P.E., an amazonian of a woman with huge breasts and a pin-head who put the girls through endless drills and bouts of vigorous gymnastic ribbon dancing. These two ruled the school. They insisted on the Hitler salute at the beginning and end of lessons; they encouraged the girls to join the *Bund Deutscher Mädel* and to inform on any girls, their families, or teachers who expressed disloyalty to Hitler and the National Socialists. The one or two Jewish students had a particularly hard time. Fräulein Weill came off worst of all.

'I'm leaving,' Sarah said finally. 'It's only a matter of time before they get rid of me anyway. There are new laws all the time. I won't give them the satisfaction.' She paused, fighting the tears back, biting her lip. 'Daniel and I have plans.' Daniel was Sarah's boyfriend, a young communist and Jewish, he was in even more danger than she was. 'We will go to Amsterdam. He has family there. Then we will go to America. Daniel says there is no future for us in the whole of Europe. I don't like to impose on you, but . . .'

'Will I help? You don't have to ask.' Edith took her hand. She smiled although tears threatened, whether for Sarah and her kind, or for herself, she couldn't tell.

Sarah went after lessons on a Saturday. Edith took her suitcase to the station. If anyone asked, she was taking English books to a friend at the University. Nobody asked. Sarah left the school as if she was just going out for the evening. She would not be missed until Monday when Edith reported that she was sick with a fever and keeping to her room. That gained her a day or two. The staff lived in mortal fear of infection spreading through the school. Her absence wasn't noticed until the Wednesday. By then, Edith profoundly hoped that Sarah and her fiancé were far away.

She claimed ignorance but no one believed her. She was told to pack her bags. She'd never been so glad to leave anywhere, even though she dreaded what would happen on her premature return. The Head's reaction had been unexpected. 'You poor girl! It must have been hideous! That Herr Hitler. Dreadful man. I was just about to send Fräulein Rolf packing.' She'd sniffed. 'Filling the girls' heads with all sorts of rubbish. I won't have those kinds of views peddled here.' Edith had burst into tears at her unexpected sympathy. Miss Jameson had patted her shoulder, suggested a few days off. The days had turned into weeks. 'Nervous Exhaustion' Dr Elliot had called it. A convenient cover for a broken heart.

She must have slept. She woke to a tentative knocking.

'*Gnädige Frau* Graham?'

A face peered round the door, thin and dark, framed with black curls. For a moment, Edith thought that it was her Lyzeum friend, Sarah.

'I am Seraphina.' The girl entered carrying a heavy ewer. She was more roughly dressed than the other girls, her hair half-hidden by a kerchief, her faded wraparound overall far too big for her, the sleeves of her blouse rolled up above the elbows. 'I bring hot water.'

Her eyes widened as they went from the washstand to the basin now by Edith's bed.

'I'm sorry, I . . .'

'No, no,' the girl put the ewer down. 'I will take away. I'll tell Frau Schmidt you are not well.'

'No, no,' Edith put out a hand. 'Please don't.'

She couldn't bear a fuss and something told her that Frau Schmidt would make one.

'I tell no one, if you don't want.' She dipped Edith's flannel in the ewer, squeezed it out and came over to the bed. She pressed the flannel to Edith's forehead with light, gentle touches. Her cracked, reddened hands smelt of lye. 'Tell me what I can do.'

She looked down at Edith, her tiny face puckered with concern. She was smaller than the others, slightly built and appeared younger, scarcely into her teens, although she was probably older than that. There were deep shadows, like brown thumb marks, under her eyes and her skin was the colour of cheap paper.

'Water. I'd like some water.'

'I bring.'

She glanced back from the door. With her large, dark eyes and delicate bone structure, the girl must have been very pretty. Would be pretty again one day. Edith hoped so, anyway. She left

142

as quietly as she came. Edith lay back. Who was she? Not German. Czech perhaps? Jewish certainly. As she'd leaned over to apply the flannel, Edith had seen the blue numerals tattooed on her bare arm. What had her life been before all that horror engulfed her? Edith had no idea. Every indication had been stripped away.

12

CCG Mess, Lübeck

17th January 1946

```
Dinner Menu
Mockturtle Soup
Fried Sole in butter
Dutch Steak with Espagnole Sauce
Castle Potatoes
Carrots
Raspberry Cream
Cheese & Biscuits
Coffee
```

```
Menu doesn't quite deliver on its pretension.
Dutch Steak should be real steak but this
is a fried hashed-beef pattie, served with
gravy and roast potatoes. The food in the
Mess is plentiful, filling and reassuringly
British. A contrast to the want all too
evident in the world outside.
```

Edith's trunk was taking an age to arrive and she was running
out of things to wear. Every day, when she got back from the

office, she expected to find it waiting but there was no sign. Finally, she asked Roz to look into it.

'I don't understand,' Roz said as she came off the phone. 'They say it was delivered *days* ago!'

Edith hurried home to find it standing in the hall.

'When did this come?' she asked.

Frau Schmidt shrugged her ample shoulders. 'When I was out of the house.'

Edith turned to the two girls, Grete and Hilde, who stared at the floor.

'Never mind,' Edith sighed. 'It's here now.'

'Grete and Hilde will take it up for you,' Frau Schmidt offered brightly.

Edith looked at her. 'Not Stephan?'

'He has bad back from war injuries.' Frau Schmidt put a hand to the small of her own back to demonstrate.

Edith caught a look passing between the two girls as they lugged the heavy trunk up the stairs. 'What *does* Stephan do?' Edith asked as they carried the trunk into her room. Sandy-haired and sullen, Stephan strolled about the place with an arrogant swagger and was rarely glimpsed doing anything. Again, that look. Edith dismissed the girls to examine her trunk. Everything seemed to be there, but someone had tampered with the lock. It could have happened anywhere, she reasoned, on its way from Coventry, but she had a feeling that it had happened somewhere pretty close to where she was now.

There was snow that night. The next day, Jack crunched up the path to collect her. Stephan was supposed to be outside clearing. There was no sign of him but when they left the house, he was leaning against the wing of the Humber, lighting a cigarette.

'Get off the car, you lazy fucker!' Jack shouted. Stephan looked back at Jack with scarcely veiled insolence as he slowly transferred his weight to his snow shovel. 'He's a wrong 'un,' Jack said as they drove away. 'You get a nose for it. Where to this morning, ma'am?'

Edith had responsibility for a group of schools in the Lübeck area. The Brigadier had outlined her task on the first morning but out in the schools, or what passed for schools, Edith found his briefing very short of the mark. She didn't blame him. It was how he dealt with a job that was beyond him.

Beyond anyone, she thought, as they crawled churned streets carved through ruins and rubble. Everywhere was crowded with people. So many people. The bridges choked with men and women, old and young, children and old people, pushing prams, pulling carts mounded with belongings.

'DPs from the east,' Jack said as he crawled forward sounding his horn.

The streams parted reluctantly then surged back around them at a steady trudge, moving with the dogged weariness of people who had walked a long way and had no idea where they could stop. As the car slowed, there was a rapping on the window. A grinning face peered in, grimy as a miner. Another appeared and another, soon children were running alongside them, hands outstretched for cigarettes, gum, chocolate, whatever they could get. There were children everywhere. If she stopped the car and asked why they weren't in school, they would just laugh and run off to range over the ruins, pick over the bombsites, pulling their own little carts behind them, scavenging for what they could find. How on earth was she going to get them into a classroom? It was hard not to despair at the impossibility of it all. She felt like the *Trümmerfrauen* removing the debris of a ruined city, one brick at a time; as if she'd been set one of those impossible tasks: reaping a field with a sickle of leather, plaiting a halter with a rope of sand.

'Where to, ma'am?' Jack asked again.

'Oh, Herr Hecht. Then Frau Holstein.'

'Frau Graham.' Herr Hecht was there to greet them. 'We are honoured. So good to see you again.'

His smile was warm with welcome and Edith felt a lift in her spirits. He was probably no more than middle aged but looked much older, his face grooved with deep lines, his hair and neatly trimmed pointed beard a pure white. He waved with a bony hand for them to follow him into the ruins of his school. He walked slowly, leaning heavily on a thin cane.

Lessons were conducted in the only room fit for habitation; the only room with any heating. An old iron stove stood in the corner; a small pile of fuel next to it, a few cobs of coke and coal, the scattering of sticks little more than kindling. The room had no ceiling. What little heat there was went up into the rafters. The children and staff worked bundled in coats and scarves. Steam rose from a large pot on the top of the stove, adding a vegetable tang to the sour smell of unwashed clothes and bodies.

The children were divided according to age, boys and girls together, four or five to a desk. They all stood as she entered. She motioned for them to sit down, get on with what they had been doing. Maths. The teachers had to teach without benefit of text-books, which had all been confiscated. More were being rewritten in London by committee, so goodness knew how long that would take. There was a general shortage of paper, so the children were using slates and the margins of newspaper pages for their workings.

Herr Hecht conducted her round his classroom. To begin with, most of the children were too shy to answer her questions but they gradually grew bolder, encouraged by Herrn Hecht's smiles and his gentle manner.

The children were well turned out: the boys' hair neatly combed and parted, the girls' plaited and ribboned, their clothes clean but a jumble mix of winter and summer wear and nearly all threadbare, patched and darned, faded fabrics rotting and splitting. There were obvious signs of malnutrition. Some of the faces looking up at her were grey and yellowish, the eyes dull and sunken, noses red and running, the areas around the mouth crusted with impetigo. The napes of those bent over their slates were pocked with eruptions, boils and rashes. At home these would be seen as marks of neglect, the parents visited, homes inspected. The parents were not at fault here.

'They do their best,' Herr Hecht shook his head. 'They give up their own clothes, their shoes, so that the children can come to school. Shoes are the worst problem. They wear out. The children grow out of them so quickly but without,' he shrugged, 'it is impossible for them to come at all.'

A look under the desks showed the pitiful truth of it. Shoes cracked and broken, the toes cut out because they were sizes too small, worn-through soles replaced by roughly shaped wooden blocks, improvised clogs bound on with rags. Some wore sandals, even though the ground was frozen, red knobs of chilblains throbbed on bare toes; others shuffled in adult boots like small, sad clowns. The children sat with their feet tucked well back, away from scrutiny. She walked the rows with Jack, careful not to shame them further, or to show how their brave dignity was moving her to tears.

At first, the children were awed by Jack. His size and, Edith realized, his uniform. Then came one spluttered laugh, then another as Jack waggled his ears, pulled hideous faces, made sticks of gum and foil-wrapped squares of chocolate disappear and appear from behind ears or out of noses.

'You are good with them,' Herr Hecht said, smiling as Jack gave one delighted boy his cap to wear.

'My sister's got kiddies.' Jack grinned and gave him the rest of the chocolate to hand out later.

It was nearing lunchtime. The children lined up to have soup ladled out to them. It was thin stuff. Hardly more than water with a few vegetable scraps floating in it. They ate at their desks, mopping up every last drop with small squares of coarse bread.

'It's little enough but more than they get at home,' Herr Hecht remarked. 'Every week I have ten, more than that, absent because they are too weak to come. What food there is goes to the man, if there is one, the older brother, older sister, whoever is working. Things will improve, Fräulein Graham.' He looked around the crowded classroom. 'Our present deprivations are merely physical. They will lift in time. I did not agree with the former regime but I am lucky. I survived.' Edith knew from Roz that he'd spent time in a concentration camp and had been sent to Belgium to do forced labour. 'Now it is better, I think. At least we are free,' he tapped his temple, 'up here.'

'I'll do what I can, Herr Hecht.'

'I know you will.'

Edith shook his hand in parting. His palm was still calloused, the knuckles swollen and prominent, the bones ribbed beneath his dry, papery skin. Edith suspected that, whatever food he had, he shared with the children, even if he himself went hungry.

'Did you see what was in that pot?' Jack cut into her thoughts. 'Not enough to keep body and soul together. Poor little sods. Freezing cold in there and all.'

'They bring in what they can, Jack.' The only fuel was what the children brought with them. 'I've tried to get more for them but nothing happens . . .'

Edith's hands clenched tight on her lap and she turned away. She didn't want Jack to see her anger, frustration and, yes, humiliation. There was plenty of food in the stores and warehouses, coal in the depots. As soon as she saw how bad things were in the schools, she'd gone straight away to the departments responsible – only to be blocked at every turn. Passed on to a succession of people who seemed to extract real pleasure from saying 'no', in making an impossible job even more impossible, and all this added to her gnawing sense of futility. She'd come here to make a contribution, make a difference. Why did she think she could succeed where others had failed? So far she'd contributed absolutely nothing and made no difference at all. She was letting down the children, the very people that she was here to help.

'Penny for 'em,' Jack said.

Edith sighed. 'Oh, nothing.' She straightened her gloves. 'It just seems impossible, that's all.'

'*Nil carborundum*, eh? Don't let the bastards grind you down.' He kept his eyes on the road as they slowly nosed their way through the still crowded streets. 'I was in tanks in the war. We used to say, "If you can't go under, you go over. If you can't go round, you go straight through." I'll see what I can do.'

* * *

149

At the next school, things appeared to be much better. The school was running smoothly, the children attending regularly. The staff were very young but they seemed to know what they were doing. The Head, Frau Holstein, was older, a hairpin of a woman, draped in rusty black, iron-grey hair in tight plaits, wrapped at the side of her head like ear muffs. She'd returned to teaching after a long bout of *Kinder und Küche* under the Nazis. Her husband had been killed in a raid so now she needed to work. Her credentials were excellent and, since she'd left teaching relatively early, her record wasn't tainted. Her Persilschein had pride of place above the blackboard in a space probably previously occupied by Herrn Hitler.

Frau Holstein was very different from Herr Hecht. Her welcome was frosty to the point of curtness. She might be getting the school whipped into shape but Edith sensed that something was not quite right.

The children all shot to rigid attention. When she motioned for them to sit down, they bent to their tasks as if their lives depended on it. The room was pindrop quiet. No fidgeting. Just the squeak of chalk on slate. If Edith asked them anything, their eyes went straight to Frau Holstein. None of them answered in a voice above a whisper and they visibly flinched from Frau Holstein's encouraging pats and smiles.

'As you see, Frau Graham, we have strong discipline here. So important for learning. You must agree.' She didn't wait for Edith to answer that but went straight on to a new thought. 'You are new here of course. Very new. Not, perhaps, very familiar with how things are working. The Brigadier is happy to leave to *us* the running of the schools. On that, he is very clear. It is not your job to interfere in any way at all.'

Edith felt herself redden.

'I don't know about that,' she said as equably as she could manage. A blazing row might upset the children and Frau Holstein would take it out on them as soon as she left.

Edith knew her type and she knew fear when she saw it. The staff showed the same quiet wariness as the children. A sliding-eyes watchfulness followed Frau Holstein wherever she went. The woman was almost certainly overstepping her authority. Discipline was necessary, of course, but Edith would not tolerate cruelty, or any kind of tyranny. They'd had enough of that, surely? And it would be all too easy. Defeat had taken away all certainty; it had made people vulnerable and frightened. Children and adults alike.

After the day was over, Edith walked home with Roz.

'You're quiet,' Roz ventured.

'It's been a long day. When I see some of it, the state of their clothes, their shoes, the way their parents try to keep them clean and smart, I just feel like howling and that wouldn't do, would it?'

'No, it would not! Who did you go to see?'

'Herrn Hecht then Frau Holstein.'

'Herr Hecht's a sweetie,' Roz smiled. 'But Frau Holstein's enough to tire anybody out.' She gave the smallest shudder of disgust. 'Rather you than me with that one.'

'Yes,' Edith frowned. 'There's something going on there. A surprise visit might be in order.'

'I'd leave it a week or so, if I was you.' Roz thrust her mittened hands deeper into her pockets. It was cold and getting colder. The Trave was properly freezing over. 'Lull her into a false sense of security. Then pounce. Come on, you need a drink!' Roz linked arms. 'Dinner at the Mess?'

'Why not?'

'Billet getting to you?'

'A bit.'

That first night seemed to have fixed the pattern for how things would be in the house. Edith felt not exactly ostracized, more isolated. Not one of them. They were younger than her and in far more junior positions. She felt like a House Mistress in a girls' boarding school. Chatter died down when she came into a room, conversation turning awkward and stilted, laughter and animation only reviving when she took her leave.

Miss Slater had taken a particular dislike to Edith, which didn't help. She was the centre of attention. The emotions that eddied below the surface of the house swirled around her but she was capricious with her favours. Any who offended, even in the slightest, became the butt of vicious jibes, left out in the cold, excluded until she made amends. It was all very adolescent, but these girls were very young. Young enough for such things to matter. Edith had heard the crying behind the bathroom door. Then there were the nicknames that Molly had given them. Rusty, Joey, Baby, Gol, Betty Boop. Names that held an edge of truth honed on cruel observation, angled to wound, or undermine. No doubt she had one for Edith and it would not be kind.

Edith laughed. 'They're a nice enough bunch. A bit young but there's one . . .'

'There is always one.'

'Her name's Molly. Molly Slater.'

'Tall blonde? Thinks she's Jean Harlow?'

'That's her. Do you know her?'

'*Of* her. Blonde bombshell. A bit of a fast piece.'

'The odd thing is, she's the billet monitor. Very thick with Frau Schmidt.'

Edith had been surprised to find Miss Slater in such a domestic capacity. It was a role that didn't really suit her. Part quartermaster, part housemother, the Billet Monitor worked closely with the housekeeper to order in food for meals taken in the billet and day-to-day necessities: tea, coffee, sugar, soap. There was an allowance, so much per person, taken out of their rations.

'*Really?* Hmm.' Roz frowned at the frosty ground. 'Wouldn't surprise me. I'd keep an eye on that. There's a lot of fiddling goes on. You wouldn't believe how much. There's a darker side of life in the Zone,' Roz dropped her voice, even though they were walking alone. 'There's an area down by the docks, notorious for brothels and black marketeering. Cigarettes, coffee, canned and packaged food, toiletries and such, traded for cameras, wirelesses, binoculars, watches, jewellery, silverware, porcelain, paintings, furniture, bicycles, even cars. They keep the illicit swag in the derelict warehouses. There are regular police raids but that never seems to make any difference. Everybody's at it. You can find half the Control Commission down there any given Sunday buying up goodies to ship back home. The whole thing's run by foreign DPs from the east. They're rapidly turning into a bunch of racketeers, according to Jeff.'

'Do you think that's the reason she's Billet Monitor?'

Added to other odd things that she'd noticed, it made sense. Something didn't ring true about Miss Slater. The stories she told about herself: her family; the house in the country, another in London; the school she'd attended. None of it quite equated. A certain vagueness on detail. *Somewhere on the South Coast, I don't remember.* A testiness when questioned. *Does it really matter?* It was as if she was acting a part. The others lapped it up but Edith could see through it and Molly knew it. One of the reasons for her antipathy.

'Oh, yes,' Roz nodded, as if it was obvious. 'Siphoning stuff off to sell on the black market. It's a big business being used to fund all sorts, not just crime gangs but underground organizations hiding fugitive Nazis, helping them escape. It's a real headache, Jeff says.'

'I was wondering if Jeff found anything?' Edith said as they sat down to dinner.

'About your friend?' Roz looked up from the menu. 'Not so far. He thinks it's rather peculiar, in fact.'

'Oh, why's that?'

'The Germans are supposed to be registered, to get rations, and so on, but she's not on any list. Maybe she's not even here.'

'Maybe.'

Was that a good or bad thing? Too soon to tell.

Roz had gone back to the menu. 'Soup that's never even *seen* a turtle and Dutch Steak with Espagnole Sauce.' She snorted. 'Rissole and gravy. Nothing here is the real thing, have you noticed?' She looked round at the other diners. 'Like this lot. Pretending to be something they're not. Living like lords. Lining their pockets. Making as much as they can out of it. The German ration's going down and in this weather.' She snapped the menu shut. 'Shall I ask Jeff to keep looking?'

'Oh, no,' Edith replied, 'it was just on the off chance, that's all.'

Edith was disappointed that her only lead, slim as it was, had come to nothing but some instinct told her not to draw any more attention to her search for Elisabeth.

They came out of the Mess, the air numbingly cold to mouth and nose, catching the throat. The town, lit by a platinum-bright moon, looked like a story from the Brothers Grimm: an icy glitter of ancient roofs and towers under a diamond dusting of stars.

'Jolly cold, isn't it? And awfully slippy.' Roz linked arms and they held each other up as they slipped and slid along together. 'Oh, before I forget,' Roz hugged Edith's arm closer. 'That chap phoned again. Captain Adams. He wants you to call him back.'

'Oh, right. Thanks, Roz.'

'Are you all right from here?' They were at the Hüxterdamm Bridge. Roz peered up at her. 'Cold getting to you? Apart from your nose, you've gone a tiny bit pale. Doesn't do to linger. Better get your skates on!'

She went off, laughing at her own joke. Edith steadied herself on the parapet of the bridge.

No lead on Elisabeth. Nothing to report to Dori. She was keeping menus and recipes as a kind of *aide memoire*, *dessous des cartes*, but so far they were just that. Recipes. Now Adams was on to her. What was she going to say to him? She'd been busy settling in, getting to grips with the job. Or not on today's showing. Distinct lack of success in all areas. She obviously wasn't cut out for any of this. Sometimes, she wondered what she was doing here at all.

She leaned over parapet. Blocks of ice clashed in the turbid, thickening water. There were more of them each day. She leaned out further. How long would you last in that? A minute? Less, probably. It was very cold; her coat was sticking to the iron. Her breath wreathed round her like smoke.

She wouldn't have to throw herself in if she stayed here for much longer. She heeded Roz's advice and turned for home. She had a sense of things moving just below the surface, like the dark waters beneath the thickening ice. The British presented an outward show of office routine and Club at weekends, but this was not the Home Counties. Roz had given the lie to that screening blandness. As for the Germans, they were enigmatic at best. It was hard to know what lay behind the mask of willing compliance. There was plenty going on that both sides had reasons to hide but how was she going to find out?

13

CCG Billet, Lübeck

17th January 1946

Refugee Potato pancakes
(Kartoffelpuffer)
Potato peelings
Handful of flour
Salt and pepper

Take potato peels cut them to very small
pieces mix them with some flour and salt fry
them on top of the stove. (Seraphina's recipe
- refugees subsist on this)

Edith got back to rather an ugly scene.

Frau Schmidt and Miss Slater had the German girls gathered together in the hall. To the others they were just 'those girls', 'this girl', or 'that girl' but Edith was getting to know them, or as much as they would allow. She chatted while they made her bed, brought her morning tea, hot water. Hilde was the most forthcoming. Blonde, fresh faced. Originally from Hanover, family bombed out in '44. She'd been sent to an aunt who lived in a village outside Lübeck. She cycled in every day. Grete, smaller, sharper featured, a native of the town and relative of Frau Schmidt. Magda, thin, dark with darting brown eyes. She was from the east and said very little about what had happened to her, very little about anything. And there was Seraphina. The others waited at table, brought hot water, changed the beds. Seraphina was treated like a skivvy. She waited on Frau Schmidt and the others and did the heavy, dirty jobs: clearing snow, hauling coal and logs, clearing out the stoves, lighting fires. Jobs that Stephan was supposed to do. Exempted by his war injuries, presumably.

Hilde, Grete and Magda were standing apart from Seraphina. They had the same look of innocence mixed with faint accusation, as if the combination would deflect blame from them. Seraphina stood, head held high, her large, dark eyes shiny with tears that she would not shed.

The other residents were watching from the stairs or the doorway of the sitting room.

'What's all this?' Edith stripped off her gloves. Some sort of hoo-ha in the billet really would put the tin lid on it.

'It has come to my notice,' Miss Slater's tone had a pompous ring that she'd no doubt learnt from some superior at work. 'It has been brought to my attention by Frau Schmidt, that Seraphina has been stealing.'

'I see.' Edith unpinned her hat.

Miss Slater looked to Frau Schmidt to take up the story.

'She is Jewish,' the older woman said with a look of contempt. 'What can you expect? I give her a chance. Now this happens. I should have known better.'

Seraphina continued to stare straight ahead. Edith wondered again what her life had been before. There was an intelligence in those eyes and something altogether refined about her looks and demeanor that this terrible time had failed to erase. Whatever her past life, Edith doubted that she'd been destined to skivvy for the likes of Frau Schmidt. But such a job was highly sought after. If she lost this, she would lose everything. They would be queuing up to take her place. Probably were already. Frau Schmidt would have someone lined up, that was certain.

'A Jew!' Miss Slater's lip curled at the word and she gave a little shudder of disgust. 'I might have known.'

'How could you not have known?' Edith said as she took off her coat. 'Did you not see the numbers on her arm?'

Of course she hadn't. Until this moment, Seraphina had been beneath her notice.

'What is Seraphina supposed to have stolen?' Edith asked. She kept her voice even, as she would do in school.

'Not supposed,' Miss Slater spat out. 'Did. She was caught red-handed by Frau Schmidt.'

Edith turned to the older woman. 'And what was it that Seraphina was caught stealing?'

'Potato peelings.'

Edith looked from one to the other. 'All this is about *potato peelings*?'

'It's against the rules,' Miss Slater countered. 'Germans are not supposed to take food home. Even scraps and leftovers.'

'Are they not? Where does it go, then?'

Miss Slater shrugged. 'Into the rubbish, I suppose.'

'Or into Frau Schmidt's basement.' She turned to the other German servants. 'Is that not so, girls?'

They said nothing but Hilde's ready colour gave them away and Frau Schmidt's blustered denial died in her throat.

'So, it's all right for Frau Schmidt to take leftover food,' Edith went on, 'and presumably the others, if Frau Schmidt can spare anything, but not Seraphina? Is that right?'

She bit back her anger, determined not to lose her temper, but no one else was going to defend Seraphina, they were all looking away, eyes averted, and she wouldn't – couldn't – put up with what was happening here.

Miss Slater's face became stubborn, sullen. 'It's against regulations. She should be reported.'

'I see. And none of us do anything against regulations? That's a very fine watch, Miss Slater.' Edith took the girl's arm. 'Mind if I take a better look?'

It was black market almost certainly. Miss Slater made to pull her arm away, but Edith's grip tightened.

'Swiss, if I'm not mistaken. And expensive.' She turned it to see the face. 'Very expensive. Would you mind telling us where you got it?'

'It was a gift.'

'Oh, from whom?'

'An admirer,' she shook her arm free. 'I've had it ages.'

'Really? And that's a nice pendant you are wearing. I haven't seen it before. Gold with what looks like a ruby at the centre. It looks old.'

'It's a family heirloom, if you must know.'

'So it will have a British Hallmark, won't it? Can I see?'

Edith held her ice-blue eyes until she looked away.

'How would I know?' She turned away in sulky petulance, a protective hand over the pendant. She rallied. 'Look here, you've no right—'

'I was merely proving a point,' Edith said, keeping her voice mild. 'You have no right, either. Neither have any of you.' Her tone hardened as she looked around at the other girls. 'How much do you pay in cigarettes for your laundry to be done? Your hair? The alterations to your clothes? We all do it but it is strictly against regulations. You could *all* be reported. I suggest we leave Seraphina alone, don't you? Is it really worth ruining anybody's life for a few potato peelings?'

No one said anything.

'I simply don't have time for this. I have to get ready. I'm going out.' Miss Slater flung the riposte over her shoulder as she ran upstairs.

'Who's for a drink?' Angela turned back into the sitting room now the show was over. 'I could do with one after that!'

The others followed in a ripple of excited, nervous laughter, anxious to dispel the recent awkwardness and presumably hoping that Edith would not report the lot of them.

Frau Schmidt shooed the German girls towards the kitchen.

'Frau Schmidt, might I have a word?' Edith called the woman back. 'I don't want to see Seraphina suffer in any way as a result of this . . . misunderstanding. And I don't want to see her being the only one stuck with the heavy work. See to it that it's shared equally between the other girls, or better still I'd like to see Stephan doing a bit more, or I might start asking some questions of my own. Like what is he doing here, anyway? And why are you two camped in the basement? Which is, as I understand it, against the famous regulations. Seraphina? Will you bring my bag up for me? I don't want dinner and I have paperwork to do.'

Edith turned for the stairs, noting with satisfaction Frau Schmidt's defeated nod as she trudged down the steps to the basement.

'Sit down, Seraphina.' Edith shut the door. 'I want to talk to you.'

Seraphina sat down, taking a fraction of the edge of the bed.

'Did you take them?'

'The potato peels? Of course. They all do. Frau Schmidt and the other girls. I wanted to make *Kartoffelpuffer*, potato pancakes, for my sister. She is hungry. Sick. She needs food. They all take food. I thought they would not mind.'

'But they did.'

Seraphina nodded.

'One rule for them, one rule for you, eh?'

Seraphina gave a weary shrug. 'Hilde, and Magda, they say nothing but Grete tells Frau Schmidt who goes to Miss Slater.' She looked up at Edith. 'I thought she is British and would be on my side. What is a few potato peels to you? I was surprised.'

'We have our own share of bigots and anti-semites.'

'It is everywhere?'

'I'm afraid so.'

'I'd like to go someplace where that is not so.'

Edith stared at the girl. She could think of no answer.

'Tell me, Seraphina,' she said. 'Where are you living?'

'We have a place in a house.'

160

'Not in a camp?'

'No.' She shook her head vigorously. 'I won't live in a camp. I don't care how bad the place is where we live. I'd rather live on our own.'

Edith took out cigarettes. 'Do you want one?'

Seraphina took a cigarette but refused a light.

'Here. Have the whole packet. Have two. And here's chocolate. For your sister. She's sick you say?'

'Yes, very sick. She needs medicine but I have no money, nothing.' Seraphina wiped at the tears that she'd refused to shed earlier. 'I don't know what to do.'

'I'll come and see her tomorrow. There, there,' Edith put her arm round the girl's narrow shoulders and offered her handkerchief. 'We'll see what needs to be done to make her better. Meanwhile, you heard what I said to Frau Schmidt, if anything like this happens again, or if she gives you heavy jobs to do, I want to know. Really, that woman. I've a good mind to get rid of her.'

'You can do that?' Seraphina looked at her with awe.

'Oh, yes,' Edith clicked her fingers. 'Like that.'

All Germans were intensely vulnerable; every aspect of their lives subject to the Control Commission. As a Senior Officer, Edith could do more or less what she liked.

'But you mustn't,' Seraphina's thin face grew deadly serious. 'She is very powerful.'

'Powerful, how?' Edith asked.

'She knows many people. They can make trouble.'

'For me?'

Seraphina shook her head quickly.

'For you?'

Seraphina nodded just as fast.

'Oh, I see. What kind of people, exactly?'

'I— I can't say. But,' she lowered her voice, looking round like a hunted field mouse, as if Frau Schmidt might be lurking, ready to pounce. 'This is not her house although she says it is. She was just the housekeeper. I heard Grete saying. The family left when the British come. Then Frau Schmidt has the house to herself.' She paused. 'Those little animals – in the parlour.'

'The porcelain pieces?'

Seraphina nodded. 'They are special. *Porzellanmanufaktur Allach*. Made in Dachau for the SS.'

'How do you know?'

'I know,' Seraphina said quietly, her small hands locked tightly. 'Frau Schmidt tells me I must not touch, even to dust. Not that I would.' Her face puckered with loathing and disgust. 'They cannot show the picture of Hitler anymore but they keep these things that are not so obvious, to show they have not changed. If you look, you see.' She turned an ornament over and signed double lightning flash runes in the air. The mark of the SS. 'That Stephan,' she lowered her voice still further. 'He is not Frau Schmidt's man. He is hiding, she is helping him.'

This all made sense. Edith could never quite square the elegant bedroom furniture, the pretty little pink stool in particular, with Frau Schmidt's ample behind. And Stephan. He looked younger than Frau Schmidt, which wasn't suspicious in itself, of course, but they seemed ill-suited. He didn't like rough work, shirked most of it, and there was something about his attitude. The sullen resentment could be a profound distaste born of shock, as if he could not quite understand how this was happening to him.

'Thank you, Seraphina.' The girl took it as her cue to go. 'No, wait a moment. These *Kartoffelpuffer*. How do you make them?'

Seraphina looked mystified. 'They are poor people's food . . .'

'I collect recipes. Indulge me.'

Edith picked up a pencil and rummaged in her bag for paper. She found the Mess menu card and wrote the recipe on the back.

What the girl had told her chimed with what Adams had said about the fear that still held sway here, of hidden forces under the surface. *Like they're afraid of something. As though the people we're looking for still have influence and power.* Seraphina hadn't said as much, but that's whom she meant. *He is hiding. She is helping him.* Did she mean hiding himself, or hiding

162

someone else? And how exactly was Frau Schmidt helping? And the porcelain animals. Crafty. A little shrine to the old regime hidden in plain sight. If anyone recognized the mark, Edith could see Frau Schmidt sliding out of it as quick as you like. *Oh, a misunderstanding! They belong to the people who had lived here before I moved in!*

Small things, straws in the wind, but this was something she could give to Adams. And at last recipes for Dori. Vienna Steak and *Kartoffelpuffer*. Refugee potato pancakes. The matching of the recipes told its own story of luxury and lack.

14

Mietshaus Moltkestraße, Lübeck;

British Hospital, Hamburg

18th January 1946

```
Moltkestraße Tea
Pine needles chopped fine
Boiling water
```

```
Used to ward off hunger by those who have
nothing else.
```

Edith directed Jack to the address that Seraphina had given her, a warren of flats down the Moltkestraße. Every room was crammed with displaced persons, from all over Europe, refugees from the East, ex-slave labourers, POWs whose countries were now under Russian occupation and who didn't want to go home.

They shared a concrete box with very little light. The windows were covered with rotting cardboard. The stove in the corner leaked smoke but gave out little heat. It was barely warmer than outside. Black mould peppered the wall above a tide line of green slime. There was a powerful smell of damp.

A woman swathed in layers of clothing stirred a pot on the

stove. She did not look up when they came in, just hunched deeper into herself. She was making soup from vegetable scraps and water. There was a battered can boiling next to the pan. She threw in a handful of something. Pine needles added their fragrance to the cold, damp air, permeated with wood smoke. The woman was no relation, Seraphina explained, they just shared the room. Her son lived there, too. He'd been hurt in the war. Seraphina tapped her temple.

He was out, and pine tea would stave off his mother's hunger. The soup was for him when he came back from scavenging for food scraps and wood.

The Germans were supposed to receive 1,500 calories a day although it worked out at more like 1,000. These people were getting far less. 600, if that. That meant malnutrition, even starvation. But coffee was being served in the Mess at this moment with complimentary toast and jam. Then lunch, always substantial, often four courses. Everyone tucking in, girls complaining about their waistlines.

They deserve it – that's what they'd say – but no one deserved this. Since when did two wrongs make a right? And these girls were victims, for goodness' sake. Would they never find any escape?

The sister, Anna, lay on an improvised bed in the corner, a wooden pallet covered with a straw mattress and a mound of threadbare, ragged blankets. She was huddled under a filthy quilt.

Seraphina apologized as Edith went over to examine the girl. 'I have no way of washing, of cleaning.'

'That's quite all right, Seraphina.' Edith bent down. 'Let's take a look at you.'

The girl's eyes flickered open. They were a most astonishing china blue. Edith pushed back her long fringe. Her forehead was cold and wet, her fair hair dark with sweat. There were fever spots on her cheeks; her breathing was laboured, difficult, with a worrying whistling note to it. Edith was no nurse, but this child was clearly very ill.

Edith nodded to Jack. 'Let's get her out of here.'

'Let's be having you, chook,' Jack bent down and picked the girl up as if she weighed no more than a bundle of sticks. 'There's blankets in the back of the Humber.' He gave the keys to Edith. The child stirred in his arms. 'There, there. Ssh. We'll soon have you wrapped up and warm.'

'Your sister is fair,' Edith turned to check on the girl in the back of the car, wrapped in brown army blankets, her head on Seraphina's lap.

'Yes. She is different, with blonde hair, blue eyes. Pretty.' She gave the ghost of a smile. 'Not like me. It saved us, really. We lived in Prague. My father worked in the University.'

'Did he teach you English?'

Seraphina nodded. 'And I learn, learnt,' she corrected, 'at school. When the Nazis came, they arrested my papa. We were taken to Theresienstadt. My mother died there. My grandfather, grandmother also. Then they took us to Auschwitz. I did not see my father, or my brother. I don't know if they live. My sister stayed with me. There's a doctor on the ramp from the train. He sees her. He pulls her out of the line. She has hold of my hand and won't let go. He calls a guard to split us up. Take her. Send me to the gas chambers. Then he asks if we are sisters. Yes, I say, twins although we look different. He is interested in this, so he takes me, too. He does all kinds of experiments on us, measuring, photographing, taking blood, other things, too . . . but we survive.' Seraphina broke off. Edith had never heard her speak about herself, what had happened to her. Perhaps she felt freer now she was outside Frau Schmidt's house, released by the offer of some kind of hope, however small. 'Then the Russians are coming, so they move us first to Buchenwald, then Dachau. Sometimes we walk, sometimes in trucks. I say to Anna, "We can't give up now. The Germans are losing. We will be free soon." Then the Americans came and set us free.' She said this without a trace of irony. 'My sister saved me. Now I must save her.'

'Where are we going?' Edith asked.

Jack was taking the road out of Lübeck, heading for the

Autobahn. As soon as they were out of the town, he put his foot down.

'Not to the local *Krankenhaus*, that's for certain. It's full to busting. She's proper poorly. She goes in there, she won't be coming out.'

The hospitals were crammed, according to Roz who billeted with someone in Public Health. Row after row of waxy pale patients suffering from T.B., pneumonia, God knows what infections brought on by the winter and the living conditions. Either that, or suffering from some form of starvation: extreme emaciation or the distended limbs of hunger oedema, the flesh indenting like putty when pressed. 'I'm taking her to Hamburg. To my wench, Kay.'

'Your lindyhopping partner?'

Jack grinned. 'That's her.'

'How do you know they'll treat Anna? It's a long way to go to find out the hospital is British Only?'

'It's mixed. Mainly us but there's a wing for the Krauts. They've got this programme going on. Sharing Knowledge to Save Lives, they call it. The Krauts don't know about penicillin, so our docs are filling them in. Better than using it all on squaddies with the clap.'

The hospital in Hamburg was bigger and better equipped than anything available to them in Lübeck. Jack's friend, Kay Winston, was tall and spare, her dark hair pinned back under her starched headdress. She appeared capable, even severe in her grey dress, scarlet cape, white cuffs and cap but her blue eyes were kind. She wore a silver service badge on the right lapel of her cape and two scarlet bands above the cuff signified her rank. Service stripes showed her time overseas. The effect was daunting. Edith could imagine Jack's squaddies quailing.

Her greeting was cool, professional. Jack introduced Edith.

'Miss Graham. I've heard a lot about you.' Her look was sharp, shrewd, the twist of her mouth hinted at humour, but it required a considerable stretch to see her lindyhopping with Jack. 'Let me look at the child. Lay her down there.'

Jack took Anna into a cubicle and put her gently on the bed.

Sister Winston's examination was deft and sure. She called a doctor to her, a fair-haired young man in army uniform under his flying white coat.

He nodded to the nurse for the curtains to be drawn. Seraphina wouldn't leave her sister and she wanted Edith to stay with her.

'Very well, they can stay.'

The doctor took Anna's pulse then listened to her chest, her back, asking her to breathe in and out.

'Again. And again, please.'

He tapped, two fingers on two fingers and listened, his forehead creased in concentration.

'What do you think?' Edith asked.

'Sounds like pneumonia. Perhaps T.B. She'll be in for a while, either way.'

'What are her chances?'

The doctor shrugged. 'Who knows? Fifty fifty? Less.' He took her wrist again and turned it to show the numbers tattooed there. 'She's gone through a lot already by the looks of this. We'll do our best.'

He moved to a nearby sink to wash. Seraphina had been watching him: his face, his hands, the movement of the stethoscope across Anna's thin body, with some intensity. Her gaze had shifted to their faces, following the exchanges, but she said nothing until they came to take her sister away.

'Where are they taking her?' She turned to Edith.

'To another part of the hospital.'

'I must go with her.'

'That might not be possible, Seraphina. They are going to make Anna better. You have to trust them.'

'No.' Seraphina's thin hand gripped the metal rail of the trolley. 'We stay together.'

'You can stay.' Sister Winston spoke in German to Seraphina. 'We need helpers on the wards to clean, help with the beds. Can you do that?'

Seraphina nodded. It was the first time Edith had seen her smile.

168

'Very well.' She turned to Edith. 'The German nurses have a hostel. I'll see if I can get her in there.'

'I can't thank you enough,' Edith replied. 'She's a good girl. Hard working. She—'

'She'll be fine. We'll look after her and her sister.'

'Will you let me know, one way – or the other?'

'Of course. I'll send a message with Jack.'

'I'll be back when I can. Meanwhile—'

'She's in good hands. We'll do everything we can.'

15

CCG Billet, Lübeck

18th January 1946

```
Billet Dinner
Cabbage Soup with Spätzle
Piroggen, Cabbage, Fried Onion
Blaubeerkuchen & Custard
```

```
Flavours of the country. Spätzle and espe-
cially Piroggen speak of the east. My Prussian
source may have recipes. Our nearest equiv-
alent would be Stuffed Pancakes. Basic Recipe.
4oz flour, 1 egg, 1/2 pt milk. Beat for 5
minutes, stand for 2 hours, fry in 1oz lard
or bake on saucers at Reg. 4.
```

It had been another long day. Edith was tired. All she wanted was a stiff whisky and a hot bath, preferably both at the same time.

'Miss Graham. Edith.' A voice came from the stairs. 'Might I have a word?'

'Miss Barratt. Lorna.' Edith looked up. 'How can I help you?'

Lorna Barratt was the tall, quiet redhead who worked as a

secretary in the Finance Department. They called her Rusty. One of Molly's soubriquets. She didn't seem to like it very much but the name had stuck.

'It's about Molly. Miss Slater,' Lorna started.

Edith sighed. 'I'm really not interested in Billet tittle-tattle, Lorna. You should know that by now.'

'I'm worried.' Lorna frowned. 'It's not just me. We all are.'

Edith could see her bath disappearing.

'Anyone in?' She nodded towards the sitting room. At least she could have the whisky. 'Want anything?'

Lorna shook her head and perched on the edge of the settee, nervously clasping and unclasping her thin fingers. She'd obviously been put up to this by the others and was feeling uncomfortable. Despite her fatigue, Edith was intrigued.

'Well,' she began, 'it's awkward, you see . . .' She paused and bit her lip. 'The thing is . . .'

'Come on, Lorna,' Edith sipped her drink. 'Spit it out.'

'Well, the thing is,' she held her hands still now, knotted together. 'We're worried because Molly, Miss Slater, has been seen out with . . .' She looked away, torn between sharing a confidence and betrayal.

'Seen out with whom?' Edith was baffled by the dramatics. It was hardly a crime, after all. Unless . . . 'A German?'

Lorna shook her head emphatically, her thick, copper-coloured hair threatening to break free of its restraining slide.

'Oh, no! She wouldn't look at one of them!'

'I didn't think so.' Edith swilled the remains of her drink. 'So, what's the matter? Is she pregnant?'

'Oh, no!' Lorna looked shocked. 'Nothing like that.' Then she paused and thought. 'At least, I don't think so. You can never be sure, can you?'

'What is it then?'

'It's . . .' The girl hesitated again, trying to find the best way to frame the revelation. 'She's going about with this chap and he's not a good sort.'

'Oh? What sort is he?'

'You know the new girl, Agnese? The one we've got instead of Seraphina?' Frau Schmidt hadn't wasted time. The girl was there the next morning. 'It's her brother. They call him Val. Molly's been knocking about with him for a while now. He's from Latvia. You know that watch? The one you spotted? He gave it to her and the locket and other jewellery and other things as well. Silk stockings, perfume, I don't know what else. She's always boasting about it. You know what she's like for showing off. He's got a motorbike and wears a leather jacket. Takes her to places. Berlin. And he's promised to take her to Paris. Then to America.'

'America? How's he going to do that?'

'She didn't explain.' Lorna shook her head. 'She says he's exciting. She says the Mess is full of chinless wonders and old men.'

Edith smiled. 'She's right there.'

Lorna gave the ghost of a smile back. 'I suppose . . . But it is practically fratting.'

'It's not really fraternization, though, is it, if he's not German?' Edith frowned as she tried to thread through the prejudice and suspicion. 'If he's Latvian, then he's a displaced person and she's free to go out with him if she wants to.'

'I know, but,' Lorna paused to collect her thoughts. 'Well, it's just not done. Not by girls.'

Men were different. Fraternization had been strictly forbidden during the first phase of the Occupation, but that had proved impossible to police when sex, like everything else, was on sale for a tin of corned beef or a packet of Players.

'And he might not *be* one – a German – but he's jolly pally with them.' Having overcome her initial reluctance to share this confidence, Lorna was willing to say more. 'He's very thick with Stephan. He drinks schnapps with him and sometimes, when he drops Molly off, Stephan goes out with him on his motorbike. Ever since she met him, Molly's been like this with the Frau.' She crossed her fingers. 'They were always going to get rid of Seraphina, if you ask me, so that Agnese could have her job. We, the rest of us, were glad when you stood up to them about that. We, we didn't agree with what Molly said. You know, about her being Jewish, and so on. We wanted you to know we're not like that. Where did Seraphina go, by the way? Do you know?'

'Her sister's very ill.'

'Oh, I'm sorry . . .'

'She's being well looked after. In hospital in Hamburg. Seraphina's with her.'

'Oh, I'm glad. I wouldn't want anything bad to have happened . . .'

But you weren't concerned enough to intervene, Edith wanted to say, but let it go. They were only girls, after all, not strong enough to stand up to Molly and Frau Schmidt.

'There's something else. Have you noticed?'

Breaking the rule *Not To Touch Plse*, Lorna picked up a pretty porcelain candelabra: pink-cheeked, rosebud-lipped cherubs, chubby arms bearing a torch aloft. It was one of a pair. Edith picked up its twin and turned it over to reveal the twin swords of Meissen.

'Not my cup of tea but valuable, I would think.'

Lorna nodded. 'But that's not it.' She turned the candelabra round in her hands. 'The thing is, they weren't here last week. New things appear, while others disappear, haven't you noticed? There's actually more here than when we came. Frau Schmidt obviously doesn't think we see it.'

Edith set the candelabra down and picked up an innocent looking bunny. The bottom was marked with the twin runes of the SS and a single word: *Allach*. She put it back. Peter Rabbit it was not.

'Have you said anything to her?'

'She says she's just bringing things up from the basement. She's always shifting things about with that friend of hers, the one that looks like a ferret.'

'Frau Kaufmann?' Edith smiled at the accuracy of the observation. Frau Kaufmann was a frequent visitor, dropping in for a chat, or to borrow this or that. She was small and thin, slightly stooped, her nose permanently pink and moist, wiry salt-and-pepper hair tied up in a headscarf and small, shiny bead eyes that were never still. 'You don't think Frau Schmidt is just "shifting things about"?'

'No. Why would she?' Lorna frowned. 'And the things don't go together, some are, well, nice, others ghastly. As if they'd belonged to different people, with different taste.'

'People who are not Frau Schmidt?'

Edith recalled the conversation she'd had with Roz about black-market dealings.

'Well, yes. That's not the only thing. I don't know whether you've noticed but we run out of things: tea, sugar, butter, coffee, cocoa, much more quickly than we should.'

'All things that can be traded on the black market?'

That was straightforward stealing. Edith pressed her lips together. She couldn't abide this kind of petty dishonesty.

'Well, yes . . .'

'I see. Well, that much is easily solved. We'll just appoint another Billet Officer. We'll discuss it over dinner this evening but I think a change of regime is in order. You seem a sensible girl. I will nominate you. Agreed?'

Lorna looked more than a little alarmed at the prospect but nodded.

'Good. A simple vote should do. Will the others go along with it?'

'I think so. Although Molly won't like it and we're all a bit scared of her,' she gave her nervous laugh, 'but, well, some of the girls are getting fed up.'

'Oh, why's that?'

'She's forever asking little favours but sometimes they're not so little and they're scared they might get into trouble.'

'Who might "they" be?'

'Well, specifically, Ginny, Frankie and Jo.'

'What kind of favours?'

'Oh, bits of information, where things are kept.'

Edith frowned, trying to remember their occupations. Public

Safety, Quartermaster's Office, Displaced Persons. It would make sense.

'There is another thing,' Lorna stopped, then went on in a rush. 'Some of us aren't sure she can, well, be trusted. Things have gone missing. Things sent from home. Soap, toothpaste, toiletries. Bits and pieces, mostly, but more valuable things, too.' Lorna's voice dropped. 'Molly either made light of it, or . . .'

'Blamed Seraphina?'

Lorna's pale cheeks coloured. 'Exactly. But we don't think that. Not now.'

Molly Slater did not grace them with her presence that evening, which made deposing her considerably easier.

The cuisine was taking a distinct lurch to the Teutonic. Perhaps the girls were getting more used to it, they ate up the *Spätzle*, the little egg noodles that made the cabbage soup much more palatable, without any complaint. The main course was greeted with more circumspection. They inspected the *Piroggen* with some suspicion, nibbling cautiously at first, but the meat dumplings were filling and savoury. First one then another declared them 'not bad'. The blueberry pudding was an equal success.

Edith stayed behind as Hilde and Magda came in to clear.

'So, who does the cooking?' she asked.

The two girls looked at each other.

'We share,' Hilde said. 'Do it together.'

'The *Piroggen* were excellent. Just right for a cold day.'

Magda blushed. Edith caught the fleeting glimpse of a smile.

'They reminded me of a time I spent at a friend's house in East Prussia before the war. The cook made something very similar. She gave me the recipe but I lost it.' Edith looked up at Magda. 'Could you write it for me?'

'Yes, of course.' Magda ducked her head. 'It is my grand-mother's recipe.'

'And the blueberry pudding?'

'I made that,' Hilde said. 'We collected the blueberries from

175

the forest last summer. Frau Schmidt preserves them in schnapps her cousin makes from potatoes.'

'So, you two do the cooking?'

'Grete helps as well.'

'What about Frau Schmidt? What about her? What's she like?'

The two girls looked at each other, then looked away.

'As a cook, I mean.'

Hilde bit her lip. Magda shook her head very slightly. Good cook or not? On balance Edith thought not, but Frau Schmidt had these two terrified. Edith had planned to ask them questions, about their new workmate and her Baltic brother, what they knew of the Schmidts' domestic arrangements, but they had the look of a goose that could see the wolf over her shoulder.

Sure enough, Frau Schmidt appeared just at that moment. The two girls flinched at her harsh, chiding bark: *Fort mit euch! Ihr verschwendet nur die Zeit der gnädigen Frau* – Be off with you! You're wasting the lady's time! They made for the stairs, Frau Schmidt driving them before her. At the top of the flight, Frau Schmidt looked back with her improbable porcelain smile and her shiny nightshade eyes.

Edith stared back, anger stirring inside. Who the hell did she think she was? What on earth was going on here? Hadn't these girls had enough fear in their young lives, without being terrified of Frau Schmidt and her kind? Hadn't they left that sort of fear behind? Edith was wondering what she could do about that when there was a light knock at the door.

'*Herein!*'

Magda sidled in and took a folded paper from her apron pocket. A recipe for *Piroggen* written out in neatly sloping *Sütterlinschrift*.

'Thank you, Magda.'

The girl was making for the door. Edith called her back. 'May I ask something?' She turned; thin fingers twisting her apron betrayed her nervousness. 'Where are you from in Prussia? How are you here?'

'From near Königsberg. The Russians came. Then,' she bit

her lip to stop it from trembling, unable to find words for what happened then. 'Eventually we escaped.'

'There are many people from Eastern Prussia here, aren't there?'

Magda nodded.

Lübeck harboured a sizeable population of East Prussians. They had come in waves. Some, like Magda, before the war ended, fleeing the advancing Russians; others later, expelled under the Potsdam Agreement, their homeland now part of Poland. Incomers from a particular locality tended to cluster together. There was a chance that Magda might know something regarding Elisabeth.

'Do you know any of them?'

'Some, I know.'

'Then I wonder if you can help me?' Edith went on. 'The friend, the one I stayed with whose cook made the *Piroggen*. I'm trying to trace her. She might be in Lübeck. Her name is von Stavenow. She's from an estate, south-east of Königsberg. Have you heard that name?'

Magda shook her head a little too fast, eyes darting longingly towards the door.

'Perhaps you could ask? I would very much like to see her. Could you do that for me?'

'I will try.' Magda released the crimped fabric of her apron.

'Thank you, Magda.' Edith held up the recipe. 'And thank you for this.' She took cigarettes from her handbag. 'Have these for your trouble.'

Magda pocketed the packet and fled.

She knew something. Getting her to part with the knowledge would be the difficulty. She seemed very frightened but of whom, or what? Edith took the recipe upstairs along with the billet menu, printed in Frau Schmidt's careful capitals. Fear was always significant.

Dori

34 Cromwell Square, Paddington, W2

Cabbage Soup and *Spätzle*, *Piroggen*, *Blaubeerkuchen*. The rush of memory left Dori reeling, falling back far into the past. Such food was common everywhere east of the Elbe. She saw her grandmother in her boots, stiff embroidered skirt, waistcoat, blouse and kerchief, feeding the geese down by the stream that chattered and rushed through their village. And in the corner of the house that served as the kitchen, wafting the fire to get the embers glowing, curtained by the bunches of herbs that hung from the beams, scraping little pieces of white dough from a wooden board, dropping them into the water. 'This is how to do it, Dorota. Now you try.' *Spätzle*. *Nokedli* in Hungarian, *Halušky* in Slovak.

Dori claimed that she could neither cook, nor sew, it was part of her legend, but of course she could. No girl growing up in a village like hers could possibly be without those talents. Her grandmother had taught her in the one room that they used for everything. She could see her father's big black boots standing next to the bed, the leather folded at the ankle, rounded to the muscular bulge of his calves; next to them, her mother's slippers embroidered with green leaves and pink flowers.

As they sat and sewed together, Dori's grandmother would tell her about her great-great-grandfather. How he had come from the north, a metal worker, marrying a girl from the village. He had laid the corner-stone where they were sitting now and had hauled great trees from the forest, shaping them into logs, building them up to form thick walls, hammering the beams holding up the steeply pitched roof of split spruce, weathered now from its first bright gold to dove grey. He had done all this himself. His name, Josef Kováč, was carved into the great central beam, along with the year the house was built, 1796, and charms for protection, petal patterns enclosed in a wheel. He had driven nine long iron nails into the wood above the door, to keep out the Devil and the unquiet dead. Dori's grandmother told her this as she taught her to embroider, sitting in the south-east corner, under the icon of the Mother and Child. Dori still had the kerchief, her first piece, the only thing she still owned from that time. 'May the Mother protect us,' her grandmother would mutter, as she bordered an apron with a repeating pattern: two triangles, one point balanced on the other, one arm up, the other down. The Mother. Sometimes, she carried flowers. 'All the patterns mean something,' her grandmother would say as they embroidered skirts, shirts, sheets and pillowcases. 'Some are for men. Some are for women. Tulips, pomegranates, they are for fertility. Hearts for love. Birds, especially peacocks, those are for marriage.' Dori shook out the piece she was embroidering. A nightdress embroidered with peacocks. Her grandmother was working on sheets with a frieze of tulips, pomegranates and hearts. She was fifteen. Betrothed to a boy from the next village. He was seventeen, tall and slender, his long, dark hair soft and slippery, his first moustache as soft as otter's fur. Dori knew she couldn't do it. She never threaded a needle again.

Instead, she hopped on a wagon and went south to Budapest. Here she met Tibor. He took her from the café where she was working and made her his mistress. She was sixteen. How old had he been? Fifty when she first met him? It had seemed impossibly old to her. He was also impossibly rich. He took her to his house in Buda, overlooking the Danube. There he taught her the Art of Love, as he put it, and much else besides.

When he was sent to Poland on a diplomatic mission, she went with him as his secretary. Things didn't go well in Warsaw. She'd outgrown him, absorbed all he could teach her and more. It made him jealous, possessive in a way he hadn't been before. He didn't like to see her slipping out of his control. She began an affair with Andrzej Taczanowski, an officer in the 15th Poznań Uhlans Regiment. He was a Count, but then they all were. 'Polish Counts are ten a penny, my dear,' Tibor had told her. What really irked him, what he really hated, was Andrzej's youth. That punctured his vanity. He could not compete with young flesh. It left him impotent in every sense of the word and he hated her for it. When he was recalled to Hungary, it was a relief for both of them.

Dori and Andrzej were married but it didn't last. Someone else had walked back into her life. Bobby Stansfield, an RAF officer in Poland to train pilots. She had met him before, in Budapest, 1936. He'd turned up with a letter of introduction from Tibor's cousin in Vienna. He'd been travelling on foot and on horseback. When she first saw him, he was dressed in a long brown hooded coat reaching to his ankles, high-backed trousers tucked into boots, an embroidered waistcoat over a homespun linen shirt. He looked like a goat herder, smelt like one, too, but so beautiful. Like an angel with dirty hands and face. The next time she saw him, he'd had a bath, a haircut, was wearing borrowed evening clothes and Dori was in love. They danced the night away but after several wonderful days and equally magical nights he was gone.

She wasn't going to lose him a second time. They fled through the chaos of Poland falling. Andrzej was killed on the first day, cut down by machine-gun fire in a skirmish with German infantry that became famous as the Riding of Krojanty. There was never any charge, Polish sabres and lances against German tanks. That was a myth but Andrzej would have enjoyed the glory of it. All she'd thought at the time was, 'Now I'm free to marry Bobby.' God forgive her for that.

Their happiness had been all too brief. Within a year, he was dead, too. It was what had brought her here. She watched her notes blacken and curl. Memory, drifting up with the smoke in some kind of alchemy, had brought her full circle.

She stood up, wiping her cheeks with a quick sweep of her thumbs. Enough of this wool gathering. She fed the last note into the Aga. It was good to know that the system was working, although she was greedy for more than tantalizing titbits. They didn't add up to a great deal: a contact that might, or might not, lead to Elisabeth von Stavenow. Doings on the black market. Goings on in the billet. Not much but something. Definitely something. That's how it was, she reminded herself, a patient gathering. A foraging, a nosing up of morsels. Edith was proving to be good at that.

Dori went up to the hall and put on her coat and hat. She had places to be, people to see. Vera had discovered that the girls they had been searching for, the ones who ended up in Natzweiler, had been on a transport of prisoners from Paris to Karlsruhe. She was going to the prison where they had been taken to try to establish their exact identities. Meanwhile, Dori was to track down any others who might have been on that transport, or kept in that prison and could have seen the girls or heard their names. It was a patient piecing of information; a matching of statements, interviews, diary entries. They had to find out exactly what had happened and the girls had to be identified beyond doubt. They had that duty to the mothers and fathers, the husbands, sisters, brothers who were waiting, still waiting, writing anxious letters asking for any news, still clinging to the last shred of hope that their girl would walk through the door, just as they had so many times before, rather than having died a hideous death in a concentration camp.

16

Schule Landstraße, Lübeck

25th January 1946

Prison Camp Soup
Fish bones and skin
Water
Kasha (buckwheat) or whatever else you can
get

Luka's Recipe – we have no equivalent unless
you count the Irish a hundred years ago,
reduced to eating grasses in the Famine.

'Where are you off to?' Roz looked up from her typing.

'Frau Holstein.' Edith had been steeling herself for that surprise visit.

'Her Persilschein checks out. Clean as a whistle.'

That was as may be. Edith went by gut instinct, not documentary evidence.

'Wish I was coming with you.' Roz blew on her chilblained fingers. It was getting colder if anything, and the heating was off again.

'You can if you like.' Edith stopped by the door. This was not going to be easy. 'I could do with some support.'

'Got to get this lot finished while I can still type.' Roz spun back on her chair. 'If it goes on like this, Jeff says, the Baltic will freeze. He's promised to take me out to Travemünde,' she added through a rapid rattle of typing. 'A sight to see, apparently. Damn!' She ripped the paper from the roller. 'How are you supposed to work?'

'I've got some fittle in the back,' Jack said as Edith got into the car. 'Spuds, and that.'

Jack had set about finding extra provisions. Each day he opened the boot on new riches: a sack of potatoes, carrots, swedes; catering-sized tins of meat, powdered milk, sacks of oatmeal, bundles of kindling, a sack of coke. Edith never asked where any of it came from. Fallen off the back of a lorry, misdirected from the docks, or some warehouse or depot. No names, no pack drill. Edith didn't know and didn't care. A few weeks ago, she'd have been petrified in case someone would find out. Now, she saw it as entirely necessary. A duty. How could you teach starving children? How could a child learn if he or she was hungry and cold?

They arrived as the children were being fed Milk Soup: skimmed milk, sweetened a little and thickened slightly with porridge oats. Frau Holstein gave grudging thanks for the extra provisions.

'An appetite for *learning* is what matters,' she said with her thin smile. 'Too much food makes a child sluggish. Too much heat makes them sleepy.'

Frau Holstein kept her classroom the wrong side of chilly. Edith asked Jack to bring in more coke for the stove.

Edith stayed for the morning classes. Before lunchtime, she told them a story while the staff got the soup ready. Thanks to Jack and his sacks, it would be a good meal that day. Like all children, they loved to be told stories. Edith was careful to tell them something full of adventure but set far away, in a different time and place.

While she was talking, a boy sidled into the classroom. His age was difficult to determine through the coating of grime and the bundled layers of clothing. He wore a Red Army greatcoat that had been roughly cut down to fit but still reached his feet, and men's boots bound about with layers of sacking like puttees. He looked young, but his eyes were old, sunken, his face etched with lines criss-crossing the patina of dirt. His skin was wind roughened and weather beaten from living outdoors in sun and cold. Hanks of fairish hair stuck out from under his matted fur hat.

He stood at the back, listening. When she had finished, all the children lined up with their bowls for soup, but he did not move to join them.

The boy watched steadily as she came towards him.

'Hello. I'm Miss Graham.'

'My name is Lukasz,' he said. 'They call me Luka.' He looked around. 'I want to know what you do here.'

'It's a school,' Edith said to him. 'Come and see.'

He had been attracted in by the smell of the soup but he did not go to the tureen or grab the chunks of coarse bread. Instead, he went to the makeshift desks, touched one of the slates, looked up at the blackboard, tracing with his finger how the letters were written.

He reminded her of a young tod fox. Wary. Inspecting new territory.

The children ignored him. Too busy with their soup. The staff eyed him with suspicion.

'Are you hungry? Would you like something to eat?'

Empty questions. Of course, he was. Of course, he would.

He looked at the steaming vat of soup, his nostrils flaring, but said nothing.

'Join us. There's plenty.'

Edith nodded to Frieda Brandt, the young teacher who was doing the ladling. He took his bowl and hunk of bread and sat down at the end of a bench. He produced a spoon from deep inside his clothes and put it down carefully. A prized object. He dunked his bread in the soup and began to eat. Not hungrily,

184

not wolfing it, but with careful, savouring deliberation. He wiped the bowl to a polish.

'Do you want more?'

Frau Holstein frowned her disapproval.

Edith was determined to fill him up, however much it took.

He ate another bowlful, keeping his bread, stowing it inside his clothes. 'Have more.' Edith offered the heel of the loaf. 'For later.'

He accepted with the gracious bow and smile of an aristocrat. Which he well might have been. Who knew his origins among the conquered peoples? The war had been no respecter of station or status. He probably didn't know himself. He looked around, as if making his mind up about something.

'I like it here,' he said finally. 'I stay.'

Frau Holstein could contain herself no longer. 'This school is for *German* children,' she hissed. She spoke loud enough for the boy to hear, as if he were an animal, without language. 'Not *displaced persons*. They have their own – places.'

Lukasz ignored her. He spoke directly to Edith.

'I will look after.' He announced. 'Sweep up. Clean board. Clean slates. Tend fire. Find fuel. Sleep here.'

He indicated a space by the stove.

'You can't let him do that! This is a school! Not a camp. Look at him! He's filthy.' Frau Holstein shuddered. 'Probably diseased. We must think of the other children. These people are not to be trusted. They steal everything.'

Edith looked round. What was there to steal?

Lukasz stared back at Frau Holstein but his eyes showed nothing. He was completely still as if any movement could tip some kind of balance.

'All he needs is a little soap and water,' Edith said mildly, 'and a decent meal.'

'Then he should be on his way. This school is for *German* children,' she said again. 'He's Polish, if I'm not mistaken. There's no room for his kind here.'

'He's a child!' Edith said. 'As such he is as deserving of educa-tion, food, clothing, as any here. He stays.'

'Frau Graham, I really have to disagree. To receive such a – boy – is, well . . .' She gave a whinnying, condescending laugh, '*completely* against regulations.'

She glanced about, seeking allies among the staff but found no help there. They looked from the boy to the two women. There was going to be a battle here.

Edith's mouth set in a thin line, her grey eyes grew flinty. It was a battle she had to win. Not just to establish her own authority but for the children, for Luka and the others like him.

'Frau Holstein,' she said quietly. 'I'd like you to collect your things and leave. Immediately. Fräulein Brandt, you will take over.'

Frau Holstein's eyes widened. Her mouth gaped. Shocked into speechlessness, it took a moment for her to gather herself but Edith put up a hand to stem her spluttered protests.

'Go. Now. Or I'll have you removed.'

Frau Holstein looked towards Jack who was frowning, arms folded and then back to Edith. There would be no argument and she knew it. Edith held all the power here. She had no other choice except to go. She hesitated for a further second then moved to her desk. She packed her bag in pin-dropping silence, all eyes upon her.

'My Persilschein . . .'

'That stays. Falsifying information carries serious consequences, as I'm sure you well know.'

Frau Holstein took one last look at her prized certificate and moved with measured slowness through her former domain. As she got to the door, she turned with hatred in her eyes. Edith held her stare in the quiet stillness of the room.

At last, Frau Holstien left. Edith turned to the expectant faces gazing at her with new admiration. They thought she'd won although she felt no triumph. She knew that Frau Holstein lived with her mother and an invalid brother and would be the only one working but sometimes one had to be ruthless. Edith would not take it further. Frau Holstein would get some sort of job but not as a teacher. She would brook no discrimination. The children were the ones who mattered. Their education was too important to be contaminated by the likes of Frau Holstein.

Luka's account of what had happened to him was sketchy. Taken east by the Russians, he'd ended up in a camp somewhere.

'Hungry, all the time hungry.'

This was all he remembered. And soup. Fish bones and skin and water. Sometimes a little kasha. Later, he was taken west again. 'Why?' Who knows why? His shrug described the enormous irrationality, the supreme stupidity of war. When the Germans came, he ran away and joined the partisans, then the Red Army.

'Then I leave. Come to here.'

That was as much of his story as he was prepared to tell. He had been caught like a feather on the great gusting breath of war, picked up and put down again. This would be the last landing place. Here he was going to stay.

Edith gave Frieda Brandt cigarettes for the widow who lived next door to the school. She would clean him up.

When Edith returned the next day, she hardly recognized him. A good scrub and a haircut made him a different child. The widow had taken quite a shine to the boy, even giving him clothes belonging to her son who had been killed on the Russian Front. She would have let him stay with her but he preferred to sleep in the school.

'I stay here,' he said. 'In case no-good DPs get in and steal.'

When Edith visited a week later, he was back in his army coat and battered fur hat. New clothes didn't smell right, Luka announced. 'They smell of dead boy.'

He kept his promise. The floors were brushed, the slates cleaned, the stove glowing. Luka was good at finding anything combustible. He wandered the town in his old uniform, roving the ruins, moving in and out of the different camps and communities, passing from one group of DPs to another. This was where he liked to be. Before he'd wandered into the school, he'd been living in the ruins; one of the troglodyte dwellers in the caved-in basements; wisps of yellowish smoke, seeping through the tumbled bricks, signalled where they lived. How old had he been when the Russians came to his village? Four? Five? For him, war was the natural state of things. It was peace that he was finding difficult. It was the same for the other children: roaming the streets, playing on the bombsites, living in the ruins, filching coal from the railway yards, hanging about the camps and temporary shelters, picking up cigarette ends – that was the life they knew. They'd be lost forever if they weren't brought into schools soon.

'Could you help get them in?' Edith asked, offering Luka a packet of cigarettes. He didn't smoke them. Cigarettes weren't for smoking. They were currency. Luka slid them into one of his many pockets. He'd see what he could do.

True to his word, Luka began to bring children like a ragamuffin Pied Piper. A few at first, then more, lured by promises of food, warmth and stories. He took to waiting for her outside the office, ready to tell her of his successes, offering to carry her briefcase. When Sergeant Jack wasn't about, Luka had appointed himself her guardian.

'It is dangerous for you,' he said as he fell into step. 'Many bad people about. No-good DPs everywhere.'

At first, Edith had taken Luka's warnings with a pinch of salt. There was no let-up in the stream of refugees, most of them Volksdeutsche thrown out of countries where they'd lived for centuries. Edith didn't think this sad caravan of the dispossessed represented any threat but there were Criminal Elements, as the Brigadier put it, already resident. She didn't exactly feel in need of protection but she welcomed the boy's company when she had to walk home alone. A couple of times lately, she thought she'd heard footsteps behind her, crunching on the snow, crackling on the icy pavements. One night, a motorbike growled, faster then slower, not quite catching up with her, then roaring past as she turned for home.

'What you thinking?' Luka asked as they walked down to the Rehderbrücke.

'Oh, nothing. Just glad of your company.'

Luka smiled. He liked being needed.

'I was wondering . . .' Edith started.

Her efforts to find Elisabeth had completely stalled. Magda knew more than she was saying but enquiries were met with that quick shake of the head. The Germans were uncommunicative. Uncooperative might get them into difficulties, but they didn't volunteer information. Roz's Jeff had found nothing. Luka might prove more useful.

'I wonder if you could help me with something,' she said as they crossed the bridge. 'I'm looking for someone. A lady. She's likely to be with people from East Prussia.'

'I don't know.' Luka's fair brows puckered. 'Maybe. But there are many here. East Prussia very big place.'

'I know that but incomers keep together, don't they? This lady is from Mühlhausen, near Elbing. Her name is Elisabeth von Stavenow. Can you remember that?'

He nodded.

'Will you help me find her?'

Luka looked up at her, head on one side, considering. He liked Edith. She'd been kind, she'd helped him and that counted with Luka; she'd fought Frau Holstein and won.

'I do my best,' he said.

Luka handed over Edith's case at the gate. Frau Schmidt was glaring from the front-room window.

'She don't like me. Nazi bitch. Same as the one in the school.' Luka scowled at Stephan leaning on his shovel. Stephan scowled back. 'He's worse.' Luka spat. 'You watch out for them,' he added. 'Worse than no-good DPs.'

'That boy again!' Frau Schmidt said as she opened the door. 'Don't be taken in, Frau Graham. They are all thieves and liars.'

17

CCG Billet, Lübeck, Travemünde

10th February 1946

```
Billet Sunday Breakfast
Cornflakes or Shredded Wheat
Sausages, bacon, fried potatoes,
       scrambled eggs
       Toast & jam
          Tea
```

```
Even though breakfasts are very British,
there are subtle differences in the texture
of the sausages, the cure and cut of
the bacon. Only the cereals from their
packets are consumed without comment or
complaint.
```

There was no coffee. It never seemed to last the week, perhaps it would now Lorna was billet monitor, but there were none of the usual grumbles about that, or alien sausages, fatty bacon, greasy fried potatoes, scramble made from powder. A billet outing was planned to Travemünde. It was even colder. Joe Stalin's weather. The Baltic finally freezing over. It was a clear, bright day and Edith wouldn't have minded going with them but she had other business.

The German girls made packed lunches: cheese and corned beef sandwiches, cake, flasks of tea. The lorry arrived at ten. Edith waved her housemates off, pleading the onset of a migraine, needing a quiet day. Before they left, she made sure that Lorna handed her the house keys. As soon as the lorry disappeared, she told the German girls they could go. She wanted the house to herself.

Miss Slater had roared off on the back of her boyfriend Val's motorbike, in leather helmet, goggles and flying jacket. Very Amelia Earhart. The Schmidts had disappeared early, off to the cousins in the country, accompanied by Frau Kaufmann. A chap came to collect them in a cart with thick rubber-tyred wheels made from some cannibalized motor vehicle and pulled by a miserable-looking pony. They took a bulging suitcase. It would come back with entirely different contents. They were not the only ones. Half Lübeck would be out roaming the country, trading whatever they had for a handful of potatoes. It is what the Germans did on Sunday. They called it hamstering.

Once she was sure that everyone had left, Edith went down to the basement. The house was built on a slope, the front higher than the back. The kitchen window looked out over the garden. A flight of steps led down to the lower basement where the Schmidts lived. Edith flicked though the keys, looking for the one for their door. Every room was supposed to be accessible. The British Billet Monitor was supposed to have keys to every door and cupboard. They were all clearly marked: Kitchen, Lower Basement. That was the one. Except it didn't fit.

'Botheration!'

None of the other keys fitted either. Her plan was about to fail at the first hurdle. She could almost hear Frau Schmidt laughing. Well, she was damned if that was going to stop her. Edith had never mastered lock picking but she knew someone who probably had and she would be glad of his company. She didn't intend to confine her investigations to the house.

She called Jack, put the kettle on and waited for the familiar rat-a-tat-tat on the door.

'Two sugars, ta. Now, what's this all about?'

'Down here. Quick.'

Jack followed her to the basement.

He studied the door for a moment. 'Her's changed the lock. Cheeky old bat! Don't worry, I've got just the thing.' He produced a ring of skeleton keys from his inside pocket. 'Won't be a jiffy. There y'are!'

The lock turned at first try.

'Phew!' He followed her in waving his hand under his nose. 'Bit niffy down here!'

The room was hot. The large stove in the corner had been well banked up. It was stuffy and overcrowded, smelling of damp and something else: sweetish and human, perspiration and unwashed clothes. The basement was not meant for human habitation. There was little natural light or ventilation. Edith felt a flicker of pity for the woman exiled from the house upstairs.

'What're you looking for?' Jack threaded his way through the heavy furnishings and mounds of clothing.

'I'm not sure . . .'

'Know it when you see it?'

'Something like that.'

'She's got a right hocking shop.' He put a hand on a pile of furs. 'Look at this clobber! Clever. You got to hand it to her. Safer here than in the warehouses by the river. Coppers are on to that. A big raid and the lot's gone. That's if the Balts ain't already filched it. Let's have a look-see at what she keeps in here.' He used his keys to open a hulking armoire. 'Blimey! No wonder she changed the locks. Take a squint at this!'

The portrait of Hitler that had hung upstairs was inside the door, along with Göring, Goebbels, and more of the Führer in different attitudes and poses. Pride of place given to a smaller photograph of him shaking hands with a younger Stephan in SS black.

'What's this?' Jack used a small pick to unlock a battered

metal trunk. Inside, neatly folded, was an SS uniform and cap, campaign medals, dagger and *Totenkopf* ring. Jack moved them carefully. Towards the bottom was a luger.

'Why would they keep all this?' Edith asked.

'Can't bear to give it up, I s'pose.' Jack sat back on his heels. 'But if anyone found the gun, they'd swing. You've got 'em both by the short and curlies, I'd reckon.' He put everything back as he'd found it and relocked the chest. 'What's that?'

'Photograph album.' Edith turned the pages. 'More Stephan in uniform. With some other woman, not Frau Schmidt. Hitler. Rallies. Marches. There's a whole lot missing. Pages and pages.' She turned the book for him to see the empty corner mountings, the slightly darker squares on the dark-blue sugar paper. 'What could be more incriminating than Stephan in full rig?' Jack shrugged. 'Do you know anything about SS uniforms? Would it be possible to tell his rank, his unit?'

'I reckon. Don't know enough about it.' Jack stood, dusting off his hands. 'All done? This place is giving me the heebie-jeebies.'

Back up in the kitchen, Edith made tea.

'Now for the garden.'

Jack went to the window. 'What's down there?'

'Not sure.' Edith stood on tiptoes to see past the frozen shrubs and brambles. 'Stephan's the only one who goes down there. That's what I want to look at next.'

Jack squinted against the glare to a crooked line of steps trodden into the snow. 'Bin traipsing there and back a fair bit. A hut, you think?'

'Maybe. To store things, gardening tools, and so on?'

'Gardening in this weather?'

'That's what I thought. Could be keeping a pig. Wouldn't put it past them.'

'Get your coat and boots. Let's take a look. If you've got a gun, bring it. Pig might be the two-legged kind.'

Outside, the sun on the snow was blinding, the foliage on the bushes and trees outlined and furred with frost. They stayed on the path. Careful to keep to the frozen footsteps.

The hut was fairly substantial. The wood was silvered with age but it showed signs of being patched here and there with newer pine. Fresh tarpaulin had been tacked to the roof and broken windows blocked up.

'Give us that gun and wait here.'

Jack approached the door cautiously and went inside, gun gripped in both hands.

'No one home.' He waved her forward.

No tools, wood or lawnmowers. The hut smelt of tar and stale cigarette smoke. A pot-bellied stove squatted in the corner, its crooked pipe zigzagging up to a hole on the roof. The sunlight found chinks in the rough planking. There had been an effort to stop up the gaps with cardboard and rags. A kind of cot heaped with blankets stood against the far wall. In the centre of the room was an old chair and a rickety table studded with candle stubs. A blackened and battered canister lid spilled ash and butts smoked down to the last quarter inch. Crushed cigarette packets and empty bottles littered the floor. Jack laughed.

'First pig I seen smokes Players and drinks schnapps. Could be friend Stephan comes down here for a drink and a smoke when the old bat throws him out.' He stepped over to the stove. The chimney was still warm. 'Or . . .'

'Or could be *he's* not using it at all.'

'Great minds.' Jack looked round. 'And whoever is might have just gone out for a piss, or to get wood, or summat. Let's go.'

'Wait. There's something in there.'

Edith pushed back the little door on the stove. Whoever was using the hut had been burning something. She took out a wad of half-charred photographs.

'Got 'em?'

She nodded, tucking them inside her coat.

Jack stirred up the remaining ashes with the gun barrel. 'Make it look like they all burnt up. Don't want them knowing we've been poking about.'

They left the cabin cautiously, but there was no sign of anybody as they walked back up the garden.

194

'Looks like we got away with it.' Jack grinned.

'That we did.' Edith grinned back, feeling slightly giddy with relief and exhilaration.

'Let's have a look at them snaps,' Jack said when they were safely back in the kitchen.

The prints were poor quality, either badly developed, or over-exposed, burnt at the sides and brittle from heat. Edith studied them one at a time before placing them on the table in rough sequence. Three men stood in the foreground, comrades posing for the camera. The man in the centre was wearing SS field grey, an officer's cap with eagle and totenkopf insignia, jodhpurs and boots. He stood square, smirking into the lens, his hand on the butt of a holstered pistol. The other two men wore forage caps, blouson jackets cinched at the waist with thick leather belts. Their hands rested on submachine guns slung across their chests. The faces were slightly blurred, but the SS man was definitely Stephan. The chap on the right was young, good-looking, grinning, arms folded. The one on the left was looking to the side, a bottle dangled from his hand.

The remaining photographs were taken from further away and a different angle, the focus on something going on behind. Edith leaned closer. The print was bleached, blurred and grainy. The terrain a pale, almost featureless expanse; undulations broken by clumps of coarse grass. Bleak, cold, it put Edith in mind of a snowy field. In the middle distance ran a crooked crevasse, a wide fissure, the base filled with what looked like lengths of timber, as if a pile of logs had tumbled down there.

'Who's these jokers with old Stephan?' Jack pointed. 'They look pretty pleased with themselves. Celebrating something?' He glanced across the sequence. 'Where are they? Why are they posing like that?'

'I've got a magnifying glass upstairs,' Edith said. 'I'll fetch it.'

'Not snow,' Jack said after more careful scrutiny. 'More like sand. Desert, mebbe? Although those ain't desert uniforms and them two ain't even Nazis. Them's German weapons, MP40s, but they look like some kind of auxiliaries.'

Edith took the glass. What *was* going on in the background? Were those little figures standing at the side of the crevasse? She moved the glass back and forth but the print was too blurred . . .

'It's impossible to see what's happening,' she said at last.

'Whatever it is, they don't want no one knowing. What you going to do?'

'Don't know yet.' Edith gathered the prints. 'Keep them safe. Until I decide.'

'It's still a lovely day. Shame to waste it. D'you fancy going somewhere?'

Edith glanced out of the window, towards the hut. There was no sign of movement, but she didn't want to be here alone.

'I'd love to, Jack.'

At Travemünde, the pale sand was crusted and frozen, crunching under foot. They walked along a sea's edge lacy and brittle with spindrift; further out arrested waves gleamed grey and green, as though sculpted from travertine. Edith took photos. They'd never believe this at home. It was like *Das Eismeer* by Caspar David Friedrich. In the Hamburger Kunsthalle, wasn't it? Was it still there now? Had the museum survived? Was the collection intact?

Jack was staring inland.

'Sand dunes,' he said. 'It's sand dunes in the photographs.'

They walked to the Strandpromenade and bought paper cups of Glühwein spiced with clove and cinnamon. There was little or no warmth in the sun. A bitter east wind blew in off the sea.

'Here, put a drop of this in it,' Jack produced a flask. They sat down at one of the rickety tables. Jack lit a cigarette. 'Ain't that your Miss Slater over there?'

She was draping herself over a motorbike while a young man took her photograph. They reversed roles. He posed by the bike, grinning, arms folded.

'Give us your camera a mo'.'

Jack strolled off to take photographs of the frozen sea. At the last moment, he turned, snapped the pair of them.

'Got him!' He handed Edith the camera. 'If that ain't the same bloke as smiler in that photo, then my name ain't Jack Hunter.'

18

CCG Billet, Lübeck

10th February 1946

*Latvian Supper Dish: Nāc rītā atkal
(slightly adapted)*
In German - Komm morgen wieder –
translates as Come Back Tomorrow.
3 eggs (2tbsp water to one of egg powder)
1 pinch salt
4-5oz flour (for stiff batter)
Half pt milk
3oz diced onion
7oz corned beef (for filling)

Another species of stuffed pancake. The
filling is traditionally leftover roast meat
but corned beef makes an acceptable substitute. Simplicity itself to make and an
excellent use for the dreaded powdered egg.

Prepare pancake batter. Make up the equivalent of eggs, add to flour, mix in milk and
salt. Let stand. Fry the minced meat (or CB)

```
with onion until browned, add bouillon (OXO),
add sour cream (if available), if not a grate
or two of cheddar would do.
```

The house was silent except for the ticking of the hall clock that was screwed to the wall. Probably the reason it was still there. Edith unwound her scarves, hung up her hat and coat, kicked off her boots, put on her 'indoor' shoes. It really was like being at school. There was a noise from the basement. The Schmidts back? Hardly. They returned late from country excursions.

'Hello? Anyone there?'

'It's me, Agnese,' the Latvian girl's blonde head appeared. 'Frau Schmidt asked me to come in. Prepare supper.'

Edith went down into the kitchen. The girl looked near to tears.

'Did she say what she wanted prepared?'

The girl shook her head. 'I don't know what to cook.'

'Let's see,' Edith opened and shut cupboards. It was going to have to be pretty basic. 'I know, let's have something Latvian, shall we?' The girl brightened a little. Everyone liked to cook something from home. 'Know any recipes? What would you have on Sunday nights, for example, before . . .'

Before everything. Before your homeland was invaded, first by the Russians, then the Germans, before you had to flee and leave it all behind.

Agnese nodded. She understood 'before'.

'At grandparents' house, we would have *Nāc rītā atkal*. In German – *Komm morgen wieder*.'

Come Back Tomorrow. Edith tried not to reflect on the irony.

Agnese explained the dish and Edith collected ingredients, making substitutions: OXO for bouillon, corned beef for leftover roast, sour cream – optional anyway. The recipe required a lot of eggs for the batter, but the dried variety wasn't so bad in pancakes.

'We'll start with the pancakes, shall we? Batter needs to stand.'

Agnese measured flour out in cups. She was missing half her

little finger and the nails on the remaining digits were bitten to the quick. Edith carefully reconstituted the dried eggs. It was tempting to be overgenerous with the powder but the result would be rubbery pancakes. The same with the dried milk. The secret was to sprinkle the powder a little at a time, whisking all the while.

She kept up a running commentary as a way of gaining Agnese's trust. She was like some shy, wild creature who could bolt at any second. She said she was twenty but looked quite a bit younger. There was a wary, frightened look about her pale-blue eyes but as they worked together, she began to relax. Her German was heavily accented, her answers halting in response to Edith's gentle prompting. She tried not to ask too many questions. It was best just to let Agnese talk. She'd lived in Riga with her parents. Valdis – Molly's boyfriend – was not her brother. He was her cousin. His parents were dead, killed by the Russians. He'd come to live with her family. Life had been hard, first under the Russians and then the Germans. Which was worse? A shrug. Both the same. Life was hard everywhere. It was war. Her father was not strong. He had a bad heart. Valdis had looked after the family. She didn't say how.

When the Russians were advancing, they'd had to leave. Why? Another shrug. Wasn't it obvious? It was cold. So cold. They had got as far as Gdynia, the Germans call it Gotenhafen. They had found a ship, the *Wilhelm Gustloff*, to take them to Kiel and safety. Edith frowned. The name rang a bell, a feeling the story would not end well. There were only a few places, so they decided that her parents should take priority. The ship was hit by a Russian torpedo. It was winter. Her parents either drowned or died of exposure out among the Baltic ice floes, along with most people on board, nearly ten thousand souls. She and Valdis had got passage on another ship bound for Lübeck. So crowded, they'd had to stay on deck. The ice was thick, coating everything. She held up her mutilated little finger. Lost it to frostbite. Somehow, they'd run the gauntlet of Russian mines and submarines. They were fortunate to be here, to have survived.

'Hello? Who's down there?' Miss Slater's voice followed by steps on the stairs.

'Fräulein Slater.' Agnese whispered. She looked alarmed, as if she'd been caught doing something she shouldn't.

'Just us,' Edith called back. 'We're preparing supper.'

'Who's "us"?'

Miss Slater's platinum head appeared, her thin pencilled eyebrows raised, her blue eyes dark with suspicion.

'Agnese and I,' Edith wiped her hands on a tea towel.

'Aren't the girls supposed to do that?'

'There's only Agnese here, as you see, and I don't mind. I like cooking.'

Miss Slater gave her high-pitched, peeling laugh. 'Rather you than me. Agnese? I have washing. I'd like you to collect it. If you can be *spared*, that is.'

The girl hesitated, looking from one woman to the other, older to younger. Miss Slater drummed her scarlet fingernails.

'We've nearly finished,' Edith said quietly. 'There's only the pancakes and we can't do them until the others arrive. You go, Agnese.'

'What were you doing?' Miss Slater demanded as Agnese followed her.

'Cooking. Frau Graham helped me.'

Edith drifted to the foot of the stairs to hear what she could of the conversation.

'That'd better be all. If I find out different, I'm telling Val.'

'Miss Graham? Can I have a word, please?' Miss Slater caught her just as she was going up to change.

'Certainly.'

Miss Slater paced up and down the hall, arms folded, hands cupped round her elbows.

'I'll thank you to stop spying on me.'

'Spying?' Edith hoped she sounded suitably thunderstruck. 'What *are* you talking about?'

'Asking questions about my private life. Interrogating Agnese.

201

And, and today, I saw you and that driver chap down on the promenade. If that's not spying—'

'Spying? I wasn't spying! And I wasn't interrogating Agnese. I was helping her. She'd been left on her own, poor little thing. As for this afternoon, it was a nice day. The first one for ages. The rest of the billet was there, along with half of Lübeck.'

Miss Slater ignored Edith's perfectly reasonable explanations.

'I'm warning you. If you carry on poking your nose in, you're going to get it put out of joint good and proper.' Her carefully developed accent was slipping into something more demotic. 'If you carry on with this, you'll be sorry, you see if you're not. You'll find yourself in a whole lot of trouble. A whole lot,' she repeated for emphasis, in case Edith had not understood.

'What kind of trouble?' Edith asked casually.

She didn't like being threatened and had begun to feel the first stirrings of annoyance but she was careful to keep her expression a suitable blend of puzzlement and innocence. She had triggered something but it wouldn't do to get on her high horse just yet.

'That'd be telling but you'd be upsetting people a bloody sight more important than you. Keep this out of it.' Miss Slater touched the side of her thin nose. 'Mind your own business in future.'

She swept past Edith and up the stairs. Edith went into the sitting room and poured herself a whisky, slightly discomforted by Molly's outrage but more curious to know what had caused it. What exactly did Miss Slater think she could do? As she sipped her drink, Adeline's drawl came back to her. 'Throw a stone in. Count the ripples. Flip a stone. See what crawls out.'

After dinner, Edith slipped upstairs to compose a message. She took a card from Travemünde.

A LATVIAN dish (see recipe). Another species of pancake. German housekeeper (Frau Schmidt) and her husband, Stephan, still very partial to the Traditional German equivalent: Komm morgen wieder. Come Back Tomorrow. They live in hope!

As ever, Edith

From the card, Dori would construe that something of interest had occurred involving Latvian Nationals, her German housekeeper and her husband. She wrote out the recipe, coded message folded into the list of ingredients for this Latvian recipe: *Nazis. SS. Photographs.*

Dori

Paddington, W2

This was the first message of any real substance. The first she had really been able to act upon. Frau Schmidt and husband, Stephan, were unrepentant Nazis. He was SS, operational in Latvia presumably. That would make him part of Einsatzgruppe A. Of interest to War Crimes. And to Harry Hirsch.

Dori opened the front of the Aga and watched the papers burn. Then she went up to the hall, to the telephone. It would take forever, if ever, to contact Harry through Mil. Gov. Bulldog in Bad Oeynhausen would be her best bet.

'War Crimes?' A distant voice crackled on the line.

'Oh, hello. I'm trying to contact Alex Drummond . . .'

There was a shout: 'Bulldog! Bird on the blower for you.'

'Drummond here.'

'Hello, darling. It's Dori.' She paused to listen. 'Edging closer but I'm not calling about that. You couldn't find me a number for Harry Hirsch, could you?' Dori waited, twisting the cord round her finger. 'I'll just find a pencil.' She wrote the number down on the back of an envelope. 'Thank you, darling. *Is* she? Perhaps she can speed things up for me. This weekend? Tell her I'll meet her. Usual place. Saturday. Around four? Cheerio!'

She cut the call. Keep it short and snappy. Bright and chirpy. Better to pass information on to Vera in person over a gin and tonic at the club at the weekend. Dori listened to the dial tone on her phone for a moment. There had been some worrying clicks lately. She'd begun to not quite trust the telephone. She replaced the receiver and tore the envelope into very small pieces. She'd give Harry a call from the club.

She put on her coat, adjusted the angle of her hat in the hall mirror. She had a small bag with her, going to Lewes to follow up on an old SOE pal who might have news of the missing girls. He was a survivor who had been in Natzweiler, among other hideous places. At first, he'd been unable to recall any women being there. Like many of the men who had been in the camps, his memory had fragmented under the weight of the horrors he'd seen. Then a scene, a face, a voice would surface. Now, he didn't just recall the women, he could describe their arrival in vivid detail. He'd made sketches. Dori's hand shook slightly as she applied her lipstick. She looked forward to and at the same time dreaded being able to identify them. These women had been her friends. There was always the tiniest gleam of hope as long as they were *missing: whereabouts unknown*.

A figure cast a shadow through the glass of the door. Anton Szulc back from his morning constitutional. She opened the door for him.

'Thank you, Countess,' he said in Polish. He was the only one who ever called her that.

He came in shaking drops of rain from his umbrella. Anton was a tall man, rather stooped, with a narrow, hawkish face. He removed his hat, smoothing back his pale hair in the hall mirror. More white than blond now, he wore it combed back, held perfectly in place by lavender-scented pomade. His overcoat was threadbare down the front edge and around the cuffs but always carefully brushed, never a trace of dandruff or dust; his shirts had worn soft but were kept spotless, laundered by the lady round the corner. In his own way, he was as immaculate as Tibor, with his white silk muffler and his black Homburg set just so.

'Anything?' Dori asked in Polish

'Umm . . .' Anton made a seesaw motion with his hands. 'Could be something. Could be nothing . . . I'll keep watch.'

Not much escaped his still-sharp blue eyes. Anton spent a lot of his day in the Square. He knew all the regulars: the mothers, the nannies with the children, the men, like him, with nothing to do. When he wasn't in the square, he was in his little room above the hall with a perfect view from the window.

He paid no rent for the room. He had no money and, besides, he was useful. Not just keeping watch. In other ways. He might look a frail old man but looks were deceptive. He was as tough as they came. He'd been an agent, a hard man in the toughest arena of all, Nazi Germany before the war. He'd stayed in post for months after war was declared, been picked up by the Gestapo, sent to a camp, escaped to Denmark and then Britain. He was a tough bird, all right, tough and resourceful.

Dori gave him ten bob for his trouble.

'Thank you Countess.' He glanced down at her bag. 'I'll keep an eye on things until you get back.'

He took out a worn wallet and carefully tucked the note inside, adjusted his hat in the hall mirror, straightened his muffler and went back outside. He turned right, narrow shoulders hunched against the raw cold of the afternoon. He would be going to the Polish Club in Princes Gate to eat *wiejska*, drink vodka and dream of returning to the home country. It would not be soon. The Soviets were in control and Anton hated them almost as much as the Nazis. If he went back, he'd be a dead man.

'I will not go back until my country is free,' he would say, his face bleak with the knowledge that it might not be in his lifetime.

He held a position in the Polish Government in Exile which operated, unacknowledged and unrecognized, out of the President-in-Exile's private residence in Eaton Square. They kept the archives there and the spirit of resistance alive as they prepared for their return as the government of a Free Poland. They might as well be preparing for the Second Coming, Dori thought, as she watched him march off with his stiff-legged, straight-backed military gait.

19

CCG Mess, Lübeck

19th February 1946

Dinner Menu
If it's Tuesday it must be . . .
Potage St Germain
Vienna Steak
Espagnole Sauce
Mashed Potatoes
Tinned Carrots
Raspberry Cream
Cheese
Coffee

Potage: Pea soup made with dried peas bulked out with onions and potatoes. Nothing fresh or green. No evidence of chervil or lettuce. The steak should be made with minced beef and veal but could be anything. The Sauce? Gravy by any other name. Dessert is a mix of tinned raspberries and synthetic cream - resembles pink zinc ointment. Cheese

is mousetrap or American. Coffee usually
the best part of the meal.

Edith had come home early. Someone had been in her room. She knew as soon as she stepped inside. Bedside cabinet left ajar. Travelling alarm folded shut. Someone had been through the chest of drawers and hadn't even bothered to push them back properly. Clothes at odd angles inside the big armoire.

On her desk, the letters in the rack were tilted the wrong way. The recipes slotted into the *Radiation Cookery Book* were misaligned as if someone had flipped through it. There were scratch marks on the brass around the lock of her writing slope.

There was contempt beneath the carelessness. Whoever this was, didn't care if Edith knew, wanted her to know. The German girls wouldn't dare. Frau Schmidt would be more careful. Which left Molly Slater. Always the last to leave. Her boss let her come in any time she liked. If this was another warning, it wouldn't work and two could play at that game.

Molly shared with Ginny. Edith knocked lightly then eased the door open. It was clear which girl occupied which side. Ginny's space was as sparse as a nun's cell. A small swing mirror on a rickety stand acted as her dressing table. All it held was a soft bristle hairbrush, a pot of cold cream and a jar of Vick. Her narrow bed lay under the window. On the sill, a couple of books, a few china ornaments that she must have brought from her bedroom at home. A group of little photographs in silver frames: a couple in a back garden, the man in uniform, must be her mum and dad; Ginny holding the reins of a horse; Ginny kneeling, arms round a spaniel. Still so close to childhood. How young these girls were . . .

She turned to examine the rest of the room. Molly's clothes from last night lay on the chair. More spilled from the chest of drawers. The wardrobe was stacked with hatboxes, filled with furs and gowns. The dressing table was strewn with makeup and perfume, the mirror draped with scarves. A carved wooden box held a hoard of gold chains, silver lockets, rings, brooches and watches. The dressing-table drawer revealed more: necklaces, jade, amethyst, tourmaline. Good stones in nice settings. A string of pearls with the silky sheen and ivory overtones of the genuine thing. Black-market booty, presumably. The bottom drawer held humbler trove: Cussons talc, Yardley bath cubes, bars of Lux. Edith closed the drawers carefully. Molly felt quite safe. No need to hide anything. None of them would dare to look.

That evening, Edith announced to Frau Schmidt that her room was to be kept locked at *all times*, apart from bed changing and cleaning. She would hold the German woman personally responsible if she *even suspected* that anyone had been in there. Edith then left to dine at the Mess, leaving the threat hanging, confident that the message would be passed on to Molly Slater.

'Hello, there.'

A voice she knew but couldn't quite place. She looked up to find Harry Hirsch standing in front of her.

'I don't know if you remember,' he smiled down at her. 'But we met at Dori's New Year's party. Do you mind if I join you?'

'Of course not! I'd be delighted,' she added, and meant it. She was, in fact, absurdly pleased to see him.

'What are you drinking?'

'Whisky and soda.'

Harry Hirsch signalled to the Mess waiter to bring drinks over. She remembered him very well. It had been the briefest of encounters but there had been something there. A hand retained in farewell, a parting New Year's kiss that had lasted just a moment too long.

He looked older, thinner, his skin sallow, bruise-coloured marks under his large, dark eyes, forehead creased in a permanent frown. His hair grazed his collar and his jaw was shadowed. Slightly worn and dishevelled, he looked as if he needed someone to look after him, which only added to his appeal.

'Forgive my appearance,' he said, rubbing his chin. 'I've only just come in. I'm starving.' He reached for a menu card. 'What's the food like here?'

'So-so. A bit boring.'

'I don't care. I could eat a horse.'

Edith glanced at the menu. Vienna Steak. 'You probably will be.'

He laughed.

'What are you doing here?' she asked.

'Interviewing DPs,' he carried on reading the menu. 'Balts as they call them here. Latvians, Lithuanians, Estonians, to give them their nationalities. There's a team of us. They need people who speak their languages. We wear civvies. They don't trust uniforms. Had enough of them in the war.' He put the card down and sighed. 'It's hard. What's happened to them, their stories. Wears you out eventually. Same thing over and over, but it never seems to get less harrowing and there is so very little I can do. Not my job anyway. My job is to sort through them all, looking for the few bad eggs.'

'Found any?'

'One or two.' He sipped his drink. 'I had a call from Dori a few days ago.' He put his glass back on the table. 'She suggested I look you up.'

'It's good to see you . . .' Edith started. Something expectant about his expression, the way he emphasized *Dori* made her stop what she was saying. She stared at him as the connections clicked into place.

'Oh, yes. Of course! It could be something or nothing,' she added quickly. What did she have really? Suddenly it all seemed very flimsy. 'I hope you didn't come all this way . . .'

'I wanted to see you.' He smiled. 'This is my excuse.'

'There's a young man. They call him Valdis or Val. His full name is Valdemārs Jansons. I checked. He could be one of your bad eggs.'

'Dori said you might have photographs?'

'I keep them in the office. Safer there.' Especially after today. 'I could get them.'

211

'Good idea.' He looked down at his wrinkled shirt and creased trousers. 'What say I make myself presentable and we could dine together?' His expression mixed hope with the smallest dash of apprehension. As if there was the slightest chance of her saying 'no'.

Edith called Jack for a lift then went back to the billet to change.

She felt a tingle of excitement. This was practically a date. She could be Stella, for one night anyway, rather than dependable Miss Graham. She selected the French navy crepe with red piping and little red cloth buttons, unrolled a pair of carefully hoarded silk stockings and found her high heels. She dressed her hair, pinning it up in a French pleat, and set about applying her makeup. She surveyed herself in the mirror. Not half bad. She smoothed the soft material over her stomach and bottom. The dress fitted much better. She chose to walk to and from work most days. The food might be plentiful but it was bland, stodgy and in the light of the surrounding deprivation, easy to resist. She applied a few dabs of Blue Grass perfume and undid her top button to reveal a little more décolletage.

Frau Schmidt took it all in from the bottom of the stairs.

'Going out again?' she ventured and smiled, a gleam in her eyes. Nothing said. Much implied.

'Yes,' Edith stepped past her. 'And remember what I said.'

Jack was waiting outside. 'Blimey! Look at you all spruced up!' His eyebrows rose. 'Going anywhere special? Meeting someone, mebbe?'

'Just dinner in the Mess. Thank you, Jack. Can we drop into the office? I have to pick something up. And no need to wait. I'll make my own way back.'

'Right you are, ma'am,' Jack said, his mouth quirking up at the corners as he started the car. 'Right you are.'

Harry was waiting for her in the bar, his black hair wet and slick as if he'd just showered. He was clean shaven and his face had more colour. The sleeves of his tweed jacket were a little too short exposing white cuffs and sinewy wrists. The top button of his shirt was undone, his maroon knitted silk tie loosely knotted. He was wearing charcoal-grey slacks and suede boots. Not the normal male attire for a Mess dinner. Edith liked him all the more for that.

'I thought we'd dine straight away. I really am starving. You can show me the photographs while we eat.'

'I'd rather not, if it's all the same.' Edith put down her briefcase. Something told her that these images were not to be perused over dinner, not to be looked at in a public place.

'We'll look at them later then. Over a nightcap. I've got some decent brandy I picked up on my way through Paris.'

Over dinner, Edith did most of the talking, telling him about her work, what she'd been doing since they last saw each other. She apologized for the food, which was worse than usual. The Potage St Germain, thin as gruel. The Vienna Steak overdone to the texture and consistency of crêpe rubber. Harry didn't seem to notice. He barely looked up from his plate. He accepted second helpings of everything and ate with the single-mindedness of a man refuelling.

'That's better.' Harry pushed himself back from the table. 'I'm sorry.' He smiled. 'I haven't been much company but I really was starving. Haven't eaten properly for days.' He patted his stomach. 'Full now. Shall we? Or would you like dessert?'

'Oh, no.' Edith grimaced. 'The raspberry cream will be synthetic pink goo and the cheese mousetrap.'

'In that case, how about that nightcap?'

Up in his room, Edith went to the desk by the window while he opened the brandy.

'Now, what do you want me to look at?'

He poured the drinks while she took photographs from her briefcase.

'These.' She set them out on the desk. First, the one Jack had taken at Travemünde.

'This is Jansons?' Harry picked up the photograph and held it under the desk light.

Edith nodded. 'He's going out with a young woman from my billet. The photo was taken at Travemünde last week.'

Harry drank his brandy and picked up the next photograph. As he studied the image, his pallor returned. He looked at her, his eyes unfocused and confused, as if he'd been jarred from a nightmare.

'You have others?'

Edith set them out on the desk.

'Where did you get these?' His voice sounded distant, mechanical, as if he was hypnotized.

'The house, where I'm billeted. There's a hut at the end of the garden. Someone was trying to burn them. A friend and I rescued them. The chap in the middle, the SS man, is Stephan. He lives with our housekeeper, supposedly her husband.' As she spoke, he continued to stare at the photographs, his hand over his mouth. 'We couldn't work out where they were, what was going on. Do you know?'

He nodded.

'I say, are you all right? I'll get you another brandy, shall I?'

Harry did not reply. Edith went to fetch the bottle. He was positively grey now, the muscles of his face rigid, his skin filmed with sweat. He wiped his mouth again. He looked as though he might be sick.

'Valdemārs Jansons is not his real name,' he said, teeth clamped together. Harry choked, as if the name had stuck in his throat. 'Excuse me.' Hand over mouth, he bolted for the bathroom.

'I'm sorry,' he said when he returned, wiping his mouth with a handkerchief, his face ivory pale. 'I shouldn't have eaten so much.'

'No, no, it's my fault. I should have warned you.'

Harry poured himself a brandy, filling the tumbler. He gulped and grimaced, putting the glass down with a trembling hand.

'How would you have known?' He passed a hand over his face. 'His name is Ivars Kalniņš. He's Arājs Kommando.' He pointed at the smiling young man posing at Travemünde. 'Latvian auxiliaries, recruited to help the Nazis. They take their name from their commander Viktors Arājs, a really nasty piece of work.' He pointed to the group photograph. 'Kalniņš and a man called Māris Ozols. This one in the middle is an SS Hauptsturmführer Einsatzkommando 2. A subdivision of Einsatzgruppe A, mobile killing unit.'

'That's Stephan.'

'He should be in gaol. Her, too, for harbouring him. Their orders—' He covered his mouth, as if to arrest the words he was about to speak. 'I'm sorry . . .' He cleared his throat and took his hand away. 'Their orders were to render the Baltic countries *judenfrei*. Free of Jews. *Judenrein*. Cleansed. Which meant all dead.'

Edith felt the same numbing, freezing horror that she'd experienced when Leo had told her about about Kurt.

'But . . . but,' she managed to say. 'That would be thousands of people!'

'Hundreds of thousands,' Harry corrected.

Edith could scarcely take in what he was saying. Just when one thought there could be no more, nothing worse to discover, further barbarities were uncovered, a fresh level of iniquity beneath the one above. It was like prising up the paving stones of Hell.

'Does that mean you know where these photographs were taken? When?'

'Oh, yes. Liepāja. I don't know the date exactly, but it would be mid-December 1941.'

She leaned over, their heads closer together.

'And this one. In the background. We couldn't quite make it out.'

'We?'

'My driver, Jack Hunter. He was with me when we found them.'

'What do you think you can see?'

'I don't know. It's so blurred. Overexposed. At first, we thought snow, then Jack thought it could be sand, but it didn't look like

215

the desert. We went out to Travemünde and he thought it might be dunes. We couldn't quite work out what was happening behind. This fissure, like a crevasse, with what looks like piles of logs, or something, at the bottom.'

'I'll tell you, shall I?' He put his hands over his eyes, pushing his fingers up to his forehead, massaging his brows as if to ease a physical pain. 'You look, but you can't see. Why would you? Sand is right. Dunes is right. This is a beach, the dunes behind the beach to be precise, in a place called Škēde, about nine or ten miles from Liepāja. Liepāja is my town. Where I'm from. The fissure, crevasse you see is a pit. The logs of wood are bodies.' He paused, staring down at the photograph, not blinking, not moving.

Edith bit her lip, nails digging into her palms, forcing herself not to interrupt to comfort his obvious distress, or to show her shock. She stayed very still to listen, to bear witness. 'This, here,' his hand shook as it hovered over the deep gash in the sand, 'is the site of a mass execution. Here, along the lip of the pit, pale, like little shadows? These are naked people. Jews. Lined up to be shot. Behind them, you see darker marks on slightly higher ground? Arājs Kommando, local police, SS doing the shooting in shifts.' He closed his eyes, seeing what was not shown. 'They're positioned like that, so the force of the shot propels the body forwards and into the pit. Very methodical. If they didn't fall cleanly, there were kickers to push them down. The people were killed in groups of ten. It went on until there was no light.'

There was a silence between them as Edith tried to take in what he was telling her. She looked again at the photograph. She could see the figures in the bleached and empty landscape, but still the image was an enigma. She turned it in her hands, frowning, squinting, looking closer and closer, as if somehow seeing would bring understanding, but what he was saying was beyond her grasp.

'You were *there*?' Her voice was scarcely above a whisper. 'My God!'

'If I had been, I wouldn't be here now. I was hiding. In the woods.' He made a strangled, choking sound, somewhere between a laugh and a sob. 'They were too busy killing to search. I saw everything.' He bit his lip, then wiped his mouth with the back of his hand. When he took it away, Edith saw blood. 'Let me tell you what happened, shall I?'

He began pacing, arms tightly folded about him.

'There'd been killings before. "Actions" the Germans called them. In July, August, Jewish men rounded up and taken to the dunes, but nothing on this scale. Then we heard from Riga. They'd emptied the ghetto. Killed everybody, thousands and thousands. Taken them to the forest, a place called Rumbula. Dug trenches. Made them lie down to be killed. One layer on top of another. Sardine packing they call it. I didn't know all that then but we knew something had happened. You can't keep a thing like that secret and the Arājs Kommando arrived fresh from the killing. Thugs like Kalniņš and Ozols taunting us, yelling *you're next*. Kalniņš was originally from Liepāja. He took a special pleasure in it. On December 13th, a Saturday, *Kurzemes Vārds*, the newspaper, published an order saying all Jews had to stay in their homes. We knew then. This was it.'

He stopped. His thin throat worked as he drained the rest of his brandy.

'People ask, if you knew, knew what was going to happen, why didn't you try to escape? They don't understand. Such a thing was impossible. We were confined to our houses. Police, Arājs Kommando, SS patrolling the streets with guns, dogs, looking for any excuse. Where would we go? We wore the yellow star. Even without it, Liepāja is a small town. Everybody knows who you are. Latvia is a small country. Anyone helping Jews would be shot and very few took that risk. We were friendless in our own country, surrounded by hostility, but even to the last minute, we couldn't believe, didn't want to believe. Hope is the last thing to go and when it is replaced by despair, so black and hopeless, all action seems – impossible.'

As he talked, so he walked the length of the small room and

217

back, turning and turning again as if trying to escape the cage of his memory. As he paced his hands fluttered, making strange little movements in the air, as if fighting off blows in a dream.

'The police began rounding people up in the early hours of the morning, taking them to the Women's Prison. They were kept in the courtyard. When it was our turn, the yard was full so they lined us up outside, facing the wall. We were there all day and all night. It was December. Cold. The next day, we were formed into columns and marched out of the city. North to the sea at Šķēde. Men, women, old, young, little children. The local police and the Arājs Kommando lined the route, so no one could escape. I was with two friends, Osckar and Jan, we positioned ourselves at the edge of the column. The police and Arājs Kommando were beating people, shouting at them to hurry. Some fell, others stumbled over them, there was confusion, the column bunched and stopped. The police waded in, beating left and right with long sticks. We seized our chance. Osckar lunged at the nearest of them. He had a knife hidden. He stabbed him in the throat. They were locked in a tussle. The police, the Arājs didn't want to use their weapons for fear of killing one of their own. The blood, the fight, added to the confusion. Men were shouting, women screaming. Jan and I broke from the column and ran into the forest.'

'Your friend?'

'Already dead. They shot after us. Jan was hit. I didn't even look back. Just heard him cry out. I ran faster. I've always been a good runner and I knew the woods. They didn't come after me, didn't want to risk a mass break-out from the column. I suppose they thought they'd find me later. I could hear shooting, volleys of shots coming from somewhere in front of me. Quite near. I had to know what was going on in the dunes. I crept closer, right to the edge of the woods. I had to see, to bear witness, or else who would believe? They didn't notice, too intent on what they were doing. I saw . . . what I saw . . . I could scarcely believe it myself.

'I waited until night and walked on through the forest,

following the coast. I came to a little harbour with small boats moored there. I stole one and put to sea. I had lived in Liepāja for most of my life, knew how to handle a boat. The Baltic in the middle of winter is not an appetizing prospect, but I'd rather die in the freezing water than down in a pit with sand kicked over me. I sailed west, making for Gotland. From there I reached Sweden and safety. My plan was to get to Britain. Join the Army.'

'What about your family?'

'My father and mother went with the Russians. Who knows what happened to them. I have a brother, Chaim, he's in Palestine. The rest? Grandparents, aunts, uncles, cousins. All dead. The worst thing, the very worst thing is, I could do nothing to save them. I just left them and ran. Like I left Jan.'

He stopped pacing and stood at the desk, looking down at the photographs.

'What you don't see is the colour. The blood streaking the sand at the side of the pit. The exposed flesh, fish-belly white in the winter light. Little children shot in their mothers' arms, babies thrown up, blown apart in the air like clay pigeons. You don't hear the whine of the wind, the screams, the moaning and sobbing, children wailing and whimpering, calling *Māmiņa! Tētiņš!* Mother! Father! But nobody would help them. Nobody. People standing round watching, drinking schnapps, taking photographs, posing for the camera, like these here. They came from miles around to see it. Like your trip to the seaside. And the guards shouting, jeering, laughing, hurling insults right until the last moment, then the quick percussion of gunfire, silence after that, then the swish of sand.'

'You were near enough to see it all?'

'I am in my dreams.'

He gave a retching, gasping sob, covered his face and began to weep. Tears squeezed between his fingers, trickling down his thin wrists.

Edith put her arm round his shoulder, drawing him to her, absorbing his trembling, feeling her own deep inside.

'I'm sorry,' he turned his face into her. 'I've never shed a tear.

Walked away from there, dry-eyed. It was as though there was nothing inside me, just hollowness. As if I'd been eviscerated. I don't know what's come over me now.'

In the face of such horror, there was nothing she could say. What he had told her was beyond language, beyond tears, beyond imagination. She drew him close, hushing, soothing. She kissed his closed eyes, tasted the salt wetness on his cheeks. She led him to the bed, stroking his neck, the back of his head. She lay down with him and took him into her, offering him the universal, primordial comfort that a woman can give to a man.

Afterwards, he was quiet for a long time. From downstairs came faint sounds: a burst of laughter, distant conversation, someone playing a piano. He put his head on her shoulder and closed his eyes. She smoothed his hair, shiny blue green, like a raven's wing. He had long eyelashes for a man. Along his jaw, a bluish shadow was already beginning to show. He looked up at her, his dark eyes heavy lidded, vacant with sleep. He gave a sigh and reached up to pull her mouth down to his.

Their lovemaking was slower, more leisurely the second time around.

When it was over, they lay talking. He told her something of his life in Liepāja, in the time before, how he'd gone with his brother to Spain, to join the International Brigades.

'You were a Communist?'

'You were either one or the other,' he shrugged. 'That's where I first met Leo.'

Leo had been to Spain in some unspecified observer capacity. He certainly hadn't taken part in any fighting, but Edith knew where his sympathies lay.

'When war looked imminent, Chaim took a boat to Italy, then to Palestine. He begged me to go, but I decided to go home to Latvia to be with the family. When the Russians came, we welcomed them. Then the Germans invaded. My parents and my girlfriend, Roza, went east. I stayed, thinking we could organize some kind of resistance.' He passed his hands over his eyes. 'We had no idea.'

'Your parents? Roza? You have heard nothing?'

He shook his head. His face was set, bleak, desolate, his eyes closed. Edith reached over and kissed him then slipped out of bed.

'Where are you going?'

'I have to go back.' She adjusted her stockings. 'I can't be caught here, there would be hell to pay.'

'Don't go yet. You're the first woman in I don't know how long I actually wanted to stay.'

'If I don't get back to the billet, I'll be missed.'

'You don't care about that, surely?' He laughed.

'Of course not, but—' she shook her head. 'It's too hard to explain.'

Frau Schmidt would have one over on her. Molly Slater would feed the mill of rumour and gossip. She couldn't risk that.

'In that case . . .' He got out of bed and padded over to her. He looked smaller, younger without clothes. His skin a milk-pale contrast to the darker tan at his neck and arms and the pelt of black hair, which tapered from his chest, flaring again over his flat belly. He put his arms round her. She could feel him stirring against her. It took a while to break away.

'No,' she said finally. 'I really must go.'

'When will I see you again? I'm leaving tomorrow. Going back to Kiel. I'll be there for at least a week.' He turned from her, grabbed the counterpane and wrapped it around himself. He shuffled back, muffled now in the folds, looking like a small boy. 'I can be in Hamburg, weekend after next. Atlantic Hotel. I'll see you there. Shall I?' She nodded and kissed him once again. 'And Edith? If you meet one of Leo's chums, don't say anything about the photographs you found. Just between us, OK?'

'Of course I won't, not if you don't think I should . . .'

'No. Don't. Not under any circumstances.' He frowned. 'I've heard that Viktors Arājs is in the Zone and they're looking for him.'

'Then finding Jansons might lead them to him. Help bring him to justice.'

'You don't understand, they don't want to punish him, they want to use him!'

Harry's hollow, bitter laugh sounded loud in the quiet room. He didn't look like a boy anymore. He looked like a man in need of solace. She let him lead her back to bed. She lay back as he began to undress her. Slowly, carefully, rolling one stocking down, then the other. She didn't want him to hurry as he laid her clothes aside, one garment at a time. His gentleness, his slowness added to her exquisite helplessness.

20

Billet, Lübeck

20th February 1946

Kaffee und Kuchen
Bee Sting Cake - Bienenstich - Hilde's Recipe

Kaffee und Kuchen - very much a <u>German</u> tradition. A chance for women of like minds and interests to get together. Bee Sting Cake (*Bienenstich*) perfect for one of these gatherings. Nothing quite like it in British baking. The cake is made from a sweet yeast dough, rather like a <u>Sally Lunn</u>. 1lb flour, 1 egg, 3oz sugar, 3oz butter, half pt. milk, 1oz yeast. Follow as for Sally Lunn p.135. Leave dough to rise for at least 8 minutes, bake regulo 6 for 20-30 minutes. The cake is topped with honey, butter, sugar and almonds, giving the finished cake a crisp, caramelized coating. When completely cold, the cake is split and filled with a pastry custard flavoured with Kirsch or vanilla.

223

She left him sleeping. There was no one about as she slipped out of his room and tiptoed down the corridor. She walked home under the frosty stars, already missing him. Two weeks seemed a very long time. She walked on, hardly noticing the biting cold. Her mind was back in the quiet of his room: the yellowy light from the desk lamp on his face, accentuating the hollow of his cheek, picking up the glitter in his eyes, illuminating the changing lines of pain as he told his story. That sob wrenched from somewhere deep inside him; the way he held his hands, like a cage to hold his tears, had moved her to a place where words ceased to hold meaning. The sex that had followed, his aching tenderness made her tingle still. She'd had a vertiginous sense of actually falling. She'd had that feeling before.

Some animal instinct broke through her reverie, a noise behind, a pricking of the spine.

She turned into a dazzle of headlights. The motorbike was coming right at her. She stumbled in a slipping scramble, pain arrowing as she turned her ankle on the kerb. She landed in a heap of frozen, dirty snow, helpless as the bike bore down on her with a growling roar. She could smell the reek of petrol, oil, exhaust fumes as the bike slewed, the wheels so close she could feel the heat from the burning rubber. The rider swerved at the very last second, laughing as he rode away.

Edith lay where she was, the initial danger over, but the pain in her ankle increased with searing intensity as soon as she tried to put weight on it. There was no one about in this quiet road. No lights in the houses, no traffic. It was easily ten degrees below. It was snowing big, feathery flakes and they were falling faster. Without help, she would freeze to death. The tears from the pain were already ice on her face.

Suddenly, footsteps running, a voice shouting:

'Frau Graham, are you all right?'

Luka held out a hand to her. For his size, the boy was surprisingly strong.

'I fell. A motorbike. Only just missed me.' Edith hobbled painfully, leaning on his shoulder.

He let out a stream of invective in three different languages. 'No-good DP. I told you.'

'How do you know?'

'He ride R51 BMW. I see him at end of road. Don't know which one he is but I find out, don't worry. I fix him good. But first lean on Luka. I get you home.'

'We look like we're in a three-legged race,' Edith laughed as they hobbled along.

'What is that?' Luka asked. He frowned as she described it. 'Tie legs together to do racing? Why they do that?'

Trying to explain took up the rest of the way.

'You all right now?' he asked when they finally reached the billet.

'Yes, thank you, Luka—'

'I come to tell you.' He leaned closer. 'I have news, about that lady. I know more tomorrow.'

He was off before she could ask more, running through the snow and ice as sure footed as a mountain hare.

Edith let herself into the darkened house, trying not to make any noise but as soon as she put any weight on her ankle, she went crashing into the hallstand.

'Is anybody there?' Ginny's voice, nervous at the top of the stairs.

'It's only me,' Edith held onto the edge of the stand, wincing against the shooting pain. 'I've ricked my ankle . . .'

'Oh, you poor thing!'

Ginny ran down the stairs and helped her into the sitting room.

'How did it happen?' she asked as she settled Edith on the settee.

Then the others appeared, curious to know what was going on. Edith's pleas not to make a fuss were ignored. Ginny went to get Frau Schmidt while Lorna, who claimed First Aid experience, knelt down to examine her. Angie and Franny went off for basins of hot and cold water. Frau Schmidt came offering bandages and advice to Lorna. At this point, the front door opened and Molly came in.

'What's going on here?' She stood, arms folded as she listened to what had happened. 'That'll teach you to stay out late in this kind of weather!' She gave her sharp, high-pitched laugh. 'I'm off to bed.'

Frau Schmidt ordered hot-water bottles to be made up, aspirins to be found. On the surface, the German woman couldn't do enough for Edith but did she detect a look passing between Molly and Frau Schmidt? Was there a glimmer of disappointment, just an initial hint of surprise that Edith was there at all?

The next day, the swelling had gone down but Edith still couldn't put weight on her ankle. She would have to spend the day resting in the sitting room with her foot up on a stool. She sent word to Roz. She would catch up on her letters home and it would be a chance to observe what went on when the British were out of the way.

She kept her letters anodyne: the weather, requests for things hard to get. Anything else would be misinterpreted, warped and twisted by Mother's continuing resentment over her absence and Louisa's bitterness at having to take her place. The row hadn't died down. Often, to fill the page, she'd describe a meal she'd had, a recipe she'd found. Louisa had started the sending of recipes and menu cards from Ted's war postings. It was an interest shared, safe ground. Food and cooking was the one thing that they had in common. The only place they got on was in the kitchen. They had been like this since they were quite little girls when Mother had let them help her. Simple things: mixing, measuring, jam tarts and scones. Louisa had followed Edith's lead. Quiet, solemn, listening to her older sister's instructions, copying everything she did. Precise and careful, she never made a mess. She'd worshipped Edith then. How things change.

Edith looked over Louisa's last missive. Minor High Street triumphs. The ration ruled their lives. Louisa was good at getting 'that bit extra' using her good looks and charm. Other than that, Mother's rheumatism was bad. Louisa had to do everything. Rory was off school with his chest again. Ted was no help. She hardly ever saw him. His new school took up all his time. When he wasn't there, he was at the RAFA or the Legion, or down the allotment, or fishing.

Like many men back from the Forces, Ted was finding the domestic world stifling, preferring his own company or the company of his kind. Edith was beginning to understand. Louisa's letters pressed heavily on the worn levers of guilt but they didn't make her want to return. Just the opposite.

Edith was composing her reply, when the doorbell rang. Frau Schmidt hardly ever answered the door yet that was her over-loud, peeling laughter. Effusive greetings subsided to animated chatter that faded down the basement stairs.

Hilde brought coffee and cake. *Bienenstich*. Bee Sting Cake. Quite a treat.

'What's going on?' Edith asked.

'Kaffee and Kuchen. Friends of Frau Schmidt.'

'Does she often do this? Frau Schmidt?' Edith asked. 'Have friends in?'

'Oh, yes,' Hilde nodded. 'Very often. When the British ladies have gone to work.'

'Neighbours?' Edith enquired. 'Frau Kaufmann?'

'Yes, she is usually here and some other ladies from other places, I don't know.'

What ladies? Edith wanted to ask but the girl's brow was beginning to pucker. Edith changed the subject.

'This is very good cake, Hilde, did you make it?'

'Yes.' The girl's face cleared.

'My compliments. You must give me the recipe.' Edith smiled encouragingly. All women who like cooking, like to have that cooking appreciated. What better way than to ask for the recipe?

'My uncle keeps beehives, so we have honey. I bring some to Frau Schmidt. And aunt has almond trees in the garden. Also cherries for *Gugelhupf*.'

'*Gugelhupf*! That's one of my favourites!'

'Mine, too.' Hilde smiled. 'It is my mother's recipe, my grand-mother's before that . . .'

Gugelhupf was a rich, yeast-based cake made in a bundt tin with the addition of fruit, raisins or in this case cherries, but Edith had never made it.

'Tell me the recipe.'

Edith was genuinely interested and it would help fill her letter to Louisa. She made notes as Hilde described what to do, remembering her home, her family, her mother and grandmother's kitchen. A whole world came spilling out with the sifting and stirring of each ingredient. Hilde and her brother trying to sneak the schnapps-soaked sour cherries before he joined the Luftwaffe and was lost to the waters of the grey North Sea. The copper bundt tin was Hilde's grandmother's. She would beat and beat with her wooden spoon, Hilde demonstrated, until the dough was elastic and silky smooth. Grandmother, bundt tin, everything, gone in the raid on Hanover that had sent Hilde north to find refuge with her aunt.

'And your aunt sends cherries as a gift to Frau Schmidt? That's very generous.'

'It's expected.' Hilde shrugged. 'We all give something. This is a good job. It is one reason why Frau Schmidt didn't like Seraphina.' She shrugged again. 'Nothing to give. Now, I must go.' Her eyes flickered to the door. 'Frau Schmidt and her friends . . .'

'Of course.'

So much to be learnt in a thoroughly domestic conversation. To be *Beziehungen*, connected, was highly sought after. It gave Frau Schmidt considerable power. So she was hosting regular meetings of women – Edith surmised that they would be coming from near and far and were likely to share Frau Schmidt's political sympathies and were therefore very probably giving aid and succour to Nazis on the run. Such groups would be made up of women, their men dead, missing or in hiding. Leo's words: find the Frau . . .

In the hall, Frau Schmidt trilled farewells as they all trooped off down the path. Edith thought of them as the Schwestern – the sisterhood. Hunched in their black coats like a witches' cabal.

The front door slammed. Frau Schmidt's heavy step outside, galoshes crunching through the snow.

A knock on the door. Hilde again. Would she like more cake? She certainly would. It was delicious. Was that Frau Schmidt going out? Yes, indeed. Where was she going? To market? A shake of the head. She went out often and *not* to market. The girl's bottom lip stuck out in a resentful pout. Hilde would have to go herself, later on, to get heavy vegetables after all the housework was done.

'Frau Schmidt has many friends. She goes to see them.' Hilde glanced to the window as if someone out there could see her.

'Who are they? These friends?'

Hilde's voice dropped to a whisper. 'It is dangerous to speak about them. It is best to be careful. Your foot. Your accident—'

'You mean it wasn't?'

Hilde shook her head slowly. The sharp rap at the window made them both start.

'There is a boy.'

It was Luka.

'Let him in, Hilde. And bring another slice of cake and more coffee.'

'I wait until Nazi bitch go out.' Luka unfolded a clasp knife, its blade honed to stiletto thinness, and cut into his cake. 'I have something to tell.' He ate with the slow, delicate care of someone to whom food like this meant a great deal, whose diet had been both monotonous and sparse. 'Yesterday, I go to railway yards. Many kids there from all over. Some from Prussia.' It was where they went to steal coal. There was a pause while he addressed another piece of cake, nibbling off the honey-coated almond flakes, turning the slice around in his hand, licking the cream like a cat. 'I ask. Any from around Elbing? "Sure," they say. I go over, make acquaintance. Tommies chase us, I show where to hide. Share a ciggie. Ask, where you from? Place in Prussia. Oh, yes? I say. Which place? Like I don't know. Not far from Elbing, they say, eager to talk. I share another ciggie, say, do you know this lady? Maybe, they say, but I know they do. I say meet

229

me today and I show best place for coal. We collect a big sack. I help them carry it back. They trust me now. They take me to a big house. Some of them live there. Nice lady give me bread and jam. Her name Elisabeth. I think she the lady you look for.' He took out a scrap of paper. A corner torn from the Lübecker. 'She live here. You want cake?'

'What?' Edith looked up from the scrawled address. 'No, you have it. And here,' she reached in her bag and took out a packet of Players. 'Thank you Luka, you've been a great help.'

Luka went to the window. 'Fräulein Roz coming. I open door.'

'What's he doing here?' Roz looked out at Luka running down the path. 'That boy gets everywhere. It's horrible out.' She shook her coat. 'Wet snow. Even worse than dry. You're better off in here.'

'Would you like coffee? There's cake.'

'I won't, thanks. Just came to see how you were. How is it?'

'Much better.'

'Good. We need you back. I've found somewhere we might use for a Teachers' Centre – just needs furnishing, of course. And there was a message from that Captain Adams. Wants to meet you at the Mess.'

'When?'

'Tonight at eight.' Roz gave a helpless shrug. 'I explained you were *hors de combat* but he didn't seem to hear.'

21

CCG Mess, Lübeck

20th February 1946

Dinner Menu
Mockturtle Soup
Fried Sole in butter
*Dutch steaks
Carrots, Castle Potatoes
Pears and Cream
Cheese & Biscuits, Coffee

Not a great deal of variety in the Mess Menus.
*Dutch Steak - find under Grilling although
can be oven Roasted. Same general rules as
Beef (see earlier recipe).

'Heard you took a bit of a tumble. All right now, I hope?'

'Fine, thanks.' Edith looked at her bandaged ankle. 'Getting better.'

'Jolly good. The Mock Turtle wasn't bad. Not that I've ever had real turtle. D'you have any idea what it's made from? Nothing to do with turtles, I don't suppose. I hear you take an interest in food.'

'Where did you hear that?'

Adams didn't answer. He kept his wide, blue-eyed gaze on her.

'You suppose right,' she replied lightly. 'It's made from a calf's head. Rather a grisly and fiddly process.'

'Really?' Bill Adams frowned. 'Doesn't sound at all appetising. Dutch Steak was all right. A bit gristly.' He searched with a toothpick for a morsel of meat. 'Anything for me? Leo was wondering. Hmm, pears and cream. Both tinned, I'd imagine. Give that a miss. Let's take our coffee and brandy in the sitting room, shall we? How've things been?' he said as he ushered her out. 'Busy by all accounts. Concerning yourself with our Baltic brethren?'

'How do you know that?' Edith looked at him, eyes wide, genuinely mystified.

'Not for you to know.' He tapped his nose and led her to the coveted wing chairs by the fire.

How *did* he know? Dori? Surely not. Harry Hirsch? Impossible. If not them, then whom? Molly. *If you carry on with this, you'll be sorry.* If Harry was right and the British were actively looking for Val's boss, Viktors Arājs, then that was not an empty warning.

'I do counsel you to be careful,' he went on. 'They are volatile people. Likely to fly off the handle. Doesn't do to go blundering about. How's the leg?' He helped her to her chair with unnecessary care. 'Comfortable? Need a stool or anything?'

Edith stared at him. She was not taken in by his exaggerated solicitude. Not for one minute. Did he know about the attack on her? Did he approve, even order it?

Edith knew she was receiving another warning. Not in so many words. Bill Adams would never use so many words, to speak in plain terms would reveal too much, but the hint was pretty hefty. She could have been seriously hurt. If not for Luka, it could have been much worse. She felt a quick flare of anger. She wouldn't be intimidated by Adams, or bested by Molly Slater, for that matter.

'Well?' he asked. 'What have you got?'

'First,' Edith looked at him, 'tell me why I shouldn't be taking an interest in the Baltic brethren, as you put it. Quid pro quo. Isn't that how it works?'

He waited for the brandy and coffee then leaned forward.

'Shouldn't be telling you this. Strictly hush, hush, but if it means fewer cats released among the pigeons, it might be worth it. There's a plan, well, it's not even a plan yet, more an idea. The Baltic States are now in the hands of the Soviets, but we're getting word of resistance from partisan groups. Nationalists. We're looking for likely chaps to send in, help them organize and so on. If we can get them in there.' He looked thoughtful, then his face cleared. 'Shouldn't be too difficult. Awfully long coastline. We're looking to ex-Arājs Kommando to do the job. They did some pretty bloody things, of course, but they could be useful. Especially their boss, one Viktor Arājs. Can't let the Russkies have it all their own way up there, can we? The game is changing, Edith. We have new enemies now.'

Adams talked on about priorities shifting and keeping ahead of things but behind his empty words, Edith could hear Harry Hirsch's hollow, bitter laugh. *You don't understand, they don't want to punish him, they want to use him!* She could see the smug, grinning, brutal faces of Jansons and that other man as they posed for the camera, slung about with sten guns, binoculars, goodness knows what paraphernalia, shoulder to shoulder with an SS officer while behind them people stood naked on those bleak, cold dunes, waiting to be shot. Harry had been right. Adams and his kind had no intention of bringing Jansons and his cronies to justice. They just wanted to know what use they could be. She knew now exactly why Harry had told her not to mention the photographs. She certainly wouldn't be doing so now Adams had so clearly explained the plans the British had to use Jansons and his kind.

'So?' he was saying. 'What *have* you got?'

'It could be something or nothing.' Edith shrugged. 'I was told to keep my eyes and ears open and that's what I've done.

The billet I'm in, the housekeeper, Frau Schmidt and her husband, Stephan, that's if he is her husband, have a veritable trove of SS paraphernalia in the cellar—'

'Is that all?' Adams laughed. 'Them and every other German—'

'No, that's not all,' Edith said evenly. 'There's a hut in the garden. It shows signs of occupation. I suspect that Stephan and Frau Schmidt are keeping someone there. Hiding them. I have reason to believe that they form part of an active Nazi network, carrying on a campaign of intimidation, dealing extensively in the black market and helping war criminals.'

'What's your source?'

'Not for you to know.' She sat back. Tit for tat.

'Ha!' He laughed, a short, sharp bark. 'Hoist on my own petard and all that. That is worth following. We're picking up information about an underground organization made up of local cells of like-minded individuals, unrepentant Nazis, better-under-Hitler types, just as you describe. A lot of them women, helping their men on the run.' Adams looked at her across the table. 'We've heard different names: ODESSA – initials stand for *Organisation der ehemaligen SS-Angehörigen* – Organization of Former SS Members. Hand it to Jerry, he likes an acronym. The other name we've heard is *Die Spinne*.'

'The Spider?'

'Exactly that!' He nodded his satisfaction, as if conferring his approval on a particularly apt pupil. 'More metaphorical, that one. We don't know if they're one and the same, or different. We don't know much of anything. Devilishly difficult to penetrate so anything you can find out would be very valuable. Whatever the moniker, the objective is to shift *die Brüder* out of Germany, help them on their way south, through Italy and onto a ship to somewhere more congenial. The Schmidts, Herr and Frau, might well be involved in this little enterprise. Well spotted, Edith. We'll keep an eye on them, of course, but we'll let them run. They might well lead us to others. Then we can scoop the whole network. That calls for another brandy.' He signalled to the waiter. 'Anything on von Stavenow?'

That wide-eyed stare was on her again with a slight twitch of the head, like a cat watching a mouse.

'Not as such.' She wasn't ready to tell him about Elisabeth. She thought fast. He needed something to chase. 'But I have information that the Americans might be looking for him. Or men like him. Men with a similar – history.'

'Ha. Bound to be! Hardly news.'

'I mean here. In the British Zone.'

'Who told you that?' For the first time, Adams looked disconcerted.

'My journalist friend,' Edith supplied. 'She has it on very good authority.'

'Hmm, yes, well,' Adams crossed and recrossed his legs. 'Good work, Edith. Keep it up. Ear to the ground and all that. But no private initiatives.' He wagged a finger. 'Pass it over and carry on caring for the *Kinder*. Sure you don't want a nightcap?'

'No thanks. My driver will be here in a minute. There he is now.'

'Ah, Hunter. Good evening, sergeant.'

Jack saluted smartly. 'Good evening, sir.'

Edith was drained by her encounter with Adams, though she thought that she'd won on points. By the time she got back to the billet, she was all but done in, but before she could get to bed, she had a card to write.

Hope you liked the Latvian Dish, I've become rather partial to it. Bienenstich – unexpected treat. Dinner tonight in the Mess. Dutch Steaks on the menu (recipes for your info). My companion showed an interest in Latvian Recipes which surprised me. Steaks not to my liking – too heavily grilled. Yours, Edith

P.S. Talking of regional dishes – I might have something Prussian for you soon.

22

44 Möllnstraße, Lübeck

25th February 1946

```
Wild Boar Steinhof
A robust dish from the north. A reminder of
times gone and places lost forever. The boar
is marinaded in a strong red wine, pungent
with juniper and thyme from the forest,
onions and carrots from the kitchen garden,
strong spices - clove and peppercorns. The
cooking is long and slow. A dish from the
past, a fragrance and flavour that lives on
now only in memory.
```

'Not far.' Edith smoothed the creased scrap of paper. 'It must be up here somewhere.'

Had the boy got it right? Could Elisabeth be here? Part of her hoped he'd got it wrong. After so long, what would they say to each other? So much had happened, so much was altered. All the dreadful things that she'd learnt about Kurt. How much did Elisabeth know? More than years measured the gap between then and now.

Edith made herself concentrate on the numbers as Jack crawled along Möllnstraße. It was the right kind of area, or had been once. Elisabeth's cousin might well have had a town house here. The handsome houses had escaped bombing but they showed every sign of dereliction and decay: roofs sagging, eaves rotting, windows boarded, wide gravel paths weed choked, steps broken, woodwork ripped away for firewood. A few were burnt out, looted by DPs or slave workers when the original residents, dead or displaced, failed to return. None of these houses would be empty. Every scrap of shelter was precious, fought over, in a city swelled to more than twice its normal size by refugees.

As they bumped along the rutted road, the houses grew better kept. These would be in the greatest danger. Edith could not see anyone at the windows or shutters but she could feel eyes watching. There was no fear of looting. Those days were over. What the residents feared now was the delivery of a British Requisition Order. Everyone to vacate the premises with what they could carry. The house taken over for billets, messes, offices, whatever the British saw fit.

There was a lorry parked at the foot of the drive to a large house. Edith couldn't see a number but she was pretty sure that this was it. Soldiers stood about smoking, lounging against the lorry's dropped tailgate, enjoying the weak winter sun, listening to an argument going on. Jack stopped the car and got out. He nodded to one or two of the men, exchanging a cheery greeting. They grinned back. Looked like their man was getting the worst of it. He was being addressed by a woman standing at the top of a flight of steps. She was speaking English, her clear, ringing voice held just the trace of an accent. Edith knew the voice immediately. She had found Elisabeth.

The sergeant stood holding a clipboard in front of him, like a shield.

'You were warned a week ago now. You should have vacated. You must leave immediately.'

'But we have many families living here.' Anxious faces watched from the windows. 'You will make thirty, more, people homeless. Women. Old people. Children. Where shall we go?'

'That's not my concern,' he went to mount the steps but she blocked his way. 'You were given notice. Alternative accommodation should have been found for you.'

'But we've heard nothing about other accommodation! How is that even possible with the town as full as it is?'

'That's not my department,' he said with triumphant finality, as though that settled the matter. 'Now *if* you'll excuse me.'

He tried to push past her. She held absolutely no power in this exchange but she was ready to stand her ground. Edith feared a tussle and was about to intervene when Jack touched her arm.

'A word, ma'am.'

He spoke rapidly, gesturing towards the sergeant and the lorry behind them.

'I see.' Edith straightened her back, squared her shoulders and moved down the drive towards them. She deliberately didn't look at Elisabeth, concentrating her attention on the requisition sergeant: small of stature, self-important, hiding inside his uniform. 'What's going on here?'

'What's it got to do with you?' He turned, his mouth a snarl beneath his bristling, shredded-wheat moustache.

'I'm the Education Officer for this District. I came to see why the children who live here are not attending school.'

'Got more things to worry about, I should reckon.' He gave a mirthless laugh. 'Like where they're going to kip. This house has been requisitioned.'

'What for exactly?'

The man looked at his sheet. 'Offices. Not that it's any of your business.'

'What is your name?'

'What's that got to do with anything?'

'I like to know with whom I'm dealing.'

'Wilkins, as it happens. What's yours?'

'Miss Edith Graham.'

'CCG type.' There was a sneer in his voice, but Edith let that go.

238

'I hold the equivalent rank of Lieutenant Colonel.'

'That's by the by, love.' Wilkins looked back down at his clipboard. 'Orders is orders. This lot out,' he pointed to the woman standing above him. 'That lot,' he jerked a thumb behind him, 'in.'

'I don't think so.' Edith took a step closer.

'Oh? And what would you have to say about it?'

'Not me. My driver. Sergeant Hunter. I think you might know each other?'

Jack gave a mock salute. 'Wotcha, Wilko.'

'And your superior. Captain Morrison, isn't it? Jack was asking if you've been down to the Böttcherstraße lately. Or has it moved to somewhere else now?'

'Don't know what you're talking about.' His voice had lost its sneer and was edged with nervousness.

'I think you do.'

He frowned, his small mouth pursed, considering. He tapped his pencil on his clipboard, in rapid staccato. Some of the men involved in requisition did a tidy amount of business, redirecting Government Issue, selling off goods and furnishings 'liberated' from the houses they took over, buying up more, arranging for the most valuable items to be shipped back to Britain, or sold on in Brussels. There was big money involved, according to Jack.

'Well?'

Sergeant Wilkins looked at her. Behind his steel-rimmed glasses, the last spark of arrogant authority flickered and died.

'I got my orders,' he said sulkily.

'Haven't we all?' Edith smiled, she knew she'd won. 'Mine are to get children into school. How can I do that when you people keep making them homeless? Now,' it was time to take charge. He was only a sergeant, after all. 'I suggest that you tell your superior that these premises are unsuitable. That shouldn't be too difficult and should get you out of a bind.'

'What am I supposed to do with that lot there?' He gestured towards the lorry.

'What does it contain?'

'Desks, tables, chairs, filing cabinets. Office furnishings.'

Edith smiled. She knew the perfect place for it. 'As of now, it has been redirected. Jack will show you where to take it.'

'If you say so.' He turned and stomped down the steps towards his men. 'No skin off my nose.'

The lorry drove off in a cloud of blue exhaust.

'Edith? It's you, isn't it? You are like an angel sent from heaven! I don't know how to thank you.' Elisabeth ran down the rest of the steps and took Edith in her arms. Then she held herself away, examining Edith's face. 'You dealt so well with him. Such authority.' She regarded Edith with a bemused smile and a slight shake of the head, as if trying to reconcile the woman she'd known with the one standing before her with all the confident assurance that her uniform gave her. 'I didn't think to see you here. Now. After – everything – but the strangest things happen.'

'I'm so, so glad to see you!' Edith blinked back tears of absolute relief and genuine joy at seeing Elisabeth. 'To know you're safe!'

The search was over. Edith breathed the slightest trace of gardenia as she took Elisabeth back into a tight embrace.

They broke apart to look again at each other, searching for what was the same, what was different. It had been seven years and five of those had been war, which had changed everything and everyone. Had Elisabeth also been sullied by the regime her husband had so enthusiastically embraced and that had infiltrated every single aspect of national life? Impossible to tell yet but she was certainly different from the woman that Edith had first met. There were shadows under Elisabeth's eyes and fine lines at the outer corners. Her face was thinner, but the hollows in her cheeks only emphasized her fine bone structure; her pale skin made her almost ethereal. She was still lovely.

Edith smiled as she followed Elisabeth into the house, brushing aside any doubts, her jubilation silencing any faint drumbeat of suspicion. The wide hall was lined with makeshift cots, to what must once have been a pleasant morning room at the back of the house. It was now divided by a crude wooden partition with a baby crying on the other side and drying bedclothes thrown over the top.

There was little by the way of furniture. A table and chair by the window. A couple of old rugs on the bare wooden floor, Persian by the looks of them, but worn to threads. Two old leather chairs stood at the centre of the room; a carved box between them acted as a table. A narrow iron bed, draped with an appliqued coverlet, occupied an alcove. A battered leather satchel and a travel-stained loden coat hung on a hook on the back of the door. The ceramic stove in the corner had not been lit.

'You may find it rather cold.' Elisabeth was wearing a thick knitted Norwegian jacket over layers of clothing but still managed to look elegant. 'I'm used to it.' She pulled the collar closer, as if she felt the cold despite what she said. 'This is my cousin Lena's house. I came with so little. What I stood up in, what I could carry in that bag. She's been kind enough to take us in. The bed is from one of the maids' rooms in the attic. At least I have a bed.' She gave a mirthless laugh. 'They are sleeping on straw mattresses up there, five, six to a room.' She looked about. 'I'd offer you something, but . . .'

'I've brought things!' Edith dived into her briefcase and took out tea, coffee, sugar, bars of chocolate and packets of rich tea and digestive biscuits to lay before her. 'It's all I could pack in, I'm afraid.'

'Real coffee! It's enough! Lena will be overjoyed!'

She came back with a tray of coffee and biscuits arranged on a fine china plate.

Edith nibbled at a biscuit out of politeness. She offered Elisabeth a packet of cigarettes, placing it on the table between them.

Elisabeth took one. 'Such luxury to smoke them. And so good to speak English after all this time! I fear I've grown a little rusty.' She inhaled deeply. 'You won't join me?'

'I don't.'

'Asthma!' Elisabeth's face lit up at the memory. 'You mentioned it that first evening when we drank all that brandy on the terrace.'

'You were drinking brandy.' Edith smiled, caught in the web of shared recollection. It had been a magical evening. 'I was drinking schnapps.'

'Williams Pear, I recall,' Elisabeth gave a faint echo of the sudden ringing peal that Edith remembered. She had always felt absurdly rewarded when she made Elisabeth laugh.

They were silent for a moment, netted in a memory that telescoped time, bringing them back to the late-evening gloaming of that last, lost summer.

The light died from Elisabeth's eyes as quickly as it had been ignited.

'I can't believe I will never go back there again. I wake up in the morning thinking I'm there, only to realize . . . It is the same every day. A purgatory that I will never escape.' When she turned to Edith, her smile was tired, automatic. 'You are here with the Control Commission?'

'Yes.' Edith looked down at her uniform. 'Education Division. I was a teacher, if you remember.'

'Of course. Remembering is all there is for me to do.' She extinguished one cigarette and lit another. 'I've lost everything. House, land, position, family. My people. All those I knew and loved. Our place. Our way of life. All gone. We'd been there for seven hundred years. Now, I have nothing.' She paused. 'The people called the moment of our defeat *Die Stunde null*: Hour Zero. I feel I'm there still, as though life is over, or has not begun. Towards the end, people began committing suicide, whole families of them. It was very common. Not through love for the Führer but because they knew that their time, everything they held familiar, was finished.'

Elisabeth sat very upright and still for quite a time, her blue eyes dark, magnified by tears she refused to spill. Of regret? Loss? Bitterness? Edith didn't know and couldn't ask her. Do tears have to be defined? And to cry before another went against her upbringing, her caste. When they'd first met, Edith had been dazzled and fascinated in equal measure. Now, she saw the woman behind the aura that her title, position, wealth and privilege had given her and was deeply moved by her but she knew better than to go to her, to touch her. Elisabeth would despise any gesture with the slightest tincture of pity. She was not the kind of woman to fall into another's arms.

But Elisabeth was still Elisabeth. There might be holes in her stockings and the knitted jacket might be worn at the elbows but it was Setesdale and the loden on the door was fur lined. Edith felt a frisson of the feeling that she'd had on first coming to Schloss Steinhof. A touch of the same social awkwardness. She looked down at her uniform, the cigarettes and packets of biscuits on the table, such shows of largesse and British authority might seem very like boasting.

'Did you feel tempted?' she asked at last. 'To end it all, I mean.'

'What?' Elisabeth turned as though she'd forgotten that there was anyone else in the room. 'Oh, no, I wouldn't do that.' Her laugh was ironic, bitter. 'Although I sometimes wish I had. No,' she repeated quietly. 'I didn't do that. I had to survive. For my daughter.'

'You have a daughter?' Edith looked around in absolute surprise, as if she might be hiding somewhere.

'Elfriede – Elfi. Would you like to see her?'

'Yes,' Edith was at a loss. She had not expected this. 'Of course.'

Elisabeth rapped on the partition. 'Lise? Can you bring Elfriede in to me?'

A girl sidled into the room, shy, her eyes cast down. She held a baby in the crook of her arm. A little dark head showed over the edge of the enveloping shawl. Edith didn't know much about babies but this one looked very young.

'Why,' she said as she moved closer. 'She's tiny!'

'She was born in the summer.'

'So you were pregnant when you left?'

'Yes, or she would never have survived. It was cold on the journey here. 20 degrees below zero, more. Infants died in nappies frozen to solid blocks of ice. Inside me was the safest place.'

She stated that as an everyday fact, as if it was something people knew. People like her. Germans. Edith sensed the gap between them, the conquerers and the conquered. 'I was sick after she was born, very sick,' she went on. 'I couldn't feed her or look after. Lise took over. She had just lost a baby.'

'Oh, I'm sorry,' Edith said to the girl in German.

'It was war, Edith.' Elisabeth spoke for Lise. 'You have no idea how hard it was. Lise became pregnant because a Russian soldier raped her. It is probably good the child is dead.'

The baby woke, stirring in Lise's arms. Edith approached carefully.

'May I see?'

Lise lowered the edge of the shawl. The baby yawned showing two tiny teeth. Edith leaned closer. The yawn widened into a smile and her eyes opened wide.

'What a dear little thing! Such big, brown eyes.'

Edith looked up. Elisabeth was blue eyed, so was Kurt. This child had dark hair and dark eyes.

'She's not Kurt's,' Elisabeth said. 'If that's the question you were wanting to ask. Thank you, Lise, you may take her away now,' she said in German, dismissing the girl. She turned back to Edith. 'It's a long story. There's so much to tell.'

She put her hands together, almost in an attitude of prayer, and began her story.

We'd been planning to go for months. We were under no illusion as to what would happen if we stayed. The Eastern Front was collapsing. Refugees had been pouring west since summer, set in motion like herds that smell fire on the wind. By the Autumn, the Nazis circulated what the Russian had done at Nemmersdorf. Children slaughtered, women, old, young, raped and murdered, their bodies dumped on dung heaps, nailed to barn doors. We assumed that it was the usual lies, propaganda, faked somehow; we didn't believe anything we were told anymore. Then refugees began to come in from the Goldap and Gumbinnen. It was all true. That was what we could expect.

We prepared in secret. Right to the last, the Nazis kept saying that the Russians would be defeated by some miracle weapon, that an army would appear from nowhere. It was a matter of will. Anyone the slightest bit 'defeatist' would be hanged. Every man, able bodied or not, old men and young boys scarcely more than children, were made to join the Volkssturm. And they were taking horses – I could not allow that. I would not let the army take them or leave them for those Russian savages to work to death or slaughter for meat. I had to save as many as possible. I had to preserve the breed. The old men and the boys saddled up with Kaspar, my Master of Horse, and drove the herd west. Organizing my people was not so easy. Some were reluctant. They had lived there for countless generations. Others were afraid. Then, from one day to the next, everything changed. On January 21st there was an order to evacuate the area. I rode to town to find that the Nazis had already left, party offices empty, files discarded, burnt papers blowing like black snow.

It was time. I sent word to be ready. We would leave that night. I ordered everyone to take the bare minimum. Most came laden but how could I blame them? When you pack your life onto the back of a cart, what do you leave? What do you take? The choices are too difficult to make. I restricted myself to the barest of necessities: change of clothing, a few photos, family papers, toiletries, bandages, valuables that were easily carried, pistol, rifle, shotgun, ammunition.

That last evening, we had a feast. We ate boar and drank Margaux, chateau-bottled Haut-Brion, Chateau d'Yquem – all the great vintages from my father's cellar. There was no point in keeping them now. When the time came, my mother ordered us to leave her. Brice stayed, he'd served the family from a young boy and was devoted to der alten Gräfin. Now they are together forever. My mother had a grave dug in the cellar for when the time came. Brice to do the honours with my father's service pistol. I assume there was room for him, too. We left the keys on the hall table, closed the great doors and left them inside.

Entombed. Sometimes I wished I'd gone down with her to the cellar, to be interred there. Never to leave.

I saddled my chestnut mare, Andreas rode the bay stallion, so we would have a breeding pair wherever we finally fetched up. We set off in a convoy, the majority in carts and wagons pulled by horses. Tractors were useless. Even if there was fuel to be had, it would freeze.

It was bitterly cold, the horses slipping on the icy roads. We were not the only ones on the move. They were coming in from every side. It took hours to get to the nearest town, more hours to get through it. The road west was clogged with wagons, tractors, handcarts, prams, people pulling suitcases on planks of wood. A solid column of misery extended in both directions as far as the eye could see, all going at the pace of the slowest with frequent stoppages for broken axles, collapsed horses, troops moving in the opposite direction. How long did it go on like this? For hundreds of miles, a thousand? By nightfall we had hardly moved. Some of my people decided to turn back, take their chances with the Russians. I don't blame them. They thought that they could carry on as they had done before but under new masters. Irenka was one of them and her daughter, she wouldn't leave her old mother, who was really too frail to survive the long journey. Our lands are in Poland now. For them it was a journey postponed and who knows what they suffered when the conquerors swept through.

To go on, go back, or strike north for the sea? No one knew what to do. Danzig was still open but for how long? The only way to it was across the frozen Haff but at least the ships were still evacuating refugees. That way was not for us. The ships would never take the horses and it had its own perils. On the ice, there was no cover. Columns were strafed, dive-bombed by the Russians. The ice stained red. Horses and wagons fell through the broken ice, whole families lost. Even for those who reached the port and got a passage out, it was hardly salvation. The ships were easy pickings for Russian torpedoes.

We rode west, cutting across country, using back roads.

Andreas leading, the rest strung out behind like a line of cavalry. We had maps but the weather was against us with freezing temperatures and strong winds blowing the snow so the horses sank up to their bellies in drifts. Across the fields, we could see the dark figures moving like a column of ghosts through the white veiling snow, always at the same slow pace, like a scene from history, from the Thirty Years' War, maybe. We were forced back onto the highway. We began to see bodies at the sides of the road. Mostly the old, but also the very young. Children. No one could stop to bury them. The ground was hard as stones. They were just left by the wayside for animals to find. After the first shock, we barely gave these huddled forms a second glance. Like everyone else, we were intent on our own survival, finding food for ourselves and the horses, shelter for the night, some warmth. We were well armed. A horse was worth a fortune but ours were beyond price.

We went across country if we could, trying to avoid the roaming, clashing armies. We knew where the armies had passed. We learnt to avoid the villages where crows robed the trees. We rode west, always west, into the setting sun. When we reached Pomerania, the people were living in the same state of uncertainty that we had endured, told that they were safe, that the Russians would never reach them, that one last heroic campaign would save them. None of them believed it for a minute, but they had been ordered not to leave. Every town, every village, still had its zealots.

By the time we reached Stettin, we could see the flash of artillery, hear gunfire, the hideous whine of Stalinorgel rockets streaking up in quick succession. The Russians were near. We struck north, across the frozen Boddengewässer to Usedom. From there we went west, heading for my cousin's estate outside Schwerin but when we got there, we discovered that she had moved to Lübeck, thinking it might be safer in the city. The Russians were over the Oder and no one knew where they would stop. When I found the great door locked, the house all shut up, I confess, I sat on the steps and wept. We got to our feet again to travel to Lübeck. But now I see her leaving, forcing us onwards, as a stroke of fortune. Schwerin is in the Russian Zone and here we are in the British Zone. The Russians were so intent on taking Berlin that the British reached here before they could. For that I am forever grateful.

Elisabeth leaned back in her chair, exhausted by her long telling. At first, Edith had wanted to ask questions: what had happened to the aged aunts, for example? But her questions lay scattered by the epic sweep of Elisabeth's story. Leo had been right when he'd said she would stay in her corner of Prussia, looking after her estates and her people, distant in every way from the Nazi regime. What greater proof could there be than this? What Elisabeth had done was heroic in the word's oldest, truest meaning. True to herself and her caste, she'd shown all the aristocratic virtues: courage, honour, obligation and responsibility, the other side of the golden coin of rank and privilege.

'What do you want from me, Edith?'

'I – I'm not sure what you mean . . .' Edith asked, shocked at this abrupt transition.

Elisabeth lit another cigarette. 'That boy, the Polish one.'

'Luka?'

'That's him. He's smart. All the kids here love him. He's a hero to them.' She stood up and began pacing. 'He holds you in high regard but he's a survivor, no moral sense whatsoever, and he's given to boasting.' She turned to Edith. 'He said you'd been looking all over Lübeck but he was the one who'd found me.' She stopped her pacing and looked down at Edith. 'I knew someone was looking. The girl who works in your billet, Magda, told me that someone from the Control Commission had been asking questions. At first, I was alarmed, but when she said it was a woman and gave a description, I knew it was you.'

'Why didn't you make contact? Send a message. Something . . .'

Elisabeth shrugged. 'I didn't know why you were searching. It doesn't do to draw attention, to be noticed. It was so under the Nazis and it's not very different now. You don't understand.

We are your playthings. You can do what you want with us. Like that odious little man with his truck and his soldiers. You have all the power.' She turned, looking down at Edith. 'So, why were you searching?'

'I was concerned. I wanted to know what had happened to you.' Edith spread her open hands towards Elisabeth. 'I thought you might be here, so many are from East Prussia. I knew you had a cousin who lived near, so there might be a chance . . .'

'I see,' Elisabeth looked off towards the window, hand cupped under her elbow, cigarette poised. 'Is it me you want. Or Kurt?'

'Kurt?'

'You have not asked about him.'

'So much has happened. There's been so much to say.' Edith found herself prevaricating. 'So much catching up to do.'

She was aware how weak that sounded. Elisabeth was clever. Intuitive. Much sharper than Kurt. She had the brains. She was seeing another side of Elisabeth now.

'So much that you do not ask about your former lover?' Elisabeth's eyed narrowed. 'The British are looking for him, aren't they?'

'They well might be,' Edith said vaguely.

'Oh, come on, Edith. You know they are. You've probably been sent to find out what you can. Isn't that the truth of it?'

Edith had no answer. Elisabeth had seen through.

'Well, yes.' She sighed. 'I won't deny it . . .' She paused to find what to say. 'But it's not all about finding Kurt. That's what Leo wants but I – I wanted to find you, too. To know that you were alive, that you'd survived.'

'The reason doesn't matter,' Elisabeth gave one of her rare smiles. 'I felt the same gladness at seeing you.' She stubbed her cigarette out and lit another. 'And I'm looking for Kurt, too. You do not ask what happened to Wolfgang, either. So, I will tell you.'

23

44 Möllnstraße, Lübeck

25th February 1946

```
B-Kost Diet: Eglfing-Haar
Minute quantities of vegetables
Fatless liquid
```

```
A diet devised to kill slowly. A recipe for
the most obscene cruelty.
```

'Life unworthy of life, was the term they used,' Elisabeth started. '*Lebensunwertes Leben*. The handicapped, the retarded, the mentally ill to be eliminated and discarded as *leere Menschenhülsen*, empty human shells, *menschliche* – ballast – no use to anyone. Useless mouths consuming resources needed by soldiers and workers to keep the nation strong. They started with the children. Did you know that? Starving them, killing them by lethal injection, then the adults. Thousands and thousands, hundreds of thousands. Asylums and Mental Hospitals, institutions built and designed for their treatment turned into killing factories, charnel houses with crematoria burning night and day.'

Edith had heard much of this from Leo but to hear it expressed this way, in a voice hollow with weary resignation at the ruthless, inhuman bureaucracy, that was something else again.

'Such a way of thinking is infinitely corrupting. Once it begins, where will it end? Who is exempted? The terminally sick, those injured in air raids, the elderly, the infirm made homeless, taking up hospital beds and scarce resources that could be used by the army? Soldiers suffering from war neurosis? What do you call it? Shell shock. No longer able to fight, so no longer useful. It is easier, quicker, to kill than to cure.

'All this was going on and we knew it. It was just another thing, among so many things, that one tried to ignore, to turn a blind eye. What could one do? Nothing. That's what we told ourselves. There weren't that many Jews in our area. When they disappeared, moved to the east to work, we half believed it. The Gypsies? They just didn't come any more. It is easy to compound a lie by lying to oneself. Easy to ignore the truth, until it arrives at your door.

'Kurt lied to me and I believed him. Or, rather, I didn't. I refused to see what was right in front of me. I just saw what I wanted to see; believed what I wanted to believe. The acceptable version of things. I lied to myself about that, about him, as well as everything else. I make no excuses. There can be no excuses. I was like the whole nation – blinded, led towards the abyss by a bunch of vicious madmen – and Kurt was one of them.'

'When we came to visit you, at Steinhof,' Edith interrupted. 'He was in the Party then?'

'He joined long before that. When he was a student.' She laughed. 'When you knew him. If you hadn't been so blinded by love, you'd have realized. But then, why would you? He was good at hiding what he didn't want people to know.'

'But you, you knew?'

'Of course. Kurt was very ambitious. Everything he did fell into a pattern. It was necessary to be in the Party. His early membership helped him get into the SS, a place at the Institute in Heidelberg, a position in Berlin. He didn't discuss the nature of his work and I didn't question him too closely. I had only the vaguest idea what he actually did. I was at Steinhof. I had the estate, my horses and my child.'

She walked to the window, gazing out as though still able to see her own lands, the formal grounds and the hills beyond, instead of the weed-choked garden in the ruins of a surburban street in a town she didn't know.

'Wolfgang grew normally, to start with, anyway, strong limbed, sturdy, tall for his age, blue eyed, fair haired, just like his father. The spitting image, isn't that what you say? Then he stopped talking. He seemed to go backwards, cutting himself off from the world, behaving like a much younger child. Kurt became increasingly concerned. He was disappointed. He wanted his son to be perfect. I just wanted him to be happy. Kurt talked about seeking treatment. I began to make enquiries. I knew Wolfgang was intelligent. He was good at puzzles. He could do a jigsaw faster than anyone. He liked to draw. Especially birds. He would watch them for hours, keeping perfectly still, so that they did not notice him, from his window, or in the garden, or down by the lake. The girls called him kleine Katze, he could stay as still as that. I'd heard of a doctor in Vienna who specialized in these kinds of children. A Dr Lehmann. Perhaps he could help Wolfie. When I told Kurt the name, he laughed. He won't be there any more, he said. He was Jewish.

'The war had started by then. Kurt was all the time in Berlin. He was involved in a new initiative that had come directly from the Führer himself. He wanted me with him. Wives should be with their husbands. It was expected. He knew of a specialist unit, where Wolfie would get the best of care, freeing me to go to Berlin. It would be better for everyone, he said.

'Katja and Irenka begged me not to let Wolfie go. They had heard rumours. About people being taken away and did not come back. But Kurt assured me that euthanasia was a mercy and anyway it applied only to the most hopeless cases, those with terribly painful, incurable diseases or who were dreadfully handicapped. It was done at the request of the relatives because in those circumstances, it was better for everyone, especially the

252

individual who was suffering so badly. Even then, several doctors had to agree and it was very rarely done. That is what he told me. None of that applied to my Wolfie. He was fit, healthy, handsome, well formed. He wasn't quite like other children, but neither was he mentally deficient. He was just – different.' She gave a shuddering sigh and stood, head bowed, lost in thought, prayer or memory. 'So I agreed.' She turned back to Edith, her eyes very bright. 'I'm sure you will I say I was wrong in this. Wrong and . . . and stupid.'

Edith shook her head, no. She refused to judge. Hindsight made it too easy. She had learnt to hold back her condemnation. She often found herself asking how we might have fared in a dark, distorting mirror world, ruled by fear and false ideas, where carers became killers, husbands betrayed wives, wives their husbands, children their parents, neighbours each other. She knew plenty who would have joined in without question, more who would have done nothing. She knew of very few who would have dared to do anything when faced with the threat of the Gestapo and the concentration camp.

'Kurt took him. He was six years. He'd just had a birthday. It was a fine day, late summer, a breath of Autumn in the air, the lindens just beginning to turn yellow against the blue sky. I made sure Wolfie was dressed up warmly in his best tweed coat, hat, scarf and mitts. He showed no emotion, but then, he never did. He did not like to be touched. Nevertheless, he let me kiss him. He reached up and wiped a tear from my face. "Why are your eyes leaking, Mummy?" That's what he said. He got into the car next to Kurt. We all waved until they had disappeared down the drive. That's the last time I saw him. He didn't look back.'

She broke off, arms tightly crossed, as if holding herself together. Edith let the silence stretch until Elisabeth was able to continue.

'Kurt . . . Kurt promised me that he would receive the best of care. The Director was a personal friend and a very fine doctor. He specialized in children of Wolfie's sort. I went to Berlin, attended receptions, parties, hosted dinners for Kurt's SS colleagues. The clinic was not far from Heidelberg. Kurt would visit when his work took him to the university there, so I had regular reports on Wolfie's progress. He's in good physical health, Kurt said, happy, being well looked after. It was coming up to Christmas; I asked if Wolfie could come to us in Berlin. Kurt said it was not advisable for Wolfie to travel so far. I asked if I could go to visit him with gifts: jigsaw puzzles, a paintbox, a new hat Irenka had knitted and a scarf and new mitts since he was always losing them. That was not advisable, either. Patients found such visits upsetting. It disrupted the routine, which was all important for the children's treatment. Kurt took the gifts himself on his next trip to Heidelberg. When he returned to Berlin, he told me about the carol singing on Wolfie's ward, the tree hung with Christmas treats and sweetmeats. Wolfie had had a fine old time, that's what he said. But it was all lies. When my son was supposed to be enjoying himself eating gingerbread and stollen, he was almost certainly already dead.'

Even though she had sensed that this was coming, Edith was shocked beyond words. Eventually, she broke the awful stillness that had grown in the cold, shabby room.

'How did you know?' she asked at last. 'What did you do?'

'In the New Year, I found a letter, dated before Christmas, saying that he had been moved to a new asylum in Hessen–Nassau. I thought that was odd. Kurt was away on Reich business, I couldn't talk to him. Or anyone else. Kurt made it very clear that it would not do to broadcast that there was anything wrong with our son.' She sighed again. 'I knew, I knew something was not right. I determined to go to the place, find Wolfgang. Take him home to Steinhof.'

Edith was about to speak but Elisabeth held up her hand. 'The next part is hard to tell, hard for me to even think about, but it is necessary for you to know. I must tell it in my own way, or I won't be able to say it at all.'

I set off immediately. I arrived in the evening and took a room in a hotel by the station. In the morning, when I asked about the asylum, the proprietor just pointed to a great red-brick edifice, crenellated and turreted, like a fortress set high on a hill above the Rhine, lowering over the pretty little town.

I set off up the hill towards it. There was a barrier across the entrance to the drive. A man came out of a small booth. He was armed, wearing some kind of uniform, more like a guard than an attendant.

'What do you want?'

'I'm here to see a patient.'

He pointed to a sign. Zutritt wegen Seuchengefahr strengstens verboten. *Entry strictly prohibited because of danger of infection. I didn't give a damn.*

'I'll take my chances – let me in.'

'Verboten!' he repeated, gripping his weapon more securely.

We might have gone on arguing but a car drew up, a Sport-kabriolett with the top down, despite the coldness of the day. The driver wore an SS uniform. He leaned out of his window.

'What's the problem here?'

'My child is inside and I must see him. I don't care about the infection.' He looked me up and down and then opened the passenger door.

'Raise the barrier!' he ordered and we were in.

His name was Dieter Brauer. Quite young, thirty or so. He was a doctor there but today was his last day. He'd come back from Christmas leave to find that he had been reassigned to the army, something that did not make him happy. I think that this is why he invited me in that day. He said that they rarely received visitors, certainly not beautiful women dressed in sable. His manner was extremely flirtatious, so maybe that was another reason.

He drove up a long drive past a line of buses, their windows covered in canvas. We got out of the car at the front of the building. He invited me to admire the view over the town and down to the Rhine. On a clear day, you could see all the way to Mainz, he said. It was not a clear day. A group of men worked below us, clearing snow. Very poorly dressed for such weather, in rags really, wooden clogs on bare feet. They moved slowly, like men in a dream. Thin, undernourished, they looked as if a sudden, strong wind would blow them away. Some of the patients, he said. Inmates, ones who could make themselves useful. What about the rest? I asked. He shrugged and looked back down the drive towards the buses. Not so many of those left now.

He'd been drinking. I smelt schnapps on his breath. He said he knew my husband. He took out a silver hip flask, offered it to me. I refused. He raised it to his lips. Prost! Then he asked when Wolfgang had been sent here and from where. When I told him, he made no comment, just said that we would go to the Children's Ward to look for my son.

The Children's Ward was some way from the main building, up on a hill by itself. It looked more like a shed, or a chalet, a temporary place. There was a balcony with a few toys scattered about: a striped ball, blue and red, some building bricks, a painted engine, a wooden tricycle. The paint on them was faded, cracked and flaked; they were frozen to the boards and looked as though they had been there all winter. What I remember most was the silence. Where children are, there is always noise, but here there was nothing, not even crying. And the smell. A cloying stench of disinfectant masking something sweetish and unpleasant. As we went in, the smell grew stronger.

We entered a small foyer with rooms off it. It was nearly as cold in there as it was outside. Double doors opened onto a ward. He threw the doors wide. We were there only for a few seconds. Sometimes, that's all you need, a fraction of that even, to see everything. The ward contained perhaps fifty beds, maybe more, placed close together, either side of a wide aisle. I say beds, but they were more like cots, or coffins, high-sided wooden boxes. Each one contained a child. The children were emaciated, some naked, or with the barest of coverings. Some were bluish grey; others yellowish white, like the skeletal effigies you sometimes see in churches. The only sound was the squeak of the nurses' shoes on the polished wooden floor. Here and there liquid eyes stared out of tiny, shrivelled faces. That was the only indication that we were not in a morgue.

The nearest nurse turned at the opening of the doors, seriously alarmed at our presence. She came towards us, arms out wide to block our view. Others came, rushing from different corners of the ward, physically barring us from entering, ushering us back, into the entrance hall. The Sister sent the others back to their charges. She wanted to know what we were doing there, what I was doing there, what was Dr Brauer thinking of, bringing a member of the public to the ward? Dr Eckhart would know about this. Brauer replied that I had come in search of my son. The von Stavenow child. Her face became a mask of false sympathy and solicitude. 'I'm sorry to have to tell you,' she said, 'but your son passed away soon after his arrival here of pneumonia and cardiac insufficiency.' A singsong recitation, no thought behind it, just a rush of words, running into each other. Pneumonia. Yes. I could understand, but cardiac insufficiency? What did that mean? When he left me, my son was strong. Healthy. He'd never shown the least sign of a heart condition. Not the least sign! 'It is something common to patients suffering from his particular affliction,' she replied, in the same sing song. 'Incurable.' She said that with triumph on her pale, fleshy face then she watched me with a kind of pitying curiosity, her dark-brown eyes as shiny as buttons. It was as if all natural human feeling had been switched off in her.

When did this happen? I demanded. Why hadn't I been informed immediately? Not long after he arrived. When would that have been? Before Christmas. Her tone was edging towards impatience. Your husband was informed. If I had no more questions, there was work to do. Brauer offered me his hip flask. This time I did not refuse.

How could it happen so quickly? 'Once they get here,' Brauer replied, 'they don't last long. They starve them. Here we follow the B-Kost, the diet developed by Pfannmüller at Eglfing-Haar. No protein, no fat. If that doesn't carry them off, they will give them something: luminal, veronal, sulfonal, trional, morphine.

Not enough to kill, just enough so they die of something else – pneumonia in winter. In summer, diarrhoea.' But why? Why would they do that? Because they don't want to lie on the death certificate. If a patient died as a result of drugs administered, it would constitute murder. What happens here is no longer under the Führer's direct order. Murder is still a crime under German law. Where is he? Where's my son? Where's his grave? I had some idea to take him home. Bury him in the family chapel. Brauer laughed. He would have been buried in a paper coffin in an unmarked grave with other children who died that day. His brain removed, along with other organs, harvested is the word they used, preserved in formalin, shipped in special containers to Schneider at Heidelberg, or to Richter in Berlin, for dissection and study. Then he will have served the Reich in some way. I had to ask him to stop the car.

I vomited at the side of the road.

Edith had listened without interruption. 'Why did he tell you all this?' she asked now. 'Exposing you to these, these *horrors*? Do you think that he disapproved?'

Elisabeth took a cigarette. Edith had to help her light it.

'Oh,' she exhaled slowly. 'There was more. He was quite reckless in his revelations. What was happening here was nothing compared to the east. Special camps designed to kill millions using the techniques they'd learnt killing the cripples. His words, not mine. Jews, of course. All organized from Kurt's office on Tiergartenstraße. I had absolutely no idea what went on there. It was just "the office". Brauer had no qualms about the work. He wanted to be reassigned there, not sent to the Eastern Front. He was bitter about that. It was the winter of 1942/1943. Things were beginning to go against us. He probably saw his reassignment as a death sentence. He was jealous. Of Kurt. Telling me this was a way to get back at him. Kurt was progressing in his career while Brauer had been written off. He wanted me to go with him for a drink, dinner. I told him to take me to the station. He looked disappointed. My seduction would have been his crowning satisfaction. To think that was even remotely possible! These people!' She shook her head, loathing clear on her face. 'It was as if they lived in a different world, completely devoid of any kind of normal human feeling and Kurt was one of them. I remember thinking that on the train. He is one of them. I went straight to Steinhof. I haven't seen Kurt since.'

She finished speaking and there was silence between them. Edith had been absolutely caught in the spell of the story. There was nothing she could say. Every word faded, discarded as wanting, inadequate. It was one thing to be briefed by Leo in London but the repressed agony apparent in Elisabeth's testimony, and it *was* a testimony, brought into graphic focus the monstrous, warped depravity of this obscene 'Project'.

Elisabeth sank into the chair next to her, eyes closed. Edith could feel her exhaustion, see it in the slump of her shoulders, hear in her shallow breathing how much it had cost to hold herself together long enough to tell that story.

'It was hard, very hard for me to tell you all that but I wanted you to know exactly what kind of man Kurt had become.' Her eyes opened and fixed on Edith. 'You are the only one who can help me find him and I want him found and I want him punished. Hanged, preferably. The child is Kaspar's daughter. I was robbed of one child. Now I have her. I want to be free to marry her father. To live the normal life of which I was deprived,' she gave a fleeting, tired smile. 'If such a thing is possible in these difficult times.'

24

Atlantic Hotel, Hamburg

2nd March 1946

```
Menu Américaine
Potage de Jour
Jambon De Virginie
Petits pois au Beurre
Pommes Croquettes
Coup Maison
Fromage
Café
```

In the British Zone, but American Menu. My
dining companion enjoyed the ham, similar to
the first time I was here, but Baked this
time. Recipe to follow.

'*Es schneit.*' Frau Schmidt said it with a certain amount of
satisfaction.

Edith looked up. Outside, the pewter-grey sky had a yellowish,
sickly tinge to it and the snow was already flying.

'I can see that.' She went back to peeling her egg. Frau Schmidt
always hard boiled them.

Frau Schmidt's grape-coloured eyes were shining and sly. She knew that Edith had been planning a trip to Hamburg, how much she'd been looking forward to it.

'How is the ankle?' she tried another tack.

'Much better.' Edith smeared margarine across her toast. 'Thank you for asking.'

'Maybe you should not go. With ankle and now snow.'

'Thank you for your concern, Frau Schmidt, but I see no reason to change my plans.'

Edith bit into her toast. It had been a week since she'd seen her but Elisabeth's story was still fresh in her mind and still as shocking. She'd been back, taking supplies for her household, help of a practical kind. They didn't talk further about Kurt and what he'd done, it would be too painful, but they both wanted to find him and they both wanted him punished. Their interests were aligned.

'I'm sorry?' Edith's thoughts were interrupted by one of Frau Schmidt's heavy sighs.

'I said I prepare packed lunch in case you are stuck in snow.'

'Thank you, Frau Schmidt,' Edith wiped her mouth and folded her napkin. 'That would be very kind. Now I really must get ready.'

She was determined to get to Hamburg, first to meet Harry and second to get out of Lübeck. She'd been nowhere else since she got here. An afternoon at Travemünde hardly counted. It had been touch and go. First, her ankle. Now this cold sweeping down from the Arctic bringing everything to a standstill.

'It ain't that bad,' Jack shook the flakes off his cap. 'It'll tack up, you see if it don't.'

He wanted to get to Hamburg just as much as Edith. He was taking Kay to a little hotel at Blankenese and a bit of weather was not going to stop him.

The heating in the Humber was temperamental. Jack drove in his greatcoat. Edith sat with a blanket over her knees. There were more in the back in case of emergencies and two Thermos flasks of whisky-laced tea.

'We'll get there, don't worry,' Jack said as he peered through the windscreen, the wipers groaning as they tried to cope with the driving snow. 'It'll be fine once we reached the *Autobahn*. I were wondering – did you find out anything about them photographs?'

'I did, as a matter of fact. I showed them to – someone I know. He's Latvian. He was able to identify Jansons. He was in some kind of Auxiliary force helping the SS.'

'What were going on in the background? Did he say?'

'Yes.' She looked over to Jack. 'A massacre somewhere in Latvia. Jews being shot then pushed into trenches. You were right. Those were sand dunes.'

'Bloody hell! I thought it was something—'

The car skidded on the ramp onto the *Autobahn*, Jack just managed to right it before they ploughed into a drift. 'Blimey! The Humber is fucking useless in these kinds of conditions, 'scuse my French. Need chains on the wheels. I keep telling them.'

The *Autobahn* was two-thirds covered. There was no more talking. Jack had to use all his driving skill to prevent them joining the already snow-covered vehicles that had been abandoned all over the road.

The snow eased as they entered the city. A thick, white blanket covered everything, accentuating the silence, adding to the sense of desolation.

Jack dropped her off outside the Atlantic. Edith checked in and went to her room. She'd hardly taken off her coat before the telephone rang.

'Fräulein Graham? I have a message. Your friends are waiting in the bar.'

What friends? Friends plural. Edith changed quickly and went downstairs.

The bar of the Atlantic overlooked the Außenalster. A long, high-ceilinged room with white-jacketed waiters gliding about, bearing trays of drinks to mostly men, in uniform and out of it, occupying deep, comfortable chairs.

Adeline was sitting with Tom McHale, drinking a martini. They both looked very glamorous. He was in blue Mess uniform and she was wearing a low-cut evening dress. The scarlet silk flattered her pale skin and her lipstick matched. Her hair framed her face in soft waves and curls.

Tom rose as Edith approached their table. Edith was struck again by his apparent youth: the wide-set blue eyes, slightly sulky mouth, fresh complexion and smooth cheeks, as if he didn't need to shave. 'Don't let those baby-faced looks fool ya,' she remembered Adeline saying. 'He's a killer over and over. Plus he's older than he looks.'

'Edith.'

'Tom.'

'Drink?'

'Yes, please. I'll have a martini. Thanks.'

'Martinis for the ladies,' Tom said to the waiter who had glided in their direction. 'I have to leave you. See you later, Edith.' He looked at his watch. 'Leaving at eight, Adie.'

He joined a group of British Officers at the bar. Army, Navy and Air Force – all the Services represented in their dress uniforms.

'This is not entirely coincidental,' Adeline looked over at Tom. 'He knew you were coming.'

'How?'

'He knows everything.' Adeline lit a cigarette. 'He's like the goddamn all-seeing eye on the dollar bill.'

'What does he want?'

'Usually, he wants information but this time, he wants me to issue a warning. He's heard you've been taking an interest in a certain Latvian individual, goes by the name of Valdemārs Jansons? Friends call him Val?'

Edith frowned. 'How does he know that?'

'He knows everything, like I told you.'

Edith glanced over to Tom watching them, his cold gaze was making her uneasy. 'Why doesn't he ask me himself?'

'It's not his way. He wants me to find out what you know.'

'I don't know anything beyond the fact that this Jansons has got some kind of relationship with a girl in the billet I'm sharing. What about him?'

'Look, I don't know. I'm just the messenger. Tell Leo or whoever's your contact to back away. This guy is ours. We have an interest. He wants you to pass that on up the line.'

'What kind of interest, do you know?'

Adeline shrugged. 'These ex-Nazi thugs have their uses. It's not what they know, it's who they know that matters. He also wants to know if you have anything on von Stavenow.'

Edith paused.

'Come on, Edith.' Adeline's eyes flickered towards Tom. 'I have to give him something.'

'I might have.' Edith sighed. 'I've made contact with his wife, Elisabeth.'

'That should keep me off a plane to the States, for a while at least. Just until I can wriggle out from under . . . You know what? I really need to powder my nose.' She stood up and nodded towards the cloakroom to let Tom know where they were going. 'Don't you want to freshen up, in case Harry arrives?'

Edith smiled as she joined her. 'You know, I think I do.'

'I'm not proud of this. Just the opposite,' Adeline said once they were safely in the ladies'.

'I'd always help you, you know that.'

'I know,' Adeline hugged her for a moment, 'and I love you for it. I won't forget this and I feel one good turn deserves another.' Adeline smiled. 'Can't let Tom have it all the way he wants it.' She turned to the mirror. 'Know what else the Nazis were good at, besides killing people? Keeping records.' She opened her evening bag and found her lipstick and began to apply it. 'We've found 750 tons and that's just so far: files, photographs, I don't know what all. I'm going to start digging on your behalf. It's not so hard when you've got a name and there can't be that many von Stavenows. Dab of powder and I'm all set.' She examined herself critically. 'Dori would be proud.'

She looked at Edith in the mirror. 'Have you heard from her at all? How's the cookbook code going?'

'I haven't heard from her directly but the code works.'

The message she'd sent about the Latvians had got through to Harry Hirsch; that was proof enough, but she was reluctant to tell Adeline. It might compromise her with McHale and she didn't want that.

Adeline seemed to know what she was thinking. 'Yes, best not to. We better skedaddle or he'll come looking for me.'

'What? In here?'

Adeline laughed, 'I wouldn't put it past him.'

There was a message at the front desk. Harry had arrived. Edith called him to see if he wanted to meet her in the bar.

'No, I'll come to your room.'

Edith opened the door at his first knock.

'Harry? I'm so glad to see you!' She put her arms round him and pulled him into the room.

He held her tight for a moment then kissed her. 'I'm glad to see you, too.'

'How long have you been here?'

'A little while. I saw you in the bar, talking to a woman. You seemed deep in conversation, I didn't like to interrupt.'

'That was Adeline.'

'Really? I didn't recognize her.'

'She looks different when she's all dressed up.'

'Was that McHale I saw, too?'

'Yes. He's here for some meeting or other. They're going to a swanky reception tonight. Do you want something to drink? I've got some whisky. Or do you want to go down? We could have dinner.' Edith picked up a menu. 'Ham or chicken.'

Harry made a face. 'I'd rather stay here.'

'I've got some sandwiches if you're hungry. Corned beef or cheese and onion.'

'Had enough of those in the army.' Harry smiled. 'Whisky will do fine.'

Edith poured two liberal measures and they sat in the chairs by the window. The curtains were still open. She stared out past their reflections into the blackness of the night.

'Adeline is acting as Tom's proxy,' Edith said after a while. 'Passing on messages. Warnings really. Like hands off our Latvian pal Valdis. I have to tell Bill Adams. He's my contact.'

Harry looked shocked. 'Why would she do that? I thought she was on our side.'

'Because if she doesn't, he'll send her back to the States.'

'He can do that?'

'Apparently.' She turned to him. 'Being here, at Nuremberg, at the centre of things, it's everything to her. And I think she is, really. On our side, I mean.' Edith paused. 'Seems both the British and Americans are interested in him, I'm guessing for different reasons, but neither seem to show the slightest intention of bringing him to justice for the crimes he committed in Latvia.' She sighed. 'It's like you said.'

'Now Latvia is occupied by the Soviets, it's a case of my enemy's enemy is my friend. We are finding this more and more . . .'

'We? Who's we?'

'A group of comrades. Like-minded people who don't like what they are seeing and are doing something about it.'

'Bill Adams said that they want this Jansons to go back into Latvia, organize resistance.'

'They wouldn't last five minutes.' Harry gave a mirthless laugh. 'That's so stupid, it's almost a good idea.'

'Why would the Americans want him?'

'My guess is that he was a double agent. Working for the Germans, spying for the Soviets, or the other way around. Whichever case, he would have contacts, maybe a network he could reactivate. Who knows?' He frowned. 'The British are already looking to use his boss Viktors Arājs in this way. It's all crazy. This new world we live in is nearly as crazy as the old. Is that all, the warning about Jansons?'

'Yes, more or less.' She didn't want to have to explain to Harry about Kurt. His involvement in the Euthanasia Project. Elisabeth's story was disturbing beyond measure and she just couldn't talk about it now. 'It's been a long day.' She tried to smile. 'Can we talk about something else, please?'

'Enough talk, then.' He put down his glass. 'Come here.'

She went into the release of his embrace. He kissed her gently, and then more fiercely as he guided her to the bed. He reached to undo her stockings, to undress her, slowly and with much care, like he had done before in the way that they'd both found so exciting. They were finding a way to be together, what each other liked, she thought with something like wonder. She angled her foot to make it easier for him to remove her stocking. The movement made her wince.

'I'm sorry. Did I hurt you?' He touched her ankle. The bruising was fading but the skin was still discoloured. 'What is this, are you injured?'

'It's nothing. An accident. It's much better now.'

'I see I must be gentle,' he touched her foot. 'You must tell me what happened.'

'Afterwards,' she said.

Later, as he smoked a cigarette, she told him about the accident, how she limped home with Luka as her unlikely saviour. She thought to make light of it, not wanting to bring the darkness back in again.

'The boy is right.' He stubbed out his cigarette. 'They are no good.'

He reached down, brushing the bruising with his fingers. Then he kissed the hollow on the inside of her ankle, then her knee, working his way up with aching slowness until she forgot about Luka, no-good DPs, meddling Americans. About anything at all.

Edith woke alone. She took Atlantic Hotel notepaper and wrote a quick note to Dori reporting on her meeting with Adeline and Tom's interest in Jansons. She'd already sent *Wild Boar Steinhof* a few days previously, her meeting with Elisabeth. She popped in last night's menu and sealed the envelope as Harry came back in his greatcoat.

'Where have you been?'

'I had to make a phone call.'

'You could have done it from here.'

He shrugged. 'I didn't want to disturb you. Come on. Let's go out. Walk by the Außenalster. A little way at least. There's bound to be somewhere we can find coffee, breakfast. It's a lovely day.'

He drew back the curtain. The sky was blue, the sun shining. There were already people out walking by the frozen lake.

On their way out, Edith dropped the letter at the desk for posting.

The steps were clear, the snow piled in big heaps. The wind had swept the walkway but the path was black with ice, they both slipped and slid, laughing holding onto each other. After weeks of dull and sullen cloud, the sky was lapis blue, the sun bright and white with just a hint of warmth in it. A sign that spring was coming. Here and there, trees showed the first dusting of blossom, delicate sepia against the china white of the snow.

They stopped at the small café Edith had found when she first came to Hamburg. The windows steamed, the interior cloudy with smoke. They breakfasted on white rolls, cherry jam and thin slices of cheese.

'What do you plan to do after?' he asked as he sipped his coffee.

'After what? After this? I don't know. I've only just got here.'

It was odd, they'd been to bed, made love, but now they were having one of those conversations, common out here, talking about what they did before, what they would do after, hardly ever what they were doing now. It was like the war. People talked about before, or after. A lovely day tomorrow.

'Will you go back to teaching?' he asked.

'No, I can't go back to my life as it was before. I came here to get away from it.' She looked around the café, at the platters of biscuits, cakes on their little stands. 'Actually, I do know what I want to do.'

The idea came fully formed, so strong that she knew it was true.

'Oh, what's that?' He smiled at her sudden certainty.

'I'm going to be a cookery writer. In fact,' she smiled, 'I've already started. I'm going to make a career of it. How about you? Will you stay on here?'

He shrugged. 'This is only temporary. A delay to my demobilization.'

'What will you do then?'

I don't know.' He stirred his coffee. 'Like you, I can't go back.' There was a bitter edge to his laugh. 'Unlike you, I have nowhere to go back to. My country doesn't exist anymore. To the British, I'm a foreigner: no matter what I do, I'll never fit in, never be entirely trusted. It's the same with Dori. Her war service was second to none. One of SOE's best operatives, no one to equal her courage and loyalty, but she was turned off as soon as her usefulness was over.'

'She's working with Vera now.'

'For how long? Vera's in the same boat. Six months, a year at most. After that, they'll both be out of a job. Female and foreign. Intelligence will go back to relying on its own kind, upper-class Englishmen who went to the right schools. I'm even more suspect. A foreign Jew with a history of Anti-Fascism. Which now means Communist. Strictly limited usefulness.' He sighed. 'My brother is in Palestine. I expect I'll join him.'

'You intend to live there?'

'Yes. The Jews need a homeland. Somewhere they belong. Everywhere they are stateless, homeless. The ones who've survived can't go back, can they? There is nowhere left for them to go to. They need somewhere of their own now. I feel that, too.'

'But Palestine is a British Protectorate.'

'So what?' He shook his head impatiently. 'They've got enough on their hands, here, at home, in the rest of the Empire.

It will happen.' He leaned forward, his dark eyes suddenly intense. 'It is already happening. They can't stop us. Refugees are already making their way there, a trickle now, but it will turn into a flood that they won't be able to stem. And we'll fight if necessary. We've learnt how to do that.' He sat back, arms folded. 'Courtesy of the Allied Armies.'

'Why aren't you there now, if you feel this passionately?'

'Because I've got things to do here. How do you think that these refugees, penniless, weakened by everything that has happened to them, is still happening to them, how do you think they are managing to get all the way to Palestine?'

'You're helping them?'

'We call it *Brihah*. It means flight, escape.' He lit a cigarette and looked at her through the veiling smoke. 'Can I trust you, Edith? What I'm about to say, you must tell to no one. You have to promise.'

'Of course, I promise.'

'This that you wear round your neck,' he leaned forward and caught the medallion, studying the scarred face of the Black Madonna. 'It's special to you?'

'Yes. Dori gave it to me.'

'And Dori trusts you?'

'Well, yes . . .'

'You wouldn't break her trust, would you?'

'No,' Edith shook her head. 'Not for anything.'

He took her hand, closing her fingers round the icon. 'Then swear on it.'

His fist around hers, the icon biting into her palm. She held his dark gaze. No words needed to be spoken. They had not known each other long but, out here, it was as if the war had never ended. Friendships, love even, could blossom quickly under the stress of leaving, separation, and the terrible gnawing fear that tomorrow would never come.

'I swear.'

'Very well,' he released her hand. 'After I got to Britain,' he said, 'I joined up as soon as I could. I was sent with the Eighth

Army to Egypt. I met Chaim again there. He was in the Jewish Brigade. I asked to be transferred and stayed with them all the way through Italy. We swore an oath to help any Jews we found. I'm still bound by that oath, and others besides. When the war was over, Chaim went to Palestine. He won't come back. Europe is too full of ghosts, he says. All of them accusing. He's in Haganah now, resisting the British, fighting for a Jewish State.'

'Why didn't you go with him?'

'There's a group of us, Brigade members. We call ourselves *Tilhas Tizig Gesheften*. It roughly translates as *up your arse business*. We aren't ready to leave just yet. There is work to do here.'

'Like getting Jews to Palestine?'

'That kind of thing.' He stubbed out his cigarette. 'I've told you more than I should have done already.'

'I'd never betray you. You must know that.'

'I'm sure you wouldn't, Edith, but the less you know the better. What do you intend to do this afternoon? I was thinking we might go to Blankenese. Have lunch there. I hear the restaurants are pretty good.'

'Oh, I've promised to visit someone.' Edith thought for a moment. 'Perhaps you'd like to come with me? We could have dinner afterwards. Would you wear your uniform?'

'Why?'

She smiled. 'You'll see.'

25

Sanatorium Langenhorn, Hamburg

3rd March 1946

*Breakfast menu served to convalescing
patients*
Ersatz coffee with 2 grammes sugar
3 grammes butter/margarine
2 grammes cheese
2 grammes human hair
slice bread
Amounts approximate

The inverse of the B-Kost Diet: Eglfing-Haar,
designed to nourish, rather than starve,
nevertheless still manages to be profoundly
unpleasant.

Under Invalid Cookery? Although it rather
breaks Rule no. 2.

Edith had arranged for Jack to pick her up. He was waiting in
the lobby. She introduced Harry.

'How do. Car's this way.'

Harry took the front seat.

'Jewish Brigade, eh?' Jack looked across at the flash on his shoulder.

'Yes, that's right. I was in the regular army, transferred when we got to Egypt.'

'I were there, too,' Jack said as they pulled away. 'LRDG. Long Range Desert Group. Bloody great it was.'

'In Italy, too?'

'Even hairier there. I was in the SAS by then. Remember your mob. Fought like demons up around Faenza. I left some good pals on a hillside there.'

'Me, too,' Harry said and they were both quiet for a while but the silence was companionable, the shared experience of loss and battle serving to draw the two men together.

Edith sat in the back, glad that they had discovered their own bond. It felt a bit like introducing a new boyfriend to a favourite brother. Jack was quick to judge and would not be budged once he'd made up his mind. She'd noticed his appraising look when she introduced him to Harry and noted the little fish-hooks threaded into his seemingly innocent opening questions. For all Jack's apparent Black Country bluffness, he was shrewd and subtle. Not to be underestimated. She tuned back into their conversation, to find that the mood had lightened. They were talking about brothels now, Jack recounting one of his stories.

'There was this whore in Naples. Only had one peg. In great demand, she was. Amazing what she could do. She'd unstrap the false un and . . .'

Time for Edith to tune out again. She'd heard that one before, anyway. When she started listening again, Jack had moved on to another cherished topic.

'The Russkies and all that raping they done, I reckon it's because the Jerries weren't grateful, see? Everywhere *we* went, the bints was chucking themselves at us. No need to rape no one.'

'It could also be because the Russians wanted revenge,' Harry countered. 'For all the things done to them when the Germans invaded their country.'

'There is that,' Jack conceded. 'And the Ivans got fuck all to trade. We always had summat – fags and that. When we got to Italy, there was this little town, practically the first place we come to, they was lining up with their shopping bags.'

'That's nothing to be proud of, Jack,' Edith interjected.

'Mebbe not but you can't stop it. War is war. Chaps is chaps.'

Jack's salty language and outré stance wouldn't be acceptable among some people but he was an unflinching and ferocious realist. Edith had to admire him for that. He lived by his own rules and had his own moral code, which was not always easy to read. He could be exceptionally kind to those he felt deserving of help. Everybody else? Watch out . . .

He'd been to see Seraphina and Anna several times, to take them things they might need, to make sure that they were all right. He had also been instrumental in getting penicillin to the hospital. Edith didn't know how he managed that. Didn't want to know. It also served as a reason to see his wench, as he called her, Sister Warren. There had to be something in it for Jack. That was one of his rules.

Anna had been moved to a sanatorium: a large brick-built house with various annexes set in its own grounds. They drove up a long, snaking drive between snow-covered lawns blindingly bright in the intense sunlight. Patients were lined up inside glittering, glass-covered verandahs; the front and sides open to the elements. Fresh air was seen as beneficial, as long as patients were kept wrapped up and warm. Much the same thing happened in Britain. Edith remembered a school friend who had developed TB and been sent to a place in North Wales where patients slept out of doors.

Edith was glad to see how well Anna looked, with colour in her cheeks, flesh on her bones, a brightness in her eyes. Seraphina looked better too, less thin and careworn, like a girl again, one with a future, a life ahead of her. She was sitting on Anna's bed and came to greet them, smiling and happy. When she saw Harry, she drew back a little. She was still shy of strangers.

Harry smiled. '*Shalom*.'

'You are Jewish and a soldier?'

Seraphina reached out towards the Jewish Brigade Star of David flash he wore on his shoulder, her dark eyes wide with wonder, as if she could not quite believe that he was real.

Harry laughed. 'Yes, I am.'

She stared at him, her eyes brimming, the tears not quite spilling. She laughed then and turned away, dabbing with a handkerchief.

'I'm sorry. It is silly of me. It's just—' she shook her head, unable to find words for what she was feeling. 'Come. You must meet Anna. She will not believe such a thing is possible.'

She led him to her sister's bed. Soon all three of them were chattering away in Yiddish.

'Getting on like a house on fire,' Jack commented. 'Harry seems to be just what the doctor ordered.'

'Yes, aren't they just. We'll leave them to it. Anna seems much better. I'm going to find the doctor in charge, ask about her progress.'

She left the ward and started off towards the main entrance and the Director's Office. She followed the signs down a long corridor with pale-green walls and black and white tiles. Nearly at the end of it, she faltered.

She saw him standing in the centre of an intersection. Corridors led off in different directions, like the spokes of a wheel. He'd stopped, as though recalling something hitherto forgotten. He was the right height, in a doctor's white coat, stethoscope round his neck like a collar. He must have been under a skylight, illuminated from above by the strong white, Nordic light. As he looked down at the files he was carrying, the sun picked out the gold in his hair, cut shorter than she remembered, the sides razored.

It was Kurt. She was sure.

All this in the time it took between one step and another. In the next second, he was gone. She saw the flick of a white coat disappearing and set off after it. She was nearly at the foyer when she collided with Harry.

'Did you see a doctor? Tall, blond. He came this way.'

'No, I—'

At that moment, he reappeared. It was clearly not Kurt.

'Doesn't matter.' Edith didn't know whether to be relieved or disappointed.

'Anna's resting.' Harry laughed. 'The nurses threw me out. See you outside?'

'I still have to see the Director.' Edith looked at her watch. 'Shouldn't be long.'

'*Gnädige Frau*, what an honour. Do sit.'

The Director settled his small hands over his ample stomach, eyes blinking rapidly behind rimless glasses. Edith hardly heard his litany of problems and complaints. She was too busy thinking about what she would have done if it had been Kurt in that corridor.

'Food is a difficulty,' he was saying, 'patients won't recover without good nutrition. To that end, they are taking part in an experiment . . .'

Edith looked up. Hadn't they had enough of those already?

He went to a shelf, took down a tin box and opened it with something of a flourish. She thought he was going to offer her a biscuit but it contained lengths of human hair, dark, blonde, reddish, coarse and fine, all combed and washed like hanks of wool. She swallowed hard.

'The hair is collected, sterilized, cut up small and nutrients extracted through special processes . . .' he explained, passing a plump hand over his own shining pate.

Edith stared at the dead hanks of hair. There was something vile, repulsive about the whole thing. Didn't they collect hair in the concentration camps? She looked away.

'The end result tastes like fishpaste. Would you like to try?'

She shook her head. 'I'll take your word for it.'

'I have a diet sheet here if you'd like to see it?'

'Thank you, Herr Doktor.' She took it from him and stood up, keen to get away. 'I won't keep you any longer.'

'I will escort you to your car.'

Harry and Jack were on the steps, smoking. They threw away their cigarettes and fell in behind her.

Across the car park, a building stood at some distance from the main complex. Tall, red-brick, with a large blackened chimney at the rear of it, the windows boarded. There was a gaunt, neglected air about it. Dr Beckenbauer had complained about overcrowding; it seemed odd to see this building empty. Perhaps it had been damaged in the bombing, but Edith could see no evidence . . .

'What's that?' Edith asked.

'A facility for mental patients,' Dr Beckenbauer replied. 'No longer used.' He offered no more information. 'Sirs, Madam.'

He acknowledged each of them with a quick bow before hurrying back inside.

26

Fischhaus Restaurant, Blankenese, Hamburg

3rd March 1946

Menu
Aalsuppe
Matjes – marinierter Hering –
Pickled Herrings
Schwarzbrot
Smoked Eel - Räucheraal
Kartoffelsalat – Potato Salad
Holsten Beer
Ice-cold Schnaps Berentzen Doornkaat

Very much a Baltic menu, eel, herring in
various guises, washed down with schnapps
and beer. My male dining companions stuck
to the herring and schnapps. One because
eels aren't kosher, the other because the
skin is black.

Edith would ask Roz to check Beckenbauer's *Fragebogen*. There'd been something unsavoury about him and it wasn't just his peculiar recipe.

'What's going to happen to the two girls when they get out of there?' Jack asked. 'DP camp?'

'Not if I can help it.' Harry stared back at the hospital as they drove away. 'They've had enough of that.'

'I'll find them somewhere,' Edith said. 'Don't worry.'

She and Roz had been talking about moving out of their respective billets, Roz declaring that she couldn't bear sharing a bathroom for another minute. Edith knew the feeling. She was tired of communal living and her room had been searched again, despite her warning. Fresh scratch marks on the brass plate of her writing slope, as though someone had been at the lock with a hairpin. Once she and Roz had their own place, the girls could stay with them, for a while at least, but what about the longer term?

'What do *they* want, do you think?' Edith asked. 'We're always deciding things for people but what do they want to do?'

'They want to go back to Czechoslovakia,' Harry answered.

'That's natural, I suppose,' Edith said. Even after everything that's happened, perhaps especially after everything that's happened, they would want to go back to what they knew. To the world they remembered. A world that wasn't there any more. 'The trouble is, it won't be like that, will it?'

'No. It won't.' Harry stared out of the window. 'It's common. We come across it frequently. They know it's all gone but a part of them secretly believes that it's still there somewhere, waiting. They're worried no one will know where they are if they don't go back and they want to find what's left of their family. It sounds brutal but there really is no point. In all likelihood, there *is* no family. They'll find nothing. All they'll encounter is hostility. Their homes will have been taken over. If they ask for news of their family, their old neighbours will just laugh and point up at the sky. That's the best that can happen. I've heard reports of new pogroms: Jews, survivors, going home and being attacked, murdered, beaten to death.'

'So? What's to be done with them?' Jack asked.

Harry did not respond. Edith knew what he was thinking: *Tilhas Tizig Gesheften. Up your arse business.* The girls would be taken care of.

They were nearing Blankenese. Edith suggested Jack went to get Kay. They could have dinner together.

'What happened back there?' Harry asked as the waiter brought schnapps.

'What do you mean?'

'At the clinic.' He twiddled a toothpick between his fingers. 'Why were you haring after that chap?'

'I thought I recognized him. He looked a bit like someone I knew before the war.'

'The chap you knew was a doctor?

Edith nodded. 'His name is Kurt von Stavenow.'

Harry looked at her closely. 'Was that a coincidence or are you looking for him?'

'The latter.'

'Is he wanted, this von Stavenow?'

Edith nodded again. She'd wanted to talk to Harry about him, about what she'd been tasked to do, but there had never been the right time, the right occasion.

'Nazi doctors did some very bad things . . .' he said, the disgust on his face belying his understatement.

'Didn't they?' Edith sighed. For no clear reason, she had tears in her eyes. 'Didn't they just.'

A slight frown, a quirking between his brows, a quizzical look in his dark eyes. He knew there was more. She didn't want to tell him about Kurt. About any of it. Not yet. Not now. Edith drank her schnapps in one. The cold, clear liquid shuddered through her, tasting like surgical spirit but giving her the lift she needed. She looked up, relieved to see Jack and Kay coming through the door.

Kay looked different out of uniform. Much younger and very

attractive. She was wearing lipstick and her short nails were painted red. With her high colour, good cheekbones, full mouth and dark wavy hair there was a little of the Joan Crawford about her. No wonder Jack was smitten.

'Jack says you went to the sanatorium to see Anna and Seraphina,' she said. 'I've been up there once or twice, keeping an eye on them.'

'The doctor in charge is a bit of an odd character,' Edith smiled. 'He was explaining his hair diet to me.'

'Did you try it?'

Edith shook her head, grimacing.

'I did,' Kay laughed. 'Looks like Gentleman's Relish. Tastes similar. I hope it works, for his sake. He's been in hot water has Dr Beckenbauer. He has to mind his ps and qs.'

'Why is that?' Edith asked, wanting to know if her instinctive dislike for him was confirmed.

'Did you notice a building? On its own in the grounds?'

'Boarded up?'

'That's the one. On one of my visits, Seraphina told me there are patients in there. She called them *muselmann*.'

'What's that mean?' Jack frowned, puzzled. It was a word he hadn't heard before.

'It means extreme emaciation,' Harry supplied. 'It's a term they used in the camps.'

Kay nodded her confirmation. 'So, I go to Dr Beckenbauer, demand to see inside. He's happy to show me. Seraphina was right. These patients exhibit signs of advanced malnutrition. They are the mental patients, he explains, they don't receive the same rations as those in the main hospital. When I ask, why not? All patients should receive the same ration, he's shocked. He didn't think the directive applied to them.'

'What happened?'

'I reported it. He got a rocket. Patients transferred. Facility closed down. Trouble is, we have the same problem with Jerry doctors and nurses as you do with teachers. To practise under the Nazis, you had to belong to the Party.'

'It's happening all the time now.' Harry frowned. 'They're letting them blend back in. Take their places again.'

'There simply aren't enough doctors,' Kay replied. 'Mil. Gov. has to keep the death rate down among the German population, so they can't be too particular. German doctors are appointed by a German committee. My guess is most of them are ex-Nazis but what can you do?'

'Where's the food?' Jack looked round. 'I'm starving.'

Harry refused his soup and lit a cigarette.

'What's this?' Jack fished out a piece of black skin. 'Looks like inner tube. Bet it tastes like it, too. I'm not eating that.'

'It's good, Jack,' Kay tasted hers. 'You should try new things.'

'I'll leave that to you.' Jack pushed his plate away. 'He isn't eating it, either.'

'I don't eat eel.'

Not kosher, Edith remembered from some lost Religious Knowledge lesson. Eels have no fins.

The two men drank schnapps and ate herring.

'What will you do when you get out?' Harry asked.

'Dunno,' Jack laughed. 'Haven't thought that far ahead.'

'What about you, Kay? Nursing?'

'No. I've had enough of that. I was at Art school before I volunteered. I'm going to apply to the Royal College. Pick up my life where I left it.' Kay touched her lips with her napkin. 'Every now and then, I just take off with a haversack, pack of sandwiches, Thermos of tea, change of undies, bottle of whisky and my sketchbook. I've visited galleries and museums in Holland, Belgium and here in Germany. I'm hoping to get to Paris. I don't advertise my interest. I don't tell many that I want to be an artist. They'd tell me to stick to nursing. You know how people are.'

'I really like Kay,' Edith said when she and Jack were on their way back to Lübeck. 'I hope you're treating her properly.'

'I thought you two'd hit it off.'

'So she's going to study art.'

'Unh, hnh.' Jack peered into the darkness ahead of him. They'd stayed longer than they should. There was black ice about.

'What are *you* going to do, Jack? You didn't say.'

'I'm going to marry her. Ain't popped the question, like,' he added, almost bashful. 'So I'd be grateful if you kept it under your hat.'

It was not quite what Edith had asked and certainly wasn't what she'd expected.

'You can count on me, Jack,' she said. 'I won't breathe a word.'

Jack could change a conversation as smoothly as he shifted gears. She still didn't know what he intended to do, or what he'd done before, for that matter.

They got back very late. All the other houses in the street were in darkness except for the billet. The curtains weren't drawn and all the lights were on, shining yellow on the snowy lawn. Even before she saw the Jeep drawn up outside, Edith knew that something was wrong.

'Looks like the Military Police,' Jack said.

'Something must have happened.' Edith got out of the car. 'I think you'd better come in, too, Jack.'

The door opened before she'd even turned her key in the lock. Hilde's blue eyes met Edith's and then slid away again. Behind the girl's usual passivity, Edith could clearly sense fear.

Edith gave her hat, coat and gloves to her. Jack stood back in cap and greatcoat, arms folded, awaiting developments.

The two military policemen were standing in the centre of the sitting room, looking large, masculine and slightly at a loss as to what to do. The German girls stood against the wall, hands clasped, eyes cast down. Angie, Ginny and Franny were huddled together on the settee, red eyed and crying. Lorna and Jo were by the window, rather less hysterical but nevertheless pink eyed. Frau Schmidt hovered inside the door, wringing her hands, fat tears rolling down her cheeks.

'What on earth's happened?'

'Oh, Edith, thank God you're back.' Angie looked up, blue eyes glassy, lashes wet and spiky. 'It's Molly. There's been the most terrible accident.'

This set Ginny off and the two of them dissolved into fresh sobs. She would clearly get no sense out of them. Edith turned to the two policemen.

'Perhaps one of you could tell me what has happened.'

'You are?'

'Edith Graham. I live here.' Edith showed him her CCG card. He inclined his head slightly as he acknowledged her rank.

'There's been an accident, ma'am. Involving Miss Slater. Fatal, I'm afraid.' He turned his red cap round in his hands. 'We need someone to identify the body.'

'I couldn't! I simply couldn't!' Angie cried.

'I couldn't, either!' Ginny looked up, her brown eyes swimming. 'It's just too upsetting.'

Franny shook her head quickly and continued to stare down at the sodden wisp of handkerchief she was winding round her fingers. Of all them, she seemed the most upset. Despite the cruel jibes, 'Good old Goll' had been devoted to Molly.

'When did this happen?' Edith asked the policeman.

'This evening. She was on a motorcycle. Icy road. No helmet, of course. It's, well, it's not pretty—'

'I see,' Edith interrupted. 'Thank you, sergeant.' As much as she disliked the Common Room hysteria, these girls were only young and they'd had a shock. 'I'll do it. I'll identify her.'

'I'll come with you,' Lorna volunteered from the window. 'I'll get my coat.'

Jack drove them, following the Jeep. They didn't have far to go. The girl had been taken to the Red Cross Hospital: a modernish red-brick building on Marlistraße, by the banks of the Wakenitz.

They followed the two military policemen down into the basement. A strong smell permeated the long cream-painted corridor, disinfectant and formaldehyde with a sweetish undertone, as though morgues could never quite rid themselves of the

284

smell of decay. Lorna put her handkerchief to her mouth. One of the policemen opened rubber-flanged double doors. He flicked switches on the wall. Pairs of low-hanging lamps cast interlocking cones of white light; their wide metal shades creating shadows on the ceiling and in the corners of the room. Tiles covered every surface; any natural light came from two small windows set high on the far wall. It was like being in a white-tiled cave.

The lights illuminated ceramic dissecting tables on thick pedestals. Three of them occupied, one vacant. The tables were curved at the head end, straight across the bottom, with a thick lip around the edge. The empty table showed a grooved and channelled surface sloping towards a centre line. Metal piping provided drainage into the floor. Lorna gulped, as if she might be sick, turning her head away quickly, as if the reality of what went on here was too much to absorb.

Edith put her hand on the girl's sleeve. 'You don't have to do this, Lorna. If you feel unwell, you can leave.'

'No,' she shook her head. 'I'll be OK.' She gave a wan smile. 'Let's get it over with, eh?'

'Very well.' Edith looked to the sergeant.

'One on the right, ma'am. With the sheet folded down.'

Edith stepped forward. She took Lorna's hand, squeezing tightly. The girl was as white as the tiles on the wall.

Molly Slater lay with only her head showing, her slender form covered with a coarse, worn sheet. The right-hand side of her face was perfect. Even her makeup was intact. Sooty lashes, thickened with mascara, brushed the bluish skin of her cheek. The platinum hair was set in rippling waves, hardly a strand out of place. The other side of her head was a mess. The silvery hair clotted and bloody, the skull beneath it misshapen, that side of her face abraded. Edith forced herself to look back at the good side, the Molly side. She might not have liked her very much, but she really was little more than a child. The closed eye showed a sweep of blue liner, irregularly applied, as though she'd been interrupted, or her hand slipped, or something. Edith felt the hot-pepper sting of tears behind the eyes.

'Is it her?' the sergeant asked. 'Miss Margaret Slater?'

'Yes.' Edith nodded, throat tight.

'Miss?' He turned to Lorna.

'Yes, it is her. It's Molly. They called her Molly, not Margaret,' she added as if that was something important for him to know.

Edith nodded towards the body on the slab next to Molly.

'And that is?'

'Miss Slater's companion. The boyfriend.' He looked at his notes. 'One Valdemārs Jansons, or so his papers say.'

There was another body on the far side of Molly, completely covered, except for a hand flopped down from under the coarse, greyish sheet. A small hand with bitten nails and missing the upper joints of the little finger. The skin broken, yellowish, like the cracked surface of a bisque doll.

'Who's that?'

'Who knows?' The sergeant shrugged. 'What the Yanks call a Jane Doe. No identification. DP most probably. Fished out of the Trave when they were breaking ice.'

Edith resisted his efforts to shepherd her towards the wide doors.

'Wait,' she said. 'I think I might know her. May I see?'

'Are you sure? Ain't a pretty sight, ma'am. Looks to have been there some time.'

'I'm sure.' Edith couldn't bear to think of her lying there, unnamed, unclaimed.

He pulled the covering cloth from her ruined face. 'Could be worse. Water's near freezing. But it's the fish, see? Eels especially.'

'Thank you, sergeant.' Edith swallowed hard. 'I think her name is Agnese. She worked in our billet. A Latvian, I believe.' She turned to Lorna. 'She's not been there for . . . how long?' Lorna shrugged and shook her head. 'I'd say a few weeks now.'

He took out a notebook. 'Any other name?'

'I don't know, I'm afraid, but she claimed to be cousin to the young man you have over there.'

'I see.' He wrote something and snapped the notebook shut. 'Thank you, Miss Graham. You've been very helpful.'

'So you knew t'other wench?' Jack asked as they walked back to the car, the younger Military Policeman going ahead with Lorna, his head bent towards her, solicitous.

'She worked at the billet,' Edith replied. 'She was missing the top joints on her little finger. That's how I recognized her. She is, was, Jansons' cousin.'

'He's a right mess,' Jack said quietly.

'Jansons?'

'Yes. Head nearly ripped clean off. I took a gander while you were occupied with the girl. That's no accident. Partisan trick. Seen it plenty of times in Italy. Wire across the road.' He made a guttural noise and passed a finger across his throat. 'Done for.'

She was bone tired. The house was quiet. The girls packed off to bed with mugs of sweet cocoa. *Für den Schock*, Frau Schmidt said and offered to make some for Edith but that was about the last thing she wanted. She poured herself a stiff whisky and went up to her room. She had postcards, menus, recipes to write and code but she couldn't think about writing. What she'd just seen eclipsed everything.

She stared down at the blank paper, thinking back. Agnese had disappeared very soon after their conversation in the kitchen. And Harry Hirsch: the Friday night she'd told him about the attack on her. He hadn't been there next morning. Making a phone call, he said. *Tilhas Tizig Gesheften.* Up your arse business. She should stop this spying. She wasn't cut out for it. Escape from its spreading, tenebrous shadow. Meddle no more. She covered her face with her hands, tears leaking through her fingers for two young women stretched out in the morgue who might well be there because of her.

27

Officers' Club, Hamburg

6th March 1946

Lunch Menu

```
Barnsley Chop - two 10oz chops cut across
the loin, served with Cumberland sauce*
Jam  Rolypoly  pudding - the  schoolboy's
favourite

*Cumberland sauce (See: Sauces for Reference)
Preparation time 8-12 minutes
Cooking  time:  10-15  minutes  (simmer  3-4
minutes to thicken)
Serves 1-4
```

'These chops are awfully good. Best I've had since I've been here.' Bill Adams tore at the meat with his sharp little teeth, getting at the pinkish flesh near the bone. He got more catlike every time she saw him. 'Why do they call them Barnsley Chops, d'you think? I'm sure *you'll* know. With your interest in food . . .'

'Named after a hostelry in Barnsley,' Edith answered equably, although the reference to food put her on alert. 'The King's Head, as I recall, although others will claim it.'

'Well, they're damned good.'

Edith had been summoned to lunch at the Officers' Club in Hamburg under the guise of an Education and Training Briefing. When she had tried to make excuses, Adams' jovial tone had turned to silky threat.

'Germans don't seem to go in much for lamb, do they? Mostly pork, veal, that kind of thing. It's always schnitzels, I find. All right in their place but can get a bit much, all those breadcrumbs, and I like a bit of lamb. New chap's English. Probably explains it. Now, where was I?' He replaced the well-gnawed bones on the plate. 'I know. The boyfriend. Jansons?' He wiped the greasiness from his hands and pushed his plate away. 'The thing is, it wasn't an accident. Head nearly severed.'

'Oh?' Edith tried to sound surprised. 'The policeman said it was icy. He skidded. Lost control.'

'That's what they've been told to say, that's what we're putting out, that's what her parents have been told, but,' he shrugged. 'Not true.'

'What happened, then?'

'Wire across the road. Caught him so.' He put the blade of his hand under his chin to demonstrate, tilting his head sharply back. 'Bike goes all over the place. She's on the back. Thrown off. No helmet.' He put out his hands, palms up in a gesture of hopeless inevitability. 'We don't want that getting out, of course. It's an accident and always will be. She could have made a brighter choice of boyfriend, but there we are. I say – you've hardly touched yours. May I?'

His fork was hovering like a paw over Edith's chop.

'Go ahead. I'm not awfully hungry.'

'Shame to see it go to waste, what with, you know . . .' He didn't finish the sentence, too occupied demolishing her chop. 'Fancy any pudding?' He looked at the menu card. 'They do a good jam rolypoly.'

'Just coffee.'

'You were here in Hamburg at the weekend, so I hear,' he said as his pudding arrived. 'Before this sad occurrence with the unfortunate Miss Slater.' He paused, spoon poised. 'That couldn't have anything to do with your Jewish friend, Harry Hirsch and his pals, by any chance?'

'How would I know?'

'How would *he* know, more to the point, I would have thought. There has to be a proper order to things.' He gestured with his spoon. 'We can't have people taking the law into their own hands. There was a certain amount of it after the war, perfectly understandable, turned a bit of a blind eye, but it can't continue. Perhaps you could pass on the message? His brother's in Haganah, so I understand.'

'Haganah?'

'Quasi-military organization, out in Palestine. Want to establish a Jewish State. Aren't too fussy how they go about it. Becoming rather a thorn in our side.'

'Do you blame them?'

'Not for me to judge. But Palestine is under our rule at the moment, keeping the ring between them and the Arabs could be a thankless task. Things are definitely changing, old loyalties, old allegiances dying, new ones forming.' He dug his spoon into the suet. He looked up from his pudding. 'While we're on the subject, this interest in food. Let's talk about that, shall we? Collect recipes do you? Menus, that kind of thing. Little snippets, like Mock Turtle, Barnsley Chop?'

'Yes, I do.' Edith looked back, keeping her gaze steady under his sudden, sharp, interrogative stare. She had to hold her nerve. He was like a sinister Bertie Wooster: his pleasant, easygoing manner always cloaking a certain level of threat. 'I've been doing it for a long time.' She smiled, spreading her hands in innocence. 'It's an interest of mine.'

'Share this interest with pals at home?' His long, slim fingers reasserted their grip on his spoon. 'Those of a like mind?'

'Yes. I send recipes, menus, anything I come across of interest. To my sister, Louisa, other friends.' Edith shrugged. 'It's what women do.' She held her hands loosely folded on the table. She wasn't sure where this was going but it wouldn't do to show any agitation. When interrogated, keep as close to the truth as possible. That was Dori's advice. Keep up injured innocence as long as you can, then go on the offensive. 'Why do you want to know about that?'

'Just keeping tabs.' He dug back into his pudding, jam oozing. 'Wouldn't want anything *sub rosa* getting out.'

'In a recipe for Mock Turtle Soup?' Edith laughed to underline how ludicrous such a thing would be.

'Well, stranger things have happened.' Adams waved his hand quickly in front of his mouth. 'I'll leave that for a moment.' He put down his spoon. 'Jam's too hot.'

'Probably a good idea. Jam retains heat,' Edith observed. 'You don't want to burn your mouth. An interest in food has its advantages. How do you know I send recipes to people, anyway? Is my mail being read?'

'Talking of messages, had one from old Leo yesterday. Reason for this meeting, as a matter of fact.' He picked up his spoon. 'He's worried you might be getting a little, ah, out of your depth. In future, if you do discover anything, it comes to me and me only. Careless talk costs lives, remember?' He emphasized each word with a jab. 'Literally so in this case.'

With that, he made a fresh assault on his pudding. She was glad of his shift in attention. She used the time to smooth her expression, keep her growing agitation off her face. Did his sinister hinting mean that he knew something, or was he just fishing? What if they had decoded the recipes? Edith went cold even thinking about it. They were definitely suspicious. Time to shift the conversation. She was tired of being treated like this, anyway. Time to go on the attack.

'I am quite aware of that, Captain Adams. I'm glad you called this meeting. I wanted to tell you in person. I no longer feel comfortable taking part in all this. I want to stop. You can pass that on to Leo. Save me the trouble.'

She had his attention now. The spoon stopped midway to his mouth.

'Oh, why's that?'

'Isn't it obvious? I don't want my mail read and I don't want to be spied on. Someone has been through my room at the billet more than once—'

'Nothing to do with us.'

Edith held up her hand. 'I haven't finished. I resent being the object of suspicion. I've given you valuable information at some risk, I might add, and what do I get in return? All this. There has to be an element of trust, Captain Adams.' She set her voice at most haughty. 'It works both ways.'

'No need to get aerated, Miss Graham. Point taken. *Do* you have anything to report? Anything at all?'

Edith sensed the tables turning. Was that a hint of desperation about the eyes, the kink of his brows?

'I might. But I'm not sure I want to continue with this, did you not hear what I said?'

'Loud and clear. Let's not fall out over a spot of overzealousness. I'll pass your feelings on to Leo. I'm sure the *last* thing he wants is for you to stop your excellent work. Now, might I call pax, Miss Graham? We're on the same side, aren't we? So what do you have?'

But they weren't on the same side, though, were they? Not really. She felt no loyalty to him. Or Leo, for that matter. Leo was using her, had used her before and would again, if he got the chance. Right from the start, he hadn't been straight with her. He had asked her to help find Kurt, but he had neglected to tell her the real reason why he was wanted.

'Any news on von Stavenow, for example? Umm, Jam Rolypoly is one of my favourites.' Adams returned his spoon to the dish. 'Is that in your culinary repertoire at all?'

Edith ignored the question. 'I might have a lead on Elisabeth,' she said.

Chuck him a bloody big bone, Dori would have said. She didn't want him circling back to the recipes. Throw him off the scent

'*Might* you? You need to follow that up, Edith. Von Stavenow is definitely *Of Interest.*'

'Why would that be?'

'The things they did won't be repeated.' He lit his pipe, sucking in the flame, making sure it was fully alight. 'Can't be, not in any *civilized* society.' He blew out a puff of smoke. 'That research, that *knowledge* could be useful, though. In the cause of medicine, humanity, and so on. Pity for it to go to waste after all that sacrifice and suffering. As we understand it, von Stavenow was involved in some very special work and it's important that we get to him before anyone else does. We wouldn't want the Russians getting their hands on him. Or the Americans.' He sucked a fresh flame into his pipe and blew out a cloud of blue, sweetish-smelling smoke. 'To tell the truth, we've been a bit slow off the mark. The Americans have been beating us to the punch repeatedly, what with von Braun and all those rocket bods, stolen from right under our noses. No. We need a feather in our cap and this one is ours.'

Edith closed her eyes. The pipe smoke was making her feel nauseous. No matter how she tried to play their game, it still shocked her that there was no mention of any possibility that von Stavenow might be punished for the crimes he'd committed, the suffering he'd inflicted, for killing his own son. She thought of Elisabeth and the unimaginable agony that underlay her dark, unrelentling description of that terrible place where her child had been sent. And they wanted a man like that? There was more morality among rats.

'I say, are you all right? You've gone a bit pale. Have a brandy. That'll bring the colour back.' He clicked his fingers to attract the waiter.

'If you do find von Stavenow,' Edith asked, her eyes on the swirl of her brandy, 'what will you do with him?'

Now, perhaps, she'd find out exactly what was intended.

'There's a research facility in the south of England. Seat being kept warm. A couple of his colleagues there already. I don't know what goes on there, exactly, it's very hush, hush, but I do know it's bloody important. Could be vital if the Ivans decide to play dirty. Nerve gas, bacteria, all kinds of nasty business.

And that could happen, Edith, mark my words. Anyway, upshot is, they want the good doctor there, not skulking about here, hiding in Stephan's shed, or somewhere similar. Or in Maryland for that matter, so any news, be sure to let me know.'

Edith thought of the vile things that Elisabeth had told her, how the brains of children were collected, harvested was the word she'd used, how they were preserved in formaldehyde, sent to Heidelberg in special containers, to Kurt's old professor, or to his colleague in Berlin.

'Is the doctor already in situ called Richter, by any chance?'

'Why, yes. How did you know that?'

His blue eyes shifted from quizzical to cold and appraising. Edith toyed with her brandy, giving herself her time to think.

'Oh,' she said eventually. 'He was Kurt's boss – before the war. I think I might have met him. I've a good memory for people.' She put down her glass carefully. Her mental repugnance had taken a queasy lurch into physical revulsion. 'If you'll excuse me, I have to go to the powder room.'

She barely made it to the lavatory before vomiting. The alcohol she'd just consumed scorched her throat. She wiped her mouth and blew her nose on the hard lavatory paper. At the sinks, she rinsed and spat. The German attendant ignored her. She took a few deep breaths to calm herself, her hand shaking slightly as she applied more powder and redid her lipstick. Her image was slightly skewed, the bevelled edges of the mirror refracting light.

'I say, are you all right? You're looking a bit dicky.' Bill Adams stood up when she returned.

'I have a migraine starting,' she said, her voice sounded thick, roughened by the rawness in her throat. 'It's probably the brandy. I shouldn't touch it.'

'My wife has them. Awful things.' His handsome feline face creased with concern. 'Let me call your driver. We must get you home.'

Jack was most concerned, giving her aspirin to swig down with tea from his Thermos and tucking a blanket round her for the journey home.

'That Adams is an arsehole, I told you ma'am. What did he want anyway?'

'Oh, nothing much. Best I don't talk, Jack. If you don't mind.'

The pain was so bad she couldn't think clearly. She closed her eyes. Careless talk costs lives.

She arrived back in Lübeck with the migraine thudding in her right temple, moving to the other side of her head. Nevertheless, she dosed herself with veganin and tried to stave off the pain long enough to compose messages to Dori. She had to report her meeting with Adeline and her conversation with Adams. A couple of things he'd said had snagged but she couldn't quite recall them now. Damn this migraine, she couldn't think straight. Concentrate on the most important things. Dori needed to know that their post was being monitored and what was intended for von Stavenow.

She picked up her pen and straightened her shoulders. Her encounter with Adams had cancelled her doubts. All thoughts of giving up were forgotten. There could be no going back. She had it chapter and verse from Adams's own mouth. They had no intention of punishing Kurt. That was confirmed. Leo wanted him found so that he could be taken to Britain where they would use him. His experience, his knowledge was useful; it didn't matter how, or by what vile means, it had been obtained. Dori was working with Vera Atkins and War Crimes to bring him to justice and Edith was proud to be helping them. Their work was so very important and it was a race against time now to see who found him first.

She worked slowly, stopping every now and then, her face crimping and releasing as the pain flared and subsided. The letters and numbers swam across the page in front of her but she gathered them in patiently as she carefully composed the messages she had to send.

Dear Dori,

I hope you enjoyed the promised Prussian dish and found the Menu Americaine of interest. No more Latvian recipes, I'm afraid – a bit of a dead end – but a selection of menus and a couple of oddities.

<u>Invalid Menu</u> – experiments continue as if nothing had happened. I'm attaching by Paperclip. Still of considerable interest. Must not be lost or mislaid.

Barnsley Chops at Hamburg Officers' Club. Rather too fiercely grilled. Indigestible. Find under Meat: Roasting and Grilling. Served with <u>Cumberland Sauce.</u>

P.S. The post is getting more and more unreliable. Hope this gets through!

Yours, Edith

Dori

Paddington W2

Brown government-issue envelopes stacked on the hallstand. One longer, creamy thick paper. Hotel Atlantic. Letters from Edith. Edith's neat, elegant writing, the royal-blue ink she used. Dori put them in order. Dated at different times but arrived all together. She would not be opening them yet, however eager she was for news.

Anton's tread on the steps. He'd been out for his constitutional. It was a cold, grey, foggy morning but Anton went five times round the square whatever the weather.

'Are they still out there?' Dori asked.

He nodded as he hung up his hat and coat.

'*Psy mysliwśkie*. Hunting dogs – part of a pack. Sometimes one alone.' He smoothed his white hair back. 'Sometimes two, sometimes three. Never the same two days running. Young men standing, smoking, sitting. What are they doing in the square with the babies and the old ladies?'

'Hmm,' Dori frowned. 'Take a look at these will you?'

He picked up the letters one at a time and scrutinized them carefully with the aid of a jeweller's loupe that he took from his pocket.

'Cheap brown paper,' he said as he ran the glass down the

sealed edges of the upper flap, then the gummed lower flap. 'Not so easy to open without leaving some trace.' The paper was dulled, cockled. There were traces of tears along the edges of the seal, the bottom flap slightly curled, the gummed part convex. Anton picked up a paper knife from the hallstand and slit one of the envelopes along the top and down the sides and reapplied the glass. 'Traces of gum. This has been steamed opened and resealed in a clumsy way.'

Dori thanked him with a ten-bob note and took the letters down to the kitchen. Flaps and seals. Definitely covert but not very good at it. She opened the letters, slitting the tops as Anton had done. The correspondence might have been read but their code had not been discovered, she was pretty sure of that.

It was hard not to think in cookery terms. Things were hotting up out there, coming to the boil. The Prussian Dish located. Plot thickening with the Balts and with the Germans. Frau Schmidt and what Edith termed the *Schwestern*, like-minded Nazi *Frauen* gathering for *Kaffee und Kuchen*, and then there was American interest to lend savour . . .

Eye of newt, and toe of frog . . .

A brew of peculiar potency. A charm of powerful trouble.

Then there was Adams and his gristly Barnsley Chop and his suspicions. The witches' charm continued in her head: *Finger of birth strangled babe, ditch delivered by a drab.* Probably tasted similar. Adams alerted by Leo, no doubt, and whoever was making a pig's ear of steaming these envelopes open. Dispatched to warn Edith off, especially since von Stavenow was due to be Paperclipped – once they found him. Dori fed the papers into the fire. She remembered her grandmother writing notes in the strange symbols of some lost and ancient script, holding them for the flames to take from fingers as bent and gnarled as oak twigs. Blessings or curses? Dori never dared to ask.

The last of the papers glowed then whitened to ash. It was all coming together now. *Make the gruel thick and slab.*

She started like a guilty thing at the shrill drilling of the front door bell. She wasn't expecting any callers. She tied on a pinny, to look suitably occupied, and ran up the stairs.

'Mrs Stansfield?' One of Anton's suspicious young men stood on her threshold, the collar of his overcoat turned up, a scarf round the lower part of his face, the brim of his hat shading his eyes. A companion, similarly muffled, stood at the bottom of the steps. 'Come with us, please.'

'Says who? Come with you where? What's this about?' Dori stood, arms folded, looking suitably put out. 'I'm busy in the kitchen.' She indicated the pinafore. 'As you can see.'

The young man planted his feet more firmly. The other one mounted the steps behind him. 'Nevertheless. We insist.'

'Oh, very well.' Dori removed her pinafore. 'If you *insist*. I'll just get my coat. Won't be a moment.'

The first young man placed his foot against the doorjamb.

Dori put on her coat and opened the drawer of the hallstand. Under cover of rummaging for a lipstick, she slipped out the little Beretta she kept there and slid it into her pocket. She applied a swipe of Chanel. Police? Unlikely. Expensive shoes and no warrant card offered. We will see what we shall see. She worked her lips together and picked up her keys.

'I'm ready.' She stepped out, closing the door. 'Where are you taking me?'

They didn't reply. They walked close, one either side of her. She sensed another behind. The two at her side stared straight ahead. Their proximity, their expressionless faces, masks of indifference verging on hostility shown to the already guilty, reminded her of being picked up by the Gestapo, although there was no gun at her back or nuzzling her ribs.

At the end of the square, they turned left and then right, halting in front of a pub on a corner not far from the station. The men stood back for her to enter. The door wheezed back slowly behind her. Dori stood on the threshold, taking in the room. A bleak white light leaked through smeared pebbled windows; cigarette smoke hung in blue drifts below a ceiling enamelled brown by accumulated tar. The walls were lined with button-backed bottle-green leatherette banquettes, torn or slashed in places, horsehair showing. Rickety round-backed chairs clustered about a scatter of scarred and ringed-round tables. The small grate was empty. The sparse clientele were still wearing their overcoats; solitary men standing, elbows on the bar, one foot resting on the tarnished brass rail. The landlord wiped the counter with a towel. Above his head, a line of dusty coloured lights hung in uncertain loops above a row of optics. They looked as though they'd been there since Christmas, 1938.

The two men walked her over to a booth in the far corner, separated off by a wooden panel topped with stained glass.

Leo was waiting for her. Crombie overcoat buttoned up. Bowler still in place.

'Thank you, Crowther.' One of her escort peeled off and made for the door. 'Burman, could you get drinks? I'll have a whisky to go with this.' He indicated a cloudy pint in a dimpled glass. 'And whatever Mrs Stansfield would like.'

'Gin. And tonic, if they have it. If not, anything they've got.'

Leo moved up into the corner. Dori slid in beside him.

'Just wanted a little chat,' Leo said when the drinks arrived.

'About what?' Dori tasted her gin. Watered and further diluted by some ghastly cordial. 'I say, could one of your young men get me a whisky? Whatever they've put in here tastes like Jeyes Fluid smells.'

Dori watched Leo as he signalled to one of the young men nursing a half pint at the bar. Leo wasn't to be trusted, not under any circumstances. As slick as a snake, he could strike just as fast. He'd been attached to SOE from one of the other Secret Outfits. Seconded in 1940. His brief was Strategy, far above Dori in the poor bloody infantry. Those were the days. Set Europe ablaze. Didn't quite work out like that, though, and when it started going pear shaped there was old Leo, quick as a wink, to conceal and disguise. Hide the cockups. Paper over. Generally cover collective arses. Thick as thieves with Buckmaster, boss of SOE, the biggest arse to cover. Less thick with Vera. Cover-ups meant double agents protected, circuits blown, SOE agents betrayed for whatever reason and that spelt 'traitor' in Dori's book. It amounted to a betrayal of the agents sent to France, the organization that sent them and ultimately the country. She had no proof it was him and whatever evidence there might have been was disappearing by the minute, but Dori went by instinct and she knew it was Leo.

The young man brought over a squat glass of whisky.

'Better?' Leo asked as Dori tasted.

'Oh, much. Now,' Dori put down the glass. 'What did you want to chat about?'

'Oh, this and that.' Leo took a sip of his beer. 'Orders come through yet?'

'Yes, they have as a matter of fact.'

'Good, good. Off soon to Germany?'

'Yes. Is that why you want to see me?'

'Something else entirely.' Leo pushed his beer away and toyed with his whisky. 'Won't beat about the bush. Are you in touch with Edith at all?'

'Yes.'

'And what do you correspond about?'

'Oh, this and that.'

'Does she send you recipes?'

'Indeed, she does!' Dori smiled her surprise that he would know that.

'Hmm,' Leo settled himself deeper into his overcoat. 'I find that odd.'

'Odd? What's odd about women sending each other recipes? She sends the same ones to her sister, Louisa.'

'I know Louisa. She's a good cook. You, as far as I know, are not.'

'So what does that prove?'

Leo knew he was on to something and wasn't quite sure what, so he'd come on a fishing expedition. He looked up, his pale-blue eyes suddenly sharp behind the magnifying lenses.

'It won't do, Dori.' He tapped the words with his fingernail on the side of his glass. 'It will not do.'

'What won't do?'

'Yes, she sends Louisa recipes, menu cards and so on. Louisa has been kind enough to show them to me, but that doesn't account for the book references.'

'Ah, that's me, I'm afraid. My secret.' She felt herself growing scarlet. She'd always been able to blush, or cry, at will. 'I can't cook, as you pointed out. Edith has been teaching me. She's going to be in Northern Germany. Cabbage Soup and Spätzle, Piroggen, Blaubeerkuchen,' Dori recited. 'It's the food of my homeland. I want to know how to cook them myself. Edith directs me to particular recipes in the *Radiation Cookery Book* and adapts them for me. Odd, I concur, and faintly shame-making for me, but there it is. You must allow us ladies our eccentricities.'

'Hmm,' Leo turned his whisky glass round and round between his pudgy fingers. Dori kept silent, letting him mull. 'It is odd,' he repeated. 'Edith has her own oddities, but she's not one for duplicity. She's doing a useful job. Wouldn't want her put off her game. No shenanigans.' He held his index finger up, moving it in tick-tocking admonition. 'I know you're up to something, I just don't know what. Yet. Whatever it is, I don't want Edith mixed up in it. How's it going in Germany?'

Leo threw out the question, a quick cast into a different pool.

'Vera's identified the three female agents who ended up in Ravensbrück. She's still working on Natzweiler.'

'Good. We need this business cleared up. Some of the parents are kicking up a stink, going to the papers, saying we're not doing enough. The *Express* loves that kind of stuff.' He drained his whisky and stood up. 'Good luck.' He offered his hand, the palm soft, slightly sweaty. 'I hope you didn't resent our little chat?'

'Not at all.' Dori returned his weak clasp with her own strong grip. 'Best to know where we stand.'

'Exactly, Dori,' Leo smiled and touched the brim of his hat in parting. '*Auf Wiedersehen!*'

His young men fell in beside him as he left the pub. Alone, Dori finished her whisky and ordered another. She drained it quickly. Leo was right. The sooner she got out to Germany, the better.

28

Lübeck Billet/Atlantic Hotel, Lübeck/ Hamburg

16th–17th March 1946

Billet Breakfast
Eggs and Bacon

Eggs pale and rubbery, made with powder,
fresh suddenly unavailable.

Hotel Atlantic Breakfast
Omelette au Champignons

'*Es regnet.*' Frau Schmidt announced with some satisfaction.
Rain was nearly as disruptive to travel as snow.

'I know.' Edith did not look up from her scrambled eggs.

'*Es regnet junge Hunde.* I tell Stephan to get the wood in dry.'

'Very wise. We say cats and dogs.'

'The roads will be bad.'

'I know that, too.'

It was the weekend. She was going to Hamburg to meet Harry.
It had been two weeks. A lot had happened. She had to see him
and a bit of weather was not going to stop her. There was

something she needed to talk to him about, something she had to know.

Jack arrived, cape slick, cap sodden. He stood dripping in the hall while Edith put on her coat.

He held out a wing of his cape for her and they made a dash for it.

'Is that Stephan?' A figure hunched in a field-grey greatcoat disappeared round the corner. 'A bit wet for him, ain't it?'

He started the car. The engine caught, then died, caught then died again.

'Bloody starter motor's been playing up. Ah, here we go.'

Jack kept his eyes straight ahead, trying to see through the slap of the windscreen wipers. Suddenly, he looked down.

'Bloody hell! What's up now?'

'What is it?'

'Nowt, probably. Brakes feel a bit spongy. Water gets everywhere.'

They drove on. The ridged, frozen roads had softened to viscous milky brown mud. In the sodden fields, dark soil and tangled mats of yellowy-green grass showed through the decayed snow. Retreating drifts revealed the remains of scout cars, lorries, even an upended tank, beside it a wooden cross, capsized and fallen to one side. The ditches were brimming. Streams coursed across roads slick with water streaming from blackened mounds of melting snow.

As they took the steep hill that led down to the river, the car started to aquaplane. Jack pumped the brake pedal, cursing.

'Nothing! There's nothing there!'

Jack's face was ashen, his jaw rigid, his knuckles white on the steering wheel. Edith clung onto the sides of her seat, teeth gritted, foot braced on an imaginary brake. They were gaining speed. She looked frantically from side to side. The river was in spate, the turbulent brown-grey waters churning great clashing chunks of ice, whole trees tossed like toothpicks. The heavy car slewed as Jack fought to control it. They were heading towards the bridge: a flimsy, temporary structure bucking and rippling under the force of the water and the impact of the floes and debris crashing into it.

'Hold on!'

For one terrifying moment, Edith thought the car was going to turn over, but it righted itself and they ended up half in, half out of a ditch just before the bridge.

'Don't open the door. We ain't out of the woods yet.'

The water was rising. As they watched, it came lapping over the banks of the river and onto the surface of the bridge.

'You stay put. There's a depot up the road. I'll go and get help.'

Jack climbed out through his window. He waded to the side of the road and began to cross the bridge, the water at his ankles. Edith stayed put, wrapping a blanket around herself. Water was seeping in under the door, her fear creeping up with it. She could feel the nudge and tug of the current from the river like some monstrous animal prying at the car.

It felt like hours but could only have been twenty minutes at most. A lorry appeared sending water up in great bow waves as it crossed the bridge to her. Squaddies jumped down.

'We'll have you out in no time, miss.'

Under Jack's supervision, they hitched a rope to the car's tow bar.

With much revving and pulling the car was finally out of the ditch. Edith let out her breath in a great huff of relief.

She rode in the back of the lorry, drinking hot sweet tea out of a Thermos.

'I suppose that's it,' she said as Jack helped her down. The Humber was already up on a ramp.

'Not a bit of it, ma'am. I'll just find a new motor. And we'll be on our way.'

'What happened?' she looked over to where mechanics were examining the car.

'Brake pipes cut.' His face grew dark and hard. 'Friend Stephan, I shouldn't wonder. You better get your mate Adams to sort them fuckers out, or I will.'

* * *

When they got to the Atlantic, Edith went straight to Harry's room. The bar was too public. Too many people, too many eyes. Harry had a bottle of Riesling chilling in an ice bucket and two hock glasses. She apologized for being late, citing car trouble without telling him exactly what. She couldn't risk how he might react.

'Any news on von Stavenow?' Harry asked as he took the Riesling from the bucket.

Edith shook her head. 'I've got an idea, though. I've made contact with his wife. She's in Lübeck at her cousin's.'

'Leo's find-the-Frau theory?'

'Something along those lines.'

'What about Adams? Seen him lately?'

Edith nodded. 'He's disappointed that I haven't made more progress. He's getting impatient, even a bit nervous.'

He poured the wine and brought it over to her. 'Did he say why they want von Stavenow?'

'Research. Seat being kept warm for him.'

'And he'll get it in the neck if he can't deliver. Adams is an idiot.' He took the chair opposite her and lit a cigarette. 'The British are too slow,' he said, narrowing his eyes against the acrid smoke. 'It takes too long for them to decide to do anything. Too much bureaucracy. Too many committees. I've got a friend, a lawyer in the Department of Justice, he's in Nuremberg preparing for what they're calling the Doctors' Trial. It's due to start later in the year.' He stood up and began pacing, gesturing with his cigarette. 'These men, doctors like von Stavenow, were in charge of an enormous laboratory, using human beings instead of rats. They probed the limits of human endurance, men left for hours in freezing temperatures then thrown into boiling water for rewarming, Gypsies made to drink only seawater, women deliberately wounded and then those wounds infected, the infection aggravated by pushing in wood shavings and ground glass. The effectiveness of different poisons, how long different gases take to kill. Experiments as cruel as they were pointless. Or maybe not so pointless.' He paused to stub out his cigarette before resuming his pacing. Edith closed her eyes and leaned back in her chair as she listened, sickened, to this black muster roll of monstrous perversions conducted in the name of science. 'There're twenty on trial and not even the worst of them. Who knows how many have already been spirited away? Certain people will think this knowledge is valuable. The study of disease agents. How they are spread. Which would make the best weapons. There will always be an enemy, only the name changes. *Hakenkreuz* to Hammer and Sickle. War is no longer about armies, it's about how many civilians you can kill.' He stood, arms folded, staring out at Hamburg's ragged silhouette. 'Look at this place. How many died here? 40,000, 50,000? Most of the buildings gone with them. If you could kill the people but leave the city? That would be worth knowing. Nerve gas. The Germans were well advanced in their research – far beyond the Allies or the Russians. For that, they will lay anything aside. That's why they want this man so much. Let him start again. Question is, will you?' He turned back to her. 'You have to find your own way, Edith.'

'Is that what you're doing?' She opened her eyes, the reason she was here refocusing. '*Tilhas Tizig Gesheften*? Up your arse business?'

'Yes, as a matter of fact.' He looked at her, his dark eyes defiant. The choice was so obvious. Why would she even ask that? 'How can we rely on any other kind of justice? Sometimes we have to deliver it ourselves.'

'Like this?'

Edith unfolded a copy of the CCG *Gazette* and laid it out in front of him.

The story was on the front page:

Secretary in Legal Division Involved in Tragic Accident

The article described how Miss Margaret Slater (Molly to her friends) had met with a fatal accident while riding pillion on a friend's motor bicycle. It did not go into detail about the nature of their relationship, or the friend's nationality. The state of the roads and last Sunday's icy conditions were the cause. *The Gazette* had a tendency to blame most disasters on the occupied country: the inclement weather, the topography, its inhabitants, or other foreign presences. Miss Slater was being depicted as something of a saint: 'loyal friend', 'great pal', 'always there with a smile and a helping hand'. Not descriptions Edith recognized. The head of her division called her 'a lovely young woman', adding 'her decorative presence will be sorely missed.' That was accurate, Edith supposed. Miss Slater wasn't the only one to be appointed more for her looks than her typing speed. Whatever her shortcomings, Miss Slater shouldn't have been receiving any kind of obituary, not yet anyway, not for many years.

Harry's head moved slightly from side to side as he read the story. When he looked up at her, his face was expressionless.

'So? That's what they would say.'

'I'm not interested in the accuracy of the *story*.' She sighed her impatience. He knew exactly what she was getting at. 'I just want to know if you had a hand in it.'

'Not personally.' His tone was sulky, verging on truculent.

'By proxy?'

'Perhaps.'

'I hope this has nothing to do with me,' Edith added, expressing the fear that had been there ever since that visit to the morgue. It was guilt she didn't need.

'Of course not.' He looked away. She knew he was lying. 'Look here, Edith, sometimes these things are necessary.'

'*Krieg ist Krieg?* War is war? Isn't that what the Germans said?'

'Kalniņš had it coming. They were never going to punish him. You know it!'

He glared at her, black brows drawn together, defying her to contradict him. She glared back. It was as though the ground between them had sundered and they were on different sides of a deep crevasse.

'That doesn't make it right to take an innocent life!'

'Not so innocent, you told me. She should have been more careful.'

'I didn't know that an unfortunate choice of boyfriend was a capital offence!'

'You don't understand,' he shook his head at her sarcasm. 'You cannot comprehend—'

'I know two wrongs don't make a right, Harry,' Edith cut in. 'They just make another wrong. You'll be telling me about eggs and omelettes next. We know where that kind of thinking leads.'

'I don't want to fight with you, Edith.' He tried to take her hand.

She understood his rage and all the reasons for it but it was still wrong for someone to die when they'd done nothing.

'No, you don't!' She snatched her hand away. 'It's not as easy as that.'

'What can I do? It was a mistake,' he nodded towards the headline, 'but there it is.'

'There was another girl in the morgue, Agnese. Kalniņš' cousin. She worked in the billet. They found her in the Trave. What about her?'

There had been no obituary for her. She was just another cadaver with no one to claim or mourn her. Her absence had been a mere cause of irritation to Frau Schmidt. *Auf diese Mädchen ist gar kein Verlass.* These girls, not to be trusted, she'd muttered, lips pursing. *Sie verschwinden ohne ein einziges Wort.* They disappear without a word, she'd added a tsk of disgust and had promptly replaced her with a niece. When Edith asked Hilde and Grete about Agnese, even the mention of her name had brought troubled looks, a flicker of fear in eyes that darted to the door. None of the girls would talk about her.

He shook his head. 'Nothing to do with us. Probably her own people. Thought she'd blabbed to you. They are vicious killers, Edith.'

'But she'd done nothing!'

'Hadn't she? There are no innocents in this. Her family took our homes, our goods, when we were herded to the ghetto. They jeered and spat at us as we were led to our deaths. They only left when the Russians were coming, running like the rats they are. How do you think she came to be here?'

Edith did not reply. He was right. There were no innocents. Herself included. That poor girl probably died because of her.

'There is one thing you can do,' she broke the brooding silence that had grown between them. It wouldn't make any of it wholly right. Nothing would make up for a life taken but something good could still come out of this.

'What's that?'

'You can get those two girls out. Seraphina and Anna. Get them to Palestine.'

'I've already thought of that.' He looked relieved, hopeful of forgiveness. 'Plans are already afoot. Now can we be friends again? Please?'

Edith shook her head. 'I'm going back to my room. I don't want to stay here with you.'

'Please, Edith. Don't. I need you!' He held his hands linked in supplication, his brown eyes pleading. 'I won't – we won't – not if you don't want to – but please don't leave me alone. The only time I can sleep is with you.'

Harry fell asleep almost immediately. Edith lay by his side, wide awake. Somewhere a church bell tolled one hour, then another. In the cold, early morning, she could not escape the thought that she had caused those two girls to die. One by talking to her, the other by talking about her. Careless talk costs lives. You don't understand, he'd said, you cannot comprehend. And she didn't. Couldn't. She looked down at the man next to her. He'd laid this guilt upon her. Ordered death to be delivered with about as much thought as ordering room service. Why was she here with him?

He shifted in his sleep, his eyes began to move under the lids at the start of a dream. His teeth clenched, grinding together, his jaw rigid, lips drawn back in a snarl. The rictus spread to the rest of his body, his hands balled into fists, the muscles on his arms corded, his limbs making small jerking movements that seemed to take the most enormous effort, as in a man fighting deep paralysis. Sweat stood out on his forehead in oily globules.

His skin was deathly cold to the touch, wet, clammy. Edith pulled the covers over him. He was shaking now, shivering, curling himself into a ball. He didn't wake, he didn't scream, or even properly cry out; the sounds he made were muffled, incoherent, beyond articulation, as if a gag, or the iron tongue of a brank, stopped his mouth, while his eyeballs moved ever more quickly under the lids, tracking unimaginable horrors. Eventually he turned with a whimpering sigh onto his side and slipped into deeper sleep. In the soft, grey light of early morning, he reached for Edith and she answered his touch, accepting his sadness, taking it with him into herself.

Edith was breakfasting alone. Harry had already left.

'Penny for them.'

Edith looked up startled, surprised and delighted to find Dori smiling down at her, looking very elegant in the tailored uniform of a WAAF Flying Officer.

'Was that Harry Hirsch I saw checking out with a grin on his face and striding off with a swagger to his walk? There goes a satisfied man, if ever I saw one.' Dori's smile grew wider. 'You always were a dark horse.'

Edith stood up to embrace her and hide her sudden rush of colour.

'What are you doing here?'

'If it wasn't so obvious,' Dori arched an immaculately plucked brow, 'I'd ask you the same thing.'

'Stop it, Dori. You know how I hate being teased.'

'That's what makes it so irresistible. You take everything so seriously.'

'You didn't answer my question. What are you doing here?' Edith touched her napkin to her lips.

'Seeing you.'

'I mean in Germany. When did you get here?'

'A week or so ago.'

'You didn't tell me,' Edith pushed her plate away, feeling more than a little put out.

'I've been busy.' Dori threw her cap on a chair. 'I hate wearing uniform.'

Whether that was true or not, and Edith thought not, Dori loved dressing up and looking the part and she was very much enjoying the glances in her direction from the men in the room. A waiter rushed over to take her breakfast order, several officers stopped in mid conversation or with their forks half way to their mouths.

'Just coffee. *Danke*. I'm really not hungry,' Dori smiled. 'Although they do a good mushroom omelette, as I recall. Thank you for the recipe.' She stirred sugar into her coffee. 'The Latvian supper dish was most welcome. Didn't work out so well for your informant. A dead end, you said?'

Edith nodded. 'Literally so. The girl who gave it to me ended up in the Trave. Her cousin is dead, too, and his girlfriend, a girl from the billet. Motorcycle accident.'

'Accident?' Dori's eyebrows rose.

'That's what they're saying. All hushed up.'

'Naturally. And the Prussian dish? Any news there?'

'Much more promising.'

'Very good. And her *Mann*?'

Edith shook her head.

'Hmm,' Dori drummed a single scarlet fingernail on the starched white tablecloth in broken, staccato rhythm. 'You've been dining out. Barnsley Chop. Such an odd name for a cut of meat. Don't you agree?'

Edith grimaced.

'Though not from what you said. British food can be so indigestible.' Dori lit a cigarette. 'To extend the culinary theme, I've had a bit of a grilling myself.'

'Oh?'

'Picked up by two of Leo's chaps. Leo waiting in the pub round the corner, wanting a little chat.'

'Really? What about?'

'About recipes.' Dori squinted through her cigarette smoke. 'You don't look surprised.'

313

'I had an inkling. Adams went on about food. Asked about my interest. Nothing on the surface. But that's not their way.'

'What did you do?'

'Threw him a bone, like you said. Told him I had a lead on Elisabeth.'

'Not that you'd found her?'

'He doesn't need to know that yet.'

'Did it work?'

'Oh, completely. He began talking about how much they want him and why.' Edith paused. 'Actually, I'd just told him I wanted to pack it all in. Seeing those girls in the morgue killed my appetite for intrigue.'

'But you didn't.'

'No. He was talking about Kurt, his work, with such, such enthusiasm, excitement, almost.' She sat forward, hands linked together on the table. 'Elisabeth told me this most harrowing story . . .' She paused, even recalling it took her back to Elisabeth's desperation. 'He – he was responsible for his own child's death! Incarcerated him in this terrible place . . .' She paused again, biting her lip, holding herself together enough to go on. 'He lied to Elisabeth, told her the boy, Wolfgang, was perfectly fine when he was already dead! And they want a man like that! I knew I had to go on with this.' Her hand shook slightly as she poured herself more coffee. 'What about Leo?'

'I managed to fob him off.'

'Did he believe you?'

'Probably not, but it hardly matters. They need you. It's when they don't that you have to watch out. We need you, too. Vera and Bulldog are very pleased you've made contact with Elisabeth. Find the Frau, find the Mann and all that.' Dori sighed and stubbed out her cigarette. 'I'll have to love you and leave you. I'm due in Bad Oeynhausen.' There was a sudden tiredness about her eyes, a blank bleakness of the kind Edith had seen in Harry. 'We're interviewing survivors from various camps – mainly Dachau, Ravensbrück, Belsen – and the swine who ran the places – trying to find out exactly what happened to the agents who

314

ended up in those camps. There are some real sweethearts. Want to see?'

She took a folder from her briefcase. Photographs of men posed in immaculate uniform, the light just right, not a hair out of place. Some held the hint of a smile, gazing off as if towards the promised future; others sat with face composed, looking straight at the camera. Each one assured of his place in the Master Race.

'And after. This gives me some satisfaction.'

Dori set out more photographs like cards in a different game. The same men dishevelled, unkempt, unshaven, dressed in ill-fitting civvies, loose collars and no neckties, faces sallow, sunken, baggy about the eyes, like the broken men one might see on any street. Only the eyes set them apart. These were guilty men, but the eyes showed no guilt; fear was there, resignation, even sullen defiance and a general furtiveness, a refusal to meet the camera's unforgiving stare.

'And now for the girls.'

They looked like any young women trying to make the most of themselves, smiling into the camera, hair coiffed, carefully made up, young and pretty, some of them even beautiful. Next to these, Dori placed images of the same women now wearing coarse dresses, their faces without makeup, greasy hair scraped back. They'd aged ten years easily, twenty. The contrast was shocking. Like the men, they showed no guilt. There was a chilling emptiness in eyes that knew the game was up and were already contemplating the gallows.

'Nice lot, eh?'

'Who are they?'

'Guards. A few commandants. Mostly smallish fry. These are the ones we've bagged. They deny everything, of course, don't know, didn't know, just following orders. We're working away at them, discovering more day by day. That's why we have to keep on. In my book, doctors like von Stavenow are the worst of the lot.' Dori collected the photographs and put them back in their files. 'Don't get me wrong, I hope they all swing, but what *they* did . . . what the survivors have told us. What was done to them, supposedly in the name of science—' She stopped. 'Terrible injuries. Really terrible. You should see them, Edith, the survivors. Young girls, pretty girls.' She shook her head. 'They'll never be the same again. But so *brave*. Determined to bear witness. Determined to see justice done. As am I.'

She looked away, eyes distant, dark with a pain that wasn't hers. Edith reached across the table.

'Harry has told me something of what they did.'

'He's been interviewing survivors too, he should know.' Dori sniffed and blinked quickly. 'Goodness, how silly. Something in my eye. Playing havoc with my mascara. Have you a hanky by any chance?' Dori dabbed beneath her eyes, repairing the damage with the help of her compact. She reapplied her lipstick, working her lips together. 'We *have* to find von Stavenow before Adams does if he's not to end up in some cosy lab in Blighty.' She examined herself briefly, critically, then snapped the compact shut. 'How was Adeline? I'm surprised at her, dogs-bodying for McHale. I know she's ambitious but there are limits. What did they want, anyway?'

'Same as Adams.'

'The Sturmbannführer *is* in demand. Any idea why?'

'Area of his research. Harry thinks nerve gas. Adeline said she was doing some research on her own account that might be useful to us.'

'Well, that's something, I suppose.' Dori waved away more coffee. 'I must be off. We're leaving early tomorrow for Karlsruhe. We've had new information and Vera wants to revisit the prison. Some of our girls were held there before being sent to a camp called Natzweiler Struthof, a *Nacht und Nebel* place in the Vosges mountains.'

'*Nacht und Nebel*?' Edith frowned. 'Night and Fog?'

'One of the pleasanter Nazi decrees. Suspected Resistance fighters, agents and others, vanished without a trace. Hence night and fog. Natzweiler is one of the places where they were disappeared.' She bit her lip to stop it from trembling. 'We know that four of our girls ended up there. Now, it's a matter of positive identification and finding out exactly what happened.'

'Dori,' Edith felt her own eyes filling as she took Dori's hand again. 'I'm so sorry.'

'No.' Dori gently pulled her hand away. 'You'll make a woman of me and this is a man's world, as you're finding out. We work in spite of the Adamses and McHales—' She stopped. The complex emotions playing over her face cleared and she smiled, the tears still sparkling in her eyes. 'You are a wonder, Edith. A natural at this. I *knew* you would be! Find out more about the *Schwestern*. Get Elisabeth in with them. You've given me the tiniest inkling of an idea. Meanwhile, I have my trusty cookbook with me and I so *love* to share recipes.'

29

Billet, Lübeck

17th–18th March 1946

Kaffee und Kuchen
Gugelhupf Frau Schmidt

We have nothing quite like it in Britain.
The nearest would be a rich tea bread
(*Gugelhupf* is made with yeast), like Bara
Brith but with more eggs and butter, gener-
ously dotted with preserved cherries (as
here), or other fruit and almonds. It is
most common in Southern Germany, where every
family has its own recipe (something else
it has in common with Bara Brith). It is
baked in a Bundt tin, traditionally copper,
deep and fluted with a central funnel. When
turned out and dusted with icing sugar, it
is so beautiful it seems a shame to cut into
it. Definitely a cake to impress!

Dori was right. Elisabeth was key to the whole thing. Edith put
her mind to how it might work.

Over the weekend, Roz had been viewing an apartment, for them both.

'It's perfect!' she said, her pale face flushed with excitement. 'Two floors, not far from the centre.'

She already had the keys. She took Edith to see it on their way home from work. Polished wooden floors and light oak panelling. The apartment was furnished. The people who had lived here had left with what they could carry but the rooms still breathed their presence. Both women found themselves walking softly, as if they were interlopers.

'At least we won't have to bring anything,' Roz said to break the spell.

'We'll need a housekeeper,' Edith said.

'Right you are,' Roz frowned. 'I'll get on to it.'

'No need,' Edith smiled. 'I've got just the person in mind.'

The next morning, she directed Jack to the house where Elisabeth was living on Humboldtstraße.

'I hope you'll take up the offer,' Edith unpacked coffee, cigarettes, various cans of this and that. She was sure Elisabeth would jump at the chance but she had to give her the choice. 'It makes so much sense. You need work, there's only two of us to look after and it'll be so much better than here.'

There was no arguing with that. Since Edith's first visit, a makeshift curtain had appeared, dividing Elisabeth's room in two.

'What about the child?'

'You can bring her with you, of course.' Edith paused. 'I want to go about this in a particular way. I want you to come to me via Frau Schmidt.'

Elisabeth folded her arms and frowned. 'How do I do that?'

'Knock on the door. Ask about a friend, a relative, someone you're looking for, from home, from the east.' Such enquiries were all too common. 'Get chatting. Does Frau Schmidt know of any work? Frau Schmidt will be impressed by your refinement, your title. She'll do her best. I'll do the rest.'

'When?'

'No time like the present. The Frau's expecting a coke delivery, so she'll be in all day. While you're there, drop a few hints about Kurt – that you're looking for him, that kind of thing. Make sure she knows his rank and that he was SS. That'll impress her even more.'

Elisabeth's frown deepened. 'Why?'

'Because she's our best hope of finding him. She has connections to organizations, Nazi orgnizations, who are in touch with fugitives, helping them escape from Germany. If she puts the word out that his wife is trying to find him then we might pick up a lead.'

Elisabeth would be thick with the Frau in no time. She would put feelers out which would offer a chance to discover more about Nazi organizations like *Die Spinne* and that would keep Adams happy. With any luck, the old bird's native cunning would work against her. That was the theory, although there could be no certainty. Nothing was certain here.

'Frau Schmidt, might I have a word?' Edith asked the next morning.

'Is it about the eggs? We cannot always get fresh,' she shrugged her fat shoulders.

'No, it's not about the eggs.'

'Is it about Fräulein Slater?' Frau Schmidt dabbed her eyes with a handkerchief that displayed someone else's initials. 'So sad. She was like a daughter. The poor thing! Her poor family.'

'Yes, it's very sad.' Edith patted the Frau's plump hand. She remembered that there was just a father. Her mother had been killed in an air raid, Molly had told her in an uncharacteristic, gin-fuelled moment of intimacy. 'Now there's just Dad,' she'd confided. 'And Mrs Powell. She's the help. His mistress, really. They think I don't know. I think they'd marry if it wasn't for me.' Now, they probably would and no one would miss poor Molly, or care one bit that she was gone. That made it worse somehow. 'Very sad indeed.'

'Is it about car slipping?' A tiny note of apprehension. 'I told you about the rain.'

'Not that either. I'm thinking about moving in with a colleague.' Edith waved away the halfhearted protests. Frau Schmidt would be glad to see the back of her. 'I know, I know, I will miss you all, too, but I need more space and a little less turmoil.' Edith paused and smiled in a way that she hoped was convincing. 'We will be needing a housekeeper. I would value your help in finding someone suitable.'

'Alas!' Frau Schmidt's first thoughts were another household, more rations to siphon. 'I cannot come, Frau Graham. With Stephan helping cousins in the country, I have too much to do here . . .'

Stephan seemed to have done a bunk. He'd made himself scarce after the 'car slipping' incident.

'You will miss his . . . help,' Edith said diplomatically. 'I wasn't thinking of you. You have too much to do here – especially with Stephan gone – and I could never take you away from these girls. So far from home and so young, you are like a mother to them. They need you.' Edith put on a suitably sorrowful expression. 'Especially now.'

'There is always Nina,' Frau Schmidt brightened. With her niece in place, she still might profit from this turn of events. 'She's very capable.'

Edith nodded, as if considering.

'Nina's a lovely girl,' she said, 'but I was thinking of someone older, a mature lady, perhaps. Respectable, naturally, with some refinement. Someone who can cook, of course, but I need more than that. Someone with good English.' That would eliminate Nina. 'To answer the telephone, for example. Many of my colleagues don't speak German. And help with paperwork. There is so much now. I was hoping that the right person might act as an unofficial secretary. I'm away frequently. I need someone who is able to act independently, who can manage the household in my absence.' She paused for a second or two, to allow her requirements to sink in. 'Do you know anyone like that?'

Respectable, mature, refined, educated, English speaking. Edith was doing everything but name Elisabeth.

'I might,' Frau Schmidt pretended to think.

'I'll leave it with you, then.' Edith looked at her watch. 'Goodness, is that the time? Jack'll be here at any minute.' As if on cue, a horn sounded from outside. 'That's him now. I must be off.'

Edith congratulated herself as she got into the car. The mention of 'paperwork' had been inspired. Edith knew how Frau Schmidt's mind worked. Elisabeth might make a useful spy. If she recommended Elisabeth, it would mean she suspected nothing. The bait would have been taken.

That evening, Frau Schmidt was there to greet her.

'I think I've found someone,' she said, her glossy curls quivered with suppressed excitement.

'Oh, really?' Edith asked as she removed her hat and gloves.

'Yes, yes! A very respectable lady, from the east. A refugee but of *very* good family. She is just what you ask. Speaks English. Very refined. The only thing is,' Frau Schmidt hesitated, 'there's a child. You didn't say about a child.'

'No, I hadn't thought of that.' Edith pretended to consider. 'How old is this child?'

'Not very old,' Frau Schmidt looked vague.

'I see.' Edith pretended to consider some more. 'Perhaps I should meet this person. Can you arrange an interview?'

'She's here!' Frau Schmidt opened the door to the living room with the flourish of a magician performing a particularly clever trick.

'Frau Graham? I'd like you to meet *Gräfin* von Stavenow.'

'I'm delighted to meet you,' Elisabeth said in English. 'And it is just plain Frau von Stavenow. I don't use my title.'

'I'll leave you, then,' Frau Schmidt beamed, proud of her protégé. 'I'll bring coffee and cakes.'

'Do sit down, Frau von Stavenow,' Edith said as Frau Schmidt left the room. 'I hope you don't mind if I ask you a few questions?'

'Of course, Miss Graham,' Elisabeth replied. 'Ask away.'

Edith glanced towards the door. Elisabeth cupped her ear. Edith nodded. They conducted the sham interview until the heavy footfall receded.

'Looks like she's fallen for it.' Elisabeth lit a cigarette. 'Very impressed by Kurt.' She breathed through the smoke. 'Can't do enough to help me there.'

There was a knock at the door, Nina came in with a tray: a chased silver pot with matching milk jug and sugar bowl; fine blue patterned china plates, cups and saucers. Edith hadn't seen any of it before. At the centre of the table, a large plate covered in a white doily held slices of *Apfelkuchen* and *Gugelhupf*.

'I haven't seen cake like this for years,' Elisabeth said, taking a piece of apple cake. 'Where on earth does she get the ingredients?'

'Most of them courtesy of the CCG. The rations are very generous, as you'll see.'

Frau Schmidt herself came to collect the tray.

'Is everything to your satisfaction?'

'Yes, indeed,' Edith put on her best smile. 'You've excelled yourself, Frau Schmidt. We've polished off most of it, as you can see.'

The plates were practically empty, although much of the cake was wrapped in a napkin in Elisabeth's handbag.

'I must say, Frau Schmidt,' Elisabeth said, brushing at crumbs. 'Your *Blitzkuchen mit Äpfeln* was divine and the *Gugelhupf*. Quite the best I've ever eaten. I don't know how you manage to produce such delicious cakes, given the scarcities.'

Frau Schmidt blushed and rubbed her hands on her apron.

'I can give you recipes, if you'd like.'

'Would you?' Elisabeth smiled. 'That would be wonderful! Then I can cook delicious cakes for Frau Graham.'

Frau Schmidt took her notebook from her apron pocket and extracted a thick stub of a pencil.

'It won't take a minute.' She sat down at the table and began to write, forming the letters laboriously in a neat, looping cursive script.

'Here you are!' She tore out the page and offered it to Elisabeth.

323

'Why thank you, Frau Schmidt.' Elisabeth accepted the sheet graciously. 'That's most kind. I will treasure it.'

Frau Schmidt smiled like a child being given full marks. Elisabeth's finely judged combination of hauteur and flattery was working wonders. She had the redoubtable Frau in the palm of her hand.

Frau Schmidt might claim it, but the recipe was Hilde's and the girl had probably made it. Edith made a mental note to compliment her.

On the day Edith was leaving, Hilde gave her a jar of cherries, handing them over with shy pride and a hint of defiance. Edith was touched by the girl's generosity and smiled at the minor act of rebellion. Perhaps there was hope after all.

30

Apartment 2a Schillerstraße, Lübeck

6th–21st April 1946

Kirschenmichel

Crumble half a loaf or so of stale white bread into a bowl, pour over a generous 1/2 pint of milk and let stand until all liquid is absorbed. Grease a baking dish and sprinkle with breadcrumbs. Separate two eggs. Whisk the whites until stiff. Cream 2oz butter, the same of sugar with the egg yolks and vanilla, fold in the egg whites, soaked bread and cherries. Bake in the centre of a moderate oven for 45 mins to an hour. Dust with powdered sugar and serve warm with custard.

Rather like Apple Charlotte – perfect for a Whole Meal Menu as an Alternative or Extra Dish as can be cooked low in the oven. With 6 runners, I'd recommend finishing at high position for 10 minutes and then lower for 12 or so. Cream the 2oz butter for 1-2

minutes. Increase amount of bread from 4 to
7 or even 10oz. (Omit 4oz butter from Apple
Charlotte recipe.)

How little she owned here, Edith thought as she walked into the
new apartment. It all fitted into a trunk and a suitcase. Roz had
even less.

Roz hung up her coat on a hat stand spiked with umbrellas
and walking sticks: *Wanderstab* plastered with little shields,
Stocknägel, nailed to the cane and chestnut shafts.

'Funny, isn't it? All this being someone else's.' She took out
a hiking staff and read the names of places they'd never heard
of: Elferhütte, Bielefeld, visited by people they would never
know. 'They're just waiting, the Germans, don't you feel it?
Biding their time, until we pack up and leave. Then everything
can get back to normal, they can go hiking again, collecting
these little badges, and it will be just as if we were never here
at all.' She put the stick back carefully. 'We're like privileged
refugees.'

Elisabeth was waiting for them: beds made, stoves lit, water
hot. She made Kirschenmichel with Hilde's parting gift to Edith.
She wouldn't allow any help with the cooking and clearing. Edith
was glad to have got Elisabeth out of the overcrowded warren
where she'd been living but it was odd to see her in this role.
She would always be more chatelaine than servant.

Elisabeth's introduction into Roz and Edith's new ménage
would not go without comment. Their move wasn't the issue,
nor was their choice of housekeeper, it was the fact that they
would share the apartment with her. That was contrary to regulations and could prove a snag. Elisabeth's daughter was staying
with Lise, her wet nurse, for the time being, so that was one less
complication, but Edith judged that it was time to tell Bill Adams.
As an Intelligence Officer, he could make problems like that go
away. She put in a call. He wanted to see her anyway. Could they
meet for a drink in the Mess?

'What's this I hear about brake pipes being cut?'

'How do you know about that?'

'Little bird. Why didn't you tell me?'

'Didn't seem any point. It was probably Stephan and he's disappeared.'

'Even so . . .' his frown deepened. 'It's not on. Getting above themselves. I've a good mind to roll the whole lot up.'

'I don't want you to do that, not yet anyway.'

'Why not?'

'At least we know who they are and where they are. *Die Spinne*. Tear a web in one place, it grows in another.'

'I see your point.'

'I've got a plan.' She told him about Elisabeth.

'Cleverly done, Edith,' he was nearly rubbing his hands with glee. 'Cleverly done! Frau Schmidt trusts her?'

'Fallen for her hook, line and sinker. Elisabeth's very charming and aristocratic. Frau Schmidt likes that.'

'Charming and aristocratic, is she? I'd like to meet her.'

That wasn't going to happen. She didn't want to put Elisabeth in a difficult position. Most of the men were Lotharios and not just the single ones. Even the Brigadier was having an affair with a woman who worked in Catering, according to Roz. With wives at home and unattached women freely available, the temptations were just too great.

'Attractive, is she?'

'Very.'

'In that case, I'd definitely like to meet her.' Bill Adams smiled and smoothed his pale moustache.

'Good idea. Perhaps I'll bring her here for dinner.'

Bill laughed a little uneasily. They both knew that Germans were *verboten*, unless employed in the Mess as servants.

'I was joking.'

'So was I.'

'All right, Edith,' Bill put his hands up. 'You win. Frau von Stavenow is safe from me. Put it down to misplaced gallantry. What about the husband?'

'Frau Schmidt is very impressed by Kurt, his rank in the SS, and so on. She's promised Elisabeth she'd help find him. She's in touch with some people . . .'

'That's *good*. Names?'

'I can give you the local women but they're small fry.'

Adams nodded his agreement. 'We want the wider network.'

'Frau Schmidt calls them the Organization. She's very cagey about it, Elisabeth says.'

Adams frowned. 'We need to know how big it is, who's involved, how widespread and if they're in touch with other groups.'

'I'll see what Elisabeth can find out.'

'You do that but be careful. These are unpleasant types, very unpleasant and we don't want any more – accidents. Good work, Edith. Another?' He clicked his fingers and the waiter came running. 'Whisky. No ice.'

Elisabeth was accepted as one of the *Schwestern*, more and more trusted. A good Nazi Frau looking for her husband. The local group were connected to other networks, who were connected to other networks. Frau Schmidt had sent out a request for information on the whereabouts of Sturmbannführer Kurt von Stavenow. Word was passing along the mycelium of Nazi organizations that were branching and spreading well out of sight of the British.

It all seemed to be working out very well – maybe too well.

'How was your weekend?' Roz started as they were walking home from work. Edith had been out all day. It was the first time they'd had to catch up with each other.

'Good, thank you. It was cold, but . . .'

Roz laughed. 'Don't suppose that mattered.'

'No, not a lot.' She smiled back.

She'd managed to wangle a precious weekend away with Harry. It was the first time she'd seen him since Hamburg and she'd had time to reflect. Although she could never condone what he'd done – the taking of an innocent life could never be justified – she did understand how his history informed his fractured morality. It was not up to her to forgive, such grace was beyond her power to bestow, but he had kept his part of the bargain. Seraphina and Anna were on their way. She knew better than to ask the details. No names, no pack drill, as Jack would say . . .

'How was your weekend?' she asked.

'Bliss!' Roz linked arms with Edith. 'Wonderful to spend all night together in a proper bed. When are you seeing Harry again?'

'Berlin. Next weekend. If I can wangle it.'

'Oh, I'm sure I can arrange some meetings.' Roz smiled.

Edith was sure she would. Another chance to play house with Jeff. At the weekends, Roz had the house to herself, Elisabeth going to the country, to a farm at Badendorf west of Lübeck, where her horses were kept, looked after by her Master of Horse, Kaspar, the father of her child.

'You know Elisabeth?' Roz began. The name sparked between them.

'Yes, I know Elisabeth,' Edith said evenly. 'Has Jeff discovered some deep, dark secret?'

'Oh, no, nothing like that,' Roz said, to Edith's relief. Interest from Jeff and Public Safety could really throw a spanner into her carefully calibrated works. 'It's just, well,' Roz went on, there was obviously something troubling her. 'Do you ever think about the child?'

'Elfriede? Why?'

'Well,' Roz had a tendency to say 'well' when broaching awkward subjects. 'Why doesn't she want the baby with her? I think that's a bit strange.'

'The baby is still being nursed and powers that be might take an even dimmer view,' Edith said lightly.

'I suppose so,' Roz conceded, 'but she hardly ever mentions her. She seems to care more about her horses. And that Kaspar chap . . .'

'What about him?'

'Have you ever met him?'

'No, he lives out in the country. You know that.' Edith tried to control her irritation. 'I thought you liked Elisabeth.'

'Oh, I do!' Roz said, keen to make amends. 'She looks after us very well.' She patted her midriff and laughed. 'Perhaps a bit too well. We don't go to the Mess very much, do we? It's just . . .'

'Just what?' Edith asked carefully, not wanting to show her growing annoyance

'I know she's your friend, and all that, but sometimes . . .' Roz paused. 'She makes me feel a bit uncomfortable.'

'Really? In what way?'

'She's awfully nice, and everything, but it's like the others. I'm surprised you've not noticed.'

'The others? You mean Germans?'

'Yes. They remind me of waiters in posh restaurants or grand hotels. They know they have to serve you and they're perfectly nice about it on the surface, but underneath they don't like it. They think they're superior.'

'Well, she was a *Gräfin*. It must be hard for a countess to take on what is essentially a servant's role.'

'I suppose so,' Roz conceded. 'I say,' she squeezed Edith's arm, 'you're not offended, are you?'

'Of course not.'

Edith fought down a desire to shake off Roz's linking arm. They walked along in silence until Roz peeled off to meet Jeff. It was their night for the Pictures. Edith hardly noticed her cheery, 'Goodbye, see you later.' She tried to dismiss what Roz had said as Control Commission prejudice, although Roz was not really like that, and it chimed with something Luka had let slip the other day as he was walking her back to the apartment. Something about Elfriede not being Elisabeth's child. When Edith asked him to explain, he just shrugged and said: *Ich weiß nicht* – I don't know – and gave a tight little smile, as if he'd said too much or not enough.

She'd dismissed it at the time as Luka getting things mixed up, as he frequently did, but . . . She walked on, hands deep in her pockets, her steps automatic, furious with both of them.

31

Apartment 2a Schillerstraße, Lübeck

22nd–25th April 1946

Frau Schmidt's Apfelkuchen
125g butter or margarine
175g sugar
3 eggs
A tenth of a litre of milk
Half a packet of baking powder
250g flour
Zest of a quarter of a lemon
1kg of soft apples
60g sugar
Spice

Beat butter to a cream with sugar and eggs. Whereupon you mix into it the spices, the milk, the flour (mixed with the baking powder), and fill the prepared cake tin. Now you add the apples, which have been prepared a few hours earlier, cut into slices, with sugar scattered and spice. Bake at a medium heat (170C) for three quarters of an hour. The cake

can also have almond nibs and sultanas or
raisins scattered over it before it is baked.

(As in Kirschenmichel, could use Apple
Charlotte recipe for reference.)

Elisabeth had made *Apfelkuchen*. She served it in the sitting room
with coffee. The cake was warm from the oven, crusted with
sugar, moist with apple and the raisins scattered through it. Edith
tasted nutmeg and cinnamon, reminders of Irenka's kitchen.

'Where did you get the raisins and spices?' Edith asked. She
didn't mention the cook. Elisabeth didn't like talking about
Schloss Steinhof: *What is there to say? It doesn't exist anymore.*

'Traded for them, like everything else. It's good? You want
more?'

Edith shook her head and drank her coffee. 'Keep some for
Roz. She can take a slice for Jeff.'

The cake was delicious but the dense texture was threatening
to stick in her throat. The slice she'd already eaten lay heavy in
her stomach. She had enjoyed the quiet evenings alone with
Elisabeth but Roz and Luka's doubts were ringing in her head
like tinnitus.

'The child, Elfriede,' Edith poured herself more coffee. 'Don't
you miss her? Neither of us would have minded you bringing
her with you.'

'It could cause trouble,' Elisabeth picked up her sewing. 'For
me. For you. It is better the baby stays with Lise. Frau Schmidt
deals in gems and jewellery, did you know?' Edith noted the
quick change of subject. 'Gets them for next to nothing. "You
can't eat diamonds" is what she says. People will trade anything
for food. She wants me to go into her business. She says I have
a good eye.'

'Are you considering it?'

'I need money for the horses.' Elizabeth threaded her needle.
'I'm running out of my own jewels.' Elisabeth paid for the upkeep
of her horses in diamonds and pearls. 'Kaspar is trying to locate

what is left of the herd. We want to establish the stud again.'

'Has Kaspar ever seen Elfriede?' Edith asked.

'No,' Elisabeth looked up sharply. 'Of course not. He's not here, is he? And it is hard for him to travel. His papers were lost.'

'He's not that far away . . .'

Elisabeth concentrated on rethreading her needle.

'You must look forward to the day when you will all be together,' Edith probed further.

'Of course.' Elisabeth said vaguely as she shook out the blouse she'd been working on. 'I've turned the collar, shortened the sleeves. I'm going to replace the buttons, brighten it up a bit. Frau Schmidt gave me these.' She took a folded paper from her workbox, a page from the Frau's notebook, identified by the thin red edging. She opened it carefully. 'What do you think?'

Edith inspected the thin discs, noting again that quick change of subject, trying to assess whether it was significant. She took one of the buttons, noting the soft, nacreous gleam as she turned it to the light.

'This is old. Real mother-of-pearl. I wonder what garment it might have been snipped from? I wonder who fastened it?'

Elisabeth shrugged, as though it would never occur to her to even speculate. She simply didn't care who had owned them, even if she had a pretty good idea.

'Traded for sewing-machine needles,' she said. 'That was a stroke of genius, Edith, I must say.'

Edith had sent home for more sewing materials. Most German women had machines, or access to one, but needles, Sylko and bobbins were practically unobtainable and thus fetched high prices on the black market. Dori's useful wampum.

Elisabeth began to sew on the buttons, fiddly work, requiring concentration. Edith found her place in her book and began to read. She'd had such little time since she'd got here. It took her a while to pick up the story . . .

Suddenly, she looked up. Elisabeth had ceased to sew and was watching her.

'What is it?'

'The Organization has been in touch with word of Kurt.'

The words came out in a rush as though she had been holding them back.

'What?' Edith stared in shocked surprise. 'Do they know where he is?'

'In Berlin.' Elisabeth retrieved the fold of red-edged paper from her workbox again. 'This is his address.'

Edith reached to take it, her heart beating harder. This was it. This was what they'd been waiting for and she'd be in Berlin this weekend. 'Why didn't you say anything before?'

'I didn't want to,' Elisabeth said as she snipped off a thread. 'You were asking questions. I feared you might be suspicious, also. Roz, I think doesn't trust me.' There was agitation in the way her accent slipped: 'v' for 'w', 'sings' for *th*ings. 'And . . .' She bit her lip, suddenly worried, wary, her voice muffled as she hunched over her sewing. 'I don't want them finding out I told . . .'

For a moment, she seemed as scared as the German girls in the billet.

'One of us?'

Elisabeth nodded. 'They hate you. These people will stop at nothing. It's not just people they're smuggling. They deal in gems, bullion, currency, tobacco, whatever has value. Proceeds are used to finance future operations, here and abroad.'

'What kind of future operations? Do they discuss those?'

Elisabeth nodded again. 'They believe Hitler is alive. Living in South America. Taken there by submarine. Bormann, too, and every other senior Nazi who isn't dead or on trial.' Elisabeth positioned another button. 'They will form a Fourth Reich. It's only a matter of time. The stories about what happened to the Jews in Belsen and Auschwitz and those other places are just that. Stories. Lies and propaganda. Pictures and newsreels fabricated by the Allies to make Germans look bad. To justify what they have done to the Fatherland, the bombing and destruction. To defend what they are doing now, deliberately starving the people while systematically robbing the nation, stripping it of everything of value. Things were far better under Hitler, that's what they say. Many agree.'

'Who?' Edith frowned. 'How many?'

'My friends from the Schrebergärten.' Elisabeth had befriended the men and women who worked the local allotments, the prospect of fresh vegetables in mind. 'Lots of people. They are waiting for Hitler to come back and save them. People like Frau Schmidt and her friends are preparing the way.'

'But that's preposterous.' Edith shook her head. 'Stuff and nonsense.'

'That is what they believe,' Elisabeth said emphatically. 'If they found out you knew, my life would be forfeit. Yours, too. They've already tried . . .'

'It was them, then? The car?'

Elisabeth nodded quickly. Her stabbing needle missed its mark. She made no sound but her finger beaded blood.

'All the more reason to stop them.' Edith fought down her own sudden surge of apprehension and took Elisabeth's hand, wrapping it gently in her handkerchief. 'This can't go on, everyone still living in terror of them. We need names, contacts. If we had that, Adams could have them all arrested. They might not like us very much, but we're here to bring some sort of order. Nip this kind of thing in the bud.'

Elisabeth swiped the tears off her face. 'I don't know what's wrong with me. I used to be so fearless.'

'Fear is insidious and you've lived with it for a long time.' Edith could feel her suspicions melting into sympathy. 'It's bound to tell eventually. It's like dry rot of the soul.'

Elisabeth sniffed and smiled, suddenly more hopeful. 'Frau Schmidt has lists. In her notebook. Names and numbers.'

'Good. Do you think you can get a look?'

'I will try Thursday. Frau Schmidt's Montags-Kaffeeklatsch.'

Kirschenmichel and Apfelkuchen. Edith sent the message in the Apple Charlotte recipe to Dori in Bad Oeynhausen.

Thursday evening, Elisabeth was waiting in the hall. She must have heard the key in the door.

'Edith, may I speak with you?' She turned to Jack who had

accompanied Edith to the door hoping for a brew and a slice of cake. 'There's tea in the kitchen and I've just taken a batch of *Bethmännchen* out of the oven.' She smiled. 'Don't eat all of them!'

With Jack out of the way, Elisabeth produced a small, well-thumbed notebook, the pages edged with red.

'Goodness! How did you get it?'

'It fell from her overall pocket. I merely picked it up.'

Names, addresses, numbers. Not just in and around Lübeck and Hamburg, but Schwerin and Rostock, and they were in the Russian Zone. Adams would love this.

'Didn't she miss it?'

'Oh, yes. She went crazy, searching the house. But she isn't going to suspect me, is she? One of the girls got the blame.'

'Oh,' Edith looked up sharply, 'Which one?'

'Hilde is her name?'

Edith felt suddenly cold, any feeling of triumph evaporating as quickly as it had formed. Frau Schmidt would surely get rid of her and for Hilde that would be a disaster.

Roz's key in the lock.

'Can you go to my old billet?' Edith asked as she came through the door. 'There's a girl there. Hilde. Bring her here.'

'Now?'

'Yes, now. Jack will drive you. Jack!'

'OK.' Roz rebuttoned her coat. 'If you say so. Oh,' she turned from the door. 'A phone call for you, just after you left. Someone called Dori? Said she'll be in Berlin at the weekend. I've fixed those meetings,' she added with a wink.

Edith was relieved when Hilde arrived. She couldn't have another girl on her conscience. Why did the innocent always seem to suffer? She went to her room to pack and parcelled the notebook for Adams. She'd send it in the morning. There was plenty here to keep him busy. This would put her in the black and keep him off her back. Elisabeth had done well to get this. There was really no proof that she was anything other than what she'd said and so far she'd done everything asked of her.

Edith had to guard against the chronic suspicion that ran like a seam through the Control Commission. The war had done terrible things to the German people, blurred the lines, made them behave in ways that were difficult to interpret.

There was a knock at the door.

'Come in.' Edith looked up from her seat on the bed. 'Oh, Elisabeth. Everything all right? I hope you don't mind Hilde coming here. I thought she might be a help to you. Another pair of hands.'

'I'm sure she will. It's not that. She brought a message from Frau Schmidt.'

'What is it?'

'An old friend would like to see you. Tomorrow in the Tiergarten. In front of the Reichstag at four o'clock.'

32

Hotel am Zoo, Berlin

26th April 1946

Dinner – Hotel am Zoo
Schnitzel à la Holstein

Ideally a veal cutlet beaten very thin, coated
in fresh breadcrumbs and fried until golden
to browning. Holstein topped with a fried egg
or two, crisscrossed with anchovies and finished
with a dressing of browned butter, parsley,
finely chopped capers and the juice of a lemon.

Not in this case. Eggs overcooked, yolks
hard, whites like crisped lace. Strips of
fish could have been anchovy but were more
likely salted herring. The few wizened capers
resembled rabbit droppings. Meat flaccid,
pallid, encased in something that had the
texture and consistency of a sodden sock.

Edith had only visited Berlin once. She'd travelled on there with
Leo after their stay at Schloss Steinhof, just for a day or two

while Leo 'nosed about'. It was a city that yielded little on casual acquaintance, rather like its inhabitants. She didn't remember it very clearly and had no affection for the place. Of that, she was glad. Fond memories would have been erased, obliterated by Allied bombing and Russian shells, replaced by the ruination she saw now. She'd seen this desolation before, of course. Horrible how one got used to it. The destruction wasn't necessarily worse than Hamburg or any other city, it was just bigger, just as the city was bigger, more spread out, going on for mile after mile.

Jack dropped her in front of the Hotel am Zoo. She hadn't expected him to drive her but he had an excuse. A new toy. A cream-and-black BMW sedan had replaced the Humber. 'Beautiful, ain't she?' Jack had said, regarding the coachwork with something between respect and lust. 'Needs a run. Put her through her paces.' Was he keeping an eye on her or did he just fancy a trip to Berlin?

They made excellent time. Harry hadn't arrived, neither had Dori. Which was good. Edith didn't want to explain where she was going or what she going to do but there was at least an hour to kill before her meeting. Her room was small. Long cracks, like a road map, zigzagged across the walls and ceiling. A skin of paint in a different shade had been applied in an attempt at disguise but that just added to the feeling that the whole building might fall apart at any minute, fracturing along the fissures. It was stuffy in here and smelt faintly of rot and other people. She opened the window. From below, came the steady chink, chink of a *Trümmerfrau* patiently chipping mortar from useable brick.

Edith couldn't wait in here. The Zoological Gardens were opposite, the Tiergarten behind them. She would go out. Get the lie of the land.

From the ruins of the zoo, a distinct trumpeting suggested that at least one elephant had survived the general destruction. Goodness knows what had happened to the other creatures once kept there. There were stories of lions and tigers roaming the city immediately after the fall. Real beasts replacing their human equivalent. A Russian vet had apparently fought to save a hippopotamus, even sleeping next to it, tending its wounds, feeding it on vodka, while all around people were dying in their hundreds, if not thousands. What a strange world this was, she thought. What a strange species we are.

Beyond the zoo, lay the no-man's-land expanse of the Tiergarten, pocked with craters and shell holes filled with green-gilded stagnant water, dotted with broken and mutilated trees. Statues of kings and soldiers surveyed the devastation. Many pedestals were empty and broken. One huge plinth held just a foot. Look on my works ye mighty. The wide walks and promenades were churned and rutted, potholed by the treads of tanks and armoured cars. Edith took the crisscrossing tracks made by the surviving Berliners in their search for firewood, the quickest way from one point to another. Edith used the soaring Victory Column at the centre of the Tiergarten as a landmark. It was the only thing that appeared unscathed. The gold figure of winged Victory gleamed in the Spring sunshine. Above her, rippled a French tricolour.

There was beauty here, among the destruction. New growth was sprouting from the boles of the shattered treas. Lime leaves, vivid green and as soft and delicate as newly washed silk handkerchiefs. Women were digging the heavy clay soil, kneeling, hands in the mud, planting, watering seeds from battered enamel mugs, turning the churned mess of what had once been flowerbeds and manicured lawns into *Schrebergärten*, allotments. Nearby, stood a low cross, lashed branches of silver birch. A grey-green helmet, pitted with rust, dangled from one of the arms.

The Reichstag, or what was left of it, was closer now. Edith slowed her pace. She looked at her watch. It was nearly four but she was reluctant to go any nearer. All the way through the gardens, different dialogues and scripts had been playing in her head but she still had no clear idea what she would say to Kurt, or what he would say to her. She wasn't even sure if she wanted to meet him at all. She could go back to Lübeck, to her work with the Control Commission. Be shot of the whole business. Just do the job that she was paid to do.

Then she saw him moving amongst the buyers and sellers

gathered under the trees. British and American servicemen, even a few Russians, poking through the contents of bags and bundles held out for their inspection, cardboard suitcases open on the floor.

He seemed to be browsing at random. She lost track of him for a moment, then suddenly he was by her side.

'Edith! I'm so glad to see you. I was worried you would not come.'

Edith stepped away as he reached to embrace her, kiss her on both cheeks, as he had done at Heidelberg station. There was a fusty, unwashed smell about him. His gabardine raincoat was shiny on the lapels and ill fitting, the sleeves too short, an epaulette missing. His hat was battered, his shoes cracked across the toes. The smile had lost its dazzle. The charm as worn and shabby as his clothes.

'You will find changes in me,' he said, uncomfortable under her scrutiny. 'I lack a woman's care.'

He rubbed his jaw, in need of shaving. There was a scar on his cheek, recent by the look of it, pink and livid.

'How did you get that?' She couldn't stop herself from staring. 'You didn't have that before the war.'

'Shrapnel.' He touched it as if it was still tender. 'It became infected. Took a long time to heal.'

'Why did you want to see me?' she asked. Suddenly, she wanted to get away from him. As far and fast as possible. 'How did you know about me anyway? That I would be in Berlin.'

He ignored her questions.

'Well, what do you want?' she demanded in the face of his silence, resisting the urge to run.

'How do you know I want something?' He gave his rictus smile.

Edith looked past him towards the trading, the buying and selling, the men following young flesh into the bushes, so sad and so utterly predictable.

'Everyone wants something.'

'I want—' he began but didn't finish the sentence. He was looking at something, or someone over her shoulder. 'I thought

341

you would come alone. I wish you a good evening.' He tipped his hat to her and turned abruptly on his heel.

Adeline was standing right behind her, camera in hand.

'Edith! I thought it was you. What are you doing here? Do you know that guy?' She stared after Kurt's retreating figure. 'What did he want?'

Edith shrugged. 'Just a light.'

'You don't smoke.'

'That's what I told him.'

She turned away, ignoring Adeline, tracking Kurt weaving his way through the crowd milling in front of the ruined Reichstag. She would tell Adeline about him when she was ready, not before. The encounter had shaken her far more deeply than she could have anticipated. Adeline's appearance was surely coincidence, but it had rescued her from an unexpected storm of emotions: revulsion, loathing, hatred, physical repulsion brought on by everything she now knew about him, everything he'd done. A few seconds more in his company and she'd have lost control, failing Dori, failing everyone.

'So, what are *you* doing here?' Edith forced her attention back to Adeline.

'Taking photographs. What do you think?' Adeline looked up. 'Light's going. That's me done.' She put her camera back in the musette bag slung over her shoulder. 'Tom McHale's in town, too. Got an apartment out by the Wannsee. Very fancy.'

'He hasn't sent you home yet, then.'

'Not yet.' Adeline laughed. 'I have my uses. He's basing himself here now. Berlin's the place to be. Things are hotting up with the Soviets. Tensions rising. There's been a referendum here on merging the Social Democratic Party with the Communist KPD. Soviets all for it, of course. The Western sectors not so keen. There's been trouble. People being snatched off the streets. All kinds of dirty tricks. It'll get worse with the Fall elections. Berlin is turning into two cities. Front line in a new kind of war. West and East. Us and them. Tom wouldn't want to miss out on that.'

* * *

Back at the hotel, they found Dori in the bar, still in her uniform.

'Drink?' she asked. 'I've already started, as you can see.' She indicated to the barman. 'Three more of these. Your last message,' she turned to Edith. 'You have an address for von Stavenow.'

'Yes, it's here.' Edith took the piece of notepaper from her bag.

Dori looked at the note, folded it carefully and put it into her bag. She looked tired. Her face was even paler than usual with tiny lines of strain around eyes that had a glassiness to them, an unfocused quality, as if she'd had more than one martini.

'That's in the Russian Sector,' she said, her expression bleak. 'Makes sense.' She drained her glass. 'I've just come from that *Nacht und Nebel* place I told you about in Alsace. Natzweiler. A secret camp,' she added for Adeline's benefit. 'Somewhere for people to disappear. Prisoners sent there didn't come back. Civilian resisters mainly, spies, foreign commandoes, worked to death in the granite quarries.' She frowned, picking a strand of tobacco from her tongue. 'They had a facility there to deflesh corpses. The skeletons were sent to the Anatomy Institute at Strasbourg University for their collection. Four of our girls were taken there. Killed by lethal injection.'

'They didn't do that . . . Surely not . . .' Edith stumbled for words to express her disgust at yet another unspeakable horror.

'No. That didn't happen to our women. They were incinerated.' Dori's laugh was dull, like cracked glass. 'It comes to something, doesn't it? When one hears that with something like relief. But they were taken there for a reason. This was a secret camp. No witnesses. A place where they thought that they could do as they liked. But they couldn't, d'you see? There *were* witnesses. Hundreds of pairs of eyes, thousands, watching, taking notice. The prisoners were nothing to them, less than nothing, but putting them in jackets marked with a cross and N and N stencilled on them did not erase the human being within. They didn't all die and they saw what happened. They heard. And now they're telling us.

'Women came to the camp. Four of them. Well dressed, young,

attractive. This was a camp of men. How would they not notice?' She stubbed out her cigarette. 'We've identified three of these women: Andrée Borrel, Vera Leigh and Diana Rowden. The fourth may have been Noor Inayat Khan, but we're not so certain. What we do know is that these four arrived in the afternoon and died that night. They were to be killed immediately. Orders from Berlin. This was unorthodox. There was a reluctance to take responsibility. This was not a moral or ethical dilemma; it was a matter of procedure. This was not how things were done. The executioner didn't want to hang them; it would create too much drama. It was up to the doctors but they weren't sure that they had enough of the right kind of drugs to kill four healthy women.'

Dori spoke slowly, her focus inward, as she carefully pieced together the story from the witness statements she'd taken, the reports she'd read. Only the tension about her mouth betrayed her emotion, the way her hand trembled as she lit another cigarette.

'Anyway,' she let out a thin stream of smoke. 'The women were locked in cells. They could have had no idea what was about to happen to them. Later that evening they were taken to the building that contained the crematorium. The other prisoners had been locked up early. They all knew what was about to happen. The camp doctors were nervous, jittery. At this point, it is hard to find out who did what. They all deny it now, of course. What we do know is that whoever administered the injections, botched the job. The listening prisoners heard screaming, someone shouting '*Vive la France*'. There is evidence that at least one of the women was put into the oven alive.' She stopped long enough to control her voice and than cleared her throat. 'Anyway, a witness, a Dutch doctor, places someone else there. Natzweiler was one of a select number of camps involved in various scientific and medical experiments involving poison gas, among other things. There was a doctor who came from Berlin to collect the results. He supplied the lethal drugs and assisted with the loading of the women into the oven. In the process, his face was scratched badly,' Dori touched her own cheek, 'deeply enough to leave a scar.'

344

'It's there!' Edith nodded quickly. 'Looks recent.' She couldn't stop the words bursting out.

'You've *seen* him?'

'In the Tiergarten.'

'Why didn't you say something?'

'You didn't ask me.' And Edith hadn't wanted to tell. But she did now. She had to.

'It *was* him. I knew it!' Dori's dark eyes were on Edith. 'Arrange another meeting. That's why you're so important. Your Verbindung.' She used the German word. Connection. 'For Vera, it's enough to find out what happened to our girls, to bring the perpetrators to justice, where that's possible.'

'But it's not for you,' Edith ventured.

'No, not for me. Vera was never in France. She never saw active duty. She just sent us there. Some of these girls were picked up straight from the landing grounds. That didn't have anything to do with Vera, but she feels responsible. She has to discover what happened, bring prosecutions where possible, inform the relatives. When she's done that, then she's fulfilled her duty. It can all be filed somewhere, tidied away and forgotten. But these women were my comrades, my compatriots. They were picked up in France, sent to Germany to die horribly. It could have been me being loaded into that oven. I saw it, Edith. I saw the iron door, the metal loader and there was a smell, faint but still there. Burnt offerings.' She shuddered. 'Some things you can't forget. Will never forget. I tell you, I'd want someone to avenge me, if it'd been my fate to die in that terrible place.'

She sighed and sat in brooding silence for a while. Edith and Adeline remained quiet, sensing she had more to tell. 'We're picking up traces of von Stavenow in other places.' She looked at Edith. 'The girls from Ravensbrück, the women's camp, had an interesting tale to tell. The women there were from different countries: France, Poland. Some Jewish, but mostly political prisoners, agents, Resistance often as not ended up in Ravensbrück. Among them comrades. Women I knew. Some

345

came in pregnant. The other women would try to keep the births secret. Babies were taken away, you see. But it was impossible. It was impossible to keep anything secret and the mothers were exhausted from the work they were made to do. They couldn't feed their babies. Crying alerted the guards and the child was taken. We interviewed a nurse, asked her, "What became of the babies?"' Dori stopped and took a deep breath. When she spoke again her voice was husky, with a slight shudder, her accent stronger. 'They had orders, she said. The babies were not to be burnt. They were to be preserved. Brains and organs removed and kept. For study. Orders from a Doctor von Stavenow in Berlin.'

Before she could shut off the image, Edith saw babies, coarse-stitched and blind, floating in jars of formaldehyde, the amniotic fluid of the dead.

'They're not going to arrest him, we know that much,' Dori said. 'It'll be a tug of war with the Russians as to who can acquire his services.'

'Don't forget the Americans,' Adeline sipped her martini. 'My turn now. I know why the Americans want him and they want him bad.'

Edith dressed for the evening in the long-sleeved cocktail dress that Dori had chosen in Peter Jones. Strange to think the shop was still there, in Sloane Square, selling elegant clothes to elegant people. Impossible to imagine.

She checked at the desk as she went down to dinner. Telephone message from Harry. He'd been delayed. However much she ached to see him, that might be a good thing. One less complication.

Adeline was alone.

'Where's Dori?'

'Gone to meet someone. We're meeting her at the Kool Kat Klub. Let's eat.'

The Soupe Julienne was a flavourless vegetable concoction, heavily favouring the potato. The Schnitzels Holstein were even worse.

'What is this?' Adeline speared a sliver of meat.

Edith cut off a tiny piece and chewed thoughtfully. 'Should be veal but more likely pork.'

'Isn't human flesh supposed to taste like pork?'

'So they say.'

'I seem to have entirely lost my appetite.' Adeline pushed her plate away. 'There's a story doing the rounds here in Berlin. Heard it from a guy who heard it from a guy who works for the *New Yorker*, so it must be true. Anyway, this is how the story goes. There's a guy walking down Kurfürstendamm, or it could be Knesebeckstraße, depends on who's doing the telling. The guy's thin and kind of bent over, dressed in an old Wehrmacht jacket, broken boots, baggy trousers, an old soldier, you know the kind, you see 'em all the time. He's blind, wearing dark glasses, has a white stick and one of those yellow armbands with the black dots on it that blind folks have here. He's tapping along through the crowds when he stops this young *Fräulein*, she's a good-looking well-built kind of girl. He asks her for help. He has a letter to deliver. Is he on the right street? "Oh, no," the girl says, "you're going the wrong way." They start to walk back together but it's slow going and the address is quite a distance. "Tell you what," the Fräulein says, "why don't I deliver it for you?" "Would you?" He's very grateful. Not so nimble after Stalingrad and what with the blindness . . . "Certainly." She takes the envelope and off she goes. After a while she looks back, worried about how he's doing. He's doing pretty well, thank you. Just about to cross the road, looking right and left to see if there's a tram coming. The glasses are gone, so's the armband. She thinks, that's strange. She's suspicious, takes the letter to the nearest cop shop. They go straight round to the address, thinking it's maybe black market. It seems to be a shoe shop but something rings phoney, so they decide to search the place. In the cellar, they find spots of blood on the floor leading to a hidden door. Behind it they find a cold store and a whole load of fresh meat. Definitely black market but there's something funny about the cuts. By the shape and the skin, it looks to be human. Up until that point, no one has thought to

347

look inside the envelope. When they open it, they find a note. It says: *This is the last one I shall be sending today.*' Adeline sat back. 'Good story, huh?'

'Apocryphal, surely?' Edith had put down her fork, even though she didn't quite believe the story. Too like Sweeney Todd.

'Yeah, most likely,' Adeline prodded the pale, flaccid schnitzel. 'But you gotta admit, it could be true. Ever wondered how these places have always got everything when people on the street are starving? True or not, says something, doesn't it? I'm figuring out ways of getting it into the piece I'm writing. It works as a metaphor and readers love that kind of thing.'

'Everything to your satisfaction?' The waiter was back to clear the plates.

'Perfect,' Adeline smiled up at him.

'Anything for dessert?'

'No thank you.' She turned to Edith. 'Ready?'

The entrance to the Kool Kat Klub was crowded with young women waiting for dates, or simply waiting. They stood around talking to the men entering or leaving, while their little brothers hovered, watching for discarded cigarette butts. The door was not much more than a hole in the wall. Ghost letters above the door, set at zany angles, announced that it used to be the Krazy Kabarett. Most of the cabarets had been closed by the Nazis, or by the war. Now they were coming back. In a city that seemed to be dead or dying, they were thriving, like the fruiting bodies of some long-dormant mycelium erupting into life.

Narrow, dark stairs led down to a cellar. The walls were painted purple and black; the low ceiling was tented tarpaulin to keep out the rain from the ruined upper stories. Under the stench of sweat and cigarettes, Edith caught the bombed-out undertone of burnt timber, rottenness and damp. The cellar extended like a long cavern to a small stage and a tiny dance floor. Tables filled the rest of the space occupied mostly by servicemen, some in civvies, some in uniform: Americans and British, even a few Russians in breeches and high polished boots. The men were accompanied by young women, scantily clad and highly made up, laughing and flirting, hectic with free drinks on empty stomachs. Other women and boys glided through the throng, delivering drinks and collecting orders.

'Dori'll be somewhere,' Adeline said as they elbowed their way through the throng at the bottom of the stairs. 'She knows the guy here. They go back pre-war.'

They threaded through tables, moving towards the tiny dance floor where a few couples swayed to a quartet playing an approximation of American jazz.

'There will be cabaret later,' a voice said in carefully enunciated English. Edith turned to a man in evening dress, white tie and stiff collar. His brilliantined hair gleamed like patent leather. His thin cheeks were chalky with powder, his lips painted violet, his eyes rimmed with black. 'Welcome, Ladies.' He bowed. 'Tonight we are very crowded . . .'

'We're with Dori.' Adeline smiled.

'Ah, Dori. Her table is over there, I think. Can I get you something to drink?' He clicked his fingers at a passing waiter. 'On the house as friends of Dori's. Vodka, gin, bourbon, brandy, Champagne? Our friends in the Four Powers are most obliging. I will send it over.'

He bowed again and left them to welcome two Red Army officers in fluent Russian.

'That's Rudi,' Dori had come up behind them. 'Looks exactly like he did before Hitler shut his old place down. Funny who made it through and who didn't. God knows how he survived. Our table is over here. Along with Tom McHale.' She waved to the American who was leaning against the bar, smoking a cigar and looking bored. 'The gang's all here.'

He smiled and started to make his way over.

'Mind if I join you?'

'Of course not,' Dori kissed him on both cheeks. 'It's good to see you. Everyone seems to be in tonight.' She nodded towards the next table. 'Including our Russian friends.'

'Hey, honey,' Tom addressed a passing waitress. 'Can you get a bottle of bourbon? For my friends on the next table.' He sat down and gave the Russians a wave. 'There aren't as many as there used to be and those are likely to be NKGB. Watching us, watching them.' Tom McHale looked around. 'Half the girls in here work for them, trading in pillow talk or blackmail.'

'In exchange for what?' Edith asked.

'In exchange for mom and pop not getting hauled off to the Gulag. The game's getting dirty.' He raised his glass to the two Russians. Just then, the telephone in the centre of the table rang. 'Goddamn! I never knew those things worked.' Tom grinned and picked it up. 'Edith. It's for you.'

Edith took the receiver. Maybe Harry had got here early.

'Hello?'

She could see a man waving. Not Harry. Jack in civvies with a group of men and a bevy of *Mädchen*. He was getting up, making his way towards them. Edith replaced the receiver.

'This is Jack,' she said by way of introduction. 'He drives for me. Jack, meet Tom, Dori and Adeline.'

Jack nodded at the assembled company but only had eyes for Dori.

'Were you in SOE during the war?'

'Well, yes . . .' Dori gave a puzzled smile.

'It's an honour,' he said, caught between bashful and eagerness, neither characteristic typical of him. 'You helped a flyer pal of mine escape through France. We saw you once on Dean Street, coming out of the French House. He told me the story. Knew you straight away. Not a face I'd forget.'

Dori gave him her warmest smile. She liked the awed attention of good-looking men.

'Why don't you join us and tell me all about him. We hardly ever heard what happened after people left us.'

Jack didn't need a second invitation. He took a chair from another table and sat next to her.

'I can't believe I'm talking to you.'

Dori laughed and flipped him on the shoulder. 'Don't be silly!'

Soon the two of them were deep in conversation. Adeline was talking to Tom. Edith couldn't hear what they were saying through the rising chatter. Every now and then Tom glanced over which made her think they were talking about her. She turned back to the stage.

The band had gone. A papier maché broken wall was trundled on by a young woman dressed in a shapeless coat, a pair of outsized men's trousers, her hair tied in a rag, her face streaked with dust. She held a trowel and a brick and clinked them together to gain the crowd's attention. She sang about the *Trümmerfrau*; the plight of German women in general, their men lost or absent. At the end of the number, she whipped off her scarf, stripped off the coat and stepped out of the trousers. She stood in silk shift and camiknickers to whistles and roars of applause. Her next song was in the languages of the Occupying Powers. It was about sex and took in everything from Soviet rape to Hershey bars and cigarettes. She finished with a bow and a wink for the girls like her. The message was clear. Do you think we'd do this if we didn't have to? The blades of satire were as sharp as ever. The audience clapped and hooted their appreciation, the women loudest of all. They yelled and whooped for the woman on stage who'd given such lusty, defiant voice to their carefully cloaked anger and despair.

Adeline shouted across the table, 'Good to see cabaret's alive and well even if everything else is dead and buried.'

Edith had the feeling that she was making notes.

The band were playing jitterbug. Couples were getting up to dance. Jack was leading Dori off by the hand. Adeline and Tom stood up to join them.

Edith sipped her drink and played with a packet of cigarettes on the table, turning it over and over.

'Have one of mine.' A man reached over her shoulder, shaking a cigarette from a pack of Camels.

'I don't smoke.'

'I know.' He leaned closer. He was now clean shaven, smelling of the Vetiver cologne she remembered. 'Meet me tomorrow morning. Same place, 9 a.m.'

Then he was gone, moving through the throng.

Arrange another meeting, Dori had said. Now, she'd done it.

33

Russian Sector, Berlin

27th April 1946

Pfannkuchen
Speciality of the city. Everyone else in
Germany calls them Berliner. Jam doughnuts,
by any other name.

Streuselschnecken
Rhubarb Snails

Similar to a Chelsea Bun (p. 136, Bread,
Biscuits and Cakes) but filled with fruit
(in this case rhubarb) and topped with a
rough crumble mixture. Schnecken (snail in
German) perfectly describes the shape of the
coiled buns and this would be an excellent
use of rhubarb which is often plentiful when
other fruit is scarce and one is looking for
another use for it once it has been stewed,
pied and crumbled.

He came out from under the trees. He must have been watching
her approach. It was early. Few people about but still he seemed

wary. He was wearing the same clothes as the day before. Same hat, same raincoat.

'You looked different last night,' she said.

'In the day, out here, it is best not to look too prosperous,' Kurt said. 'Come. I know a place, not far.' He put a proprietorial arm round her shoulder. 'A small café. We can talk there.'

He took her to a place near the Brandenburg Gate. How quickly these places had popped back up again, business as usual between the ruins and the rubble. Small tables covered in oilcloth. The coffee served in thick cups.

He ordered coffee and a little plate of jam doughnuts.

The coffee came black, coarse ground and bitter tasting, more than a little of the ersatz about it. Kurt bit into one of the doughnuts, red jam oozed from the centre.

'You have to try,' he dusted sugar from his fingers. 'They are a speciality of the city.'

She picked one up, the crisp dough still warm from the fryer, coated in ground sugar.

He was still wearing that ring, heavy gold and carnelian. She remembered the last time they'd been together like this, outside that café in Heidelberg and marvelled how little she felt for him now. Gone was the lovelorn girl, her heart torn into bleeding pieces. Gone was the woman who had run the bath to overflowing to hide her sobs as she mourned the loss of love. He had betrayed her, many times over, now it was her turn. For her. For those lost women. For Elisabeth.

'What are you thinking?' he asked. He still pronounced *th* as *s*. She remembered trying to teach him, them laughing together.

'Oh, nothing.' She tore open the doughnut. 'Just wondering where they got the ingredients.'

'British, Americans. They trade like everybody does.' He dusted the sugar from his hands. 'But we're not here to talk about that.'

What were they there to talk about?

'You have been looking for me,' he said it as a statement of fact. 'Now you've found me.'

'I found Elisabeth,' Edith corrected. 'Elisabeth found you.'

'What does she want? Do you know?'

Edith thought quickly. 'A divorce. She wants a divorce.'

'And you?' He sat back. 'What do you want?'

'Not me, exactly.'

'If not you, then . . .' His face cleared. He gave that tight smile, hope sparking light into his blue eyes. 'Leo!'

'Yes,' Edith spread her hands. 'You have it in one.'

He sat forward, excited now, hands tightly clasped to control his agitation.

'When? What will happen?'

'You will be contacted,' Edith got ready to go. She didn't have the first clue. If there were plans, no one had told her what they might be.

'Edith, wait,' Kurt caught her hand and held it. 'Don't leave yet. I have more to say. This is my best chance. I know that. My only chance if I'm not to end up in Moscow but I must see her.' He looked up at Edith, his eyes at their most pleading. 'We parted badly. If she wants a divorce so be it, but I won't go anywhere unless you promise that she will see me.'

'It's really not in my power,' Edith took her hand from his. 'But I'll make sure they know.'

Back at the hotel, Dori and Adeline were waiting in her room.

'And? What happened?' Dori asked.

Edith took off her coat. 'I told him Leo wanted him,' she said simply.

'How did he react?'

'Like a drowning man who's just been thrown a life buoy. What I didn't know is why *you* want him. No, that's not right.' She turned to Dori. 'I know *why* you want him, but don't know what the plan is, if there is one, of course.'

'Of course there's a plan!' Dori looked stung.

'So? What is it?'

Dori sat back in her chair, thinking fingers steepled. 'Okay. The plan is . . . The plan is to get him out. Out of the Russian Sector for a start, then out of Berlin and on his way south. To

Italy. For that we need help from the Americans. They use ratlines all the time to get "visitors", as they call them, out of Europe.' She looked over to Adeline. 'Adeline's arranging a meeting with Tom McHale tonight.'

'You're going to help him escape!' Edith looked from one to the other, completely at a loss. 'I don't understand . . .'

'No,' Dori cut in. 'He's not going to escape. He's not going to escape at all. Just the opposite. But we need to be in an arena where we can take control. He's no good to anyone in the Russian Sector, is he?'

'So you're giving him to the Americans? They want him as much as Leo does and for the same reasons!'

'We want them to *think* they've got him. Then we'll step in.'

'Double-cross them?' Adeline frowned. 'That's a big risk, Dori.'

'I know!' She turned on Adeline, eyes blazing. She didn't like being questioned like this. 'I'm working with War Crimes and Drummond. We know what we're doing – you'll just have to trust us!' She turned her dark gaze, still sparking, to Edith. 'Now, I've got a question for you. How did you know to meet Kurt in the Tiergarten?'

'A message. From Frau Schmidt.'

'How did she know you would be in Berlin?'

'Elisabeth, I suppose.'

'So, Frau Schmidt knows that you, a British Control Commission Officer, are looking for a German war criminal and she's setting up a meeting with him in the Tiergarten? No, no, no!' She shook her head rapidly. 'That doesn't wash in any way!'

'What do you mean?'

'You could have arrived with a troop of Military Police ready to cart him off to Spandau. Think about it, Edith!'

The telephone rang. Adeline answered.

'Driver's here.'

Dori stood up and put on her coat. 'I arranged for Jack to come and pick us up. I told him to wangle a Jeep. I want to have a look at where Herr Doktor von Stavenow lays his head.'

* * *

Edith thought about it all the way through the Brandenburg Gate, into the Russian Zone and down the wide thoroughfare. Bare now of trees. Unter den Linden, without the limes. Of course. It was obvious. There had been no message from Frau Schmidt. Which meant it came directly from Elisabeth. Which meant that she must have been in touch with Kurt somehow. Edith stared, distracted, seeing, but not seeing. Elisabeth hadn't said anything about that. Not a word . . .

'Up here. Turn left.' Dori was directing Jack.

It was impossible not to feel exposed here. The city was really no different, but this side felt even more desolate, the streets empty of people, the walls adorned with huge photographs of Stalin, painted hammers and sickles, Communist slogans in Roman and Cyrillic script.

'Now right. Left again.' Dori consulted the note on her lap. 'This should be it.'

The curving street was residential, or had been. They looked out for house numbers scrawled on walls, or pillars, or in a few cases still on the actual buildings.

The house stood alone. The dwellings either side reduced to a few jagged walls jutting from reefs of fallen masonry.

Jack coasted the last few yards. The Jeep came to a stop outside a small café. Jack made a show of trying the engine, the turning motor sounding harsh and loud in the quiet street. He got out and opened the bonnet. Dori went into the small café to ask for help. '*Danke*. I'll try across the road,' she said loudly and walked across to Kurt's house. Jack took off his jacket and dragged a bag of tools from the back.

'It'll be the carburettor full of muck. It's the petrol. Full of God knows what.'

Edith and Adeline went to the café and sat down at one of the rickety tables to watch as Dori went up the steps and peered at numbers. Had Elisabeth been in touch with Kurt? Edith thought back. She'd shown her the address on Monday. Not really time for messages to go back and forth. *That was when she showed it to you*, the insidious, precise little voice of suspicion whispered. *You don't know how long she'd had it . . .*

Adeline jogged her arm. 'She's in!'

A man was coming out of the building, tipping his hat to Dori, holding the door open for her.

She showed you the address because she knew you were going to Berlin at the weekend, the voice in her head continued to reason. *Then she set up the meeting . . .*

Adeline nudged Edith again. A small woman was coming out of the café, wiping her hands on her washed-out wraparound apron. Edith explained that they had broken down. The woman nodded, pushing a lock of dark hair, streaked with grey, back under her faded kerchief. So the other lady had said. No telephone. She indicated the drooping web of lines. The other side, maybe. Meanwhile would they like something? The *Streuselschnecken* was very good.

'*Das klingt schön,*' Edith said. '*Und Kaffee bitte.*'

The lady went into the café. Adeline lit a cigarette and stared across the street. Jack carried on peering into the engine, muttering to himself and making a play with various spanners. Of course, they had been in touch with each other. It had been in Kurt's eyes when he'd asked about her . . .

The proprietress came out with coffee and cakes on a tray, a plate for them and one for Jack. He wiped his hands on an oily rag and leaned against the side of the Jeep.

'Ta, love.' He took a swig of coffee and scoffed his cakes in two bites each. He made a thumbs-up sign. '*Sehr gut!*'

The cakes were warm. Edith bit into one. The filling was a surprise.

'Rhubarb?'

The woman beamed. 'Yes, growing in the garden.'

'It's very good. I haven't come across that before.'

'English?' The woman looked from one to the other. 'American?'

'I'm English.' Edith pointed to herself. 'My friend is American.'

'Pleased to meet you.' She spoke in English. 'That is correct?'

Edith nodded.

'I like to practise. We don't see so many of you here. I am Frau Becke.' She laughed. 'Named for my trade. I know.'

'Can I have the recipe?' Edith asked.

'Of course!' Frau Becke's small, lined face creased with pleasure at Edith's interest. She patted her pockets, 'I write it for you.'

'No need,' Edith smiled back. 'You can tell it to me. That's fine.'

Edith took out notebook and pen to write down the recipe, it would go in the cookery book she'd told Harry she was going to write. Louisa would like it. Something else to do with rhubarb. And it would stop her mind ranging back and forth looking for clues, following a breadcrumb trail of duplicity across this whole new hinterland of deception that had suddenly appeared.

She forced her attention back to Frau Becke who was running through the recipe, indicating the dry ingredients with her hands, from cupped palms to a pinch. The table became her worktop as she mimed mixing, rolling, spreading on filling, rolling again and cutting. Edith noted each stage down. The recipes were like a diary, fixing times and places, people and faces. She would pair this with the *Pfannkuchen*. Her time in Berlin.

'Sprinkle on the *Streusel*. Heat the oven medium hot and bake the rhubarb snails—'

'Snails.' Edith looked up.

'It is not the right word?'

Edith thought of the fat little coiled buns as she wrote *Schnecke*. 'Yes, it's perfect.'

'Bake five and twenty minutes.'

'Thank you.'

Edith shut her notebook. She took out Reichmarks and a packet of cigarettes and put them on the table. She could be wrong, of course. There could be some other explanation. Edith took temporary refuge in that thought. It stopped the creeping feeling that she'd been completely fooled.

They all looked up at the sound of a car slowing down to cruise past them. The car stopped. Two men in civilian clothes, hats and long overcoats, got out.

'*Polizei.*' Frau Becke muttered. '*Gestapo.* Same as before.'

She scooped up the money and the cigarettes and disappeared inside.

Just at that moment, Dori came out of the house. She turned smartly to the right and set off walking.

The two policemen stepped towards Jack.

'Oi! Mate!' Jack shouted in English. 'Can you gis a hand? *Gib mir Hilfe?*' He nodded towards the engine. '*Ist kaputt.*'

The men stopped and took a look. They bent over the open bonnet examining the innards of the Jeep with reluctant curiosity. Jack got into the driver's seat.

'Hold that down while I try it. That's it. What do you know? Started first time. *Verschließen?*' One of them released the catch. The hood fell down with a slam. 'Thanks, mate. *Danke.*' He was revving the engine hard now. 'Hop in, girls.'

Jack executed a neat U-turn and roared off towards Friedrichstraße. He slowed when he reached Dori, stopping long enough for her to jump in.

'Think we've got away with it,' he said.

Edith turned round. The long, green, shiny snout of the German car was just visible, nosing out of a side street, chrome grill glinting.

'I wouldn't be so sure.'

Jack looked in the mirror. 'OK. Hang on to yer hats.'

Jack drew alongside a green-and-cream tramcar, pulling past it. He turned the wheel sharply, crossing the lines then cutting sharp right into a street narrowed by heaps of bricks and rubble spilled across the potholed surface like intersecting mounds of scree.

'Still behind us?'

Edith and Adeline turned, trying to see through the dust thrown up by the Jeep without losing their grip on the sides.

Edith caught a glint of glass. 'Yes, they are.'

Jack took a left and tucked the car behind the fallen frontage of half-destroyed building. The wall ran at a fractured diagonal, starting high up and descending in a series of jagged steps.

'At least it ain't a Tiger tank,' Jack whispered.

Nevertheless, they all crouched instinctively at the sound of the car approaching, nosing along cautiously, like a predator seeking out its prey. Edith felt the sharp prickings of fear as she listened to the low growl of the engine, the wheels bumping over the detritus that littered the road. The thin skin of bricks seemed flimsy protection. Then the engine noise changed as the car reversed sharply and left in a skidding crunch of tyres.

Jack waited until the sound had gone altogether before reversing the Jeep and turning towards the road. He pulled out cautiously. The coast was clear.

'Phew! That was—'

'Don't speak too soon.' Dori nudged his arm. The German car was coming up fast, getting ready to overtake the slow-moving Jeep.

'Right!' Jack shouted. 'If that's the way they want it.'

He jerked the wheel, pulling the car into a side street that had been only partially cleared. The piles of rubble practically met in the middle.

'We'll never get through there!' Adeline grabbed Edith's arm.

'They won't, that's for sure. Hold on tight.' Jack used the sloping rubble as a ramp and took the Jeep up on two wheels to get through the smallest of gaps. For one frightful moment, it felt as though they were going to overturn, then the Jeep bounced down onto the road again. 'That should fix 'em.' Jack laughed. 'I haven't had this much fun since I was bombing round Normandy in a scout car.'

He waved two fingers and roared away.

'Reckon I know where we are now,' Jack said, 'there should be a crossing point. Bridge over the Spree.' He nodded towards the oily, slow-moving river. 'Full of bodies, so they say.'

'They say that about everywhere, Jack,' Dori stared down at the black, turbid waters choked with all kinds of wreckage.

The crossing point back to the British Sector was on a bridge. The Russian soldier frowned down at the various documents while Dori spoke to him in rapid Russian. She offered him a cigarette. He took the packet, inspected the rolled cylinders of notes packed inside and raised the barrier. The British checkpoint waved them through after a cursory glance at their papers. It was Sunday afternoon and the guard was keen to get back to a fresh brew-up and his game of cards.

Jack dropped them at the hotel. There was a message from Harry. *Delayed. Sorry. See you later.* She folded the note and put it in her pocket, glad that she had other things to occupy her.

'Did you find anything?'

Dori had hardly spoken except to get them through the check-points.

'Research papers. My guess is he's been back to the Charité to get them. Gives him something to trade.' Dori dug into her pocket and took out a tiny cassette of film. 'It's all on here. I'll pass it on to War Crimes.' She took out a miniature camera, gave it to Adeline. 'There's more in this.'

'A Minox,' Adeline took the tiny silver lozenge of a camera and turned it over. 'Where did you get it?'

Dori shrugged, hands in pockets. 'We were issued with all kinds of kit during the war. Some didn't make it back to the stores. Can you develop it?'

'I guess. Might take a while.'

Adeline had converted the adjacent bathroom into a temporary darkroom. She'd tacked *Out of Order* to the door. Such inconveniences were not uncommon, to be met with a shrug and a trip to the next floor.

Dori stared out of the window, distant and abstracted, still in her coat, arms wrapped close, as if she was cold.

Some of Adeline's latest photographs lay on the table. *Trümmerfrauen* passing rubble hand to hand; women standing in line, waiting outside shops, waiting for trams, just waiting; a young woman stretched on a sunlit bench, eyes closed, in winter coat and hat; an older woman in a head scarf, pushing a pram, her feet wrapped in rags; a couple pulling a cart between them, yoked like mules; a woman pegging washing across a space where a fourth wall should be, her apartment now a balcony. Children at play. A boy had made a slide out of a steel girder. Two others were turning a tank tread into a car. Two little girls piled up stones in some arcane game. How resilient these children were, she thought, how inventive. They had lost everything. Homes. Fathers. Mothers. Their young lives had been shattered like their surroundings by a war that was no fault of theirs but they still managed to conjure a playground out of a bombsite. If this country had a future, it lay with them.

There was a darker side. Photographs of graffiti scrawled on walls that showed the things the children sometimes drew in the classroom, especially those from the east: soldiers with guns, bodies on the ground, men hanging from lampposts, crude depictions of rape. The things these children had experienced, the things that they had seen, they would carry those images the rest of their lives. Sometimes it was hard to keep hope alive. Only real security, good food, warm clothes, comfortable homes, proper education would turn this black tide of horror and they were very far from providing any of these things.

Edith picked up another photo. Two girls, a few years older. Dressed in polka-spot halter tops, sitting with GIs, the men's presence shown by a trouser cuff, a cap on the table, a uniformed arm. The girls nursed bottles of Coca-Cola, their eyes hidden behind dark glasses, their pale faces puffy, pan-cake makeup covering skin eruptions. Tell-tale signs of bad diet. The puffiness and makeup made them look older, but Edith placed them in their early teens. Bodies barely pubescent; painted fingernails bitten to the quick.

A quick scrawl in china pencil: Germany As It Is Now.

Dori turned, as if she'd made her mind up about something.

'I found something else. It was on his desk.' She held up an opened envelope. Basildon Bond notepaper. The address written in Elisabeth's large, distinctive, European cursive. 'How much do you trust her now?'

Before Edith could reply, Adeline stepped into the room.

'Are you ready? I think you should both come see what Dori found.'

34

Bauhaus Apartment, Wannsee, Berlin

27th April 1946

Smoked Ham McHale
Thinly sliced onions melted with a generous amount of butter in a skillet. Two thick slices of uncooked, smoked ham then cooked quickly - five minutes, or so. Half a bottle of red wine added with a shake or two of pepper. Cooked for another twenty minutes until wine reduced. Served with red cabbage and creamed potatoes.

Edith followed Dori into Adeline's improvised darkroom. It smelt of developing fluid and perfume.

'What did it say? In the letter?'

'There was no letter. Just the envelope but it proves that they've been in touch.'

'This is as good as I can get.' Adeline pointed to a printed reel, still wet, pegged on a line between the nylons and silk stockings. 'I need a proper dark room to enlarge them.'

Various groups of men in uniforms, high-ranking SS officers, standing around, hands in pockets, smoking cigarettes, smiling, laughing, their women in evening dress or fur coats and hats. Dori pointed to one photograph with a crimson fingernail, isolating it from its fellows. A group sitting round a table at what looked like a summer evening garden party.

'The man standing is von Stavenow.'

Edith moved close.

'And this woman, seated in front of him. Is that Elisabeth?'

Edith peered closer, until the image blurred. Yes, Elisabeth was there, in the fall of her hair, the tilt of her head, the way her eyes challenged the camera, the way she held her cigarette.

'Yes, I think so. There could be some innocent explanation, though . . .'

'Oh, yes? Look who she's with! See him?' Dori pointed to a heavy-set man, sitting sideways to the camera, heavily brillian-tined hair catching the light. 'See his collar patches? Oak leaf clusters. That makes him a General. See him?' She moved her finger to the younger man at his side. 'High-ranking Gestapo. And this one,' she pointed to a fourth man sitting on her left, his hand on the arm of her chair. 'Wehrmacht. The von Stavenows kept big-shot company.'

'I know him.' Adeline picked up a hand lens. 'That's Ernst Kaltenbrunner. Chief of the RSHA, the Reichssicherheit-shauptamt, Himmler's outfit, Reich Security Main Office, sister organization to the Gestapo. He's in the dock at Nuremberg. I've been staring at his ugly mug, day in day out.'

'Do you know the others?' Dori asked, her dark eyes searching, hopeful that she might.

Adeline shook her head. 'Should be able to tell more when we've got decent-size prints.' She turned to a distant ringing. ''Scuse me, that's our phone.'

'We have to identify them,' Dori continued to stare at the still-wet image as if it might give up its secret. 'Establish Elisabeth's connection.'

Edith peered at the miniature woman in the tiny print. 'What if it's just a social occasion?'

Part of Edith wanted to be mistaken, didn't want to think

this of her. She could perhaps understand that Elisabeth might have been in touch with Kurt for some reason. Maybe her letter had been full of accusation, maybe she couldn't resist the temptation to pour out all her bitterness and recrimination, but to see her laughing and smiling, surrounded by a bunch of high-ranking Nazis? That was a suspicion of a different order.

'You said she was never in Berlin.' Dori turned on Edith.

'I didn't say that,' she snapped back. 'She was his wife! She had to be there. It was expected. I just said she wasn't there all the *time*!'

Dori sighed her frustration. 'I can't believe how far you're prepared to go to make excuses for her!'

'I'm not making excuses!' Edith glared. 'I think we just need to be sure!'

'No point in arguing.' Adeline came back, holding her hands up. 'Edith, you need to get ready to see McHale. That was him on the phone. He wants to see you and not anyone else.'

'Why?' Edith was genuinely mystified and not a little alarmed.

Adeline shrugged. 'Just get ready. That's the way he is. If we want von Stavenow out and on his way south, you better get out to Wannsee. I'll run you over there.'

'What am I supposed to say to him?' Edith felt panic mounting.

'I'll come to your room with you,' Dori linked arms, all her annoyance seemingly forgotten. 'We'll have a little chat and a stiff gin to steady the nerves, then we'll pick out the right thing to wear.'

Tom McHale's apartment was in a modernist building overlooking the Wannsee.

'Nice spot.' He looked out of the large window. 'Right by the lake. Impressive, don't you think?' He turned back, inviting her agreement. 'Bauhaus. Belonged to some high-ranking Nazi. The normal thing for the Nazis. Declare Bauhaus degenerate, *ungerman* and whatever else, while keeping it for themselves.' He gestured round the white-painted room with its polished oak floor, glass-topped table, leather, bentwood and metal furniture.

'Whoever lived here had taste. Some of this was his. The rest I've collected.'

He stroked the curve of one of the chairs, his touch covetous. The walls were hung with Braque, Matisse, Picasso, Chagall. Presumably, also collected along the way. Maybe he was looking after them until the owners could be located, although Edith doubted it. He would likely have the whole lot crated up and shipped back to the USA. He wasn't alone in this. Lorry loads of furniture, china, silverware, carpets had been shipped back to the Home Counties. It was a temptation that many felt unable to resist. As they saw it, they were only looting the looters.

'But we're not here to discuss architecture and furniture design, are we?' He turned away from the window. 'Too bad Adie couldn't stay. Had to file copy.' McHale gave her that disconcerting smile of his, open and wide, while his eyes stayed the same, ice on a sunny day. 'But that's Adie. Always on the job.' He stretched, arms above his head, showing off his lithe, athletic build. 'Hope you're hungry, Edith. You're interested in food, recipes?'

Edith looked at him sharply. 'That's right. How do you know?'

'I have an excellent memory.' He tapped the side of his head. 'Hash with beets. What did you call it? Bubble and Squeak? There's a great kitchen here. It even has a refrigerator. You want a drink? I've got scotch or bourbon.'

'Bourbon would be fine.'

'Ice?'

'Not for me.'

'I'll be right back.' He was already disappearing out of the door.

He returned carrying two glasses, the liquor trickling through the ice. He was wearing loose-fitting gabardine trousers, a striped polo shirt, unlaced tennis shoes with no socks, boy's clothes that made him look scarcely out of his teens. He threw himself into the chair opposite her, sprawling like an adolescent, his long, loose frame making the steel and leather look almost comfortable.

'I like to cook. Did Adie say?'

'Yes, she did.' Edith sipped her whisky.

'I do like to cook.' He smiled and swirled his drink, the ice tinkling against the crystal. 'We have that in common.' He boosted himself out of his chair in one fluid movement. 'Care to give me a hand?'

Edith followed him into the kitchen. 'What are you cooking?'

'Ham. This Bavarian ham is so good. Seems a shame not to take advantage. And red cabbage. That's in the oven. Creamed potatoes. Also in the oven keeping warm, and apple and horse-radish sauce.'

He began cutting onions, very fine, with quick, even strokes of the knife.

He tipped the onions into the foaming butter and turned down the heat.

'Look at that.' He held up a thick slice of ham. Dark-pink flesh with a layer of opalescent fat and a thin, deep-brown rind. 'Isn't that perfect?'

He parted the frying onions carefully and nestled each slice into the pan. He looked at his watch.

'Five minutes each side. Then I'll add the wine.'

Tom moved round the kitchen with an exuberant delight, like a child playing with the grown-up things, while his cook, house-keeper, or whatever she was, had the night off. If they bothered at all, men cooked differently from women. Less instinct and more precision. They approached it as they would any hobby, making model aeroplanes, running train sets. Everything was arranged. All the ingredients chopped, measured and weighed. Nothing else in sight.

'I don't often have the chance to do this,' he said as if sensing her thought. 'Helga doesn't let me in the kitchen.'

'Does she not?' There was always a Helga, or a wife, to do the day-to-day mundane stuff.

'And the food here is such good quality.'

'You don't see a lot of it about.'

'And whose fault is that? There's plenty out there. Ham,

sausage, butter, cheese, potatoes – all hoarded against the black market.' He passed a hand over his head. The light picked out reddish glints in his chaff-coloured hair. 'We need to get a proper currency. You can't have a country run on cigarettes. Just a splash of wine and we'll leave it to simmer.' He dipped a spoon into the sauce and invited Edith to taste. 'More pepper?'

'Perfect as it is.'

He laid out the thick slices of ham on fine china plates, pouring the sauce over them.

'Edith, can you take these in? I need to open the wine. Should have done it earlier. Given it time to breathe.'

He was opening a bottle of Chateau Lafite. Another of the spoils of war.

They sat down at the table and Tom poured the wine. He passed Edith the dish of creamed potato and the red cabbage.

'What do you think of the *Kartoffelpüree?*'

'Very good.'

Edith was saying very little. Dori had told her to let him do the talking.

'Cream and a grate of nutmeg. How do you like the red cabbage? It's my Swedish grandma's recipe.'

Edith took a forkful. 'Sweeter than the German version. Less pungent. I like it.'

'And the ham?'

'Delicious,' Edith answered with a smile, going along with the deliberately elliptical pattern of the conversation.

He smiled back, satisfied. 'Cypriot recipe, believe it or not. Greek boy gave it to me. Had his head blown off on a beach near Salerno. We buried him next to the temple of Poseidon. Ancient Greek town, Paestum. It's nice there. I mean to go back one day.' He paused for a moment before going on in his falsely bright way. 'Now we have Peach Cobbler and cream.'

'Sounds wonderful'

'What d'you think?' he asked as they were finishing the pudding. 'Good?'

'Excellent.'

'My ma's recipe. Hine?' McHale offered after he'd cleared away the dishes. He picked up a bottle off the sideboard and read the label. 'Reserve. There were some very fine cellars out here. Amazing what the Russians overlooked. Couldn't drink it all, I guess.'

'I won't, thanks.'

He took out a cigar, cut the end and reached into his pocket for a lighter. 'We found humidors as well.' He rolled the Zippo. 'Senior Nazis didn't stint themselves.' He puffed on the cigar once or twice, then examined the glowing tip to see if it was evenly alight. 'So, Edith, let's get down to business. What do you want from me?' He took another draw, exhaling aromatic blue smoke.

'Who says I want something?'

'Now, Edith,' he grinned. 'Come on!'

'On the contrary, I'm here to offer you something.'

'Like what?'

'I can give you Kurt von Stavenow.'

This was where she delivered what Dori called 'the pay off'. And it worked. She resisted an impulse to smile as McHale almost choked on his cigar. Those wide-apart, pale-blue eyes were on her now, engaged and expectant. With something else there, she hadn't seen before. A kind of respect.

'Really? His wife, too?'

There was an urgency to his tone, as though they wanted *her*, specifically. Why would that be?

'Her, too. That's guaranteed.'

'What do you want in return?'

'He's in the Russian Zone. You have to get him out of there and on his way out of the country. I know that you can do that.'

He looked slightly disconcerted. He had to be careful now. That was not for public consumption. He drew on his cigar while he framed his reply.

'Let's say that we do help people.' He gave a small smile and carefully nudged off a column of accumulating ash. 'Let's say he is of interest. There are hundreds like him. Thousands. We

369

can't put them all on trial. That would be pointless. We have to move on. We've got the main culprits. The trials are set. If some of the smaller fish get away,' he made a swift swimming motion, 'so be it. Truth is, we don't want them here. The big guys are already in the States. The rest? Some may have their uses and maybe your Kurt is one of those. Otherwise, they can go to South America, or somewhere, play at being Nazis, dream of the Fourth Reich, whatever it is they want. They're a spent force. Dreaming is all it will ever be. There's a new war starting. A new enemy. We have to turn our minds to that now.'

'Move from the old war to the cold war?'

'You've got it exactly.'

'So you will help get him out?'

'Well, he's no use to anyone except the Russians where he is now. That's enough of a reason.' He masked his eagerness in a show of indifference. 'I'll see what I can do.' He proffered the bottle of Hine. 'Sure I can't tempt you?'

'Quite sure.'

He poured himself another finger or two and swirled the rich burnt-sienna liquid round his glass.

'What do you want?' he asked. 'What's in it for you? And Dori. What's in it for her?'

Edith half wished she hadn't refused that brandy.

'I don't want to go into details,' she answered, deliberately evading his question. 'I'm not privy to Dori's thinking.'

'Best guess then?'

'I'd say,' she thought hard, sensing snares all around her, 'I'd say she thinks he knows something about the fate of the SOE agents she's seeking. A chance to question him could be part of the deal.'

'Uhn, hnn,' Tom nodded, eyes half closed against the smoke from his cigar. 'And them? The von Stavenows? What do they want, d'you think?'

'They want to get out of Germany, Europe preferably but . . .' She stopped. She had to be careful, very careful now. Keep her face straight, expressionless, show him nothing. 'Most of all . . .'

she heard herself say. She was finding it hard to breathe. The message to meet, the letter on his desk, the photographs. It suddenly all clicked together. It was so obvious, why had she not seen it? Elisabeth didn't want a divorce. They hadn't parted on 'bad terms', as Kurt had put it. 'Most of all,' she began again, 'they want to be together. That's what they've always wanted.' She tried to gain control. 'That's what this is all about and he won't go without her.' She took more air. 'I do know that.'

'Are you okay?' Tom was out of his chair.

'Asthma,' Edith managed to say. 'Your cigar.'

'Oh, God, I'm sorry.' He mashed the remaining rolled tobacco into the grey ash. 'I had no idea.' A bell sounded out in the hallway. 'Ah, there's Adeline,' he said, with something like relief.

'Hey! Are you okay?'

'I wouldn't say that exactly.'

'Did he fall for it?' Adeline asked.

Edith didn't answer. She just stared out into the darkness.

'Doesn't matter.' Adeline started the car. 'If you said Dori wants to get von Stavenow to Italy to throw rocks at him, Tom wouldn't care. He's planning the double-cross already. The point is he wants von Stavenow and Frau and you're delivering them all tied up with a bow. I managed to get those photos blown up at the Press Agency,' she went on. 'Musette bag on the back seat.'

Edith unwound the ribbon that fixed the cardboard file. The now enlarged photograph showed the summer party in detail. Glasses on the table, ashtrays, champagne in an ice bucket. Elisabeth at the centre of the group with Kurt behind her, his hand on her shoulder. No mistaking her and no mistaking the gesture.

'Max at the Press Agency recognized the mystery men,' Adeline was saying. 'The weasely-looking Gestapo guy? Horst Kopkow. Heydrich's protégé, Senior Counter-espionage Officer. The Wehrmacht guy, balding with the big ears? Reinhard Gehlen. Chief of the FHO, Military Intelligence on the Eastern Front. Classy company. There's a little date in the corner, see?'

1943. According to her account, Elisabeth had left Berlin by then but, of course she hadn't, that was just another lie. Edith let the photograph fall back onto her lap and wound down the window, short of breath again. The betrayal was vast, spreading, out and out.

'Say, are you okay? Do you want me to stop the car?'

Edith shook her head. 'No, I just needed some air. Have you told Dori?' she asked, hoping to move her mind on to something else.

'Just left her now. It's my guess Elisabeth worked for one of those guys.'

'Worked for them?' Edith turned. 'She's never worked in her life!'

'I wouldn't be so sure. I find the women interesting. What were they doing? They couldn't just be *Kinder, Küche, Kirche*. To begin with, maybe, but not after they started losing in '43. With so many men called up, they'd have to join the workforce. To run that kind of bureaucracy, all that minute-taking and typing, women would do that, surely? Behind the scenes work, routine administration.' She leaned forward, brows furrowed, eyes on the road. 'The young guys, the junior guys who might have been doing it before would be needed to fight. Who's going to take their places? Women. I bet Elisabeth stepped right up to the plate. She was in Berlin. As a good Nazi, she'd want to do her bit. She'd be right at the heart of government. And you know what they say? If you want to know anything, don't ask the boss, ask his P.A.'

Edith's eyes went back to the image lying on her lap. Love's veiling glamour can be hard to dispel but here was Elisabeth's duplicity in enlarged black and white. Of course, parts of Elisabeth's story had never added up. Not just how she'd spent the war but before. Kurt's line of work as an SS doctor. How could she *not* have known? *I do not like this life*, she'd said on the terrace at Steinhof. She seemed to be enjoying it in these photographs.

Some things Elisabeth said had never made proper sense.

372

That's why she'd been so furious with Roz, with Luka. She glanced away from the photograph and back again. Kurt's hand on her shoulder. The closeness clear to see. Edith's feelings for Kurt had made her easy to deceive but the affection that she'd developed for Elisabeth made the betrayal much deeper.

'I was hoping that it might be somehow – innocent,' she said, almost to herself. She looked over at Adeline. 'But it doesn't look that way, does it?'

'No, it doesn't.' Adeline continued to stare out into the fragile cone the headlights cast into the looming blackness. 'One time, I was with the 82nd, April '45, pushing deep into Germany. We came to this town. White flags everywhere, white sheets hanging from the windows, but nobody was throwing roses. People just standing in the streets looking puzzled, as if they couldn't believe this was happening. The surrender was recent. I went with a patrol to secure the town hall. First thing I noticed was how quiet it was, just the rat-tat of gunfire in the distance, like rice falling on a kid's drum. As we went up the stairs, the silence seemed to grow, thicken. We took a long corridor to the right. Door at the end of the passage. A heavy door in some dark wood. One of our guys pushed it open with his gun and we stepped inside. First thing we saw was a man at the desk; head down in a pool of blood. Then a woman slumped in a chair, a streak of blood dried by the side of her mouth. We turned around to see a girl. Very young and quite beautiful, dressed in some kind of uniform, lying on a leather sofa, head back, mouth slightly open, eyes glassy. A fine layer of dust covered everything: the furniture, the man's shoulders, the pool of blood in front of him, the eyes of the girl on the sofa. The mayor and his family. All dead by their own hands.' She paused. 'What I'm thinking is, what about the ones who *didn't* kill themselves? What are they doing now?'

Adeline fell into silence, as if still in that room with the dead girl and her parents. Out of the window, the lake flashed silver between the dark bars of the pines. Elisabeth had told her about just such incidents at that first meeting. Edith remembered her saying: *Oh, no, I wouldn't do that . . . I had to survive. For my daughter.* Then Luka hinting that the child wasn't hers. Was that another lie? Was it all lies? Spun to work on Edith's regard? Gain her sympathy? Edith glanced again at the woman smiling out of the photograph. So charming, so plausible. So beautiful. She'd thrown her glamour over Edith, caught her in the web of her story. Edith's feelings of being duped were receding. She felt the first deep stirrings of anger. No one liked being taken for a fool.

'I'll find out what Elisabeth was involved in,' Adeline was saying as they entered the broken outer rim of the city. 'You and Dori work on what she's up to now.'

Harry was in the hotel bar sitting in a booth by himself. He didn't seem to notice her and Edith had to fight a desire to walk straight past. She had a feeling that this meeting would be goodbye, that he was going back to Palestine, and she didn't know how much more she could take. The day had been so long, she barely remembered the morning and the encounter with McHale, the revelations about Elisabeth, had left her drained. At that moment, he looked up and she felt some of the burden of the day begin to lift away.

'Edith! Where have you been? Do you want a drink?' He was already signalling the waiter. 'Whisky and soda?'

'I've been around,' Edith's shrug was vague. 'We must have just kept missing each other.'

'You look tired. What have you been up to?' He finished his drink as the waiter brought another. 'Aren't you going to tell me? What's kept you so busy, kept you away from me?'

'I don't want to talk about it.' The whisky was cheap, diluted. She put the glass aside.

'I hope it's not anything to do with Kurt von Stavenow.'

Edith looked up at him, too tired for dissembling.

'How do you know?'

'I met Dori. She said you'd seen him. Here in Berlin. She also told me that he's in the Russian Zone, which means he'll want to get out, and that you were having dinner with McHale.' He leant forward. 'Keep out of it, Edith.'

'Why?'

'Because it's dangerous! A murky business, getting murkier by the minute. Ratlines. That's what the Americans call them. Aptly named. Stretching from here to South America, a conduit for Nazi vermin, organized either by the SS old comrades or the Americans. I can't think of a more ruthless pairing. And then there's the Catholic Church lending a helping hand. You'd be mad to get mixed up in it. Leave it to—'

'The professionals? They are the ones smuggling them out!'

He shrugged. *Touché.* 'Why are you so involved, anyway? Why do you want to get him out?'

'I don't.' She shook her head. 'It's not about that.'

'What is it about?'

'I can't really tell you but it's not what you think. What he did was heinous,' she said quietly. 'He shouldn't be allowed to get away scot free. You aren't the only people to think that way.'

'Why didn't you tell me about this?'

'I don't know. I didn't—'

'Think I'd be interested?' he finished her sentence for her. 'Not at the top of our dance card? Why not? The Jewish wards were the first to be emptied, you can be certain of that. And what they learnt from the Euthanasia Project allowed them to kill with ever greater efficiency. T4 set up the Extermination Camps at Sobibór, Treblinka. Hundreds of thousands of Jews died there. Millions, probably. We're interested, all right. What about Dori? What's she got to do with it?'

'She's been working with Vera Atkins. Something to do with their agents being executed at a place called Natzweiler.'

Harry sat forward. 'Natzweiler-Struthof?'

'You know this place?'

'Oh, yes,' Harry's thin fingers knotted together. 'Jews were taken there from Auschwitz. They were gassed, their corpses defleshed to add to the Jewish skeleton collection. What was von Stavenow's role? Do you know?'

'Dori thought he might have been present when the agents were killed.'

'What about Leo? Where's he in all this?'

'Nowhere, as far as I know.'

'But they want him, don't they? This von Stavenow. You told me so yourself.'

'Yes, but Leo's not involved, not directly . . .'

'So it's Dori and Vera on a solo hunting trip?'

'No, they're working with War Crimes.'

'I wouldn't be too sure about Leo. He'll be in it somewhere.' He looked at her, trying to read her face. 'There's less and less appetite for bringing these people to justice. Too time consuming and expensive. The new policy seems to be to use them against the Russians or let them slither away. All this War Crimes stuff is being "discouraged".'

'That's more or less what McHale said. No one's interested in going after them any more, punishing them for what they've done.'

'We are, Edith.' He took her hands and held them tightly. 'We are.' His eyes took on a sudden, dark intensity. 'We are a patient people. We remember for millennia. They will never be safe from us. No matter how long it takes, no matter how far they run.'

She felt a shiver pass through his thin body, as if he was tensing himself in readiness for this unknown future. His grip slackened and he held her hands more loosely, his eyes distant now, looking into a future that was unlikely to include her. He leaned forward, as though there was something more, something he wanted to tell her. She thought she knew what it was, but didn't want to hear it. Not yet.

'Let's go to your room, shall we?' She looked around. The bar was filling. The crowd approaching the noisy stage of drunkenness. This was no place for goodbyes.

'I was expecting you earlier,' he said as he turned the champagne in its silver bucket of melted ice water. 'It'll be warm now.'

They took it into the bedroom and drank it anyway.

His lovemaking was so slow and considerate and achingly tender that all her suspicions were confirmed. *There's a leaving at the end of this, there has to be* was her last fleeting thought before all consciousness was lost in fierce oblivion.

Afterwards, they were quiet for a long time, neither of them saying anything, just lying still together, hardly moving, wanting to stay in the exquisite languor of the moment.

Eventually, Harry sighed and leaned up, stretching for his cigarettes.

'I'm leaving,' he said as he lay back on the bed.

'When?' Soon, she knew, but she had to ask it.

'A couple of weeks at most.' He exhaled. 'My work here is done. I'm being demobbed.'

'Where will you go? What will you do?' Although she knew the answers to those questions, too.

'To Israel.' He no longer called it Palestine. 'To join my brother in Haganah, play my part in the struggle. The British have no appetite for it. They'll be gone in a year. I want to be there when it happens.' He stared at the glowing tip of his cigarette. 'I want to be present at the beginning, to help build a new state, a new country which will be my country.' He stubbed out his cigarette and turned to her. 'Come with me, Edith. We can start a new life there. Together. I don't want this to be goodbye.'

'Neither do I.'

'Come with me then! The country is beautiful. You'd love it there – and there is so much to do. It will be exciting. We can make a new beginning. My brother lives in Tel Aviv. We can stay with him, to start with, anyway. You can write your cookery book. We'll go through Italy, Greece. You can collect recipes . . .'

Edith had not been expecting this. She'd steeled herself to part from him. She knew he was going and soon. His life lay elsewhere, and theirs could only be a brief affair. So she'd denied what she felt. Made up any number of narratives that it was for the best.

'But I'm not . . .' She looked away.

'Jewish? You can convert. Anyway, I don't care. I want you.

As you are. You are an unusual woman, Edith.' He sat up in bed. 'Most of the women I meet show too much, or there's nothing to discover. You are different. So much of you is hidden but each time we meet, I find out more.' He leaned over to look again into her face. 'I could go on doing that for the rest of my life and still not know it all.'

'This is so sudden—'

She didn't know how to answer him. She wanted this more than anything else in the world, and yet—

'Not for me. I've thought about it a lot. All the time, in fact.'

'I can't.' She bit her lip. 'Not now. I have to see this through.'

'I understand,' he stared straight ahead, arms folded. 'I'll be taking more or less the same route through Italy as the Nazis do,' he said after a moment. 'If the plan is to follow this von Stavenow, I can recommend safe places, leave word with comrades. If I can help, I will. Be careful, Edith. Each party involved will be watching, waiting to double-cross the others. It'll be a case of who jumps first.'

'I know.' Edith sighed. Everyone lying, led by the von Stavenows. Subterfuge upon subterfuge. Who knew where the truth lay? If it even existed.

'Afterwards. When it's over. You can come to me.'

Afterwards? She couldn't think that far ahead. She loved him, had done since that freezing night in Lübeck, but there had always been a goodbye at the end of it. His words were like a sudden flare lighting up a landscape that she hadn't even known was there.

'You're right.' He reached to turn out the light. 'It probably wouldn't work.'

'That's not what I'm thinking. It's just so – sudden. It's what I want – more than anything – but here I am, turning you down!'

She turned so he wouldn't see her tears spill.

'Hey,' he took her chin to turn her face around and gently touched her cheeks with his fingers then his lips. He smiled down at her. Her tears were her answer. All he needed to know. 'Don't cry, Edith. The offer's there. Always. I'll leave my brother's address.

I'll wait. However long it takes. I know about things that have to be done. I know you won't want to let others down.'

'Dependable type, that's me.' Edith smiled through her tears.

He laughed softly. 'That's why I love you. When it's over. You will come to me. Promise?'

'Yes.'

'That's enough talking.' His hands began to move over her body. 'I can think of better things to do.'

35

Alte Küche, Berlin

28th April 1946

Breakfast Hoppelpoppel
A kind of omelette. Potatoes fried with ham
and onions until crisp and browning. Eggs
mixed with a little cream and seasoned with
salt and pepper poured over the mixture with
a sprinkling of parsley and grated cheese.
Allowed to set over a lowish heat. Finished
under the grill until cheese is melted.

When Edith woke, Harry had gone. She dressed and left his room quietly. Back in her own room, she ran a bath, glad that there was more to their affair than the excitement of clandestine arrangements, the fierce intensity when they were finally together. That could feel tawdry – and horribly temporary. Being here, surrounded by all this devastation, it was like being in a place where the war had never ended; the febrile whirl of sudden passions, furtive sex, casual affairs and endless drinking still went spinning on. He'd given her a way out; a chance to live a normal life in a place where one could look forward, instead of backwards into death and destruction. A sudden shiver ran through her and she gripped the sides of the bath, shaken by the powerful conviction that she should have gone with him. Someone walked over her grave . . . The bath was cold, that was all. She shouldn't have stayed so long in the water. She stood up and reached for a towel, rubbing at her goose-pimpled flesh.

There was a knock on the door.

'Just a minute.'

She wouldn't say no a second time. She snatched her robe from the back of the door, her heart beating disconcertingly fast.

Edith stepped aside as Dori strode in, stripping off her gloves.

'No need to look quite so disappointed. Who did you think it was? Harry?'

Edith didn't, couldn't answer.

'I saw him leaving looking very hang-dog and sorry for himself and you're not exactly overjoyed to see *me* are you, darling? Did you think he'd come back to sweep you off to the Promised Land?' Dori didn't wait for a reply. She lit a cigarette and exhaled slowly. 'Adeline went off to Nuremberg early this morning. She says your dinner with McHale went well.'

'Well, he's offered to help . . .'

'Thought he might. He'll get von Stavenow out of the Russian Zone and on his way to Italy. Then he'll try to double-cross us.'

'That's what Harry said.'

Dori looked up sharply. 'You didn't tell Hirsch?'

'He guessed. Some of it anyway.'

'Well, he won't say anything. He's not exactly a stranger to this kind of thing, is he? We thought you'd do well.'

'We?'

'I met Bulldog Drummond last night. Jack was with him. Old comrades, apparently. Both in the SAS.'

Edith nodded. That didn't surprise her. There was something about both of them: a casual, complete physical assurance that disguised a compressed strength, a power they kept hidden. She remembered Drummond's hands. The flat strength about his wrists, square palms with the blunt fingers and those nicely kept nails. Hands that could kill, could squeeze the life from a man like wringing out a dish cloth, probably had done many times.

'When Jack went off to telephone his girl, we had a quiet word. We'll wait until the Americans have got von Stavenow as far as the South Tyrol. That's where we'll nab them.'

'I really don't understand.' Edith spread her hands. 'Why don't the Americans just take him once he's in their zone?'

Dori regarded her with a mix of affection and pity. 'Because we'll have Elisabeth. You can bet she'll be part of the deal.' Dori stubbed out her cigarette and fished in her bag for her makeup. 'Bulldog's arranged your transfer.'

'What?'

'To Bad Oeynhausen. He can arrange pretty much anything. You won't be going there, of course. That's just for show.' She looked at Edith in her compact mirror. 'I say, you do want to come, don't you? Didn't think to ask. Sort of assumed . . .'

'I wouldn't miss it. I want to see justice done,' Edith said with sudden conviction. 'The von Stavenows get their come-uppance.'

She saw Kurt's hand on Elisabeth's shoulder. The closeness that had always been there. She'd been duped, used by them. Her affection for Elisabeth exploited. That cut deepest. How many more lies had Elisabeth told? About the boy? The child, Wolfgang? Edith suddenly felt very cold.

'Not a word when you get back to Lübeck,' Dori put down her mirror and took Edith by the shoulders, looking into her face. 'Not a hint. Elisabeth must suspect *nothing*. The whole enterprise depends on it. You understand?'

Edith nodded.

'Good.' She returned to her makeup, dabbing powder. 'I hope you're packed, darling. Jack's bringing the car round. He stayed last night. Couldn't let the poor lamb go back to some ghastly barracks.' She was back to her usual arch, teasing banter with a flash of the outrageous. The dark, serious mood gone with a click of her compact. 'I'm cadging a lift to Hamburg, I hope you don't mind. I don't know about you but I'm starving. Sex always makes me hungry. Thought we might go somewhere for a spot of breakfast before the off.'

The Alte Küche was off Kurfürstendamm, not far from the ruins of Kaiser-Wilhelm-Gedächtniskirche. They found a table and ordered coffee and three plates of *Hoppelpoppel*, a mix of ham, potatoes, cheese, eggs and cream. Edith was surprised at how hungry she was. Jack pronounced it as good as a fryup.

'Not so keen on the stringy cheese.' He wiped his plate with a hunk of dark bread, 'But I'll miss this grub when I get home.'

'Think I'll pop to the *Damen*.' Dori finished her coffee. 'Hope it's not too gruesome. Edith, do you want to go? It's a long trip.'

'I'll wait outside.' Jack stood up. 'Want to check on the motor. Don't trust these blighters. Have the hubcaps off and the petrol siphoned in no time.'

'I've seen worse, but I've seen better,' Dori commented when they found the facilities. Her nostrils flared at the stench of ancient urine and drains. The only ventilation came via a tiny rusted window in the far wall.

'This transfer,' Edith said through the thin partition. 'When will it start?'

'It has to be soon.'

'How soon?'

'Soon. You have to be ready to go. Holiday in the Tyrol. Very scenic.'

'Why the Tyrol?'

'Because that's where they all go. The whole area used to be Austrian until a blink ago. Absolutely swarming with old Nazis waiting to be moved on to Rome or Genoa and take ship for South America. Good hunting country. That's what Bulldog's calling it. Operation Hunting Trip. Ha!' she gave a humourless laugh. 'We'll bag him from right under McHale's nose.'

'But you won't have jurisdiction there.'

'Exactly. Neither does anybody. We just have to get them to Austria, where we do.'

There was a rustle of underclothes, the clank of a chain and

383

flushing. Edith emerged to find Dori leaning on one of the cracked basins, smoking a cigarette. There was no soap. Edith swilled her hands under a dribble of rust-tinged cold water, took one look at the hand towel and dried her hands on her handkerchief.

'Where does Drummond comes into this?'

'He's looking into the fate of his chaps – they should have been treated as prisoners of war. Instead, they were shot.' She balanced her cigarette on the side of the basin and began to apply lipstick. 'Some of their chaps, ours too, were betrayed, picked up immediately they were dropped. Eighteen agents by our count. Nazis waiting when they shouldn't have had a sniff of them. We want to know how they knew. Could be that there was a traitor at the heart of SOE. Either that, or they were deliberately sacrificed.'

'To what purpose?'

'Like chaff dropped from a plane to deceive and confuse.' Dori worked her lips together to an even carmine. 'To hide the fact that a circuit was blown, to save their own hides, or something more sinister.' Dori leaned forward, hands on the crazed lip of the basin, studying her reflection in the cracked mirror. 'We just don't know. It's like a cobweb in the darkness. We want the spider at the centre.'

'How's nabbing Kurt going to help you find out who that could be?'

'Not him. *Her.* Consider the company she kept. Kaltenbrunner, Gehlen, Kopkow.' Dori counted their roles off on her fingers. 'Security, Military Intelligence, Counter-espionage. Adeline's gone back to Nuremberg to ferret in the files. Of course, we want von Stavenow but it's looking as though she could be an added bonus.'

'Tom McHale doesn't seem to think what happened during the war matters very much any more,' Edith stared at their reflection in the cracked and clouded mirror. 'He says the world has moved on.'

'He would say that, wouldn't he? And he's wrong. He should

be more careful. Once a traitor, always a traitor, in my experience.' Dori caught her arm. 'A word before we go. Careful what you say in the car.'

'You mean in front of Jack? You can't suspect Jack? He's straight as a die.'

'This is strictly need to know and he doesn't.'

It had begun to rain. Jack stepped out from the narrow alleyway where he was sheltering. He looked up at the sky.

'What do they say? Something about *Hunde*?'

'*Es regnet junge Hunde*,' Edith supplied. High up on the wall behind him, a rusty window, half open. Had he heard any part of their conversation?

'Well, anyway,' he looked up at the sky, 'it seems to be slackening off now. All set?' He flicked his cigarette away. An old man picked it up in a quick, furtive, fluid movement, nipping the end and dropping it into his pocket. 'Dori following on, is she?'

'She's just paying.'

He smiled. 'She's quite a girl.'

'Yes,' Edith looked at him. 'You two seemed to get on very well.'

'You could say that.' Jack's smile became distant, as if reviewing some private satisfaction.

'What about Kay?'

'She wouldn't mind. Well,' he shrugged, 'not all that much. I've been talking on the blower, keeping her sweet. Besides, she knows me. Me and Kay, we got an understanding. What happens in Berlin, stays here, if you take my meaning.'

Edith stepped towards the car. 'I won't breathe a word.'

The car stopped at the checkpoint. They were about to leave the British Sector of Berlin and enter the Soviet Zone of Occupation. Russian soldiers waited in their green caps with the red star, weapons held in readiness. A gloved hand came through the open window with a gruff demand: 'бумага, паспорт. Papers. Passport.' A graphic reminder that the game was changing into McHale's Us and Them.

Dori turned up her astrakhan collar and closed her eyes. Jack was silent, absorbed in his driving. Edith stared out of the window. The passing landscape was pine forest and heathland. Armies had passed through here. A burnt-out tank stood stranded on high ground; the rusted remains of an armoured car nose down in a ditch. Here and there lay reminders of civilian flight: the skeletal remains of a pram, a sodden bundle, colourless, shapeless, abandoned to rot by the side of the road. She was reminded of Elisabeth's hasty departure from Prussia.

'Elisabeth told me the most amazing story . . .' She began to tell it, adding in all the little details she remembered so vividly. Dori appeared not to be listening, Jack was concentrating on his driving, but it was a way of passing the time.

'Another checkpoint up ahead.'

The car slowed, jolting over potholes. Dori opened her eyes.

They watched as their papers were given the same frowning scrutiny, the slow turning of the passports. They stared ahead, doing their best to look indifferent when the barrier creaked jerkily upwards.

'Don't like being in Ivan's territory,' Jack said as he accelerated away.

The land was the same either side. Undulating country, fields dotted with cattle, greening with new crops, stretched off towards dark forests, unknown and enigmatic. The Green Border began on the Baltic. Lübeck was only a couple of miles away from it. An arbitrary line marked with sagging strands of barbed wire strung between rough-hewn poles from the forest. It followed the contours of the land, an inexorable progress up hill and down dale, through farmyards, railway stations, even houses, all the way to Czechoslovakia. The Great Divide had begun. The line had been drawn. A visible border for an invisible war.

In the distance, a horse-drawn cart heaped with sacks was clopping along a muddy track. There were no barriers on the little unadopted roads that connected villages and farms across the newly constructed border. The Soviets didn't have the manpower for that. Edith was reminded of the Frau's weekend trips to the country. She sat up.

'That's how they did it,' she said.

Jack glanced up into the mirror. 'Do what?'

'Move people, messages, anything, across the country along with sacks of food. There's no barriers on the minor roads.'

'Do you mind if I drop you off first, ma'am?' Jack asked as they neared home. 'It's just if I take Dori to Hamburg, I can go and see Kay. Two birds with one stone, like.'

Dori smiled. 'What a way you have with words, Jack.'

'I didn't mean—' The back of his neck reddened.

'That will be perfectly all right, Jack,' Edith replied. 'Good idea.' She turned to Dori. 'When will I see you?'

'Can't say but soon.' Dori stared out of the window.

They had hardly spoken. Not in front of the servants. Operational rules apply. Edith's eyes met Jack's in the mirror. He gave her a mock salute. Could she have been wrong about him? Had she made too many assumptions based on his accent, his manner, his uniform, his rank? Her judgement of him began to slide. What did she really know? Never said what he did before. What he was going to do after. Never said much about himself at all. She'd been wrong about Elisabeth, maybe she was wrong about him, too.

She had never treated him like a chauffeur, as some of her CCG colleagues did with their drivers. There was no barrier between them, no sliding glass. She'd long since stopped thinking of him as her driver. He was a friend, a constant presence. If she'd wondered why he was always available, she'd put it down to one of his many wangles. She'd trusted him. Perhaps too much.

36

Apartment 2a Schillerstraße, Lübeck

April–May 1946

Rote Grütze

A summer pudding made with purely red fruits:
redcurrants, strawberries, raspberries. I
prefer just redcurrants if enough are available. Roughly pureed fruit, heated with sugar
(the pudding should retain some tartness),
the mixture then thickened with cornflour.
Traditionally, the thickening agent would
have been groats and in some places semolina
or sago are used. The whole is brought to
the boil slowly, stirring constantly until
clear and thick, then simmered for three to
five minutes. White wine, lemon juice and
vanilla can be added at this point, but why
mask the taste of the fruit?

Edith was back earlier than expected. Voices coming from the
kitchen. Frau Schmidt's hectic laugh. Edith removed her shoes and
walked on cat feet, trying not to make floorboards creak. Outside
the door, she heard a few unflattering remarks about herself and

more besides. Elisabeth wasn't holding back. Two loyal Nazi wives together. Part of her cover, Edith might have thought, but the benefit of that doubt had been removed. It didn't matter now. The debris of shattered illusions had all been swept away.

A scrape of a chair leg on the floor heralded the Frau's imminent departure. Edith felt a new strength as she stole silently to her room. Everything looked the same but it wasn't. Part of her still wished she'd gone with Harry but she'd have to leave those dreams at the door for now. There was other business here and it would take all her reserves to deal with Elisabeth.

Voices in the hall. She waited for the outer door to close and went to find her in the kitchen.

'Edith! Goodness!' Elisabeth turned from the sink. 'Where did you spring from? You gave me quite a fright.' She dried her hands on her apron. 'I didn't hear you come in.' Her slight frown said *what had she heard?* 'Would you like coffee. Cake?'

'I've been home a while. I didn't want to disturb you. Was that Frau Schmidt?'

Elisabeth's ivory skin coloured slightly. Let her worry.

'She wanted to see how we are settling in.'

'Nice of her. What did she really want?'

'She is untrusting.' Under stress, Elisabeth's English slipped. 'Of you. Us. My intentions.' She bit her lip. 'Did you find Kurt?'

'Yes. I met him.'

'You did?' Elisabeth coloured further. 'And how was he?'

The merest flicker of a look crossed her face before she busied herself with the coffee pot. Just enough to confirm that Elisabeth knew very well where he was and how he was. Carts patiently clopping across the country, messages passed from hand to hand, pocket to wallet. Planning, plotting. They'd been in cahoots ever since the organization found him in Berlin. They must have thought her a real mug.

'He wants to see you,' Edith said, keeping her voice as neutral as she could manage. Elisabeth's hand stilled. 'I told him you want a divorce, but even so. He's in the Russian Zone now, so we need to get him out and heading south.'

'What can I do?'

'Convince the Frau of your good intentions.'

Elisabeth reported that arrests had been made. A side effect of sending the Frau's notebook to Adams. He was very pleased with himself. He called Edith to tell her how well he had done. He'd left Frau Schmidt and the *Schwestern* alone for now, small fry beneath his interest, but it had left them nervous. Elisabeth would have to smooth feathers, wait for normal service to resume. No sign of Edith's transfer. She found distraction in her work but the waiting was getting to her.

'Productive time in Berlin, I see.' Brigadier Thompson interrupted her thoughts.

'What? Yes. Very.'

'Excellent.' He brandished her report. 'I've made a few emendations.'

He dropped the paper back on her desk and left for the day. Edith didn't mind staying late. She found it hard to be in Elisabeth's company.

Youth Becoming Delinquent. One of the Brigadier's pet projects. Teenagers hanging round stations and like places, pilfering, pickpocketing, black-market dealing and 'Getting Up To No Good' by which he really meant prostitution. Going into the shadows of the ruins to service the servicemen for a packet of cigarettes, a bar of chocolate, a tin of corned beef. It had to be 'Stamped Out'. There was a great deal of debate around this subject, much anguish and wringing of hands, but it always centred on the delinquent youth. No one ever questioned why men thought it perfectly acceptable to buy sexual favours from children for food.

The Americans had the right approach. The teenagers, boys and girls, needed somewhere to go where they could be together with coffee, Coca-Cola, even. Why not? A club. A Youth Club. With ping-pong, that kind of thing. There could be a library, maybe, with books and comics and newspapers, a radio, a record player for dancing. The Yanks were as keen as mustard but it would cost money and she couldn't see Thompson waxing ecstatic.

Much to her surprise, he was all for it. She set about finding volunteers among the younger teachers, discussing ways to get the teenagers involved and retaining them, looking into twinning with youth groups in Britain. This work was important, her time here suddenly finite, which reminded her that she needed to do something about Luka. Unlike the rest of it, that was easily solved. There was a child refugee scheme being set up. She'd put in a call in the morning and get him on his way to Britain. She'd have to find him first, though. She hadn't seen him for a while.

A week went by. The *Schwestern* remained quiet and no sign of the transfer and Adams was beginning to pester, eager for more. *You did well there, Edith. Leo very pleased. Anything new from the delectable Gräfin?* He mustn't know anything about what they were planning but how much longer would she be able to hold him off?

Then, there it was, in the morning post with the routine memos and directives: 'Miss E. A. M. Graham. Transfer with Immediate Effect'. She was careful not to show any emotion as she dropped the letter onto the others to be signed by the Brigadier.

'Shall I take them into his nibs?' Roz asked as she collected the pile from Edith's desk.

Edith glanced up at the clock. Nearly lunch time. His mind would be on lunch at the club.

'Why don't you? Tell him they need signing immediately. Wait 'til he's done it.'

'OK.' Roz took the papers from her.

'Then let's go down to the Trave, have our lunch there. It's a lovely day.'

'I have some news . . .' Edith started, she'd been dreading telling Roz that she was leaving, but now was the time.

'I do too!' Roz linked arms. 'Jeff and I are getting married, next leave or even sooner. I've been putting off telling you because it'll mean breaking up the billet and I've so much liked living there with you – and Elisabeth, of course.'

'Oh, Roz,' Edith squeezed her arm. 'That's splendid! I'm so happy for you!'

'You don't mind?'

'Not a bit. The thing is, you see, I'm going, too. I've got a transfer to Bad Oeynhausen.'

'Gosh!' Roz's eyes widened. 'You kept that under your hat.' Then her face clouded. 'You keep the whole show going. The Brig will put the kibosh on it, I bet.'

Edith laughed. 'He's probably signed the order already. I put it in with the bumf you just took in to him.'

'Oh, very good!' Roz grinned. 'Jolly clever. You're a cool one, I must say. I'd have been skipping round the office. I'll file it before he realizes what's happened.'

'Too late if he does.' Edith looked over at the salthouses, their distinctive crowfoot outlines mirrored in the still water. 'I'm only going back to collect my things then I'm off.'

'That soon?' Roz clutched her arm. 'Never mind, it's a good opportunity. Headquarters means promotion.' She turned to Edith. 'I say, let's celebrate. Toast both our futures.'

They sat at one of the little tables that had been set out down by the river now that summer seemed finally on its way and toasted each other with steins of beer. Edith promised to be back for the wedding and certainly for the christening. She smiled. Apparently double congratulations were in order. No wonder Miss Esterhazy was in a hurry to become Mrs Jeffrey Grant.

Edith collected her things and called her driver.

'Where to, ma'am?'

The man opening the door for her was a stranger.

'Where's Jack?'

'On leave.'

'Oh,' Edith felt deflated, some of her ebullience leaching from her. She'd wanted to say goodbye to him. 'Just take me home.

No, wait.' She looked across the road. 'On second thoughts, I'll walk.'

Luka. She'd been searching for him all week and suddenly, there he was, leaning against the wall opposite.

'I've been looking for you,' she said.

'I thought you maybe angry with me.'

'Why would I be?'

He didn't answer that. He took her bag. 'This is heavy.'

'Yes, I'm leaving.'

He looked striken. 'Where are you going?'

'I have a transfer to a place called Bad Oeynhausen.'

'It is far, this place?'

'Yes, quite far.'

'They can do that. Make you go?'

'Yes. I have to go where I'm posted.'

'I won't see you?'

'No, I'm afraid not.'

He looked up at her. She was astounded to see tears filling his eyes. Suddenly, she was reminded that he was just a little boy.

'No, Luka. It will be all right.' She dropped down on one knee to face him. 'Here.' She reached in her handbag for an envelope; she'd been carrying it with her for just this moment. 'Go to see this man, in this place. Tell him I sent you. Give him this letter. He will arrange a new life for you in England. Would you like that?'

He sniffed and looked around. 'It will be better than here?'

'Oh, yes. Much better. You will have a family. New clothes to wear. New things—'

'Not clothes of dead boy?'

'No! Your own clothes. Your own things. Toys,' Edith said, although she'd never imagined him playing with toys, or playing at all.

They walked on in silence as Luka thought over this unexpected proposition, weighing whether to accept it.

'Can I have dog?'

They were nearly at the apartment now. He put the bag down.

'I'm sure you can. You will be able to have anything you like.'

He stood for a moment weighing up her proposal. 'Will there be race with three legs?'

'I'm sure there will.'

'Then I take it,' he said with finality. 'I go. You come see me?'

'Of course I will!'

Edith reached down, crying and laughing as she hugged him to her.

Elisabeth opened the door.

'I've had word,' she said, wiping her hands on her apron. 'Frau Schmidt and Frau Kaufmann. They brought Papers. A new identity. A list of people and places for me.' Elisabeth's eyes slid sideways. Something, or someone was making her nervous. 'Your friend is here.'

'*Guten Abend.*' Dori's voice came from the kitchen. She was at the stove, stirring a mixture as red as her nails, her other hand holding a cigarette.

'*Rote Grütze.* I remember you like it, Edith.' Elisabeth took over the stirring. 'The first summer fruits from the garden. Always a special time. Hilde brought a *Körbchen* from her aunt and my friends in the *Schrebergärten* had fruit to trade.'

'My transfer came through this morning.'

'Ah.' Dori already knew. 'Guess what I've got?' She waved a hand towards the kitchen table. 'Vermouth and real olives. I might not be any good at cooking but I can mix a proper martini. All we need is gin. I'm sure you have that.'

Elisabeth set the pudding to cool in the larder and Dori mixed a jug of martinis.

'Cheers,' Dori raised her glass. 'Chin, chin. Here's to it. Getting on like a house on fire, aren't we, darling?' she said, as she clinked glasses with Elisabeth. 'All sorts of people and places in common from before the recent conflict, isn't that right?'

She was at her most dazzling, her most charming and most disarming.

There was wine with dinner, a Riesling that Dori had also

brought with her, then the famous pudding. Tart, not too much sugar. Bright red. Like arterial blood.

After dinner, the table was cleared. Dori laid out a map of Germany, Austria and Northern Italy.

'Right. Down to business. This is the plan. We'll be travelling together by train. Me under my own name, Dorothy Stansfield, Elisabeth as my translator. I've got papers for her. That will get us through the American Zone and into Austria without any problems. You, Edith, travel as yourself, going on holiday.' She tracked the route, using a teaspoon as a pointer. 'Once we reach Innsbruck, we split up.'

'Why do we have to separate?' Edith asked.

'Because my need for a German translator becomes redundant when we reach Italy and I can't get a German citizen through the official border. Elisabeth and I will be taking the scenic route over the high passes. It's the only way. That's what these papers are for. We will be assuming different identities, using false papers. The *Schwestern* came up trumps for Elisabeth. Just the ticket, I must say. Good, but not too good. That is what the people who are to get us over the border and down into Italy will expect. I've got a similar type of thing. War Crimes knocked it up for me. I'm Frau Brunner, looking for my Nazi husband. There are a couple of Brunners on the run, so it's good cover. Elisabeth is Frau Kushner which is the name von Stavenow is using now. Elisabeth and I will wait in this place,' Dori pointed to the map, 'Steinach am Brenner. The smugglers take people over in groups.'

'Where am I going?' Edith asked.

'You go on by rail, leaving the train at a little town in the Tyrol called Vipiteno Sterzing. There's a guest house on the main square – Hotel Aquila Nera-Schwarzer Adler. Take a room there. We will be staying at Pensione Sterzberg. The proprietors are Nazi sympathizers. That's where von Stavenow, now known as Herr Kushner, will fetch up.'

'When are we going?' Edith looked up from the map.

'Tomorrow. Sleeper from Hamburg to Munich.'

'In that case, there will be much to do.' Elisabeth stood up. 'Goodnight.'

The next morning, Dori was already on her first coffee and cigarette.

'Just had a lovely chat with Rozália. You didn't tell me she was Hungarian. Oodles in common. I definitely knew one of her aunts and might have had affairs with an uncle or two.'

'Where's Elisabeth?'

'Gone to say farewell to the infant and to make arrangements for her care.' Dori's eyebrow lifted. 'Want coffee? There's some in the pot.'

Edith poured herself a cup and came back to the table.

'Elisabeth is definitely our girl,' Dori said after a while. 'Your Miss Esterhazy agrees.'

'You interrogated Roz? Really, Dori—'

'Just confirming! A little gentle questioning. *Très discret*. Elisabeth likes nice things. Jewellery. Clothes. Who'd want to be buried in deepest Prussia when you are young, rich, good-looking, your husband's a Nazi officer and there's fun to be had elsewhere, at least while you're winning, and who'd go back to Prussia with the Russians on their way?'

'She was in Berlin for part of the time, at least.'

'You aren't still defending her, surely? She was in Berlin *all* of the time,' Dori said emphatically. 'And the child and this Kaspar. Has anyone seen him?'

'Kaspar? No.'

'He doesn't exist. Even if he does, he's strictly there to look after her precious horses. He's never going to get into the Gräfin's silk knickers. She's a Prussian aristocrat to her fingernails. I know them. She'd rather be torn apart by her own stallions.'

'The baby's real enough.'

'Not hers, I'll bet. You can buy anything in Germany for a handful of ackers, even a baby. She's good. I'll give her that. It is a bloody convincing story. Crafted to get your sympathy. We'll just have to make sure ours is as good as hers. It's got to last as far as Vipiteno. Being up in the mountains with a bunch of Nazis and those who aid them could leave me more than a little exposed.' Dori lit another cigarette. 'She's important. The *Schwestern* appeared just after I arrived. One of them, a large body, much given to nodding and smiling or, in Elisabeth's case, bowing and scraping.'

'Frau Schmidt.'

'And a smaller one. Older. Pink nose. Beady little eyes.'

'Frau Kaufmann,' Edith supplied. 'Friend of Frau Schmidt.'

'They seemed pretty skittish, so I made myself scarce, but I stayed close enough to overhear. You should have seen how they treated her. She could have been Frau Himmler. Afterwards, I got a little bonus. The contact list brought by the *Schwestern*. People and places from here to Switzerland and beyond.'

'How did you get it?'

'Picking pockets is a particular talent. Done in minutes while I was helping with the cooking.' She mimed using the Minox. 'And back in the apron pocket.' She held up a tiny roll of film. 'I thought we might pop this in the post to your friend Bill Adams. It's about time you gave him something. It'll keep him busy and distracted. I'll post it for you. I need to wire Drummond.'

Edith wrote a quick note to Adams. She dashed off a card to Louisa, included the *Rote Grütze* recipe and a casual mention that she might be going for a bit of a holiday. To Italy. Then another card to Harry. No time to agonize. Keep it simple. Keep it short.

> *I'm taking that holiday to Northern Italy. I can be contacted poste restante at* Vipiteno Sterzing, *Trentino-Alto Adige/Südtirol, South Tyrol. I miss you. If the offer is still open, I accept with all my heart!*
>   *Much love, Edith*

She sealed the envelope and addressed it to him at BAOR Quarters, Bad Oeynhausen, hoping that it might get to him, that he hadn't left yet. It was an act of faith, a bottle thrown into the sea. She delivered her post to Dori's waiting hand. To her annoyance, Edith found herself blushing like a schoolgirl.

'I don't suppose he'll get it,' she said, trying to sound as if it didn't matter.

'You never know.' Dori smiled. 'There's ways and means.'

After that, Edith was busy packing. A small suitcase and a knapsack, Dori instructed, no more than you can comfortably carry for a reasonable distance. Spare skirt, couple of blouses, two frocks, one a bit dressier, underwear, nighties, toilet bag. Her Mason Pearson hairbrush had disappeared, her best lipstick, too. A damned nuisance but no point in going on looking. She would have to make do with Rimmel and the comb in her handbag. Time was tight. They were getting the midday train to Hamburg.

ITALY

1946

37

American military train

10th May 1946

```
Buffet Menu
Crème Tomate
Crevette au Mayonnaise Russe
Poulet Roti
Pommes Chateau
Asperges au Hollandaise
Filet Mignon
Shortcake au Fraises
Welsh Rarebit
Café
```

```
The menu in French, but the food American:
tomato soup or shrimps in a kind of pink
mayonnaise, chicken or steak with roast pota-
toes and asparagus. Strawberry shortcake.
Welsh Rarebit as savoury. American rations
far more generous than the British equivalent.
```

Edith hadn't been back to Hamburg Station since her arrival in the depths of winter. Now, people milled about the great concourse in frocks and shirt sleeves. The place smelt of soot and smoke laced with lilac from untended gardens, the sourness of broken drains and a sweetish undernote of decay. Eau de Hamburg. The noon sun shone down through the great arches, the strong light split into golden shafts filled with swirling motes of dust. The squeal of iron on steel, the urgent snorts and long exhalations of arriving and departing engines sent roosting pigeons whirling up into the blueness past glinting shards of glass still gripped into the twisted ribs of the roof.

The military train stood at Platform 4. A young Rail Transport Officer stood checking papers at the barrier. Dori swept up to him, Elisabeth in tow. She was in her WAAF Officer's uniform, which suited her tall slenderness and dark good looks. She managed to be both austere and alluring at the same time. The papers she had obtained for herself and Elisabeth would get them through as far as the Austria–Italy border but she was not one to leave things to chance, even here. Her combination of haughtiness and charm left him reeling. He hardly glanced at Edith's papers, just nodded her through, while staring after Dori's legs in seamed stockings with awestruck lust.

The train wasn't crowded. An attendant met them at the door and saw to their luggage. They had the four-berth sleeper compartment to themselves.

'So far, so good,' Dori got out her compact and applied a fresh coat of lipstick, a dab of powder. 'I'm going to the buffet car. Anyone coming with me?'

'I think I should stay here,' Elisabeth replied. 'Not to attract attention.'

'Hmm,' Dori snapped shut her compact. 'Probably a good idea. Edith?'

'I'll keep Elisabeth company.'

'Need to get the lay of the land,' Dori stared out of the window, studying the people dotting the platform. 'Have a scout about. See who else is on board.'

Edith had taken a seat by the window. Elisabeth sat opposite, her attention caught by something outside. Edith had her back

402

to the engine and had to peer to see what Elisabeth was looking at so fixedly.

The furthest platform had no train standing there. None leaving, none arriving. It was distant from the other platforms, foreshortened, as if it was not really part of the vast station. It stood like an island. Beyond it lay sidings full of rusting engines, smashed wagons, twisted rails. A dumping ground for the detritus of war. The platform itself looked like a scarecrow encampment, black with people and their piled-up belongings under ragged awnings, rigged to keep out the hot May sun. People sat huddled, arms round their knees, staring out at the busy station, the trains leaving and arriving, studying the passengers who were boarding and alighting – coming from somewhere, going to somewhere – while they were going nowhere. Others lay sprawled while the makeshift awnings flapped above them like black, tattered flags. Children ran about between them or leaned listlessly against their mothers, or each other. Occasionally someone would stand up and find a place to relieve themselves, quite openly.

'*Ostvolk,*' Elisabeth said quietly. 'People from the east.'

They had fetched up here from East Prussia, Pomerania, Poland and even further east: Ukraine, Belarus. Some might have come from the south. Sudeten Germans from Czechoslovakia and where else? Who knows? Moving west, always west. Moved on from one place to another because no one wanted them. Lawyers, doctors, farmers, dentists, musicians, their wives and children, forced to take this trek by road and rail, the old, the very young, the weak abandoned by the wayside, buried there, or left to rot. On, ever on. But this was the last stop. There was nowhere else to go. So they sat here, waiting for someone to rescue them.

'Someone will come and pick them up,' Edith said without a great deal of conviction. 'Red Cross, UNRRA, the British. They are building Nissen huts in the streets.'

'For Hamburg people. Not these.'

Edith did not disagree. The residents of Hamburg were still living in the bunkers and cellars of their bombed-out city.

'Schleswig-Holstein has already been declared a black area. It's full, so is Hamburg.'

'But nobody has told these people this, so still they come.'

It was overwhelming and the truth of it was, no one knew what to do.

The last door slammed, a whistle blew. A deep hoot announced that they were about to depart and the engine began its long, laboured chuffing as it drew them away from the station.

'Where's Dori?' Edith asked. She had not come back yet.

'I'll go and see, shall I?' Elisabeth volunteered.

After a little while, it was clear that she'd lost her, too, but Edith didn't mind. She liked being on trains and she liked travelling alone. She got her book out of her bag: Graham Greene, *The Ministry of Fear*. Leo boasted an acquaintance with Graham Greene, albeit slight, so she felt a personal connection. She'd got it out of the NAAFI Library. She'd have to post it back.

Yet the book lay on her lap, unread. The devastated city gave way to less scarred suburbs, then countryside: a farmer driving cattle to milking, a boy walking down long rows of potatoes. The fields became barren heathland, clotted with flaring gorse, dotted with twisted pines. Here and there, the rusting remains of war: a burnt-out tank, a field gun tipped on its side, the skeletal remains of a truck. Then a tract of forest, great scaly trunks reared as the train plunged into cuttings; thick, twisted roots clinging to red, sandy soil. Every so often, they would steam through a station: a small village strung along the railway; a town of thin copper-clad spires, red roofs and turrets. Gone before Edith had time to wonder about who lived there. On through Lower Saxony, glimpses of distant castles on gothic crags; isolated farmhouses with logs piled up against the oncoming winter, even though it was barely summer, the wood stacked under steeply pitched roofs reaching almost to the ground. The shape and the design of these Saxon dwellings hadn't changed much since the Iron Age. We are a deeply conservative people, that seemed to say. Our history goes back a very long way.

There was little sign of the war here. Only the cities showed real scars. The empty, sentinel steeples of Hanover looked like Hamburg or Berlin.

Time to go and find the others. Edith had gazed on enough destruction in her time here.

Dori and Elisabeth were in the dining car, entertaining two American officers who stood up like schoolboys when Edith joined them. They seemed young for the marks of rank they carried but when she came closer she saw a bullet crease disappearing into a blond hairline; eyes that were no longer young. There was a weariness there, as if they'd seen plenty of things they'd like forget, creases at the corners from staring down gun sights and into the sun.

'Don't let me interrupt,' Edith said as she sat down.

'Would you like a drink, ma'am? I'm Lew, by the way.' He was older than the other. A colonel. He smiled, his pale-blue eyes crinkling. He ran a hand over his dark-auburn hair.

'Yes, please.' Edith smiled back. 'Whisky.'

'No ice, I'm afraid.'

'No ice is fine with me.'

Edith sat back and sipped her drink. Dori was being especially winning, looking up from under her long lashes, fixing the younger of the two with her large dark eyes as he lit her cigarette. She was keeping up a stream of flirtatious banter threaded through with casual-seeming questions. Where were they stationed? Where were they heading? What did they do?

Lew grinned as the younger man sought to monopolize her. 'Your friend is quite a girl.'

Edith smiled. She knew how Dori worked. Befriending American officers would minimize problems when crossing into the American Zone and maybe there was something more to it than that . . .

The talk moved on to swapping war accounts, as most people did at first encounter. Elisabeth scooped the pool.

'By January we knew we had to leave . . .'

Elisabeth began the story of her dramatic escape on

horseback before the Russian advance. The searing cold, the impossible distances, the rocket whine and artillery fire of clashing armies; the endless columns of refugees, whole provinces on the move. The Americans listened with rapt attention, nodding now and then, to encourage her to go on or because she was confirming what they thought already. They were predisposed not to like the Russians, the new enemy, and this eyewitness account of rape and slaughter was exactly what they wanted to hear.

Everyone had war stories, embroidered to add texture and colour, to make vivid the plain linen ground of day-to-day wartime life. People would, no doubt, continue to do so until the bright myth became the memory, but this was of a different order. Edith sat back in her seat, listening. Elisabeth didn't make this up. She was sure of that. The telling contained too many tiny details: the warning of crows in the trees near the villages they had to avoid, the infants encased in the frozen carapaces of their nappies. Such observations took her story out of the realm of invention. That's where the power of it lay. Edith watched the expressions shift and change on the faces around her: horror, disgust, sympathy, admiration – all the emotions she'd felt on that first hearing. Elisabeth couldn't play her in that way now. The deep sympathy she had first evoked had long gone.

They ate together. The talk turned to lighter matters. At Kassel, the train halted. American border police came along the carriages, inspecting papers. The presence of a colonel meant that theirs got little more than a cursory glance. There was a call for those leaving to leave now.

'We're changing here.' Colonel Lew picked up his cap. 'Come see us if you're over in Frankfurt.'

They all smiled with that combination of regret and relief that comes from knowing that you will never see that person again.

'Tom's men,' Dori said as the doors slammed. 'Keeping an eye while keeping us entertained. Two more have taken over.'

She nodded towards the two officers settling themselves at a table. 'Time to turn in, I think.'

The train stopped at Nuremberg while they were breakfasting. The two Americans from the night before had been replaced by another pair a few rows down and across the aisle.

'He really doesn't trust us, does he?' Dori breathed, smiling in their direction. They quickly looked out of the window, instantly absorbed by the passing scene. 'Not them I'm worried about, though. It's those two.' She took out her mirror as though checking her makeup. 'Third table, right-hand side.'

Edith glanced down the train. Two men sitting opposite each other reading newspapers. As she got up to leave, one of them folded his paper carefully and followed her.

Edith went back to the compartment to find her place had been taken.

'Adeline!'

Edith hugged her fiercely, absurdly glad that she was here. Soon, Dori and Elisabeth would be leaving and she hadn't been looking forward to going on alone.

'Got on at Nuremberg.' Adeline resumed her seat. 'Dori wired me which train you'd be on. She thought I might like to come along. Escaping Nazis will make helluva good story. Also, I've got information of the sensitive kind.' She patted the musette bag by her side. 'Where's Dori? Elisabeth with her?'

Edith nodded. 'They're still at breakfast.'

'Good. I've got something you need to see.' Adeline took a file from her bag. 'I looked up the guys she was with in the garden party photograph. Guess what I found in the Nazi photo archives?' Adeline set out photographs. 'Elisabeth with Gehlen.' Elisabeth in a fur coat and hat walking next to the Nazi officer, going through a gate, barbed wire each side. 'And here she is again, this time with Kopkow.' Elisabeth in an office somewhere, taken from the side. She tapped the file. 'I got evidence that shows that Elisabeth worked for the both of them at different times.' She sat back. 'Looks to me as though Elisabeth might be the draw here. Intelligence, British and US, would be interested in using Elisabeth as a bullshit detector on the stories these men are spinning to them and whatever else she knows.' She paused. 'That's not why Dori wants her, of course. These men sent her agents to the gas chambers.'

At Munich, they boarded the British military train to Vienna. No one seemed to follow them.

Munich's ruins were replaced by bright meadows and dark forests. Adeline took photographs.

'Isn't Berchtesgaden here someplace?' she asked.

'Further east,' Elisabeth replied. 'Even more remote.'

'Didn't Hitler have plans for the Nazis to hold out there? The last redoubt? What did they call it?' Adeline frowned as she lined up another shot. 'Alpen something?'

'Alpenfestung,' Elisabeth supplied. 'I don't think it was a serious plan.'

'Is that a fact?' Adeline turned the camera on her. 'You don't mind do you? It's just I like snapping faces and you are very photogenic.' Elisabeth blushed slightly. 'Even better. No, don't pose, like you are, looking out the window, that's nice. So what was it about then? This Alpenfestung? Sure fooled our guys.'

'It was a trick. They wanted the Allies to believe they could hold out in these mountains indefinitely.'

'But why?' Adeline carried on snapping.

'Who knows?' Elisabeth shrugged. 'Maybe they wanted to believe it themselves.'

Edith watched the two of them. She'd seen Adeline do this before, question someone while taking photographs at the same time. It both disarmed and disconcerted. Adeline said it gave a more honest portrait.

'We'll be at the border soon,' Dori remarked. 'Just popping out for a smoke.'

'I'll join you.' Adeline got up, taking her musette bag, leaving Edith and Elisabeth alone in the carriage.

'They can smoke in here.' Elisabeth looked enquiring.

'They know I don't like it.'

'The border,' said Elisabeth, looking out of the window. 'It will be all right?'

'Sure to be,' Edith replied, although she had no idea.

'Two British officers smoking out of the windows at either end of the carriage,' Dori said quietly as the train came to a slow halt.

They were entering the French Zone of Occupation. The border guards inspected papers with fastidious politeness. They touched their caps, everything in order, and went on to the next carriage.

'That went smoothly.' Dori tucked the papers back in her bag. 'Our friends still out there?'

Edith looked out into the corridor and nodded.

'Time for a change of plan. We get off at the next station. You two stay on until Innsbruck. Take a turn round the town, have coffee, cake, take some photos. Stay a day or two, then get a train to Vipiteno Sterzing. If our friends are still with you, go past the town and double back.'

Dori reached up to the rack and took down the case that she'd brought with her.

'Goodbye, then.' Dori hugged Edith, then Adeline. 'You two be careful.'

'You, too, Dori,' Edith kissed her cheek.

'Yeah,' Adeline held her tight. 'You stay safe.'

The train slowed and stopped. Passengers alighted to change trains or stretch their legs. Dori and Elisabeth disappeared into the Ladies' Waiting Room. One of the British officers stayed at the open window of the train, watching. The other roamed randomly, as if merely exercising cramped muscles while he kept an eye on Edith and Adeline who were innocently strolling, taking in the sharp clean mountain air, enjoying the pale sunshine, looking up at the mountains serrated against the sky. The man on the train was becoming more and more agitated, nervously scanning the platform for a woman in uniform and her companion. From the corner of her eye, Edith saw Dori and

Elisabeth, arms linked. Two German women of a certain age and class. Dori on the outside, now in a pale-grey duster coat with the collar turned up, a feathered hat down over one eye. Elisabeth, similarly attired. Dori carried a small suitcase. Everything in it would be appropriate to a good Nazi wife in search of her husband, right down to underwear, handkerchiefs and items of toiletry. The beretta she carried was a present from her SS husband. French clothes, perfume, makeup, picked up by him in Paris. Dori was undercover. Her British uniform would be lying in the waiting room, discarded like a shed skin.

38

Hotel Aquila Nera–Schwarzer Adler, Vipiteno Sterzing

17th May 1946

Torta ai Carciofi
Angelina's Recipe
Pâte Brisée (pie pastry)
6 artichokes
3 eggs
5 spoons of Emmenthal cheese
Oil
Salt
Pepper
1 lemon

Clean the artichokes, cut them into slices
and place in a bowl with water and lemon.
In a frying pan, heat a little olive oil,
add the drained artichokes, season with salt
and let simmer for about 15 minutes.
Eventually add a bit of water. In a bowl
beat the eggs, add the grated cheese and

cold artichokes. Season with salt and pepper.
Roll out the dough and fit into a pie tin,
prick with a fork and pour the artichokes.
Fold the edges of the dough on artichokes
and bake at 190 degrees for about 20 minutes.
Serve with a cream cheese.

Vipiteno Sterzing was a small place. Too small. Little more than a market-place and a long, narrow, main street. The borders might have shifted but the place remained resolutely Austrian. The clock tower still displayed the double-headed eagle, the motif repeated on the decorative ironwork outside the shops and houses. The German language was ubiquitous: in sign and script, spoken in the street by men in Tyrolean hats and Lederhosen.

Sitting outside the hotel on the main square, drinking espresso, they were attracting attention. Not all of it friendly. This region was not occupied. The people lacked the servility routinely displayed by the Germans, whatever their true feelings might be. The English, the Americans had no presence here. Its residents were not beholden, not dependent on anybody. There was no one to remind them constantly to feel guilty about the war they'd lost, the damage they had done. They were free to feel anything they liked and Edith sensed hostility. Seething with Nazis, Dori had said. The last redoubt had not happened, but Nazis were likely to have drained down through the border to settle and be joined by others who were waiting for papers, marking time in their onward journey to who knew where.

'Don't stare,' Adeline stirred sugar into her coffee. 'Relax. Enjoy the sunshine.'

'I keep wondering which ones are Nazis. I feel as though they are all watching us.'

'Most of them, probably,' Adeline answered. 'And sure they are. At least it's only suspicious Nazis watching us. No sign of any British or Americans.' Edith was not sure how comforting she found this observation. 'Wonder what this guy wants?'

A little man was approaching from across the square. He addressed them in German although he was very obviously Italian: small, wiry, dark-complexioned with thinning black hair swept back over his scalp. His eyes were a yellowish brown behind his thin-rimmed glasses. His wide smile showed a glint of gold.

'Signora Graham? It is nice to see you here.'

Edith looked up at him in surprise. 'How do you know my name?'

'I was asked to look out for you. We don't get very many visitors. And who is this lovely lady?'

Adeline didn't say.

'You are?' Edith asked.

'I don't introduce myself. I'm so sorry. My name is Signor Rossi. At your service.' He bowed to Edith, 'I have a nice place with a view of the lake. Pensione Alto Adige. I extend an invitation for you to come tomorrow. Four of the clock. I prepare Marende. Very nice. Special to the region.' He leaned close. His breath smelt of garlic and cloves. 'For you and a German guest, you understand? Take the path north around the lake,' he added more loudly. 'First house you see. A nice walk for you.'

He beamed his smile at her but there was no matching warmth behind his gold-rimmed spectacles, no light in his dull, clay-coloured eyes.

A tall figure loomed over him. 'This fella bothering you?'

Signor Rossi took one look and scuttled off across the square with a muttered, 'I welcome you tomorrow.'

'Sergeant! What in the world are you doing here?'

Edith should have been surprised to see him, but somehow she wasn't.

'On holiday.'

Jack sat down at the table. He was wearing long khaki shorts, army socks folded over his hiking boots, a pale-blue Aertex shirt and a short-sleeved cricket pullover. His face and neck were tanned, his arms and legs a convincing brown, as though he really had been on a walking holiday.

'I'm here with Kay. Honeymooning, in fact.' His grin was slightly sheepish now. 'Finally tied the knot.'

'Oh?' Edith looked at him. That did surprise her.

'Spur of the moment, like. Kept it small, you know. German padre at the hospital. Just a few of me mates and a couple of her nursing pals.'

'Where's Kay now?'

'In the church looking for frescoes. *Bier, Birra!*' He shouted to the approaching waiter. 'And make it quick, Alphonso! What did the Eyetie want?'

'He invited me to Pensione Alto Adige for Marende to share with a German friend. Four o'clock tomorrow afternoon.'

'Did he? I know it. Below Pensione Sterzberg, where Dori's staying. I've been here a couple of days. Having a recce.'

'She's here?' Edith was relieved to know that Dori arrived safely, even if the information had come from a most unexpected source. What exactly was Jack doing here?

'Last night,' he went on quietly. 'I'll let her know. Send word with Giorgio our *padrone*. Ex-partisan. He can be trusted. Thanks, mate.' Jack swept the beer from the waiter's tray, took a long draught and shuddered. 'Can't stand this stuff. I'm gasping for a pint of Holden's Mild, or even Bank's at a pinch.' He drained his beer and stood up. 'Better get on. Kay'll be finished in that church soon. It's only the size of a rabbit hutch.' He looked down at them. 'Don't say nothing to her about any of this business.'

'Of course not.' Adeline and Edith spoke together.

'See ya later. In the bar at seven, say?'

He left with a wave and went into the hotel.

'What's he doing here?' Adeline asked. 'Is he here as your faithful German Shepherd? Or is something else going on?'

'Yes, Adie,' Edith shook her head. 'I'd like to know, too!'

Jack came down to dinner with Kay on his arm. They looked very much the honeymooning couple. Kay tall and tanned, with just a dash of lipstick, her dark hair caught in at the nape, falling onto the neck of her short-sleeved summer dress. Jack in grey slacks and a blue open-necked shirt, his unruly curls slicked back and tamed. His skin had a close-shaved, polished look and was that cologne? Kay's influence, no doubt. He was quieter in her presence, more subdued.

They drank their aperitifs on the terrace under the wide, low eaves of the hotel. The grey-paved expanse of the square was empty apart from a few women dressed in black scurrying to Evening Mass in the small, squat church next to the clock.

'Doesn't look much, does it?' Kay sipped her Cinzano. 'But it hides real riches. The frescoes are marvellous.'

'Not to be missed, eh, Kay?' Jack said, picking up their conversation. He winked at Edith. 'Tomorrow morning might be a good time for you to go and have a look.' He waved his empty beer glass and looked around the table. 'Anyone want another? Hope dinner's soon. I could eat a dead dog,' he laughed. 'Probably will be.'

Dinner was a fixed menu, a mix of Austrian and Italian dishes cooked by the innkeeper's wife. The guests sat round a long table in a wood-panelled dining room decorated with trophies: tusked boar, delicate chamois, scimitar-horned ibex, the spreading antlers of red deer. As they were the only guests, they had the table to themselves. Their host, Giorgio was small and dark with glasses, like the man in the square, but there the resemblance ended. Giorgio's brown eyes had a brightness, as if he was always close to laughter, his curling smile was genuine, no gold teeth in evidence. He poured the wine, a dark Marzemino. His wife, Angelina, served the food. Quiet, self-contained and darkly pretty, she smiled at their praise, her high colour heightening further as she tucked a curl of black hair back under her white cap.

There was much to praise. First, she brought them a huge plate of antipasti: dry-cured ham tracing-paper thin, circled by smoked sausage and layered with almost transparent slices of rose-coloured juniper-scented speck. Giorgio brought out wire baskets of bread, wheaten and rye, speckled with fennel seed and caraway. The antipasti was followed by a savoury tart. Edith had to ask what it was. *Torta ai Carciofi.* Artichoke hearts. Edith had never tasted anything like it before and immediately asked for the recipe.

'How are things at the hospital?' she asked Kay.

'Busy, as always.' She wiped her mouth with a napkin. 'Although fewer T.B. cases now the weather's improved. Anna and Seraphina came to see me. Did Jack say?'

'No, he didn't.' Edith looked over at Jack. He'd finished the wine and was calling for *grappa*. Kay would have her hands full there.

'I know what he's like,' Kay said, guessing her thinking. 'Can't change him. Wouldn't want to. Now, the Jewish girls.' She returned to the previous topic with a bright smile. 'Anna is fully recovered, thanks to you. They said they were leaving. Off to Palestine. Didn't say how and I didn't ask. All organized by your friend, Harry, to start a new life there. I hope they find it, I really do. God knows they deserve it, all they've been through. We've had a couple more in, you know. Jewish girls, from Poland. They were in Ravensbrück. Young, pretty and such strong spirits despite terrible injuries. Really terrible.' She put down her fork. 'What was done to them, it doesn't bear thinking about. We're doing what we can, but they'll never be the same. I don't know how they could do it. Doctors, nurses deliberately harming, mutilating young flesh. They are going to testify. The girls, I mean. At the trial of those responsible. Brave of them to do it but they are very determined. I hope the swine swing for what they did.'

'*Dolce, Signora?*'

'No thanks,' Kay dabbed her lips again. 'I've rather lost my appetite. He's very fond of you, you know.' Kay nodded to towards Jack who was clinking glasses with Adeline. 'Doesn't normally care for CCG types – his words, not mine. One of the best officers I've served under. That's what he said. That's great praise coming from him.'

Edith felt herself colour. 'Don't know what I might have done to deserve that accolade.'

'You're straight, that's what he said. Never afraid to do what's right, never mind the brass hat and red tape brigade. He hates all that.' She turned to Edith. 'I don't know why we are here, Jack wouldn't say, but I don't believe it's just a honeymoon, despite all his flannel, and I don't believe meeting you here is "just a coincidence". He'll tell me if he wants to, if not? Better I don't know. He's been up here before, you know.'

'I knew he'd been in Italy.'

Kay nodded. 'He was here or hereabouts at the end of the war. You've heard of the last redoubt?' Edith nodded. 'He was here to clear it out. He'd always been a bit vague about what he did during the war. You've heard his patter: "A bit of this, a bit of that, a lot of the other." Makes out he was a ducker and diver, a bit of a skiver.' She smiled and shook her head. 'Nothing could be further from the truth. He was in Special Forces. Did you know?'

'Well, yes . . .' Special Forces. S.A.S. That's where the connection lay. Bulldog Drummond. This was his 'show'.

'I didn't. Didn't know what he did. One night – it was after he came back from Berlin – he got very drunk – so drunk he could hardly stand and, you know Jack, he can hold his liquor. And he was,' she searched for the right word, 'emotional. Which was unusual. Doesn't show his feelings, not ever. A smile and a laugh, that's Jack. Not this night. I asked, what was the matter? Said he'd had bad news. He'd met someone, an officer, I think.'

That must have been Drummond, Dori had mentioned meeting them together in Berlin.

'He was over in Germany,' Kay went on, 'looking for his men, Special Forces, who'd been dropped behind enemy lines. There were hopes that they might turn up as POWs, one or two were still trickling in, but there was no sign of them. They'd tried everything. Even held a séance.'

'What are you two so thick about?' Jack sat down between them, a slightly owlish look on his face. The bottle of *grappa* in front of him was two-thirds empty.

'Nothing, Jack,' Kay said. 'Just talking.'

'Is that right? If I didn't know better, I'd say you were spilling beans.'

Jack gave a lazy smile but his eyes had a glitter about them. Hard to tell whether he was angry, or more than a little tipsy.

'It's my fault, Jack,' Edith said. 'I encouraged Kay to speak out of turn.'

'Want a tot of this?' he offered the bottle. 'Come on, join me.' He poured two glasses. 'They were men I knew. Trained with 'em. Fought with 'em. It's hard to understand but that kind of friendship, it's closer than most marriages. I knew Bulldog'd be looking for 'em. *If these did not die well, it will be a black matter,* that's what he'd said. Any sign? I asked when I saw him in Berlin. He's as drunk as I've ever seen him. "'Sfar as we can tell, Sergeant," he says to me, "they did not die well." He's found 'em, all right. Buried in some wood. Naked. Hands tied. Shot in the back of the head. Should have been treated as prisoners of war. He recruited me to help find the bastards who done that.' He looked out to the deserted square. 'Some of them might be hereabouts. Come on, our wench.' He held a hand out to Kay. 'We're s'posed to be on honeymoon. Time for bed. See you in the morning. Enjoy the frescoes,' he added, looking at Edith. 'Around eight. After Mass.'

39

Hotel Aquila Nera-Schwarzer Adler, Vipitino Sterzing

18th May 1946

La Prima Colazione
First meal of the day

Bread rolls or toast, with unsalted butter
and jam (or just jam) cornetto (croissant)
biscotti. Served with cappuccino (coffee with
hot milk). In Alto Adigeo (Südtirol) cheese,
ham and eggs form part of breakfast, a clear
Austrian influence. Brioche substitute for
cornetti.

Edith woke to the thin, oddly cracked sound of the town bell.
She looked at her watch. Nearly eight o'clock. She got dressed
quickly and went out into the square, hurrying through the
stallholders setting up for the market. Women, heads covered,
dressed in black, were already out looking along the stalls piled
with fruit and vegetables.

The church was dim after the brightness outside. It took a
moment to adjust her eyes. Bunches of candles flickered and

flared, windows glazed with veined, translucent alabaster let in a dim, golden light. The church was almost round, as wide as it was long, without side aisles. Edith was reminded of Templar churches, Byzantine basilicas. She could see what Kay meant about the frescoes. The wide arched roof was completely covered, so were the walls. It was like stepping into a painted cave.

The church was almost empty. Two black-clad old women, heads covered, sat hunched outside a tall confession box, telling their rosaries in a steady buzzing drone like a fly trapped behind glass. Another woman knelt at a pew about half way down the church. Dressed in black but obviously much younger than the crones in the side pews, she knelt, straight backed, hands clasped, her head half covered by a dark, filmy scarf. Edith slid into the pew beside her.

'You took your time.' Dori didn't look round. 'Haven't been on my knees this long for quite a while.'

'Sorry. Bit of a late night.' Edith knelt down. The pew smelt of old wood, incense and plaster dust. She bent her head to her folded hands in a parody of piety. 'Jack's idea to meet here?'

'A church is good cover. A good place to rendezvous.'

'How are you faring? Do they believe you?'

'On the surface, can't do enough. Mein Host swears he helped my husband on his way back to Germany. We're staying in Pensione Alto Adige. It's just a bit higher up the hillside from Pensione Sterzberg where you will be meeting Kurt. They are both owned by Rossi. I've been given the best room. Lake view and everything. But it's wearing a bit thin, to be honest. I'm beginning to feel a bit spare. *Hail Mary, full of Grace,*' Dori intoned, beads clicking between her fingers. '*The Lord is with thee. Blessed are thou among women.*'

'Do you have to?'

'Don't want to attract attention. *Blessed is the fruit of thy womb, Jesus* . . . Anyway, I am a Catholic. A little rusty, perhaps, but it soon comes back. Puts me quids in with the locals. A positive boon. Catholic Church hand in glove. Helping the escapees, providing all sorts of goodies: papers, passports, safe havens in nunneries and monasteries, all the way from here to Rome. *Holy Mary, Mother of God, pray for us sinners, now and at the hour of our death. Amen.*'

'Amen,' Edith joined in automatically. 'Maybe you should have this back.' She held up the medallion she was wearing.

'No,' Dori gazed down at the sad, scarred face of the proffered Madonna. 'You may still have need of Her. You're going to meet von Stavenow this afternoon.'

'Is he there?'

Dori shook her head. 'No, not yet. Expected later today. Mein Host is in a high old tizz getting things ready.'

'Where's Elisabeth?'

'Out for the day. Off bright and early. To Merano probably, to get new papers, would be my guess.' She passed the beads through her fingers. 'I admire her more and more and trust her less and less. She's clever and quite, quite ruthless. She's got a photographic memory; did you know that? The routes we took? One glance and she knew them. One of the guides tried to give us the runaround. He went for a walk with Elisabeth. I think he fancied his chances. He didn't come back.' She recited a few more *Hail Marys*. 'The evidence Adeline found puts her at the centre of Nazi Intelligence, she'd know names, places, circuits within the Soviet Union, contacts who may still be active. Worth a great deal in anybody's money. I'm guessing that their plan is to make their way from here to a port, probably Genoa, where the Americans will be waiting with lovely new identities for their onward journey and tickets to happy ever after. She's good, I'll give her that. Did you see her with those yanks on the train? They'll never forget that encounter.'

'It's a very powerful story.'

'You can say that again. She didn't make that up. The thing is, all the time she was telling it, I was thinking: how did she get herself stuck in Prussia? This is how I think it went. By July '44, Russians to the east, Allies to the west. Everyone knew it was coming unstuck. Panic. Some of them try to blow up Hitler and get strung up by piano wire for their pains. There's a general covering of tracks. This was when our Joes and the SAS chaps were rounded up and dispatched. People start making plans. Clandestine approaches to the Allies, a hasty remove to the Alpine Redoubt. Individuals start thinking about their own survival, so Sturmbannführer von Stavenow and his good lady wife come up with their personal strategy. Number One: they don't want to be in Berlin when the Ivans arrive. Number Two: they have items that might be of interest to the Allied Forces. How to kill large numbers of people quickly. The key to major espionage circuits. Both are smart enough to see this could be useful currency after the war. They aren't going to keep sensitive materials in Berlin. My guess is they kept such in Prussia. Along with easily transportable valuables, gold and jewellery.'

'And the horses,' Edith added. 'She would never leave the horses.'

However much of Elisabeth's story was fabricated, her love for her horses was genuine. The thought of them falling into the hands of the Red Army would be enough to send her back to Prussia, whatever the risk or personal cost.

Dori inclined her head, accepting the point. 'And the horses. She's dispatched to the Schloss while he gets himself and his lucky patients sent north. But she gets caught. Ivans advancing on all fronts. The only way out is to take to the saddle, which she does, fetching up in Lübeck in time to meet you.'

'How did they know I was going to be there, though?' Edith asked. It was all speculation but it sounded plausible – until the last part. That was a coincidence too far.

'Ah! That's the *really* interesting question,' Dori said with a note of triumph.

'So how did they?'

'Search me, darling, but I have my suspicions. Tell me, when did Leo know about you applying to the Control Commission?'

'Early on. He was one of my character referees.'

'And how did you end up in Lübeck?'

'I don't know. I thought they sent people to where they might be needed—'

Pennies were dropping, puzzle pieces falling into place. 'You don't think—'

''Deed I do. Leo can wangle anything, he's on all sorts of committees and there's always the Club. It makes sense, doesn't it? Von S. a target. The *Gräfin* has relatives in Lübeck. She's likely as not to fetch up there . . .'

'He set me up from the start!'

'You were perfect! Known to the subjects, totally above board, no taint of skullduggery. He must have been rubbing his hands. And you're good. You took to it. He knew you would. They *trust* you. She does, anyway. *I'm* the enemy. Not you. You're the only one who can get close to von Stavenow. So now you need to make the meeting. See what he wants. And keep him talking. As long as possible. That's very, very important.' She stood up. 'We'll do the rest. No,' she put a hand on Edith's arm as she made to rise too. 'Best not leave together. Stay here. Look at the frescoes. Hans von Bruneck. 1402. Very fine.'

Dori left the pew without looking back. When she reached the aisle, she bowed her head to the altar and dropped into a graceful curtsey of genuflection.

Edith gazed up at the frescoes. Softened by time, the colours muted to darkened pastel, rubbed away to shadows in places, tableaus and scenes ran around the whole church, one after another, crowding in on each other. Angels soared across the ceiling. Saints suffered a variety of martyrdoms; the Passion, depicted in a number of small scenes, surrounded the plain wooden crucifix fastened to the eastern wall: the Agony in the Garden, the Crucifixion. A sad-eyed Madonna looked down over all.

She closed her eyes and leaned forward, hands clasped tightly together. She didn't know how long she stayed like this. Perhaps she was actually praying. At length, she stood up. Time to leave. She walked towards the door. The great Doom painting spread above her. The dead rising from their graves, pale and naked, angels on one side, devils on the other. Christ in Judgement, sorting out good from bad. Sheep from goats.

* * *

Giorgio brought her breakfast: coffee and brioche, a plate holding three kinds of cheese, slices of salami and thinly cut ham. The others had already breakfasted, he said. Signora Hunter and the American Signorina had gone by train to Verona to see the Roman edifices and the Basilica San Zeno Maggiore. Signor Hunter had gone for a hike and would be out all day.

Edith ate her breakfast slowly. She had time to kill. She noted down what was on the table, asked about the various cheeses, was that fennel in the salami?

Giorgio answered her questions and brought her more coffee. 'My Angelina, she has prepared the recipe for you.' He smiled. 'The *Torta ai Carciofi*.'

'Thank you.'

Edith followed him past a larder, stacked with round cheeses, dark as a cave, into the kitchen. A long, cool room, lit by small windows and an open door that led to a garden already green with thick growth: silver-stemmed artichokes, peas ravelling over netting, beans winding up sticks, tomatoes bursting from their stout wooden frames, rows of radish, beetroot, carrots, white-stemmed chard, purple radicchio and lettuces: bright green and frilly, dark, coppery – varieties she didn't even know. She caught the scent of lavender and rosemary, bees already busy among the purple and blue flowers. Mint, Italian parsley and oregano grew in terracotta pots by the door.

Angelina was already at work preparing lunch, humming as she washed vegetables at a stone sink. A box stood on the draining board packed with bunched white and red onions, bundles of herbs: sorrel and rocket; wild asparagus, as thin as whips, the purple-tipped, fat-blanched spears of its cultivated cousin. Another box on the floor held celery and white-bulbed, green-fronded fennel.

'The Signora,' Georgio said.

'*Scusi*,' Angelina turned, drying her hands on her apron.

'No, no! Don't let me disturb you. I was just admiring your garden.' Edith smiled. 'It reminded me of home. My brother-in-law, Ted, would love this! He loves to grow vegetables.' The image of Ted, digging on his allotment brought sudden tears springing. 'You have so many different varieties,' she went on quickly. 'Ones I've never seen before and he loves to grow new things.'

Angelina nodded, smiling as Giorgio translated.

'*E la ricetta*,' she reached into her apron pocket and brought out the recipe neatly written in thick pencil on white greaseproof paper.

'Thank you.' Edith put the recipe into her bag. She looked round the kitchen. 'May I stay for a bit?'

She felt the day stretching out in front of her. A yawning gap of time before the appointment she was destined to keep at 4 p.m. She could feel anxiety growing, gnawing at her with little sharp teeth. If she could just stay here, at least for a while, in this airy, sunlit kitchen with its smells of wood smoke from the oven, bread rising on the scrubbed pine table, green things growing in the garden, cheeses under their lacy covers on the long sideboard. She wanted to be doing something. Chopping, mixing, rolling out and shaping would help to calm her. She'd always found cooking a comfort and a solace.

Angelina wouldn't hear of Edith helping but she allowed her to stay and watch as she prepared lunch. Her English was limited and Edith hadn't used her Italian much since college but cooks don't really need language. It's all in the look, the scent, and the movement of the hands.

Angelina promised to prepare a picnic. Edith would spend the afternoon down by the lake. She bought sun-faded sepia views of the little town, the Market Square and Clock. It was time she wrote home. She took the cards out onto the terrace and closed her eyes for a moment to imagine a gentler sun. She'd never felt so close to them, or so distant.

Giorgio brought her a pot of coffee and with it a bundle of small brown packets. He laid them on the table, almost shyly. '*Per tuo cognato. Dal nostro giardino.* From our garden. We keep from year to year.'

The packets were carefully labelled: *lattuga*, *cipolle*, *cavolo nero*, *prezzemolo*, *oregano*, *carciofo*. Giorgio's translations carefully printed underneath.

'Thank you, both of you!' Edith smiled, although his kindness had brought fresh tears.

She bought one last postcard and begged an envelope from Giorgio. She put in the little packets and the recipe for *Torta ai Carciofi*. Ted would be delighted with the seeds and Louisa could make pie from the plants that he would grow.

40

Pensione Sterzberg, Vipiteno Sterzing

18th May 1946

```
Marende (local name), Brettljause
              (German)
A  snack  (often  served  in  the  afternoon),
more  Austrian  than  Italian,  consisting  of
speck,  sausages,  local  cheeses  and  pickled
cucumbers,  served  on  a  wooden  board  with
farmers' bread - Vorschlag - a round, flat
domed  loaf  with  a  fine  texture,  thick  crust
and  slightly  sour  taste,  and  wine.
```

Dori watched from her balcony in the upper chalet.

In the distance, the cracked town bell was striking four as she tracked Edith walking from the side of the lake up towards the Pensione Sterzberg. Behind her, a jetty jutted out into the water. Dori studied the small boats moored there then swept her glasses along the lake's edge. She caught stealthy movement under the overhanging branches. She looked away instinctively, as if to stare would draw attention. Edith was taking the flight of steps leading up to the first-storey entrance of the Pensione.

* * *

Boxes of geraniums edged each step, the scent strong after the heat of the day. Edith crushed a leaf between her fingers, breathing in the sharp, peppery smell. Double glass doors stood open, the panes pasted with peeling posters advertising ski competitions, local attractions. The pine of the doorframe oozed, adding a resinous, creosote tang to the geraniums' pungency. A stand of curled postcards stood at the end of the empty reception desk.

'Ah, Signora Graham.' Signor Rossi's small, sleek head appeared from behind the postcards. He smiled, a flashing of gold. 'I'm sorry if you are waiting.' He waved his small hands in apology. 'Come, Herr Kushner is this way.'

He led her past a small bar, into a cavernous dining room. The pine-panelled walls were heavily varnished and dotted with painted shields: the black, red and gold of the old Empire, dragons, gryphons, lions rampant, representing who-knew-which noble families, expressing a patriotism for a place with no independent existence. Between the heraldic shields the inevitable hunting trophies, stuffed heads and skulls.

They emerged through open doors into the sunlight, blinding after the darkness of the house. Edith put on her sunglasses. Kurt was sitting at a table, drinking wine. He was wearing a high-collared, green loden coat, stags'-horn buttons undone, a natural linen Trachten shirt open at the neck, cavalry-twill breeches tucked into high polished boots. He was dressed as though nothing had changed, as if he was still the prosperous *Graf*, owner of vast estates, out on a hunting trip. Signor Rossi added to the illusion; he could not have been more obsequious. Kurt hardly acknowledged his presence.

'Edith!' Kurt stood as she approached the table. 'Come. Sit. Wine?' He was pouring a glass, whether she wanted it or not. '*Lagrein*. It is local.' He replenished his own glass and held it to his nose. 'Not bad, actually. *Prosit!*'

Edith lifted the heavy roemer glass. The dark wine was warm and syrupy from standing in the sun. Edith caught a whiff of rancid *salumi*. On the table between them, Rossi's Marende:

drying bread, curling cheese and thin slivers of sweating speck. Cut too early and left too long.

'Marende. Will you join me?' Kurt opened a white napkin with a flourish. 'I'm famished.'

Edith shook her head.

'Such a treat after Germany. There is so much food here. I can't get over it.'

Kurt made a show of selecting slices from the plate but he merely nibbled at what he had taken, despite his protestations of hunger.

Edith put her goblet down on the table. 'What am I doing here, Kurt?'

'Cannot old friends—'

'We're not friends, are we? Not anymore.'

He pushed the food aside and her took her hand. The ring he wore glowed blood red in the sunlight. Edith tensed at his touch.

'Time is short and I want you to understand,' he leaned forward. Edith caught the wine on his breath, the slightly rank scent of food, mixed with the vetiver of his cologne. 'First, my work. Whatever you have been told will be lies and propaganda. What I did was important. We learned a great deal. Don't mix me up with the fanatics but since the matériel was available, it was sensible to use it.' He folded his arms. 'Those dead, or dying, or destined to die could still serve a useful purpose.'

Edith took him to mean the Jews, reduced further to 'matériel'. She kept her silence. She would let him talk. See how far he would go to justify what he had done, what others had done; how far he'd try to excuse the inexcusable. Let him condemn himself out of his own mouth.

'Of course, such processes are unpleasant to the medically untrained, just as an autopsy might be, or a dissection.' He mistook Edith's look of distaste and disgust for general squeamishness. 'I would cite the importance of the research carried out by one of my colleagues, Dr Mengele, on the pairs of twins that came into his care.' Edith stared at the table, unable to look at him. He was retreating into science now, seeking to hide his lack of humanity behind the specious screen of medical detachment. 'It is necessary work. Important work. We need to know what makes people different. If we can find the inborn causes that create that difference, then we can discover the very keys to life.'

Edith thought of Anna and Seraphina; the Polish girls Kay had cared for and all the myriad, nameless others. Her mouth felt numb and she had to swallow. She was glad she hadn't touched the food.

'*Is*,' Edith managed to say. 'Not *was*?'

'Oh, the work will go on! Perhaps not in the way it was performed, such . . . freedom – may not come again, but what we discovered is of great value. Not just what makes persons,' he paused to find an acceptable term, 'degenerate and how to mercifully end life but how better to treat disease and to know the effect certain . . . substances have on the human body.'

'The better to kill people, you mean?'

'The better to *treat* and to *save*! In order to do that it is important to know how the human body changes when put under,' he searched again for an acceptable word, 'stresses.'

'So, you don't think that anything you did was wrong?'

'On the contrary it was, as I said, necessary work.'

'Even,' Edith fought hard to keep her voice from shaking, 'even when it was your own son?'

'You have no children Edith. You cannot understand what it is like to know that your son will never grow up to be a man, have children of his own.'

'And Elisabeth?'

'Oh, she was in full agreement, whatever she might have said to gain your trust and sympathy. It was a mercy, believe me. Wolfgang could never have lived a normal life. We were there together to ease his passing.'

So she *had* been there. The story she'd told about her visit to the hospital had not been fabricated, rather it had been recreated, reimagined in reversed polarity where evil became good. To be able to do that travelled so far beyond natural human feeling that Edith profoundly wished Elisabeth *had* lied, had made the whole thing up. In the face of such enormity, there was nothing to say. All words fled away.

'It is progress.' Kurt's continuing justifications filled the silence. 'To eliminate weakness. To promote strength. For the greater good. Ultimately, it would have led to the improvement of the whole human race. One day the world will understand the wisdom of such actions.'

'I hear there's to be a special trial at Nuremberg,' Edith finally found her voice, clear and strong. 'Just for the doctors. I hope they hang you all.'

'A few will be sacrificed,' he shrugged. 'For show, that's all. There is much interest already expressed, in what we can offer to the world. The Russians, the Americans, the British all want what I can tell them. The Americans are, of course, by far the better option. I understand from Agent McHale that I have to thank you for making that possible.'

He smiled. An unrepentant Nazi with no regard for human life. He swept back his thick, blond hair with his right hand, a characteristic movement. He was the kind who had always relied on his good looks, his charm, even though his face had coarsened; his blue eyes had lost their brightness, they were dull and hard, like unpolished lapis. And that scarring on his face. Two deep, parallel grooves gouged deep into the flesh. Put there by a woman's long, sharp fingernails; a last, defiant wounding, to mar his beauty, mark him for life as a murdering swine.

'Now, there is no more to say.' He reached for a cigarette. 'I don't like goodbyes, you know that. I just wanted to thank you for bringing my Elisabeth to me, for all you have done for us.'

She stood up and walked to the edge of the balcony. She heard the scrape of von Stavenow's chair behind her, heard the spin of his lighter, smelt the tang of smoke from his cigarette. The setting sun was catching the snow on the distant mountains, turning them to rose gold and copper. Below the peaks, a jagged line of pines showed, Hooker's Green against the deepening blue reflected in the steel mirror of the lake. The view was famous, that's what people came here to see.

It was over. She'd done what Dori had asked of her. What happened now was up to others. She was free.

Germany seemed distant to her. Home, more so, yet she could see them clearly: mother sitting in her armchair, the French windows open to the smell of roses after rain; Louisa in her kitchen, pushing back her heavy hair with her wrist, waiting for the rattle of Ted's key. She would not be going back, not now, not for a long time, if ever, so this was a farewell of sorts.

Harry was waiting for her. She would be starting a new life. She saw him now, that slight quirking between his brows, there even when he smiled, as if happiness was an accidental surprise. I will be there soon, my love, to smooth that furrowing. I will be there quite soon now.

She looked up to a sharp, mewing cry. A hawk, or could it be an eagle? Turning and turning in a gyre, higher and higher . . . A sound pulled her back. It came with no warning; no sudden shudder of premonition. A sharp crack, as of a twig breaking. High above, the bird wheeled in its flight, heading towards the mountains with a flick of its powerful wings.

Dori watched from her balcony in the chalet above, the higher elevation and relative position afforded a good view of what might be happening in Pensione Sterzberg. She saw Edith come to the edge of the balcony, saw von Stavenow follow, saw him light a cigarette and felt a flutter of alarm. Edith was very exposed standing there. As, of course, she was . . . She swept her binoculars across the opposite shore and caught a sudden flash in the trees. Binoculars, maybe, or a rifle sight catching the sun . . .

She turned to run.

The first shot sent the birds on the lake rising up in a sudden cacophony. The noise grew, echoing away up the narrow valley. Rifle shots. One percussion followed by another and another. Dori felt heat on her cheek, a stinging, warm wetness, heard a whining yip close to her ear. She crouched down as she ran, using the flimsy balustrade as cover. When she looked back, she could no longer see Edith, just von Stavenow racing down towards the jetty. She leaned over the balcony and fired shot after shot. The Beretta was useless at any distance. Nevertheless, she carried on firing until the hammer clicked and clicked and clicked.

Below, an engine caught, stalled, caught again with a deep rumble and sustained roaring. Waves slopped and lapped on the shore. A small boat was pulling away from the jetty and heading for the middle of the lake, turning in a wide arc on its own creamy wake.

Dori ran down the steps from her balcony, crossed to Pensione Sterzberg and raced up the flight on the outside of the chalet. At the top, she grabbed onto the balustrade, sending a geranium flying, petals scattering. Edith lay where she had fallen. Blown back by the force of the shot, surprise still on her face. There could have been no moment of recognition, no time to react. Dori knelt and tried for a pulse, knowing there wouldn't be one, feeling for it anyway.

Nothing. She was dead.

Dori removed her glasses, one lens shattered, the other darkened with blood. Her eyes were half open, their greeny, grey blue already clouding to a sea-glass dullness. Dori gently closed them, brushing a scarlet petal from her cheek. She touched the waves of golden hair spreading out like a halo, merging with the crimson pool that darkened the wooden floor. There was nothing she could do.

She was aware of people around her. Rossi's hands paddling the air. Cries of 'Orrore! Orrore!'; maids, women from the kitchen crossing themselves, hands at their mouths, eyes wide, one girl crying, her face turned into the shoulder of an older woman while Dori crouched over Edith, glaring up at them, as protective as a mother cat.

'This is a mess.'

Drummond strode through the group. He walked round, head down, inspecting the body.

'Carabinieri?'

433

He turned sharply to the people standing on the fringes. Rossi shook his head.

'Well, don't. No police,' he said briskly and took a bundle of *lire* from his pocket. 'We'll take care of this.'

He knelt down next to the body and examined the hole drilled in the temple.

'Head shot. Neat job.' He looked at the Beretta still in Dori's hand.

'I shot after him but . . .' she shook her head quickly.

He looked down at the small gun. 'Next to useless.'

'A sniper in the trees over there,' she shook her head again and gave a shuddering sigh at the futile hopelessness of it. 'Somewhere. Other side of the lake.'

Drummond's narrowed eyes scanned the opposite shore. 'Long gone now. That's for certain.'

'Von Stavenow got away in a motorboat. It went up the lake.'

'We saw. We had to leave the inflatable in case he spotted us. Came in by foot. Another few minutes and we'd have had him.'

Dori bowed her head. 'I didn't anticipate—'

Drummond helped Dori to her feet, lifting her gently. She leant against the balcony, her knuckles whitening as she gripped the varnished rail, sticky from the day's heat.

She hardly registered Drummond's men, dressed in boots and khakis, moving onto the balcony to stand guard, arms folded.

'You,' Drummond turned to the hotel proprietor, indicating the hotel servants still collected together. 'Get this mob out of here, show's over, and brandy for the lady. *Pronto!*'

'I'm all right.'

She looked out at the water. It had regained its calm, mirror surface. The famous view that people came to see. She couldn't look at Edith, at the hole in her temple, small and round, bluish at the edges, leaking blood. Dori closed her eyes, tears threatening to spill.

Drummond covered her hand with his own. A surprisingly tender gesture.

'Don't break down,' he whispered. 'We don't have time for

it now.' He gently pushed back her hair, turning her face to expose the wound on her cheek. 'You're hurt.'

'It's nothing.' She put her hand to her cheek. It came away wet.

She looked at the blood on her hand and turned away. He was right, she mustn't break down now, but she was close to it, damn close to it, closer than she'd ever been. This was all her fault. Should *never* have involved Edith in this business. Should have taken better care of her. It should be me lying there. She braced her arms against the balustrade to stop herself shaking. It should be me.

'No point in taking on,' Drummond said quietly. 'Let's concentrate on the job in hand.' He looked out at the lake. 'Where do you think he went? To meet the lady wife?'

'I suppose so. Merano.'

'I want to see her room.' He glanced down at Edith. One of the women had covered her with a sheet. 'Come with me, Dori. These chaps will look after things here.'

Drummond looked round for the hotel owner who was hovering by the door, eyeing the body with nervous concern, weighing up the consequences and wondering how he was going to remove the stain from the wood of his balcony floor.

'Show me her room. Now.'

Rossi hesitated then shrugged.

Rossi led the way to the chalet above. Dori looked around the room. All Elisabeth's belongings had been removed. All that was left was the lingering musk of her Worth *Je Reviens* perfume. Drummond opened the wardrobe and the drawers. All empty. A leather suitcase stood by the door.

'This hers?'

The proprietor nodded quickly.

Drummond hauled the case onto the bed. It was locked. He took a knife from his pocket and selected a blade. The locks opened with a pop. He began to rummage through the contents.

'No, *Signore!*' The proprietor ran forward, hands fluttering in objection. 'Is not your property!'

435

Drummond hit him hard, an open palm across the side of the face, sending the gold-rimmed glasses flying.

'Where is she, you little shit?'

'I don't know!'

'I think you do. At least you know where she's going to. A lady doesn't leave all this behind. She'll want it sending on. To where?' He picked the little man up by his shirt and slammed him against the wall. 'Where did she say to send it to? Tell me.'

'I can't say, please, *Signore!*' The words came out in a squeak. His face was oiled with sudden sweat. Dori could smell his fear, sharp and rancid. 'I have to live here! If I tell you they kill me!'

Drummond hoisted him higher, twisting the collar into a ligature.

'If you don't tell me, I'll let my boys loose on you. They'll rip you apart and throw the bits into the lake for the fishes. How'd you like that, eh?' Drummond slammed him harder, the man's head hitting the wall with a dull cracking sound, dislodging flakes of plaster. 'Eh?'

The little man went limp. Drummond let him drop and stood over him, legs apart, waiting for him to recover.

'No, no, please!' He looked up, pleading as Drummond reached down to haul him up again. 'No more! I beg!' He hid his face with his hands and scuttled crablike, trying to escape.

'You better tell me, then.' Drummond squatted down to his level.

'She say send to Roma. Rome!'

'Where in Rome?'

Drummond reached for his throat. The man cowered back, trying to evade his grip.

'Vatican. German College.'

Drummond leaned back, as if he was satisfied, allowing the man to scurry out of his grasp. He picked up his glasses and was off down the stairs.

'Rome! Lying little toad.' Drummond stood up and wiped his hands on his trousers as though the contact had soiled them. 'The case says Genova. All carefully labelled. Good mind to let the boys loose on him. Throw what's left into the drink. But we'll let it ride for now. Let him tell them what a clever little chap he's been, throwing us off the scent.'

Adeline and Kay were sitting outside the hotel in that soft golden light peculiar to evenings in Italy. They were smiling, Giorgio about to take a snap of them with Adeline's camera. Dori walked towards them, eyes cast down to her long shadow. Time divided into before you knew and after. The moment before you could be laughing, talking, just as they were, and then came after when there could be no more jokes, no innocent, idle chatter. Nothing would ever, could ever be the same again.

'What's the matter? What's happened?' Kay rose from her seat. 'You're hurt. Has there been an accident?'

Adeline was on her feet, looking behind them. 'Where's Edith?'

Dori shook her head, the tears that she'd been holding back spilling. How many times had she seen smiles and laughter freeze like that? Seen eyes wide in a moment of foolish wonder then the crumpling contraction of grief and despair? Too many times – in London pubs and Paris cafés, forest clearings and lonely airfields. It should be me, she thought, not for the first time, not for the last time. It should be me.

'It all went tits up,' Drummond said. 'Edith was shot. Edith's dead.'

Only the slight shake in his voice softened the brutality of his words. He would not, could not show more emotion. Feelings always had to wait until 'afterwards'. It might not be for days, weeks, years but it always came.

'Where is she?' Adeline demanded, looking from Dori to Drummond, her voice rising, her face creased with shock and anquish. 'Where have they taken her? I must go to her. Stay with her. It's not right that she should be on her own.'

'To the local doctor's office, Signora,' Giorgio supplied gently. 'That is where they will take her. Angelina will go with you. Make sure everything is done.'

He went inside, turning round the 'open' sign on the door to 'closed'. Angelina came out with him and put an arm round Adeline.

'Where's Jack?' Drummond asked Kay as they watched the two women cross the square.

Kay turned, frowning at the harshness in his voice.

'He's just got back. He went straight up to the room.'

'Dori, come with me.'

Dori followed him into the hotel and up the stairs.

'Open up, Sergeant.' Drummond hammered on the locked door. 'Or I'll break it down.'

Jack let them in. Towel round his waist, torso still wet from the shower.

'So? What happened?' Drummond stood, arms folded, confronting him.

Jack sat down on the bed and covered his face with his hands. 'I went over the other side of the lake to cover the balcony, like you said. It was rough terrain, lots of trees and rocky outcrops. Took me a while to get into position. Turns out someone else had the same idea. Through the 'scope, I could see Dori watching from the balcony above. Edith and von Stavenow below, sitting, talking. Edith suddenly stands up, comes to the front of the balcony, von Stavenow following. Then bang, bang, bang. Shots from somewhere below me. Von Stavenow jumps over the balaustrade and down onto the grass. I got off a good few and I saw Dori fire. I think one of us winged him. Then he's in a boat and away. After it dies down, I wait. Chap comes out of a shallow cave just below me, cool as you like. So I bash his brains in, stuff him back and block the entrance.'

'Any idea who he was? Who he might have been working for?'

'No identification. No labels in his clothes. Eytie Carcano M19 rifle, French scope, Mauser ammo. Good kit. A professional. Knew what he was doing.' Jack picked up an empty brass cartridge case and gave it to Drummond. 'I saw Edith go down,' he said quietly. 'Is she . . .'

Dori inclined her head.

'Thought so. That's a shame.' He gave a heavy sigh and pinched the bridge of his nose. 'That's a damned shame. She was good, a good woman.' He bowed his head so they couldn't see his face. He coughed to clear his throat and wiped his eyes with his fingers. 'You should've given her close cover.' He looked up at Dori. 'Got him while you were at it.'

'I could say the same thing.'

'Stop this,' Drummond put up his hands. 'What's done is done. That's not going to help anyone.'

41

Verona

19th–20th May 1946

Risotto al Radicchio
A speciality of Verona. Risotto made with
radicchio and red wine. The recipe is cooked
in the same way as a classic risotto but
with red wine instead of the customary white.
The roughly torn leaves of a radicchio lettuce
(Rosso di Verona) are added after the rice,
then a glass of Valpolicella. The wine and
radicchio give this risotto its distinctive
reddish colour. Sounds unlikely but tastes
perfectly good.

Stella Snelling's Memorable
Mediterranean Meals

The von Stavenows would be heading south. Drummond had
bought tickets for the last train to Verona. They would stay
overnight there and go on to Genoa the next morning. Jack and
Drummond had tucked into the corners of the carriage by the
door. Kay was asleep, her head on Jack's shoulder. Dori stared
at the reflected scene, her thoughts too busy for sleep.

Adeline had gone with Edith's body.

'She's not going on her own,' she'd said. 'I'm going with her. Someone has to see her safe home.'

The plain, pine coffin looked small inside the ancient, spindly, glass-sided hearse drawn by plumed black horses. It was odd, incongruous, to see it pulling up at the station but how else do you transport a coffin? Drummond's men jumped down from where they had been riding with the driver and formed up with Jack and Drummond to become the bearers, arms linked to take the weight. They carried the coffin onto the northbound platform where the train waited in huffing clouds of steam. Passengers stood back, bare headed, as they passed, the women crossing themselves. It didn't matter that this was a stranger's coffin, after so much death, it was time to show respect again. The coffin was loaded into the goods van. Drummond's men and Adeline climbed in after it. The sliding door slammed shut, a whistle blew, the impatient hissing turned to slow chuffing, the wheels began to turn and she was gone.

They found a small hotel near to the station and booked in for one night. Two rooms. They were travelling as couples. It seemed less complicated.

'*Mangiare?*' Drummond demanded.

The man behind the desk looked at his watch and shrugged, palms out.

'*È tardi.*' It's late.

Drummond produced *lire* and began counting off notes.

'*Un momento, signore.*' It was late, he repeated, few places were open, but the *lire* did the trick. '*Venire, venire.*' He ushered them out and down a side alley to a small restaurant. '*Il mio fratello.*'

His brother opened the place for them. They ate by candlelight surrounded by chairs stacked on tables. Clattering came from the kitchen as his wife went about preparing something. They didn't know what and weren't given any choice. The brother brought plates, a basket of bread in the crook of his arm, an

441

earthenware jug of wine dangling from one hand and a fistful of glasses clutched in the other. He took spoons and forks from his top pocket and poured the wine. It was rough stuff, blackish red and harsh tasting, but it brought them back to some semblance of life.

'What now?' Jack took a piece of bread and tore it into pieces, dunking it in his wine. He'd hardly spoken.

'You go to Rome. See if you can pick up any sign of them there. We'll go to Genoa.' Drummond took a hunk of bread. 'I'll get in touch with our chap in the Consulate. Get him to check sailings and passenger lists. See who's been visiting the Argentinians, see if our friends at the Red Cross have been issuing any interesting passports to poor, benighted, stateless Germans. This bread's as dry as a nun's knickers.' He threw down the piece he'd been chewing. 'I hope the rest of the food's better than this.'

The red risotto didn't look too promising, but it tasted fine.

'*Come si chiama questo piatto?*' Dori asked.

'*Risotto al Radicchio,*' the patron said with some pride. '*Specialità di Verona.*'

'*Ricetta?*'

He smiled, softening at her interest. '*Sì, signora.*'

'Recipe?' Drummond looked sceptical. 'I didn't even know you could cook.'

Dori took out a notebook. 'Maybe I've changed. I'm thinking of starting a new career as a cookery writer.'

Drummond laughed. He clearly didn't believe her but Dori was quite serious. The idea had just come to her and she suddenly knew that it was the right thing to do. She would even write under Edith's *nom de plume*: Stella Snelling.

The patron brought more wine and his wife from the kitchen. She dictated the recipe in Italian. This much and that much, pinches and handfuls, mezzo litres and quartos. By the time Dori had written it down, the wine had been replaced by rounds of grappa. Drummond dished out a fan of notes and they went back to the hotel.

Drummond looked round their room.

'I was going to sleep in the chair, but—'

'There isn't one.' Dori felt a twitch of a smile, the first in a long time.

'There's always the bath.'

Dori kissed him hard. His hand gripped her through her slip, the other going to her breast. There was nothing subtle about his lovemaking. He was quick and brutal, but that's what she wanted. To blot out the events of that day, to burn it all away, to make her feel alive again. They broke apart, sweating, both partly dressed.

'Here.' He retrieved his trousers from the floor and reached into the pocket. 'I saved this for you. It's yours, isn't it?'

He held out the icon that Edith had been wearing.

'She wanted to give it back.' The icon swung between them, the silver chain stained, the face darkened still further. 'I thought she might have need of it. In the church. I—' her voice cracked, stopped by a surge of memory: the smell of incense and ancient stone, that light floral perfume that Edith wore, the warmth of her arm as they knelt together. And then, and then a scattering of scarlet across dark crimson, echoing cries of '*Orrore! Orrore!*'. In dreams, at random moments she would be taken back to that exact time, that precise place, she would see both scenes, over and over, added to all the others on the spooling film reel of her guilt. 'I – I put her in harm's way.'

'We all did. She didn't deserve what happened, that's for sure.' He brushed the heavy dark hair from her neck and fixed the chain with a surprisingly delicate touch. 'I remember talking to her about it on the train. We all carry something. Stupid superstition, I suppose.'

'What do you carry?'

He looked suddenly shy and Dori wondered if she'd over-stepped some invisible line as if showing her might take away the power.

'No harm you seeing.' He picked up his shirt and took some-thing from the pocket. 'Found it in the desert.' He dropped it into her palm. A small wheel, about the size of a shilling, made from tightly coiled gold wire and surprisingly heavy in her hand. 'Roman, sacred to Mithras, soldiers' god, or so some clever sod told me.' He leaned back, his compact muscular torso braced against the headboard. 'So, at who's door? The Nazi *Bruderschaft*?'

Dori lit two cigarettes, passed one to Drummond. 'That's what they'll want us to think.'

'Who then? Leo? McHale?'

Dori shrugged, 'Could be either. Neither. Both. Waiting to pull the double-cross.'

'Why Edith?'

'Isn't it obvious? Shooting her allows the von Stavenows to escape. He shot at me, too. Get rid of both of us, no one the wiser and on their merry way.'

'We'll get them,' Drummond said, his grey-green eyes as hard as serpentine. 'We owe it to Edith.' He stubbed out his cigarette. 'Early start. Get some kip.'

'Why are you sending Jack to Rome?' Dori frowned, a new thought dawning. 'Are you not sure about him?'

'Can't be certain of anybody in this business.' He rubbed at his jaw. 'He was Special Branch before the war, did jobs for Leo. Might be working both sides of the street. Better to be safe than sorry.' He reached to turn off the light. 'Anyway, the von Stavenows might still turn up and the poor sod deserves a bit of a honeymoon.'

42

Grand Hotel Savoia, Genoa

21st May 1946

Ristorante Al Porto Antico
Roasted Branzino

Bass, spitting on a charcoal grill, the coals
encouraged to a brighter fierceness by the
use of an ancient electric fan. The fish
served with the silver skin blackened and
splitting to reveal white flesh, perfectly
tender, scented by dill. Served with golden,
crusted potatoes scooped from a wide, blackened iron tray and a scattering of tiny
Taggiasca olives of Liguria, reddish in colour
and deliciously sweet, scented with thyme,
bay and rosemary. The best, the only way to
cook this magnificent fish.

Accompanied by a Ligurian Rossese di
Dolceacqua. Bright to the eye, with the fresh
tang of herbs and blackcurrant. An intensely
aromatic wine. The slightly resinous bouquet
whispers of its Greek origins.

In Genoa, they took a taxi from the station to the Grand Hotel Savoia overlooking the port. Drummond booked them in at the desk.

'They aren't here yet,' he said. 'Just checked the register.'

'We're staying at the same place?'

'Why not?' He looked round at the opulent interior, all marble floors and red and gold furnishing. 'Didn't know for sure that they'll tip up here but this is where they all stay. The ones with money, anyway. With a few bob stashed away. Or . . .'

'If they are being sponsored?'

'*Essatamente.*'

Double doors led from their room out onto a balcony overlooking the harbour. Drummond had slid a few extra notes over the counter to obtain that view. One good thing about the Italians, they were eminently bribeable.

'I've got a few people to see. Why don't you go shopping?' Drummond peeled off more *lire*. 'Buy something smart for this evening. I thought we'd dine at the hotel.'

Dori took him at his word. There was plenty of choice on the Via XX Settembre and the streets around. She managed to find a Madeleine Vionnet evening gown in black silk, a wrap and a bag to go with it, even a pair of heels. *Le signore tedesche, German ladies*, the woman in the shop told her, selling everything to raise the fare.

Back at the hotel, she had a bath and washed her hair. She looked at her face in the mirror, removing the sticking plaster Kay had applied. The wound was healing well. If she arranged her hair just so, it hardly showed.

After her bath, she lay down on the bed, meaning merely to rest through the heat of midday. When she woke, it was late afternoon. Drummond was leaning on the balcony, studying the harbour through binoculars.

'Consular Offices. We've been warned off. MI6 and all that,' he said with his back to her, his voice bowstring taut, vibrating with the anger he was suppressing. 'Don't upset the Cousins. The von Stavenows are off limits. Looked after every step of the way. There's a big liner down there. The *Don Giovanni*, waiting to load up with Nazis, due to sail to Argentina tomorrow. I'm going to check the passenger lists in the morning, but it's my bet they'll be on it.'

'They're here?'

He turned round, square hands gripping the binoculars so hard, Dori thought he might tear them apart.

'Arrived this afternoon. My guess is he'll be outside the Consulate getting visas from the Argies. The street is full of tall blond men in Homburgs standing in a queue.'

'Is there nothing we can do?'

'Take a pop at him, you mean?' He gave a ragged, humourless laugh. 'I wish I could. "Hands off, Bulldog," that's what I've been told. Our chaps have done a deal with the Yanks. Leo waving his paws in the air hoping for scraps.' He put down the binoculars and came towards her. 'Put your glad rags on. We'll start with cocktails in the bar. Don't want them feeling they're home and dry.' He looked at his watch. 'We've got a bit of time, though.' He kissed her neck. 'You smell very good. I wonder what we can find to do between now and cocktail hour?'

The bar was full of people in evening dress. Dori's new gown could have been made for her and the dress suit Drummond had cadged off someone at the Consulate fitted him perfectly. Dori took his arm. They made a handsome couple.

A man in a white tie and a tailcoat was playing tinkling jazz on a grand piano. The tables were occupied by couples, hardly speaking. There was an air of waiting, of quiet tension about the room.

'Teutonic-looking lot aren't they?' Drummond remarked. 'You could add another chapter: The Rats of Hamelin Lose their Master and Make a Run for It. What are you drinking?'

'A Negroni, since we're here.'

'Whisky for me,' he said to the barman. 'And whatever that

is for the lady.' He turned around, drink in hand. 'Look at them. Dressed up to the nines. Practically wearing their iron crosses. Think they're safe now. Almost home and dry. No more yes, sir, no, sir, three bags full, sir. Subservience doesn't sit well with the Hun.' He turned away and studied the room in the mirror behind the bar. 'Should be in gaol, the lot of them.' His gaze ranged over the rest of the tables. 'The Italians are as bad. Bunch of Fascists. And the Argentinians for that matter.' He finished his drink and ordered another. 'Makes me sick. What a crew. Here they come. Trunks have arrived, I see.'

Kurt and Elisabeth. He looked tall and slender, graceful in black evening dress. Dori was gratified to see one arm strapped and under his jacket. One bullet must have found a home. She was wearing a finely pleated, pale-cream Delphos dress. Pre-war Fortuny. The silk shimmered as she walked, the simple, graceful lines following the contours of her figure. Murano glass beads glinting down the sides of the gown. A diamond collar glittered above the high neckline, matching earrings caught the light. They made their way between the tables, arm in arm, looking enough like film stars to turn every eye in the room, smiling from side to side, accepting the general gaze as if it was their due.

'What are we going to do?' Dori asked, watching them to their table by one of the long windows overlooking the harbour.

'Nothing,' Drummond replied without taking his eyes off them. 'Can't do anything. Of special interest. Under the protection of our friend Tom McHale, not to mention Leo and everybody else up to and including the Pope himself, I shouldn't wonder, as part of the new crusade to save the world from the Communists. So, it's nothing doing, Bulldog. Let them scamper away into the Pampas with the rest of the rats.'

He leaned back against the bar staring intently, willing them to look back. When they did at last, he gave them a wide grin, mirthless and ghastly, and raised his glass in mock salute. The von Stavenows' gaze arrested for a moment then moved on with no other visible sign of recognition.

'Fuck off to you, too.' Drummond drained his glass. 'Come on, let's go.' He sniffed. 'It's getting too ripe for me in here. Take you to a little place I know. Food's really good. Authentic.' He laughed, again there was no humour in it. 'You can add to your collection with a genuine Genoese recipe.'

Dori wanted to leave just as much as he did. She and Drummond were on the side of the victors but it certainly didn't feel like it. It felt the opposite, as though victory had gone to Kurt and Elisabeth. She watched the two of them, leaning towards each other, close, intimate, hands clasped across the stiff, white linen. They appeared to be laughing. Elisabeth leaned towards him, saying something. A waiter rushed over to ease back her chair as she stood.

'I'll be with you in a minute.' Dori checked her bag. 'I'll meet you outside.'

The ladies' powder room was all cream marble, gold taps and green onyx basins, silk-backed Venetian chairs in front of banks of mirrors. Dori dropped *lire* into the bowl on the attendant's table and gestured with her head towards the door. The crone scooped up the notes and was gone.

Dori locked the cubicle and waited. Whatever orders Drummond had received didn't extend to her. Or to Elisabeth von Stavenow. The outer door opened and closed again. A toilet flushed, water ran. Dori counted to twenty, then twenty again, and eased back the catch.

In the mirror, she could see into the powder room proper. A woman was sitting at one of the chairs, makeup placed in front of her, lipstick, compact, mascara, like an actress getting ready for a show. She was intent on her own reflection, brushing her hair with a Mason-Pearson brush.

'I think that belongs to Edith,' Dori said from the door.

The brush stopped in mid stroke and then continued, taking the hair back from the forehead and to the side, following the deep, shining waving line.

'She won't be needing it, will she? Not any more.' Elisabeth continued to brush out her hair, bringing up the shine. Satisfied at last, she shook her head, her hair falling into perfect waves and folds of bronze and gold. 'What are you doing here, Dori?' She snapped open her compact. 'It's too late to stop us. You missed your chance.'

'Edith. You used her.'

'Didn't you?' Elisabeth began to apply mascara with brisk upward strokes. 'The British Secret Service, the Americans. You all used her. Naïve, an innocent. The perfect vehicle. We both used her. Let's not be coy about it. She was surplus to requirements.' Elisabeth shut the mascara box and uncapped her lipstick. 'Not a good thing to be.'

The lipstick was carmine red in a Marcel Rochas silver tube. Dori had given one just like it to Edith. She watched Elisabeth applying the colour, working her lips together. What kind of woman would steal another woman's lipstick? Such pettiness was deeply revealing. In that moment, Dori knew. Elisabeth had ordered the kill.

'That's Edith's, too.'

'Not her colour,' Elisabeth said as she examined her reflection in the mirror. 'It was wasted on her.' She turned her head this way and that looking for flaws. Satisfied, she collected her makeup and put it away in her handbag. 'Now, I must go.'

'I don't think so.'

Dori held her hand down by her side. The Beretta was small, snug in the palm. She raised it slowly. Elisabeth watched her in the mirror. They both knew that she wouldn't miss, couldn't miss at this distance.

'*Maman je dois faire pipi!*'

A shrill voice, a child's voice. The door banged open. Dori lowered the gun as a little girl ran into the room. The child stopped in mid pace to stare at the two women with her big dark eyes.

'*Je suis désolé*,' her mother came in after her. '*Excusez-nous.*'

'*Pas du tout. Nous avons terminé. Pas devant les enfants.*' Elisabeth whispered to Dori, 'That wouldn't be nice.' She smiled,

450

touching her lips to Dori's injured cheek. '*Lebe wohl, meine Liebe. Lebe wohl.*'

With that she was gone. The kiss on Dori's cheek felt like a fresh wounding. The red came away as she rubbed, staining her fingers like blood.

Drummond took her to a little *osteria* in the old port close to the water. It was dark inside, cave like, lit by candles guttering in wax-encrusted bottles set on rough wooden tables. The menu was chalked on the wall in Ligurian dialect. It didn't really matter. They only served fish. Branzino.

'Rossese di Dolceacqua, nothing very special,' Drummond poured the wine. 'Doesn't have to be if all you want to do is get drunk. They've won, Dori. We've lost. Here's to 'em.' He raised his glass. 'Bottoms up. Fuck 'em, I say. I hope the ship hits a mine in the mid-Atlantic. One of theirs, preferably.' He grinned. 'Wouldn't that be ironic?' He sat back. 'Oh, well, can't win 'em all.' He lapsed into silence for a while and sat brooding, arms folded. 'I do hate to lose, though,' he said finally, his voice low, almost distant. All his anger and frustration distilled into absolute resolution. 'I do so hate to lose.'

'I do, too.' Dori joined in his mood. 'How could I have let her get away from me?'

'Life goes on, eh?' He finished his wine and poured them both another.

'Not for Edith.' Dori bit her lip hard and looked away, almost overwhelmed by a sudden surge of sorrow and despair.

'I say, don't take on, old girl.' Drummond took her hands in his. 'It's like in the war. Chap'd go down, wouldn't come back, quite often several chaps, but it was bad form to sit about moping. Does no one any good. Get up and get on. Which is exactly what we are going to do, so cheer up,' he chucked her under the chin. 'Let's see a smile. That's better.' He gave her an answering grin. 'We'll have a bloody good dinner. Food's excellent here, better than that ghastly hotel. Nothing worse than Italian bloody *haute cuisine*. Then we'll work out what we are going to do.' His smile disappeared. 'Because this is not over.'

The decks of the liner were crowded with people, waving and smiling down at the crowds on shore. It could have been a Pathé Newsreel, except there were no streamers and the flags strung from the funnels were faded and ragged. Corrosion stained the grey paint, seamed the water line red and wept down from the hawsehole that held the anchor chain. The ship had seen better days.

'Bit of a rust bucket,' Drummond was leaning over the balcony balustrade. 'Let's hope it doesn't make it.' He trained binoculars on the passengers leaning on the rails. 'No wonder they're all smiling. Getting clean away. Won't be smiling soon.' He laughed. 'That thing is a tub, she'll roll all over the place.'

'Can you see Kurt and Elisabeth?'

He shifted the binoculars. 'Just leaving the hotel. Got them right in my sights, I could get both of them if I had Jack's Lee Enfield. He's in a light suit, pale-grey fedora; she's in a polka-dot dress, black hat, red feather. That should make it easier. Ready?' Dori nodded. 'Let's go.'

They left the hotel. She indicated for Drummond to go left while she stayed behind and on the right. They tracked the von Stavenows through the streets leading down to the Porto where the ship was waiting. It was easy to keep them in sight, the grey fedora, the bobbing feather, difficult to get close enough to kill.

At the dockside, there was a melee of leave takers and those boarding. A hold-up had developed, the crowd bunching. A man in uniform stood at the bottom of the companionway checking documents and tickets. Dori could sense the tension building around her, shouts of *Was ist los!?* There was a surge in the crowd as impatience turned to a panicking realization that their chance of escape might be snatched away at the last moment.

Drummond gave her the nod. The von Stavenows were almost at the companionway, near the centre of the surging, spreading queue. They would be distracted, occupied by their anxiety to get on board. Dori insinuated herself between the sweating, jostling people, squeezing through any small gap, working her way nearer while Drummond did the same from the opposite side. The silencer made the gun heavy, unwieldy, not ideal at such close quarters but necessary if they hoped to get away. Dori measured off the space between them and the targets in yards, feet, finally inches. She would take her; Drummond would take him.

Dori was so close now that she could smell her sweat masked by talcum and sweetish, musky perfume; see the damp circles under her arms, blue polka dots rendered slightly transparent by the dampness between her shoulder blades. Just one more ebb of the crowd and she would be close enough to jam the barrel into the fifth intercostal space between her ribs, angled up to make absolutely sure that the bullet ripped through her heart.

'Excuse us ma'am. We can't allow that.'

Two men moved in on her. The gun was wrenched from her. Strong hands clamped her arms to her sides. She saw Drummond struggling with a similar pair. He managed to butt one of them with a quick jerk of the head. The man recoiled, blood blooming from his smashed nose, but he didn't let go. The other man administered a sharp rap on the back of his head. His captors braced themselves to take his weight.

If there had been a disturbance in the crowd behind them, the von Stavenows didn't notice. The delay had been cleared away. They were free to go on board. As they climbed up the swaying metal gangway they were laughing and smiling like the rest of the passengers, not quite believing their luck. They paused at the top, turning to wave as if they were royalty.

The gangplank was brought in. The hawsers were cast off. The anchor rattled up. The engines started, the propellers churning the water, horns sounded and the ship steamed out into the bay accompanied by the whistles and hoots of smaller vessels. The von Stavenows joined others at the rail, staring back at the receding port, the last of Europe, before turning to go down to their cabins to begin their new lives.

'Aren't you going to wave them goodbye?' McHale stood by

Dori's side, with a firm grip on her arm. He gazed out at the receding liner.

'What have you done to Drummond?'

'Oh, he's OK. Got a hard head. My guys have taken him back to your hotel. There will be no more of this.' McHale looked at her, his pale-blue eyes almost colourless. 'You tell him that from me.'

The Grand Hotel Mirabeau, Lausanne

11th November 1989

```
Tisane Verveine
```
Common Verbena made into a tea. Verveine is
also known as Herb of Grace, Herb of the
Cross, Enchanter's Plant. In French, Herbe
aux Enchantements, Herbe du Foie, Herbe
Sacrée, Herbe aux Sorciers.

That was more than forty years ago. Dori added a creased, black-and-white photograph of Drummond to those ranged in front of her. After McHale's intervention, they'd left Genoa, roaring off in a 'borrowed' Alfa Romeo, seeing where the road took them, north to Milan and then into Switzerland. Drummond still furious, driving through the Alps with thrilling recklessness. Only his skill as a driver saved them from crashing over a parapet and launching into nothingness. He'd pulled up outside this very hotel just as the sun was setting over the lake. They'd stayed for a week, swimming, hiking, sailing on the lake. Champagne in their room, dinner in the restaurant, more champagne afterwards and making love long into the night. Then Drummond had gone north and out of her story. She'd gone south. To Milan, then to Rome.

She'd found Jack there, watching the German College like a faithful hound while Kay absorbed the riches of the Eternal City. He was still suffering, harrowed by guilt that he'd failed to save Edith. Whatever Drummond's doubts, Dori believed him. She'd rarely seen a man so cast down. The birds had flown, she'd told him. He might as well return to Germany. After his tour of duty, he'd gone back to the Police. Special Branch. Much later, he would have a part to play in Leo's eventual demise, doing the honours for MI5.

From Rome she'd intended to go straight to Brindisi, then to Greece and on to Palestine but she'd found herself, heart sick and exhausted, in a tiny place on the coast, cobalt sea beyond blinding-white salt pans, a dusty road shaded by umbrella pines the only way in or out. She'd needed time to think and time to heal. That's where she'd hit on the idea that a new career as a cookery writer would be the perfect cover for a life in espionage. So it proved to be, but that was a story for another day.

Impossible to follow the von Stavenows; they had slipped away, taken out of view on Time's tide. Now they had fetched up again, as a bottle tossed into the ocean in one place might wash onto some far-distant shore.

Outside, the sun was rising, spilling gold and silver onto the lake. Time to rest. She'd been up all night. She'd take a nap before her appointment. It was not yet over and she would need to be alert, have her wits about her. She put the *Do Not Disturb* sign on the door and set her travel alarm for 9.30. That would give her time to bathe, order some coffee and get everything ready.

A white-coated waiter pushed the trolley into the room. Coffee in a silver pot. Two cups, a jug of hot milk, one of cream, a sugar bowl with a silver spoon. A squat kettle on a little burner to keep the water hot and a dish of little bags containing different teas and herbal preparations.

'Shall I pour, *madame*?'

'No thank you. I'll wait for my visitor.'

'Very well, *madame*.'

He closed the door quietly. She worked quickly. There were things to do before the appointed time.

The rap on the door was assertive, almost peremptory. She resisted the temptation to look through the peephole. She had a feeling that there would be an eye on the other side.

The woman came into the room, still that long, slow stride, while Dori quietly turned the lock on the door. As svelte and assured as ever, her grey dress and jacket expensive, immaculately tailored to accentuate her carefully preserved slenderness. Her shoulder-length hair held the same deep wave. The gold was not the shade that Dori remembered but the tinting was convincing.

'You're looking very well, Elisabeth.'

Elisabeth stopped and turned, surprised at the use of her Christian name.

'I'm sorry,' she came closer, looking into Dori's face.

'You don't recognize me.' Dori gave a tired smile. 'Dorothy Stansfield. You knew me as Dori. Don't you remember?'

'I—' she faltered, a temporary loss of assurance in a woman who was rarely nonplussed. 'Of course, but it has been many years now.'

'Indeed. And those years have been kinder to you than they have to me.' Dori closed her eyes with a sigh and held her hands tightly clasped. 'I've come to avail myself of your er, special services,' she spoke euphemistically, in the terms the clinic used. 'I'm tired, Elisabeth. Tired of living. I want to end it. That's what you do isn't it? End it for people.'

'The clinical side is not my area, of course, but . . . Yes. That is a service we provide. If you are sure.'

'Oh, I'm certain.'

'Is there anyone,' Elisabeth looked round as if that person might be hiding, 'anyone with you?'

'No, I'm alone. I never married again. Have no close relatives.'

'We have to be certain . . .' She walked to the window, as if wanting to change the subject. 'This is a nice room. Lovely view.'

457

'Indeed. A nice place of exit.'

'Oh, we don't do it here.' Elisabeth looked shocked. 'The hotel would not like it.'

'Death bad for business?'

'Something like that, yes,' Elisabeth agreed, solemnly. She never did have much of a sense of humour. 'Many of our clients use this hotel before . . .'

Dori nodded. 'Quite so.'

'I have attendants waiting downstairs,' Elisabeth went on. 'You will be taken to our special facility. It is very pleasant there. Very,' Elisabeth searched for the right word, 'peaceful.'

Dori did her best to look comforted.

Elisabeth moved to the desk. She examined the photographs laid out there, touching them cautiously then withdrawing her fingertips, as if the likenesses might be coated with a toxic substance.

'What is this?' Again, she seemed disconcerted, nervous even.

'A way of saying goodbye, I suppose.' Dori was quick to reassure. 'Many of your clients must have something similar, a photo album to sift through the memories. Don't they say that, at the end, life flashes before you in moments.' Dori gave a dry laugh. 'In my case it took most of the night. Won't you sit down, Elisabeth? Join me in a cup of coffee?'

'Thank you, no,' Elisabeth gave a little shudder. 'I never touch caffeine. So bad for the skin.'

'A tisane, then,' Dori indicated the tray. 'The Swiss do those things so well.'

'Nothing, really.'

'I'd be so pleased if you would join me.' Dori reached for the kettle. The tremor in her hand wouldn't be lost on Elisabeth.

'Let me,' she said, half rising from her seat.

'No, I can manage. This is the very last time I'll do anything quite as normal as take tea with somebody.'

'Very well. A tisane, thank you.'

'Verveine, menthe or camomile?' Dori read the labels.

'Verveine will do very well.'

Dori dropped the little bag into a cup and poured on the water.

'It's kept hot by a little burner. Isn't that clever?'

Elisabeth nodded, humouring her. She sipped the hot liquid, leaving a lipstick imprint on the cup. 'You are not here by accident, are you? How did you find us?'

'It was Adeline. She found you. Do you remember Adeline? The American journalist? We agreed. When it came to a certain time . . .' Dori paused. 'She was alone, like me, you see. She did some research and discovered your Institute. There aren't many places in the world that offer your kind of service. We didn't realize it was you and Kurt, not at first,' Dori lied. It was one of the things she'd always done well. 'A happy coincidence, you might say.' Dori took a sip from her own cup. 'I rather like these herbal beverages. Refreshing and good for one, so they say.'

'Yes,' Elisabeth inclined her head. 'Although this is rather bitter.'

'Why don't I add a little sugar?' Dori sifted a spoonful from the sugar bowl into the cup. 'They do say the bitter ones do you the most good. Verveine is cleansing. And healing, as I recall. The Ancient Egyptians called it "the tears of Isis", did you know that?'

'No I didn't.' Elisabeth continued to sip, frowning a little, pursing her lips as though the sifting of crystals had done little to take away the bitterness.

'Tell me, Elisabeth, do you think of those days at all?'

'No. It was a long time ago. The water has flowed under many bridges since then.'

'I do. I can see you now standing with Kurt at the rail of the *Don Giovanni* steaming off to South America. Argentina, wasn't it?'

Elisabeth inclined her head. 'We were only there for a short while. We spent more time in the US. Kurt worked at a research facility in Maryland. It was a good place for the horses. We re-established the stud, preserved the breed. After that, we moved here, to Switzerland. Kurt set up his own clinic. It has been most successful. I will carry on the work now he's dead. Skiing accident.'

Elisabeth answered the question Dori hadn't asked. From the Euthanasia Programme to this. Finding ways to kill people. Their progression had been seamless.

'Anyway, it was Adeline who tracked you down.'

'You have some kind of pact?'

Dori smiled. 'Something like that.'

'That is very common.' Elisabeth nodded her understanding. 'But she is not here?'

'Alas, no. She didn't make it. Heart failure.'

'So it's just you.'

'Yes, just me.'

'Diseases of the nervous system can be most distressing.' Elisabeth's eyes rested on Dori's hands. 'We have many clients who have suffered so.'

'Oh, I'm sure.'

Dori had had enough of the hypocrisy, the false sympathy, the patronizing pity, the secret superiority that the living and healthy felt for the dying stranger.

It was time to bring the performance to a close.

'Except there's nothing wrong with me.' Dori held her hand out in front of her. 'Steady as a rock.'

'I'm sorry,' Elisabeth frowned. 'I don't understand . . .'

'You will soon enough.' Dori sat back.

'If you are not here for that . . .' Elisabeth's blue eyes showed the slightest tremor of alarm which flared to panic as she made to rise and fell back in her chair. She looked back into Dori's implacable stare, truth dawning.

'What is happening . . . ' Her voice had dropped to a rasping whisper, the words slowed, like a record played at the wrong speed.

The cup dangled from Elisabeth's fingers, its remaining liquid spilling.

Dori leapt forward, deftly catching it and returning it to the tray. She smiled. 'There's enough diamorphine in that to fell half the hotel.'

Dori sat back to watch, hands linked loosely in her lap. Elisabeth's eyes remained open, fixed, the pupils contracted to pinheads. Dori had dealt death many times but she'd rarely seen someone actually die slowly. She was going to enjoy this. It had been a long time coming.

'You must have thought you'd got away with it, you and Kurt.'

Elisabeth uttered a sound, guttural, animal. All speech lost now. A plea for mercy? A bit late for that. A cry for help? No one to hear.

'What does it feel like?' Dori asked. 'To die the kind of a death you've dealt to countless others, you and Kurt, including your own son.' She paused to see if her words were registering. A slight tremor of the head. She could hear. 'Edith. Do you remember Edith? That story you told her about your son, Wolfgang, was that his name? She *believed* you. What decent human being wouldn't? And she was decent, as decent as they come. Edith's been dead these forty-odd years. You robbed her of her life, too. Did you think you'd got away with it as you steamed off on that liner? No punishment? No retribution? Did you think you'd won? I'm here to tell you different.' Dori stood up, stepped across the space between them and planted a kiss on Elisabeth's forehead. '*Lebe wohl, meine Liebe. Lebe wohl.*'

There would be no more talking. Dori watched Elisabeth slump sideways, her mouth sagging open, eyes filming to a grey dullness. She waited until there was no longer any movement then tested for a pulse. With a brush of her fingers, she closed the eyes. It was done.

Now there were things to do and she didn't have much time. She tidied up the cup, the tray, the room, wiping away her finger-prints as she went.

In the bathroom, she put in tinted contact lenses and did her makeup, swiping on blusher for more colour, patting on a modicum of powder. She'd always had good skin. She pencilled in her brows, applied a little liner and shadow, brushed on mascara. It was amazing how the years dropped away with a little definition about the eyes. She uncapped her lipstick. Yves

461

St Laurent *Rouge Pur*. Red lipstick could be a disaster on an older woman but it always added a hint of glamour. She brushed her hair, sprayed it a flattering platinum and wound it into a chignon. Change the hair, change the face. Dori had always been a mistress of disguise. She stripped to her petticoat, went to the wardrobe and slipped into the black Chanel suit, a diamond brooch at the collar. She eased on a pair of mid-heel, black patent court shoes and viewed herself in the mirror. Not bad. That extra bit of height made her feel much more herself. She packed everything into her Louis Vuitton travel bag, put on a pair of sunglasses of the kind favoured by Jackie Onassis, picked up her Chanel handbag and left without a backward glance.

She summoned the lift and went down to the foyer. No one noticed her passing, least of all the two young men in white jackets waiting with a wheelchair.

There were always taxis waiting outside. She took the first in line.

'Cointrin Airport, please.'

In the taxi, she sorted through a selection of passports. After all these years, she'd be travelling under her real name: Dorota Zophia Kováč. The others went into the first bin she encountered. There was no reason to ever change her name again. At the Swiss Air counter, she bought a first-class ticket to Tel Aviv. Harry would want to know. The last debt had been paid.

Acknowledgements

My aunt, my mother, my grandmother and their friends whose handwritten recipes I found slotted between the pages of the cookery book that provided the inspiration and impetus to write this book.

Brenda Hillier and Maria Pia who gave me their own and their family recipes for me to use.

Meike Blatnik for introducing me to Dirk and Lotte Foks who acted as my guides in Lübeck.

Writer friends: Linda Newbery, Adèle Geras, Yvonne Coppard, Julia Jarman, Cindy Jeffries and Susan Price for their help and support; Clare Mulley for advice about the SOE; Leslie Wilson for her help with German and Helena Pielichaty for sharing her own family's recipes with me.

The Polish community in Leamington, old and new, for their help with food, recipes and the Polish language.

The Imperial War Museum, the British Library, Warwick University Library as well as my local libraries in Warwickshire and Coventry. Without these libraries, research would be impossible.

The Leamington History Group for sharing Luftwaffe maps of Leamington Spa.

Sylvia Levy-Nichols for providing a magical place to write.

My old agent, Rosemary Sandberg, who was there for me when I needed her. My previous agent, Rachel Calder, for her input into the developing manuscript; my current agent, Stephanie Thwaites at Curtis Brown, who saw it through.

My editor Kimberley Young, Martha Ashby, Laura Gerrard and everyone at HarperCollins, and Rachel Kahan at William Morrow, for their meticulous care and dedication.

My cousins, Ann Bannister and Stephen Price, for sharing family memories and family history.

Catrin for accompanying me on the spy walks and other London research trips; for being there at the beginning and helping me to see it through to the end.

Terry – for everything.

Q&A with Celia Rees

Miss Graham's War was inspired in part by an extraordinary family history. Can you tell us a little bit about it?

The book began with a cookery book of the kind given away with gas cookers: *The Radiation Cookery Book*. The cover boards were stained and faded, the back had gone and it was held together with parcel tape. I found it among my mother's effects and I'd never seen it before. The pages were interleaved with clippings from old newspapers, magazines – and handwritten recipes. I recognised my mother's writing, and my aunt's and what I took to be my grandmother's. I guessed that it had been my grandmother's book, passed onto my aunt and then to mother who had kept it after her sister's death. To my knowledge, there were no existing letters between these women, so these recipes were the only connection. The old cookery book suddenly seemed very precious. I knew that there was something I wanted to write about here but had no idea what it could be. Years later, I was in the Imperial War Museum in London with my daughter. We were in the gallery devoted to espionage. One of the wall panels said that after the Second World War, the British Zone in Germany had been a hotbed of spying. My aunt had been there then, working as an Education Officer. One of us said, 'Perhaps Aunty Nancy was a spy. . .'. We both laughed. My Head Mistress maiden aunt a spy? The idea was absurd. But maybe not. . . I suddenly saw how I could use *The Radiation Cookbook* and *Miss Graham* was born.

You paint the post-war backdrop so vividly in the book. How much historical research did you do, and how did you set about it?

I did a great deal of research, some of the reference I used is listed below. It wasn't all that easy because although there is a huge amount of material about the Second World War, there is far less about the immediate aftermath. I began with a research plan: mapping this new territory, working out what I needed to know about food and cookery (because they are so central to the book), what was happening in different locations, what the lives of my characters might entail. Once I was able to navigate this new landscape, I could begin to shade in my different characters, what they had done in the war – such a huge event in everybody's lives – and what they might be doing afterwards. The more I read, the more details emerged that I could integrate into the book to give it life and colour. When I thought I knew enough, I could begin to write. But the research didn't end there. As I write, I carry on, finding the specific detail I need, accurate to the period, and those little 'extras' which will make the time, places and people live on the page.

What was the most fascinating detail that you discovered about the era or real-life characters through your research?
This book covers some very dark areas of the Second World War and post-war history. I was deeply shocked and disturbed by some of the reading I had to do: the doctors and nurses involved in the Euthanasia Programme; the hideous brutality of the *Einsatzgruppe* massacres in Latvia; the strange occult beliefs held by Hitler and many of the Nazi High Command; the utter chaos in Germany after the war ended; the hypocrisy of the USA and Britain in searching for and recruiting Nazi scientists even before the war had ended, regardless of what they might have done. The list goes on. Matched with that was the heroism of the female SOE agents captured and killed by the Nazis at Natzweiler-Struthof and other concentration camps. There's the courage of the women who had been subjected to medical experiments in Ravensbrück and who re-lived their trauma to testify at the Doctors' Trial; the brave and beautiful SOE agent Christine Granville, aka Krystyna Skarbek, my model for Dori, her redoubtable boss in SOE F Section, Vera Atkins, and her indefatigable post-war search for her missing girls. I discovered so many inspirational stories, like that of Marion Dönhoff who, in the depths of winter, led her people from her estate in East Prussia to escape the advancing Russian forces, travelling seven weeks on horseback

before reaching Hamburg. Many found their way into the novel but in different forms. It is a work of fiction, after all.

How did the character of Edith form in your mind? Did you have a clear picture of her journey from the beginning?
My aunt directly inspired the book and her life gave me the character of Edith. She was born 1/1/1900, an auspicious date, but on the surface she led an entirely unexceptional life. She taught in Coventry, never married, lived at home with my grandparents. After my grandfather died at the beginning of the Second World War, she looked after my grandmother. So far, so predictable. Then, in 1946, much to the consternation of the whole family, she went to work for The Control Commission in the British Zone in Northern Germany. The Control Commission was tasked with re-construction. She was fluent in German and was taken on as an Education Officer, with the equivalent rank of Lieutenant Colonel. Much to the further consternation of the family, she liked the life there and stayed on, well into the 1950s. She only came back to Britain for my grandmother's last illness. She took up her work in schools again, becoming a Headmistress. I remember her talking about her time in Lübeck and the photographs she had of the devastation: ruined cities and sunken ships. As a child, I absorbed the family narrative about how irresponsible and selfish she'd been, but as an adult I saw her differently. I admired her striking out, rebelling against the role convention had assigned for her, her sense of purpose and her compassion. All her life, she worked tirelessly for the Save the Children Fund, never forgetting the plight of those refugee children in Germany. I also liked that she had a hidden life: her fluency in German; her 'friendship' with a German boy before the war; the trips abroad she'd taken with her cousin; the holidays she took in Germany, Austria, Switzerland, often on her own; her lifelong friendship with an American whom she'd met in Germany. She flew to America to see him, the year before her death in 1984. She once told me, 'However old you get, you're the same person inside. Only your body lets you down.' I've never forgotten that.

Edith's friendship with Adeline and Dori is a wonderful strand of the story. Why did you want to highlight the theme of female friendship?

Friendships in wartime are made quickly. I liked the idea of three very different women with different personalities, life experiences, even nationalities, but then something draws them together into abiding friendship. Each has something the others lack and they freely give and receive from each other, which is the essence of many friendships between women. Edith's character came first and is central, the others pivot around her. I wanted the other two to be very different from Edith. I chose espionage agent and war correspondent, partly for the plot but also because there were plenty of women who took up roles in these essentially very male arenas and were brilliantly successful against all odds and opposition (*'no suitable job for a woman'*). I wanted to celebrate them because, too often, their roles have been overlooked, the part they played passed over, and essentially unrecognised.

Do you enjoy reading historical fiction yourself?

As a young reader it was my favourite genre, closely followed by horror. I still read historical fiction. I've always loved history and it is a great way to learn about periods and places I don't necessarily know much about. As a writer of historical fiction, I can always learn from some of the brilliant authors writing in the genre. Of course, I also read other things: contemporary fiction, crime fiction, spy novels and classic gothic.

If readers are interested in learning more about the post-war period and unlikely spies such as Edith, are there any reading materials you'd recommend?

Below is a selection of the books I used when I was writing *Miss Graham's War*. The list is by no means comprehensive, but these books were the books I consulted most in order to understand the period and the lives of those living through it. If you want to know more, do go to the area that interests you and see what you can find there.

Spies & SOE

Helm, Sarah, *A Life in Secrets: The Story of Vera Atkins and the Lost Agents of SOE*, Little Brown

Mulley, Clare, *The Spy Who Loved: the Secrets and Lives of Christine Granville Britain's First Female Secret Agent of World War 11*, Pan Macmillan

SOE Manual: How To Be An Agent in Occupied Europe, William Collins: National Archives

Greene, Graham, *The Ministry of Fear*, Vintage Classics

Greene, Graham, *The Third Man*, Penguin Books

Food & Fashion

Collingham, Lizzie, *The Taste of War: World War Two and the Battle for Food*, Allen Lane

Knight, Katherine, *Spuds, Spam and Eating for Victory: Rationing in the Second World War*, The History Press

Patten, Marguerite, *Victory Cookbook*, Chancellor Press

Summers, Julie, *Fashion on the Ration*, Profile Books

Walford, Jonathan, *Forties Fashion: From Siren Suits to the New Look*, Thames and Hudson

Germany

Sereny, Gitta, *Into That Darkness*, Vintage Books

Arendt, Hannah, *The Portable Hannah Arendt*, Penguin Classics

Lower, Wendy, *Hitler's Furies: German Women in the Nazi Killing Fields*, Vintage Publishing

Dönhoff, Marion, *Before The Storm: Memories of My Youth in Old Prussia*, Knopf

Douglas, R.M., *Orderly and Humane: The Expulsion of the Germans after the Second World War*, Yale University Press

Vonnegut Jr., Kurt, *Slaughterhouse 5*, Dell Publishing

Steege, Paul, *Black Market, Cold War: Everyday Life in Berlin, 1946 – 1949*, Cambridge

Clare, George, *Berlin Days 1946 – 47*, Macmillan

Friedlander, Henry, *The Origins of Nazi Genocide: From Euthanasia to the Final Solution*, University North Carolina Press

Schmidt, Ulf, *Justice at Nuremburg: Leo Alexander and the Nazi Doctors' Trial*, Palgrave Macmillan

Kurlander, Eric, *Hitler's Monsters: A Supernatural History of The Third Reich*, Yale University Press

Feigel, Lara, *The Bitter Taste of Victory: In the Ruins of the Third Reich*, Bloomsbury

Post-War Europe

Sebestyen, Victor, *1946: The Making of the Modern World*

Best, Nicholas, *Five Days that Shook the World: Eyewitness Accounts form Europe at the end of World War 11*, Osprey Publishing

Thomas, Merrilyn, *The Cold War (Beginners Guide)* Oneworld Publishing

Anders, Edward, *Amidst Latvians During the Holocaust*, Occupation Museum Association of Latvia

Beckman, Morris, *The Jewish Brigade: An Army with Two Masters 1944-45*, The History Press Ltd

Lewis, Damien, *The Nazi Hunters*, Quercus

Jacobsen, Annie, *Operation Paperclip: The Secret Intelligence Program that Brought Nazi Scientists to America*

Sands, Philippe, *The Ratline*, Orion Publishing

Women Journalists & Photographers

Gelhorn, Martha, *The Face of War*, Virago

Burke, Carolyn, *Lee Miller*, Bloomsbury

Ed. Penrose, Anthony, *Lee Miller's War: Beyond D-Day*, Thames & Hudson

Hollingworth, Clare, *Front Line*, Jonathan Cape

Chapelle, Dickey, *What's a Woman Doing Here?: A Reporter's Report on Herself*, William Morrow